MONSTERS, MAGIC, & MAYHEM

BUBBA THE MONSTER HUNTER SEASON 4

JOHN G. HARTNESS

PART I

INTO THE MYSTIC

1

———

I didn't say much on the drive back from Muscle Shoals. Wasn't much to say, really. I had a whole lot to process, but it wasn't the kind of processing that ended up with me in the bathroom with a copy of the funny papers. It was more the kind of processing that ended up with a normal person laying down on a shrink's couch, or for me, the kind of processing that ended up with something, or somebody, getting broken.

We'd just saved the soul of the music industry from a demon that wanted to auto-tune everything to sound like a bad Florida Georgia Line cover band, which is my idea of the ninth circle of Hell. In the meantime, I'd been party to some downright scandalous dreams, and in the middle of my very own reenactment of *The Devil Went Down to Georgia*, my mama came back and sang with me.

My mama was back. The woman I'd last seen tied to a pole and about to be set on fire by my crazy-ass werewolf brother. The woman I'd pretty much told to stay the hell out of my life forever. The woman who walked out on Pop, Jason, and me when I was a teenager because she couldn't put up with Pop's life as a Monster Hunter. She was back.

Oh yeah, and she was a fairy.

Not like Skeeter. As far as I knew, she was straight. That ain't anywhere on the list of stuff I want to talk to my mama about.

A real fairy. Like pointy ears and magic shit, fairy.

If that wasn't enough damn surprises, she proceeds to tell me that I've got a sister, that she's in trouble in Fairyland, and that we've got to go there and save her.

I've been to Fairyland. It wasn't a whole lot of fun. If given a choice between Fairyland and Disneyland, I'm gonna pick Disney-land every time. Even in the middle of summer with twenty thousand preschoolers. Still taking Disneyland. Mice suck, but fairies are worse.

So, I don't think it surprised anybody when I pulled into the driveway, got out of the truck, walked right inside, and pulled a twelve-pack of Budweiser out of the fridge. I walked straight out to the back deck, popped open the first of what I anticipated to be many beers I would drink that afternoon and on into the evening, and sucked the sides flat on the can before I came up for air.

I heard the sliding glass door open behind me. I didn't turn around. I could tell it was Amy for a couple of reasons. One, Joe has a heavy tread from the engineer's boots he wears all the time. Two, Skeeter knows better than to interrupt me when I'm thinking about Mama. He was with me when she ran off, and he saw what I was like then. I was with him when his mama died, so I returned the favor. Mamas have always been a subject we didn't talk about. Ever.

I just assumed it wasn't going to be Mama following me out on the deck because she was never a stupid woman, and it would take an exceedingly stupid woman for her to think I wanted to talk to her right then.

That left Amy. Probably the only person in the world I wouldn't hit square in the mouth for trying to talk to me right then. There's a good thirty percent chance I wouldn't deck Skeeter, and Joe got maybe another five percent for being a priest. But I wasn't gonna hit Amy, no matter what. And she knew it.

She walked up beside me and put a hand on my arm. "How you doing out here?"

"I don't know." I told the truth. There's no point trying to be brave with the woman you wake up whenever you have nightmares, which is pretty often. Not to mention the fact that she'd been in the room when Mama sang with me, and she saw what that was like. It was magic, and it felt worse than anything I'd ever gone through in my life. And I once wrestled a naked Sasquatch.

"Is there anything I can do?" she asked. One thing I like about Amy. She ain't one for platitudes or bullshit. She wasn't gonna tell me that it was all going to be all right, or it was all going to work out, or whatever other crap she thought I might want to hear, or need to hear, or whatever.

"I don't think so," I said. "I got a lot of beer here." Then something hit me. "You might want to lock up Bertha." I slipped out of my shoulder rig and handed the holster with my Desert Eagle to her. "I don't think I want to shoot anybody, but I can't promise I'll feel the same way in an hour."

"I'll put her in the gun vault. I'll put all the hideaway pistols in there, too." She turned to go back into the house.

"There's a Glock in a holster duct-taped under the table," I called after her.

"I know, Bubba."

"There's a Sig nine-mil taped behind the headboard of the bed."

"I know."

"There's a little Ruger stuck in the middle couch cushion."

"I know about that one, too. I know about all the guns you've got tucked away, Bubba. I'll secure them all. You can get as drunk as you want; I won't let you shoot your mother tonight."

"No promises about tomorrow morning?" I asked.

"Depends on what she has to say for herself tonight," Amy said, turning back to the sliding glass door.

"There's one in a Ziploc bag in the tank of every toilet," I added.

That one stopped her. "Jesus Christ, Bubba! How many pistols do you have stashed around here?"

"I can't always keep track. A dozen or so. You were just asking about pistols, right?"

She rolled her eyes at me and went into the house. I reckon she decided that if I couldn't remember where the guns were sober, I wouldn't be able to find them drunk. Sometimes I wonder if that woman knows me at all.

I slammed about four beers before Skeeter made it out onto the deck. I'd moved from leaning over the deck to sitting in the ratty recliner that I kept out there to watch the sunset. It used to be in the den before Amy started spending time at my place. She decided it was unfit for anyone, man or dog, to ever sit in and had to leave the house. So, I put it on the porch. She pretended it wasn't there, and I pretended I still had some semblance of control over my home. I think I heard that was called "compromise."

Skeeter walked out and started putting kindling in the big clay fire pot over on the corner of the deck. He didn't look at me, just reached over and grabbed a beer. "You okay?"

"No."

"Didn't expect so."

"What the hell am I supposed to say, Skeeter?" I yelled. A crow flew up out of a cedar tree a dozen yards off the deck. I might have been a little louder than I expected. That happens around beer three or four, usually. "I mean, shit. She's been gone twenty years, and last year I find out she ain't dead. So, I keep Jason from making her dead and tell her I don't ever want to see her again. Then she shows up outta nowhere with my best friends and tells me that she's a *fairy*? How do I react to that? Do I just say, 'Welcome home, nice ears'? 'Cause I don't damn think so. I don't know what to think. I mean…I mean…goddammit." I leaned forward and put my face in my hands. There were all these feelings rolling around inside me, and I couldn't make heads or tails out of any of them.

I sat there for a minute, just leaning forward, and then I felt a pair of skinny arms wrap around me. One of Skeeter's bony wrists went around my shoulder, and the other one ended up in my ear, but it was the thought that counted. He hugged me something fierce for a minute, until I shrugged my shoulders. He got the hint and went back to building up his fire.

"I'm here for you, brother. Always have been."

"I know, Skeet. I know." We sat there for another minute. I popped the top on another Bud.

"You gonna need another twelve-pack," Skeeter said.

"You got Cheeto breath," I replied.

"What has that got to do with anything?"

"Nothing, I thought we were just saying obvious shit."

I sat out there most of the night. Skeeter came out a couple times to check on me. Amy sat out with me for a couple hours. Joe came and sat down and looked at me kinda awkwardly like he thought he was supposed to be all "spiritual advisor" and stuff, just because he's a priest and all. I ran him off when I could tell he didn't have nothing to say and wasn't gonna drink with me. If a preacher don't drink and ain't got nothing to preach about, what's the damn point?

The house was dead quiet when I went in around three in the morning. I closed the door from the deck and turned like I was going to the fridge. Out of the corner of my eye, I saw movement, and I froze.

"Don't worry, Robbie. I'm not going to pounce," Mama said from the old wooden rocking chair in the corner by the cold fireplace. That chair had sat empty ever since I brought it into this house from Pop's place down the hill. Mama used to rock me and Jason in it when we were babies, singing to us in her clear, sweet voice. Seeing her in it now brought back a whole lot of memories and drug up a whole lot of feelings I wasn't sure I was ready to deal with. But it looked like I wasn't going to have much of a choice.

"I suppose you want an explanation of where I went when I left and how I came to return and tell you that you have a sister," Mama said. She was sitting in the dark, nothing for illumination but the light from the half moon and the stars streaming in the glass door casting deep shadows across her face and making her expression even more otherworldly than her ears.

I set my empty Budweiser box down on the floor and walked across the room to take a seat on the couch facing her. I wasn't close enough for us to touch, but she wouldn't have to raise her voice to make me hear her. "Yeah, I reckon I want to know about all that. But that ain't all I want to know."

"I'm sure that's true," Mama said. Her voice was soft, like it was a delicate thing that could break if she spoke too loud. "What else do you want to know?"

I stared at her, sitting in shadows, her long dark hair blue-black in the moonlight, the tip of one pointed ear screaming out her alienness to me, making me wonder about everything. Did Pop know? What does this make me? What would this do to any kids I might have? Did Jason know? Is this why he went nuts?

I didn't ask any of those things. I sat there looking across the room at her for a long time, just taking in every new line on her face, every strand of silver shooting through the black sky of her hair, every crinkle at the corner of her eyes.

"Why did you leave?" I asked. It was all I wanted to know. It was all I'd wanted to know for twenty years, since I realized she was gone and wasn't coming back. I spent years wondering what I'd done, what Jason had done, what Pop had done to make her leave. What could make her leave the family she'd built, the home she and Pop created? What could make her leave me?

She nodded, like she expected me to ask the question. I'm sure she did, but I wasn't real sure I wanted to know the answer. I held my breath when she opened her mouth.

"I think you ought to wake up the others," she said. I cocked my head to the side, looking I'm sure like a dog that finally caught the car he'd been chasing.

"Why?" I asked. "I don't think this is any of their business."

"But it is their business, Robbie. The reason I left is all tied up with the reason I came back, and your sister, and why we have to go find her and save her. If they're going to help us, and I could see by the looks in their eyes that we'd have to kill them to keep them from trying to come with us, then they deserve to know what they're getting into and why."

"And you want to do this now? In the middle of the night?"

"Some stories are best told by the light of the moon, son. Mine is one of them."

2

———

My story starts before I was born, like all tales do. My parents were Fae royalty, the King and Queen of the Winter Court. They were much in love, and the realm of Winter was a happy place, sparkling like the dawn on a snowy tree. At first.

But the Fae are a mercurial people and long-lived. These are not qualities that make for a lengthy partnership, and when I was just a child, barely twenty mundane years of age, my mother, Mab, the Queen of Winter, cast aside my father and sent him from her sight.

I knew they were fighting, of course. My mother was not what one would call shy and retiring, and her voice cut through walls like a brisk January wind. My father gave as good as he got, his booming shouts thundering over her shrieks of rage turning the entire castle into a blizzard of angry words and hurtful accusations.

Even though I knew they were fighting and I knew my father to be desperately unhappy, I was surprised when he knocked on my bedroom door late one night.

I wasn't sleeping. We require only the barest minimum of actual sleep, a few hours across several days will suffice for us. I was reading, tales of fancy about men and their miraculous inventions. I thought them nothing but stories, these wild books about automobiles and airplanes, about engines and machines. I had no concept of such things. Why would I? We had magic, after all.

When my father knocked, I closed my book, carefully marking the page with a winter rose I had picked from Mother's garden just that afternoon. I opened the heavy canopy around my bed, put on a robe against the ever-present chill, and went to the door.

"Who is it?" I called through the heavy wood. I could have simply opened the door, of course. I was never safer than in my rooms at the heart of Winter's Palace. No one would dare assault our home—it was unthinkable. And I knew every soul within these walls, having grown up underfoot in the kitchens, tripping the maids in the hallways, and teasing the guards standing their posts.

But there is a certain decorum expected of a princess, as my mother never failed to remind me, so I called out before I opened the door.

But I didn't open the door. The knob turned under my hand, and my father pushed into the room. I backed away from him, stepping on the hem of my robe and nearly tumbling to the floor.

"Father!" I cried. "What is wrong? Are you injured? Has something terrible happened?"

I looked at him for the first time, and I saw a bright red handprint on his face and a tiny trickle of blood at the corner of his mouth. I knew immediately what had happened. They had finally taken their bickering too far, and Mother had done something she could not come back from—she had struck Father.

Father was a warrior. More than simply a soldier in the armies of the Fae, he was a general, a hero in both the skirmishes against Summer over territorial lines and in the more serious wars against goblins and orcs that constantly wanted to attack the lands of Unseelie and Seelie alike. He had not been in the field for some time, but he still carried his sword everywhere, and he always walked like he expected an enemy to launch an attack at any moment.

Well, the enemy that had assaulted him was one he could not take the field against. Mother had struck him. I did not know why then and do not to this day. I did not ask what was said; I simply reached up to his face and dabbed the blood away with the corner of my robe.

"Get your things. We are leaving this place. I cannot abide her another night." Father walked to my wardrobe and flung the doors wide. He began pulling riding breeches and shirts from the large closet willy-nilly, throwing them onto my bed. More than half the things he flung aside landed on the floor, but he never looked back to see.

I stepped forward and took him by the wrist. He stopped and turned to me. "I have to go," he said. His voice was tight, and I could see by the throbbing vein in his temple and the cords of muscle standing out at his neck that he was holding himself in check with the greatest of difficulty.

"I understand," I said, keeping my voice low and calm. I spoke to him like I did to Thunder, the skittish war horse in the stables that never let anyone save my father or Rogim the Stablemaster ride him. "You cannot stay with her any longer. If you do, you will return to a place that you do not wish to revisit. So, you must go."

"You must go with me," Father said through gritted teeth.

"Yes," I said, picking up some of the clothes on the floor and putting them on the bed. That act, that mundane act of stooping to pick up an ice-blue blouse, snapped him out of his rage-induced trance. He shook himself all over, as if he were a dog climbing out of a river, and looked at me with sad eyes.

"I am sorry, Ygraine," he said. "I have tried. For years, I have endured the sniping, and the belittling comments, and the infidelity, but tonight..."

"Tonight, she struck you," I said with a nod.

"Tonight, she struck me," he confirmed. "I told her long ago that I would tolerate many things from her: I would turn a blind eye to a great deal of horrid behavior for the sake of the love I bore her and for the sake of the child she bore me. But I warned her, I am still a man. I am still a man, and I am still a warrior, and I will not be struck.

Tonight, she has crossed that line. I cannot retaliate in kind, for if I do, it will mean only two things."

"Your death for laying hands on the queen," I supplied the first, and most likely, outcome. The throne passed to my mother through blood. The Fae are always ruled by queens, and the duty is passed down to the firstborn daughter. Our "kings" are truly prince consorts, king in name only. Some queens entrust much of the duty of rule to their consort. My mother was not such a queen.

"Or civil war within Winter," Father said.

I looked up at him but saw nothing of jest upon him. He was a popular consort, and many called him king in all sincerity, not the empty title so often bestowed upon men of his station. He nodded down to me, lips pursed in a tight scowl.

"The generals are all loyal to me, and much of the Guard. Your mother has never been popular with the people, and even less so with the members of the Court who have endured her temper. Were I to attempt it, I may very well be able to take the throne by force."

I thought about it and decided he was quite likely correct. Mother was a capricious, temperamental, and often downright dangerous monarch, prone to overreaction to the slightest insult, real or imagined. I had long heard muttering among the guards and servants about her behavior toward them and could only guess how the men who fought her wars felt about the treatment they received should they darken the doors of the castle.

"What will you do?" I asked.

"I must leave," Father said. "I will not be put down like some rabid dog for defending myself. Your mother is no fragile snowflake—she is Winter itself. She is the most powerful sorceress in the realm, and even should I wish to harm her, I doubt I could. But I have no desire to."

I looked up at him, and his blue eyes were sad under his mop of curly dark hair. His trim beard was shot through with gray where none had been just a few short years before, testament to the strain of living with Queen Mab.

"I love her, El," he said, pulling me close. "Gods help me, I still love her." He took me by the shoulders and held me at arms' length. "And that is why I must go away. Tonight. I can no longer live with a woman who has no love or respect for me, and if I stay here, it will either be the end of me, or the end of Winter."

"Where will you go?" I asked.

"I do not know," he said. "But we must leave now, before a servant tells her that I was seen rushing to your rooms. She will never let you leave with me, not her heir. So, if we are to go, it must be now."

I didn't say anything, just turned to the bed and started sorting clothes into piles. "Meet me at the stables in half an hour," I said. "I need to assemble my things, and we can't be seen leaving the castle together with packs. I have a friend among the stable hands who will let us out the Merchant's Gate."

He smiled down at me, warmth flooding his face. "I will see you there, my daughter. We will go far from this place, somewhere your mother can never find us, and we shall be happy."

I hugged him, almost crushing the air from him with the ferocity of it. "I will meet you there. Now go, before she decides to come here and berate me for being born of a worthless sot like you."

I motioned him to the door, and he dashed out, my tall, handsome father. He stopped at the door and smiled at me, knowing that in less than an hour we would be free of mad Queen Mab and her temper, creating a new life for ourselves somewhere in a hidden corner of Faerie.

That was the last time I ever saw my father.

3

I packed nothing. Not a stitch of clothing, not even an apple to eat on the road. I dressed like my bedroom was on fire, in the plainest garb I owned. I pulled on breeches that I often used when mucking out my favorites horse, Paisley's, stall. I threw on a tight-fitting undershirt and a loose, shapeless shirt I had pilfered from my father's rag bag over it. I tied my hair back in a low ponytail to cover my ears and put a thick woolen tunic over everything. I belted on a light sword and a knife, then tucked a pair of throwing knives into the tops of my riding boots.

I glanced in a mirror as I bustled to the door, looking at myself in this rough-hewn disguise. My clothes were obviously made with quality, and I would not fool anyone looking closely, but from a distance, I more resembled a boy from a middling prosperous family than a Princess of Winter. My clothes were faded tones of gray and once-white, rather than the sparkling blues and silvers of the Court. My three-year-old boots, while well-made were scuffed and worn, obviously several years old, and spoke of a family that had money for luxuries such as boots only every so often. I left the two newer pair sitting in my closet, one of them never worn.

I knew I was leaving behind a life of unparalleled luxury and comfort for one of hardship and possible danger. I had my magic and my wits, but there were many in Faerie who would love to hold a bargaining chip against my mother, and the life of her heir was one she would be unable to ignore. I knew all this, and still I threw open the door to my bedchamber and strode down the halls to the stable as though I had not a fear in the world.

Nothing could have been further from the truth. I carried no food because my stomach was in such knots that I became ill at the very idea of eating. I passed through the kitchen and picked up a pair of waterskins from a hook by the door, my only concession to my body's needs. I crossed the courtyard into the stable, waterskins in one hand and my heavy hooded cloak in the other.

"Wake up, Barris!" I called. "I need to ride at once."

The tow-haired stable boy peered over the edge of the hayloft, straw poking out from his hair. "Whossat? Princess? What you doing here in the middle of the night?"

"I'm leaving, Barris. I have received a message from the gods and must go at once to the Forest of Ekwan to pray for guidance." Ekwan Forest lay far to the south, a three-day ride in the best of circumstances. By the time Mother sent someone there after me, I planned to be far west of our citadel. I knew she would send a second rider north; that's why I had no intention of going in that direction.

Barris climbed down the ladder without further complaint or question and moved to Paisley's stall. I called out to him. "No, Barris. I won't be taking Paisley. Saddle Cinnamon instead." It pained me to leave Paisley, but she was a lovely animal and very distinctive. Pure white in color, with obvious breeding in her lines, she was an amazing horse. Cinnamon was brown, slow, and plain in every way. If you did not know horses well, you would never know that she was bred from lines of old war horses and cart horses, taught from birth to carry a rider for days on end, capable of managing any terrain with almost no trouble at all.

Barris saddled Cinnamon without a question, accustomed as he was to the quixotic nature of the Fae in general and of the household of Queen Mab in particular. He brought her to me as I finished packing a light pack of oats and a few apples to keep the horse happy if we had trouble finding forage. My mother's tendency to coat her land in snow made it challenging to keep a mount fed unless you knew where the way stations were, and I would be unlikely to stop anywhere that Mab might have magical minders looking for me.

"Thank you, Barris, and I'm sorry," I said as he brought the docile animal out to me.

"Sorry for what, my lady?" the slightly dim boy asked.

"Sorry for this," I said. I held my open hand up to my face, palm up, and blew across it. A shimmer of dust flew into Barris's face, and he collapsed to the stable floor, unconscious. He would awaken within an hour, with no recollection of the past few minutes. Hopefully it would provide enough of a lead for my father to be unable to pursue me.

I put my foot through the stirrups and hopped into the saddle, petting Cinnamon's neck when I was settled. I leaned down and spoke softly into the horse's ear. "Let's go, girl, but softly. We don't need to alarm the gate guards."

The guards nodded at me, then raised the massive iron portcullis. It wasn't an ordinary occurrence for one of the Court to leave under the cover of darkness, and less typical for it to be one of the royal family, but it also was not so unheard of as to be challenged. They would remember my passing and which way I turned out of the gate, so I went half a mile in the wrong direction, then doubled back once I was out of sight of the castle and took the Western Road.

I rode until sunrise, then led Cinnamon off the trail into the woods. I left her lightly hobbled and fashioned a pallet for myself from branches and my saddle blanket. With my head on my saddle for a pillow, I wrapped myself in my cloak and slept for a few hours.

I woke to the sun high in the sky and the sensation of the wards I had set around Cinnamon and myself being tested. "Hello," I called out. I felt no fear. I was a strong sorceress, if young, and we were within the boundaries of my mother's kingdom. I had full faith in her ability to keep the most unsavory of the Fair Folk from our lands, so anyone crossing my wards would be a bandit at worst, and a charitable soul with some breakfast at best.

"Hello, young human," came a growling voice. *Or an animal,* I thought. I opened my eyes to see a giant wolf standing over me, its head cocked to one side. "Why are you sleeping in the forest? Do you not have a den?"

I sat up and rubbed my eyes. "Good morning, Wolf," I replied. "I have a den, but I had to leave it. I grew weary, so I slept in the forest. Is it yours? I apologize if I trespass." I have always found that it is best to treat wolves with the utmost courtesy. They are lovely animals but can be prickly if they feel they are being disrespected.

The wolf chuffed at me, a laugh of some sort, I suppose. "The forest belongs to no one but herself, little fairy. If she allowed you to sleep here, then it is beyond me to challenge your right. But you are likely not warm, and likely hungry as well. You may follow me to my den, where you will sleep among my cubs and share their food."

"I thank you, Mother Wolf," I replied. "I am not one who is bothered by the cold, but I will happily share your food." I was telling the truth, by the way. I am the Heir of Winter. The cold no more bothers me than does air.

I saddled Cinnamon, who watched the wolf warily but maintained her placid poise. I led the horse behind the wolf to a cave to the west, near the road but farther back than where I slept. I looped Cinnamon's reins around a low-hanging branch, loose enough for her to pull free if there was trouble, and went inside. It was a cozy cave, big enough for me to stand upright at the front, but quickly narrowing until I was forced to creep along on my hands and knees after just a few minutes. I crawled deeper into the cave, my eyes adjusting to the total darkness, and soon found myself buried in a pile of warm fur and discontented yips as I crawled right into the middle of four wolf pups.

"I told you it would be warmer here," Mother Wolf said as I snuggled into the pile of fur. She was right, it was very cozy. Even though I am unharmed by cold, I can feel its touch, and the warmth of the cubs was welcome.

"Sleep now, and when you wake, we shall eat," Mother Wolf said. I would have agreed with her, but the warmth and comfort of being surrounded by doggie snores and dream-barks had already overwhelmed me. I closed my eyes and drifted off almost instantly.

I woke some time later all fuzzy-headed and covered in wolf pups, which while pleasant enough, is a little hard to breathe. I wormed my way out of the pile of fur and paws, took a few moments to handle my morning ablutions near a stream that ran beside the cave, and knelt at the mouth with Mother Wolf.

"Thank you for your courtesy and hospitality, but I must be on my way," I said.

"You have not yet eaten," said the wolf. "I have caught a fat rabbit; you should tear off a leg before you go."

"I cannot," I said, my mouth watering at the thought of nice roasted rabbit. "I would have to build a fire and cook the rabbit, and I must be away before time for that."

"I never understand why your kind finds it necessary to ruin good meat with fire," the wolf said with a sniff. "But I understand. It is your way. I hope you are well, young hairless one."

I nodded to her. "Thank you, Mother Wolf. I hope all your cubs grow to be strong and hale." I wrapped my cloak around my shoulders, saddled Cinnamon, and walked back to the Western Road. I mounted my horse and rode off into the afternoon sun. With any luck and a clear road, by midnight I would be convincing the Witch of the Western Wood to open a portal out of Faerie and to my new home.

And that is where our tale becomes interesting.

4

———————

As soon as I set foot in the Western Wood, I knew I was unwelcome. A huge oak leaned over the path and turned its branches to me. A face appeared in the bark and said, "You should go home, princess. You are not wanted here."

That's clue enough even for a starry-eyed little girl to understand. I looked up at the tree and said, "My apologies, fair dryad, but I have no home to go back to. I have left the life of Queen Mab's daughter and seek to make my own way in the world."

"You will have neither way nor life if the Mad Queen hears those words," the dryad said. She stepped out of the trunk of the oak, her branch-arms drawing back within herself. "Why have you left the Winter Queen's Court?"

"My father, Oberon, has left her, and I feared for my safety. I must find sanctuary from Mab's displeasure," I said, seeing no reason to lie to the tree spirit.

"There will be no sanctuary for you in the lands of Winter. Mab is our queen, and capricious though she may be, we live to serve her. None will shelter you within her boundaries."

"This I well know," I replied. "That is why I have come to the

Western Wood. To leave the lands of Winter behind and travel to the human lands."

The dryad drew back, the leaves of her hair trembling in shock. "Why would you do that, you silly princess? The lands of man are built with cold iron, that heartless rock that sucks the very magic from our bones. Even the oldest trees there have lost the ability to speak."

"I must go there," I said. "There are few places Mab cannot follow, and the lands of man are among them. I must find the Witch and convince her to send me there."

"What do you have for payment, princess?" the dryad asked. "Jewels? A crown?"

I looked at my feet. "I have nothing."

The dryad laughed, making her leaves shake in that dry rustling sound again. "Then you may as well return to Mab and throw yourself on what minuscule mercy she has, for the Witch grants no favors and logs no debts. She will be paid or you will not pass through her circle."

"That is not for you to say, Oaklet," said a gnarled old woman who slid between the trees with the grace of a panther and less sound. She was hunched over a walking stick, with hanks of gray hair falling over her face and spilling out from the hood of her tattered brown cloak. Liver spots dotted her twisted twig-knuckled hands, and a hooked nose stuck out crooked on her craggy face, which held more wrinkles than teeth at this point.

"You are Mab's child?" the ragbag woman asked in her voice like an uncoiled hinge.

"Aye, ma'am," I replied with a slight curtsey.

She laughed at the gesture, a hacking, coarse thing that sounded like a woodpecker tapping into rotted wood. "Such manners, child. Your mother-queen has taught you well. Tell me this, child. Do you fear me?"

"No, ma'am," I said honestly.

"Do you find me beautiful?" the hag asked.

"No, ma'am," I repeated, just as honest.

She chuckled a little at that. "Would you believe me if I told you that I once had men falling at my feet asking for my hand?"

"No, ma'am," I said for the third time.

This time, the Witch cackled, throwing her head back and flapping the wattles on her neck in the air. "Good, child! For I was born ugly and got better at it with every passing year. There were never men, or women, plying me with sweet words and empty promises. You are an honest child. It is no wonder you wish to leave Mab's court."

"Will you help me?" I asked. "I have nothing to give you. I left the palace in a rush, bringing nothing with which to barter."

"I will help you for the cost of the only thing you have—a promise."

"I will give it," I said, the words tumbling from my lips pell-mell, like a spring down a mountainside.

"Be careful, child. You should not agree before you have heard the terms. Nonetheless, I will take your promise for aid in a future endeavor. I do not yet know what help I will require from you, save that I will not ask you to betray or harm your king or kin."

"I agree to your terms," I said.

The old woman grinned and turned to walk deeper into the wood. "Then follow me, princess. We shall find you a path out of Mab's domain and into the world of men."

I followed her for hours as she wove a twisted, turning path through the forest. Several times I was sure that we had done little but retrace our steps, only to have a seemingly familiar stretch of trail turn into something completely unknown. We hiked across rocky mountain trails, trudged through nigh-invisible swamp passages, and padded long across carpeted glades of evergreens.

Finally, as my feet ached and my legs throbbed, we stepped into a clearing, and I could see the sun for the first time in hours. I looked up, and rather than the frosted blue-white sunshine of the Winter Court, I saw the warm yellow smile of a spring afternoon. There was no frost licking the limbs of the trees above me, and the sea of golden dandelions before me swayed in a warm, gentle breeze that kissed across my cheeks and tickled my hair across my ears.

"Where are we?" I asked, a hint of wonder creeping into my voice.

"This is the land of Georgia," the Witch said. "You are in the world of man, now. Your magic no longer works here, and you are human in all ways that matter."

I reached up to touch my ears, the very visible reflection of my Fae-ness, and found them odd. No longer were they gently swooping, graceful ovals coming to a point after several inches of travel. Instead, they were these awkward, floppy things with fleshy lobes hanging from them and drab rounded tops. My mouth curled up in an unintended sneer, prompting another screeching cackle from the witch.

"Everyone does that at first," she said, once she finished laughing at me. "You will soon enough become accustomed to the dangly bits and to all the other myriad pains and trials of being a human woman. But know this—you may not stay."

"What do you mean?" I asked.

"You are of the Fae, and that will never change. You do not belong here, and the longer you stay, the more your body will reject this world, and this world will begin to reject you. This is not a world of magic, but you are a creature of magic. You cannot simply separate the magic from the girl—to do so would be to remove everything about you. Eventually, this world will destroy you. You will weaken and grow sick, and if you do not return to Faerie, you will die."

"How long can I stay? Can I come back after I leave?" I was frantic. I had escaped Mab, only to find that I would have to return.

"You can remain outside of Faerie for twenty of this world's years. No more. As that time draws to an end, you will feel yourself begin to change. When the pains begin, you must return to Faerie for as long as you have been gone. Only then can you return to this world without consequence."

"So, if I stay here for a year, I have to stay in Faerie for a year?" I asked.

"Exactly. You can return before your time is up, but you will become grievously ill immediately. Do not try to cheat magic. It knows," she said in a grim voice. "Now, I must leave you. I make many such trips, but I never stay more than a few hours. Be safe, child of Mab. I hope you can stay here for many years, for the Mad Queen will not forgive you easily or quickly."

With that, the old woman turned and walked back into the woods. She took a few steps into the shade, stepped behind a giant maple tree, and simply vanished. I walked around that tree four times without finding any sign of her.

"Well," I said to the empty air. "I suppose now I should begin to find out what a 'Georgia' is." I heard a strange whirring sound coming from the south, so I struck off through the pines toward the source of the noise and my new life.

The whirring noise was, as I now know, a highway. The Witch had transported me to a patch of woods just north of Atlanta, right off Interstate 85. I knew nothing of these strange machines that flew by me faster than any carriage I had ever seen. I looked in awe as these boxes of red, green, blue, white, black, and every color I had ever imagined flew by my face at breathtaking speeds. Some screamed at me with terrible noises, some ignored me completely, but I knew I wanted nothing to do with them. They were loud, and they belched horrible odors into the air. The entire path stank to high heaven, reeking like the den of a thousand fornicating goblins.

I must have stood on the side of the interstate for thirty minutes before one of the odd creatures passed me, then slowed and pulled off the road into the grass some fifty yards past me. A hatch opened on the side of the carriage, and a man got out. He was a big man by my standards, having lived my life around the slight frames of the Fae. He had his long hair tied back in a ponytail, and a smile shone through his beard. I knew instinctively that this was a kind man, one I could trust.

Even with that, I kept a hand on the dagger at the small of my back. I thought he looked trustworthy, but I had been wrong before. Once upon a time, I even thought my mother was sane, after all.

"You okay, miss?" His words were strange, but I understood them, even though his speech was heavily accented.

"I am, I believe," I said.

"Your car break down?" he asked. I stared at him blankly, having no idea what he was saying. He repeated himself, then shook his head. "You got no idea what I'm talking about, do you?"

"I don't think I understand what you are saying, no," I said, hoping I was answering his question. He seemed nice enough, and perhaps he could help me find shelter and safety.

"Are you hurt?" He slowed down his speech even more, almost to the point of comedy, but it helped.

"No," I said. "But I am alone and far from home. Can you help me?" I watched his eyes for any signs of pleasure or flashes of greed at my words but saw nothing but a touch of sadness and perhaps empathy for my plight.

"Well, I don't know how much help I can be, but I've got some food and can get you a place to sleep that'll be out of the rain."

"Rain?" I asked. I honestly thought perhaps the word meant something different here, for the sky was perfectly clear.

"Oh yeah, you definitely ain't from around here," the man said. "It don't look like it right now, but it'll be pouring down in about three hours. 'Round here we got a word for that. We call it July." He laughed at his own joke, and I smiled vaguely. I had no idea what he meant, or why it should be funny.

"I'm sorry," he said, when he was finished slapping his own knee. "Why don't you get in the truck, and I'll take you home where you can get something to eat. Then we can figure out a place for you to sleep and make some plans for tomorrow. How does that sound?"

Something to eat sounded wonderful. I'd not eaten a bite in hours, and I was famished. The forest had contained nothing, not even berries or nuts. I followed him to his truck and stood behind it as he walked around to the right. He opened the door and gestured for me to get in.

"Don't you have more than that little sack?" he asked, pointing to the pack on my shoulders.

"No," I said. "I left in a rush."

He gave me a steady look, then just nodded. I slid into the truck, and he closed the door. He walked around the truck, got behind the wheel, and cranked up the old blue Ford. The truck rumbled to life, and he grasped the top of a stick protruding from the floor and jiggled it into position. The vehicle lurched forward, and we merged back into the steady stream of northbound traffic.

And that was how I met your father and came to live in the cabin with him.

I stayed in the cabin with your father, deplorable though his housekeeping skills were, for some time. His father, your grandfather, came to eat dinner with us every evening, and every night I slept on the sofa in the den. We had been living together for about a week when he stopped me as I got up after dinner to go read in the rocker by the fire, as was my custom. I learned a great deal about humans from their literature, and I had nearly exhausted the meager library your father owned in just a few days.

"Sit down a minute," he said as we finished clearing the dishes.

I sat. Your grandfather had not joined us for our evening meal that night, so we were alone in the house. "What is it?" I asked.

"We need to talk about what your plans are," he said. "I don't mind you sticking around here. As a matter of fact, I kinda like it. You certainly are easy on the eyes, and the place smells a lot better with you here than with just me and Pop. But if you're thinking about staying, I reckon we need to talk about a few things."

I stood. "If one more evening is not too much trouble, I'll be gone in the morning." I had no intention of answering any questions about my origin, certainly not from a man who carried a pistol everywhere he went, even inside his home. It was only later that I learned exactly how important that habit was.

"You don't have to go, but if you want to stay, there's some stuff you need to know."

I stopped. He wasn't asking me things, but telling me? What secrets could this plain-spoken human possibly have? His round face was as open as any I had ever encountered, and there was not a disingenuous bone in his body, at least as much as I could tell in the few days we had shared the space.

"What would you like to tell me?" I asked, taking my seat once again.

"Well, this would be a whole lot easier if Pop was here, but I reckon the fact that he ain't is part of the reason I feel like I got to tell you in the first place."

I sat silently, waiting for him to continue. I had no idea what he was talking about, so I just allowed him to continue at his own pace.

"There are things in the world," he started. He shook his head and let out a little laugh. "This is one of them kinda talks like parents have with little kids, except it usually goes the exact opposite of the way this one is gonna go."

I waited.

"So, you know how when you're a little kid, and you're scared of monsters under the bed, or in the closet, and your mama or daddy comes in and tells you that there ain't nothing in your closet and that monsters ain't real? Well, I hate to be the one to break it to you, but monsters are real."

He looked at me, but whatever reaction he was expecting, I didn't give it to him. Of course I knew that monsters were real. I was a Princess of the Fae, after all. I had been raised around goblins, and nixies, and pixies, and even the occasional troll attack. Why was this even a subject for debate?

Then I realized that in this world, monsters were considered mythical. It all made sense to me in an instant—the machines, the hiding of my ears, the lack of magic—this was truly a mundane world, with almost no magic whatsoever. I tried my best to fix a look of shock on my face, but I feared it was too late.

Regardless, your father continued. "There are real monsters out there. There's vampires, and werewolves, and zombies, and ghosts, and ghouls, and all kind of things that you only hear about in books or stories. But that ain't all. There ain't just monsters. There's people who fight the monsters, too. People like me. And Pop. We're Monster Hunters. That's where he is tonight, out on a hunt."

"Why are you telling me this?" I asked.

"I reckon if you stay here much longer, there's a chance that I'm gonna have to leave you here by yourself some night 'cause I don't make it back from a hunt before you go to bed, and I wanted you to know why."

I tried to put a small tremor in my voice to appear a timorous little thing, not a woman trained in the use of magic and blade. "Do you think any of those things can find us here?"

He looked shocked, as though he had never considered the possibility. "Oh no! Me and Pop do a good job of keeping where we live real separate from where we hunt, and...well, to be honest, there ain't ever been anything left alive when we're done with a hunt. So, I ain't never worried about anything tracking us back here."

"So, your father is out on a hunt this evening and that made you think that I needed to know about your life?"

"Yeah," he said, a slight blush creeping up his face. "Well, that and...well, I reckon I kinda wanted..."

"Wanted what?" I asked. He was so cute with the pink almost blinking through his beard.

"I kinda wanted to see if you would mind if I courted you a little bit, and I wanted to make sure you knew what you was getting into if we went on a date."

By now the blush had reached all the way into his hairline, and I had to take pity on him. I leaned across the small kitchen table and took his hand. "I appreciate that. And I think I would very much like it if you courted me a little bit."

He grinned across at me. "Are you teasing me?"

"A little bit," I said with a smile.

We sat for a long time like that, holding hands across the table. He told me stories of the hunts he had been on, and I deflected his questions about where I grew up and what my family was like. I trusted him and felt strongly that he was to be very important in my life, but I still did not want to reveal myself completely to him. I suppose a small part of me was worried that he would see me as just another monster, something to be destroyed. I couldn't bear that, so I kept my true nature hidden from him. I kept it hidden from him the entire time we were together.

Your grandfather returned the next morning to find us asleep together on the couch, your father's arms around me as we slept, fully clothed, thank you very much, in front of the television.

"Well, I was starting to wonder if you was a little light in them loafers, boy. Not that there's anything wrong with that," he said, startling us both awake. I will admit that your father wasn't the only one blushing at that.

The old man stood in the kitchen, covered in the drying blood of who knows what creature, looking to us for breakfast. I poured the orange juice, your father cooked eggs and grits, and we sat down to eat ignoring the gore coating your grandfather from head to toe. This became a routine of sorts—we never discussed the hunts or the family business after that first night. It was something the Brabham men did, and I was not involved in any way.

We were married that winter, and a few short years later, you were born. I knew when I first held you that you would break my heart, and I counted the days until I knew I would have to leave you. Then Jason was born, and my fair-haired boy was just as dear to me as you were, my giant man-child firstborn.

The hardest thing I ever did was leave you both, and the second hardest was to return. I walked away from this world at the last possible moment. I began to feel myself become weaker, and had I remained here even a few weeks more, I would have become deathly ill and been unable to make the trek back to Faerie.

The day I walked away from here, I drove to the spot where your father first met me on the side of the road, walked into the forest, and stepped into the clearing. It was still there, unmolested after two decades. I lay down on the grass, surrounded by toadstools, and closed my eyes. When I opened them again, I was home.

And I wept for the life I left behind.

6

———————

The moonlight had given way to the pink of sunrise by the time Mama stopped talking. We all looked at her for a long time, saying nothing. Over the course of her story, Amy, Skeeter, and Joe had come out of their rooms and sat down at various places around the room. Amy sat cross-legged on the floor in front of me, her head leaning back on my knees. Skeeter was on the other end of the couch, his legs curled up under him covered up in a blanket we kept on the back of the sofa pretty much just for him. Joe sat in my recliner, leaned forward with his elbows on his knees and his chin propped up on his hands.

"So, you're back now..." I kinda let my question trail off into nothing.

"Because I wanted to see my children," she said. "I missed my family. I missed my husband. I missed my boys."

"Yeah, that didn't work out so good, I reckon." I was applying for Understatement of the Year with that one. The first time I saw Mama, a little more than a year ago, Jason had her tied to a stake and was ready to kill her as part of the kickoff party to his attempted monster revolution. She had to watch as I killed my brother in front of her, then I told her I never wanted to see her again.

I meant it, too. But she showed up with the rest of my gang when I most needed backup to save the world from a demon invasion, or at least some really shitty country music. So, I reckon she listened about as good as I usually do.

"I've had better reunions," she agreed. "Jason was..."

"Batshit crazy," Skeeter offered.

"Troubled," Joe countered.

"Nuts," Amy said right in time with the others.

"An asshole," I concluded. "But you missed the mess with Pop. I killed him, too. Cut him down with Great-Grandpappy Beauregard's sword." I pointed to the corner of the room, where the sword leaned up against the wall. I didn't carry it too often anymore. A little too much blood of people I cared about on it for my tastes.

"I know," Mama said. "Jason took great joy in telling me of your battle with your father. He seemed to think it would turn me against you."

"Did it?" I asked.

"No. Even in Jason's telling, it was obvious you had no choice. Your father was driven mad by the lycanthropy. It happens in some cases. You had no choice, Robbie."

"Bubba," I corrected.

"I don't think I'll be calling you Bubba, dear," she said, and there was some of that steel in her tone that let me know that no matter how old I got, she was still my mother.

"So now what?" I asked. "You're back, so am I supposed to just open my arms and welcome you home? And what's this about a sister? I thought you spent twenty years in Faerie missing a family, but it sounds like you just got started right in on making a replacement." I didn't bother to hide the sneer in my voice.

"That is uncalled for," she said, and I could see from the twitch in her jaw that my words hurt. I didn't really care.

"Bubba," Amy said, looking up at me. "Don't."

"Don't what?" I asked, my voice rising. "Don't call her out on her bullshit after she waltzes back in here after all this time? Don't refuse to welcome her back with open arms just because she decided she needs something from me? What am I exactly supposed to not do?"

"Don't act like you don't love your mama with every damn piece of your body, you stupid bastard," Skeeter said, getting up from the couch and stomping across the room to the deck.

"Skeeter, wait!" I said, watching the screen door slam behind him. "Shit."

"Yeah, pretty much," Joe said. "I'll go." He stood, but I waved a hand at him.

"Nah, this is on me," I said, standing up. Amy slid up onto the couch where Skeeter had been, and I walked toward the porch. I stopped right in front of Mama's chair. "I'm sorry," I said. "I was out of line. I ain't sure I've forgiven you yet, but I don't need to be a dick about it."

"Apology accepted, son. Now go talk to Skeeter."

I nodded and walked out onto the porch.

"Go away," Skeeter said, looking straight ahead as the sun started to peek over the hills.

"No," I replied.

"What?"

"No," I repeated. "I ain't going nowhere, Skeeter. That ain't what we do. We don't leave one another. You didn't leave me when Mama bailed, or when Britt got killed, or when Jason stabbed me, or any other time you should have. I didn't leave you when your mama died, or when you told your daddy you was gay, or when that dude from Atlanta dumped you, or even when you decided to become a ball-room dancer. You're stuck with me, so deal with it."

"You're an asshole."

"You ain't wrong," I agreed.

"I miss my mama every single day. I know you did, too. But now yours is back, and instead of getting down on your knees and thanking God Almighty, you're in there giving her a bunch of shit over stuff she couldn't help." Skeeter turned to me, and I could see the tears cutting tracks down his cheeks. "That makes you a Grade A, USDA Prime asshole."

"I can't disagree with you, Skeet. I just couldn't help myself. There's been so many times over the years that I wanted to say something to her, to ask her why, to tell her about something cool in my life, to have her hold my hand through some of the shit we've walked through...I just couldn't keep from being a dick. 'Cause I thought if I was enough of a dick, I wouldn't have to be so damn scared."

"Scared of what, Bubba? What the hell do you have to be scared of now?"

"Scared she'll leave again," I said, and I felt one big tear roll down my own face and get lost in my beard along with more than a little bit of beer and maybe a morsel or two of last night's dinner.

"You can't be scared of that, brother. You just got to take the time you got and cherish it. Everybody leaves one way or another, Bubba. Or we leave them. Shit, in our line of work it's way more likely that we'll be the ones leaving somebody behind. But if we focus on that, then we don't get to do no living. And that ain't nothing but dying while walking around."

"Shit, Skeeter, when did you get so smart?"

"I've always been the smart one. And the pretty one. You're just here to shoot shit and deal with the grateful women."

"I reckon I can handle that."

"Then let's get back inside and see what we're gonna do to save your sister." He turned and walked back into the house, leaving me outside with the stars, my thoughts, and one horny-assed hoot owl making a shitload of noise trying to get laid.

I took a deep breath and walked back inside. Skeeter was back on the couch, and Amy was sitting next to him now. I heard noise from the kitchen, so I figured Joe was putting coffee on. "There's bacon in the fridge," I hollered. I heard the refrigerator door open, then close, and a few seconds later, Joe's head popped into the living room holding a yellow Styrofoam tray from the grocery store.

"Bubba, are you alright?" he asked, and the look on his face was full of concern.

"Yeah, I reckon I'm fine. Why?"

"This is...turkey bacon."

"Oh, that's on me," Amy said. "*Somebody's* cholesterol was creeping up at his last checkup, so we've been making some changes to his diet." She gave me a sideways look. I kept my mouth shut for once.

Joe looked like somebody had just hit him in the head with something heavy. And given some of the spots me and Joe have been in, I know exactly what he looks like when somebody whops him upside the head. "Okay...I'm just going to go cook up this...turkey bacon and scramble half a dozen eggs. Coffee oughta be ready in a few minutes, then we can continue this conversation over some breakfast."

"I'll make the toast and grits," Amy said, getting up from her spot on the couch. "You three figure out the plan and fill us in over food." She walked into the kitchen with Joe, leaving me and Skeeter alone in the den with Mama.

"My two sweet boys," Mama said. "Look how you've grown. Even you, Skeeter. You're not so little and frail anymore, are you?"

"No, ma'am, I reckon not," he said.

"I'm sorry about your mama. She was a fine woman. I know you miss her."

"Every day," Skeeter said. "But that ain't what we're here for right now."

"He's right. So how about you tell me about this sister?"

"When I returned to Faerie, I couldn't go back to the lands of Mab. The second I stepped across the boundaries into the Winter Kingdom, she would know, and the punishment for my escape would be severe. I couldn't go to the Summer Court because even though my father now sat at the side of Titania, my status as Daughter of Mab and Heir of Winter would make me a bargaining chip at best, and a hostage at worst. So, I went into hiding."

"Are there places you can hide in Fairyland?" I asked.

"Not every acre of Faerie is aligned with Summer or Winter, my son," Mama said. "There are places, like the Western Wood, that stand independent of the Courts. These places are remote and rare. The Wood is allowed to be unaffiliated because of the strength of the

Witch, and her alarming tendency to turn people into frogs. Not to mention her appetite for frog legs."

I might have grinned a little at that idea. Skeeter shuddered, but I've had to deal with a few people who would be better off deep-fried.

"The mountains of Finalor are such a place. I returned to the Western Wood, then used another spell from the Witch to travel unseen to the foothills of Finalor. There is a small town there, nestled up against the mountains along a river that brings runoff down from the melting snow high above it. The town is called Hannes, and that is where I hid for most of the next twenty years."

"Not really explaining the whole sister thing yet," I prodded.

"Don't push, Robbie. It's unseemly," she scolded.

"Unseemly is kinda right in my wheelhouse," I said. Skeeter kicked me, one bony foot thrusting out from under the blanket he had across his lap. "Fine," I said. "I'll keep quiet."

"That'd be a first," Skeeter said.

"I met a blacksmith there, and over time, we began to speak socially. I mourned the loss of your father, and my family, for I knew it was unlikely that I would be able to return to you. But with the passage of years, the pain of losing you lessened, and I began to see the blacksmith. After a number of years, we wed. Some years after that, a daughter was born to us. She was a beautiful child, and we raised her in that little town with no knowledge of her lineage, or of her mother's travels to your world. I had put all that behind me."

"Until Jason," I said.

"Until Jason," she agreed. "I don't know how he managed the feat, but he sent a redcap to the village hunting me. It slaughtered my husband and brought me through a mushroom ring to the bonfire that Jason had planned for me."

"Wait," I said. "Jason knew who you were? What you were?"

"Not at all," Mama said. "He had one of his sorcerers cast a spell to find me, and they located me in Faerie. I disguised myself immediately when the redcap arrived, and Jason had no idea that I was anything other than his human mother, hiding from him in Faerie."

"Well, he was kinda right. You were his fairy mother, hiding from him there," I said. "Sorry," I added quickly, seeing the pain that flashed across her face. "I know it wasn't by choice. But how much time had passed for you?"

"Time moves differently in Faerie than here, so while over twenty years had passed here, it had been over a century for me."

I stared at her. "A century? You remember that in this world that a hundred years, right?"

"It is the same everywhere, Robbie. A century is one hundred years."

"So, to you, it was over a hundred years ago the last time we saw each other?"

"One hundred fourteen years, eight months, and three days between the time I walked out the door of our home and the time you rescued me from Jason," she replied. Her face was tight, like it was taking a huge effort to hold herself together, and now I was starting to understand why. Not only had she carried a torch for my dad for over a hundred years, she'd kept her memories of me and Jase for that long. All the anger kinda flooded out of me right then, and I realized how much she'd been hurting, and for how long.

"Wow," I said in a small voice. It was all I could say.

"When you told me, in no uncertain terms, that you were not interested in seeing me again, I returned to Faerie, determined to put my life there back together, to finish raising my daughter as the brilliant, fierce, strong young woman she is, and to never again attempt to contact you."

"So, what brought you here?" I asked. I held up a hand. "Don't get me wrong, after a lot of thinking about it, I'm really glad you're here. But I don't understand why."

"The Puck has taken my daughter, Robbie. When you encountered him last year and thwarted his games, he became angry with you. The woman he thought he loved turned out to be completely uninterested in a life outside of the Courts and left him. He blames you for his pain, and when he met you, he could sense me as a part of you."

"When you left, he came to the village and kidnapped your sister.

He took my daughter and fled with her. Only you can help me get my daughter back. Only you can save your sister, Robbie."

"Not only him, ma'am," Amy said, leaning against the doorjamb. "Bubba doesn't travel alone. He's got friends."

"Good friends," Joe added from beside her.

"And family," Skeeter said, holding out a fist to me.

I pounded fists with my best friend, nodded to Joe and Amy, and stood up. I held out a hand to Mama, pulling her to her feet. "Let's go eat some breakfast, then go to Fairyland, beat the shit out of Puck, and save my sister."

7

———

I pushed back from the table, a ton of turkey bacon and a three-egg omelet with pepper jack cheese and Texas Pete tucked safely away in my belly. "Okay, when do we leave?" I asked, looking at Mama.

"Leave for where?" she asked.

"Well, we gotta go to Fairyland to kick Puck's ass and get back... what did you say my sister's name was?" I asked.

"I didn't. Her name is Nitalia. And how do you plan to get to Faerie? It's not called Fairyland, by the way."

"I know," I said with a grin. "I'm screwing with you a little. I don't know, I figured we'd go to that patch of woods you came out of back when you first got here."

"That won't work," Mama said. "It's a movie theatre now."

"Oh. That sucks. Well, how did you get here?" Skeeter asked.

"I crossed over using a spell and cashing in the last of the favors I had built up with a pixie wizard over the years. The way I came to this world was a one-way trip, unfortunately."

"Well, shit," I said.

"How about the game?" Amy asked. We all turned to her. "You know, the game that sucked you into Faerie the first time?"

"Oh yeah," Skeeter said. "That Pokémon rip-off that Puck made."

"He took the app down and closed all the portals after I freed his girlfriend. We got him what he wanted, so he didn't need to steal any more human children," I said.

"No, now he has graduated to stealing Fae children," Mama grumbled.

"I've heard of some folks in the hills of Tennessee that are descended from the Fae. Their magic is centered in their music. Maybe they can create a portal," Joe chimed in from the sink where he was washing the breakfast dishes. Sometimes it's real good to have somebody around whose job title includes "servant." Even if it says "servant of God" and you ain't anywhere close to holy, usually you can get them to pick up the place a little bit if they get bored. Idle hands and all that jazz.

"I know those folk," Amy said, polishing off her orange juice. "They're under constant DEMON surveillance. They have no connection to Faerie anymore and no idea how to make contact. They've been on this side of the veil for too long. They have magic, but they're so many generations removed from Faerie that they don't even have lore on crossing over."

"You know a bunch about that bunch," Skeeter said.

"I spent three months trekking around Appalachia researching them when I first joined DEMON," Amy said. Her gig with the Department of Extra-dimensional, Mystical, and Occult Nuisances was the way I stayed out of jail a lot of the time, and every once in a while got to ride in a black helicopter. "They're harmless and very insular. Even if they had the ability to cross over, the odds of them using their magic for an outsider are extremely low."

"I might have an answer," Joe said. "It won't be easy to find him, and it will likely be even more difficult to convince him to render aid to a representative of the Church, but I would expect him to have some knowledge in this area."

I cocked an eyebrow at Joe. "Who are we talking about, buddy?"

"His name is Roy McEvoy, and he used to be a liaison between the

Church and a Hunter in New Orleans. He retired when he met someone and wanted to get married."

"Why do I get the feeling that there's a lot more you're not telling us?" I asked.

"Because there's a lot more I'm not telling you," Joe said. "It might be better if we just went to see Roy instead of discussing it too much. Let it suffice to say that he used to be a priest, he isn't anymore, and he has a few issues with the Church and her leadership."

"Well, shit, Uncle Joe, who doesn't have a few issues with the Church?" Skeeter asked.

"Most people haven't been excommunicated," Joe replied.

Amy let out a low whistle. The nuclear option of disobedience to the Church, excommunication was the kind of thing usually reserved for politicians, murderers, and fantasy writers. I didn't know what a priest could do to get the axe, but if he could get us to Fairyland, it sounded like we were going to go meet an ex-priest.

"Well, if he's our best option, I reckon he's what we got," I said. "Where is he?"

"He left Louisiana when he left the church. The last I heard, he had a place in the woods outside Shelbyville."

"That's a couple hours from here," Skeeter said. "Let's load up. We could be there by lunch."

"Everybody grab your gear and meet here in half an hour," I said. "Me, Amy, and Mama will ride in the truck. Skeeter, you and Joe take your car. Not the Beetle. The other car."

"You want me to bring the Groover?" Skeeter asked.

"Yeah," I said. "I think we're gonna need the cargo room."

Twenty-five minutes later, Skeeter rolls up my driveway in a jacked-up PT Cruiser tricked out like an old rat rod, complete with jet black paint and flames going down the side of it. It looked tough as hell, until Skeeter got close enough to hear and your ears started bleeding from the show tunes he was blasting from the radio.

Joe turned to me, fear in his eyes. "Come on, Bubba. You know I love my nephew, but three hours in a car with just him and the Broadway channel on XM is enough to kill a man. Please let me ride in the truck. I'll ride in the back with the guns, just don't make ride with the entire cast of *Wicked*. The last time I took a road trip with Skeeter, I knew every word to the *RENT* soundtrack within the first two hundred miles."

"Coulda been worse," I said. "He was on a Gilbert and Sullivan kick in high school. I still sometimes wake up in a cold sweat hearing *Pirates of Penzance* in my sleep."

We piled into the cars and rolled north to Shelbyville, a little town surrounded by a lot of trees. A lot of trees. Joe directed Skeeter to a driveway almost invisible in a patch of woods to the west of town, and we turned off somewhere long past where civilization ended. The gravel track was no problem for my big pickup, but Skeeter's little Cruiser bottomed out on the ruts more than once.

"Why did you tell him to bring that thing, Bubba?" Amy asked. "You know it's not worth a damn in any kind of rough terrain. He could have driven my Suburban if you wanted me to ride with you to keep you on your best behavior."

"I don't think I need anyone to keep Robbie on his best behavior, sweetie," Mama said from the back seat. "And I expect his desire for Skeeter to bring his own car has more to do with some customization that's been done to the vehicle than to the seating capacity."

Amy looked at me, and I shrugged. "She ain't wrong. Skeeter's got the Groover tricked out. There's a serious computer hooked to a sat phone wired up as an internet tether in the back, and he's lined the body panels with armor plate. All the glass is bulletproof, and those tires are run-flats. There's a button for nitrous in the gear shift, and in a pinch, that little car can hit one-twenty in a straightaway. I didn't know what we were going to run into here, so I wanted to make sure him and Mama were as safe as they could be when we went in."

"While I appreciate the sentiment with regard to Skeeter, I don't know why you're worried about me," Mama said. "I won't be staying with the car, and I can certainly take care of myself."

"I know you think that, Mama, but we don't know what we're

getting into here. I want to know that everybody with me can take care of themselves if I get hurt."

"Are the rest of your companions impervious to harm from most non-magical means?" Mama asked. "Because I am. Remember, Robbie, I am not just your mother, and I never was. While I played the dutiful housewife to keep my secret safe from your father, I am still a Princess of the Fae, of the Royal House of Winter, and I am magic incarnate."

I felt a chill through the air as her temper flared. The windows fogged up, and all of a sudden, I could see my breath in the cab of the truck. I looked at her in the rearview mirror, and all the soft edges of her face had melted away with the last vestiges of her illusion. She looked back at me with ice-blue eyes, pale skin, and black hair shot through with icy white.

"Well, then," I said. "I reckon you're coming with us."

"Damn straight," she muttered, and sank back into the seat.

"Just once I'd like to meet one of these shy, retiring women I hear tell of. I ain't never known one my whole life. I don't want to go out with her or anything, I just want to see her. Like Nessie, or a UFO."

"Not Bigfoot?" Amy asked with a smirk.

"Hell no! I have seen more damn sasquatches, and more *of* those sasquatches, than I ever want to see in my life. I had anxiety about measuring up to that furry jackass for months."

"Well, I for one am glad you got over that," Amy said, giving me a naughty grin.

"Children," Mama said in a warning tone. Dammit, now my monster hunts were starting to feel like a middle school dance, complete with chaperone. I needed to get her to Fairyland, and soon, so I could go back to pretending to be an adult.

After a good fifteen minutes of bumping along the half-maintained road that looked and felt more and more like a deer track with every turn, we pulled into a clearing about thirty yards across. In the middle of the clearing was a small frame house with a wraparound porch, a nice little hunting cabin, or maybe the kind of place that a rich city moron would buy for "getaway." It backed up onto a good-sized pond with a dock stretching out into it. I didn't see any kind of boat, so I figured whoever lived there just walked out on the dock to fish or whatever.

A battered old GMC pickup sat next to the house, as much rust as green paint showing on the hood and a long crack running sideways across the windshield. The only thing that looked real out of place was the satellite dish off to the right of the house, on the other side of a tiny garden that consisted of a dozen head of cabbage and six tomato plants. There was a row of what might have been beans planted, too, but I couldn't tell from the truck. This wasn't some kind of DISH network satellite—this was a big-ass, old-school dish, the kind people used to have back in the 80s. There was a generator tucked up beside the house, too, one big enough to power a building for several days. There was definitely more going on with this dude than you'd think from his choice of homesteads.

I put the truck in park and got out, leaving Bertha and her shoulder holster hanging on the back of the driver's seat. If anything went sideways, all I had was a little Judge revolver at the small of my back and a Buck hunting knife on my belt. Well, and a federal agent, a priest, a tech wizard, and my fairy mother. On further analysis, I decided I'd probably be okay.

Mama and Amy got out of the truck, and we all instinctively spread out, so no one shot could take out too many of us. Joe and Skeeter did the same thing when they got out of the Groover, and Joe stepped forward, his hands held high.

"Roy!" he called out. "It's Joe! Remember me? I work with Bubba, the Hunter from Georgia. We need your help."

"Piss off!" The voice was sandpapery and sharp, and I couldn't quite tell where it came from.

"We can't, Roy. We need to get to Faerie. I know you can send us there," Joe called.

"I don't know what you're talking about," the voice replied. "But I know you got five seconds to get your ass back in that ugly car before I put a bullet in your leg."

"Hey!" Skeeter protested. "What the hell is wrong with my car?"

"Stow it Skeeter," I said. "Mr. McEvoy," I called. "My name is Robert Brabham. People call me Bubba. We have to get to Faerie, and you're the best chance we have to do that. Could you please come out and talk to us?"

"I reckon we can talk, but it ain't gonna do no good. Especially not if you got him or any of his ilk with you." A man stepped out from the woods to the left of the house, a shotgun in his hand. He spat in Joe's general direction, then lowered the weapon when he got a good look at us.

"I'm sorry, folks," Roy said. "But I can't open the door to Faerie no more. If the queen finds us, she'll kill me."

"Holy crap, you got beef with Mab, too?" I asked. I turned to Mama. "Does my dear sweet granny just murder everybody she runs into?"

"I ain't worried about Mab," Roy said, and I'm pretty sure that's the first time anybody's ever uttered those words in that order, if Mab is anything like Mama described her. "It's that crazy Summer bitch that I'm afraid of. She gets hold of me, she'll yank my arms and legs off like a snotty kid playing with a fly."

"You exaggerate, husband," came a voice from the house. We all looked up as one of the most beautiful women I've ever seen came down the steps to stand next to Roy. Her hair was golden blonde, and she wore a tan of rich gold. Her eyes were a sparkling green so rich I could tell their color from a dozen yards away, and when she smiled, it seemed like the air became warmer.

"Titania would not kill you, my love," the woman said. "My mother is harsh, but not cruel."

"Wait a second," Amy said. "You mean to tell me that you're..."

"Yes," she said. "I am Tanara, Daughter of Titania, Heir to the Throne of Summer."

"Or you were until you came to hide here in the world of man," Mama said, stepping forward. She stood straighter than usual, and her black hair whipped around her in a perpetual chill wind. Her blue eyes glinted like ice in her pale skin, and the tips of her pointed ears poked out from her blowing ebon locks. She looked like Tanara's polar opposite, which I reckon she was in a lot of ways.

"Ygraine?" the blonde woman said, puzzlement etched in her furrowed brow. "What are you doing here?"

"I have to go home, Tanny," Mama said. "Puck has my daughter, and I have to get her back."

The two women stared at each other across the expanse of grass and dirt. Then after a long moment, Tanara nodded and said, "Well, I suppose if we aren't going to murder each other on sight like we're supposed to, we may as well go inside and have some tea."

8

"So does this mean that you're my aunt?" I asked the curvy blonde once we were all settled Roy's living room. Roy's place was even more rustic-looking than mine on the outside, but the inside was really swanky. There were two sofas, a big flat-screen TV, a couple of movie theatre recliners with cup-holders in the arms and a bunch of buttons on the side, and a glass-topped coffee table with fish swimming around inside it. I wanted to ask Roy how he fed the fish but decided we had more important stuff to deal with.

"What's wrong, Bubba? Having some impure thoughts about your fairy godmother?" Amy asked with a grin. I blushed a little because she wasn't too far off. Tamara was a good-looking woman, soft in all the right places with a hint of sharp edges. I wasn't sure I'd want to try to pick her up even if I wasn't dating a woman who carried a gun, but it would probably be worth the scars.

"Ygraine and I are half-sisters, both of us daughters of Oberon, so yes, human, I suppose I am your aunt. I would appreciate it if you never mentioned that fact again, in this world or any other." She looked at me with undisguised disdain, taking in my hair, my beard, and my tattoos with one sweeping glance. I guess the biker chic/heavy metal redneck look I cultivate just ain't for everybody. Her loss.

"My name's Bubba, Aunt Tanny," I said, holding out my hand with a huge grin. I've always had a talent for making uncomfortable people feel way more uncomfortable, and I was milking that for all it was worth with my newfound snotty-ass aunt.

She shook my hand, managing to only look mildly horrified. "This...behemoth is your son, Ygraine? What kind of beast was his father?"

"Werewolf," I said, my voice grim. "My father was a Hunter, then he got turned into a werewolf by my psycho brother. Then I killed him. A year or so after that, I killed my brother. I don't have the greatest track record with family members," I said. The Summer Princess turned a little pale, and I let a little grin escape as I turned around and walked back to the couch. Mama shot me a dirty look, but I just shrugged. Everything I said was true, and if she wanted me to play nice, maybe Auntie shouldn't have been an asshole.

"Why does Puck have your daughter, Ygraine? What could the Goodfellow possibly want with the child?" Tanara asked once I was seated.

"I have no idea," Mama said. "I just know that he took her, and I intend to return her to safety before she is harmed."

"You're kidding, right?" Skeeter asked.

Every head in the room spun around to stare at my friend. "What?" he said. "You really don't see it? It's a power play. It's the most obvious thing in the world. This is Puck, right? Like *A Midsummer Night's Dream*, Puck? He's a trickster. A con artist, a sham, and an angle-shooter. This gives him leverage against both Courts because your daughter is royalty of Winter *and* Summer."

"Because Oberon left Mab and is now with Titania," Joe said.

"Exactly," Skeeter agreed. "That means that Ygraine and her daughter..."

"Nitalia," Mama supplied.

"Nitalia," Skeeter continued. "You two are the only people with a halfway legitimate claim to either throne."

"Or both," I said. "That makes sense. As the granddaughter of Mab and Oberon, Nitalia has a legitimate claim to the Court of Winter and Summer. That's got to be why Puck was interested in her. But what is he going to get out of it? I met that little bastard, and he doesn't do shit without some way for it to benefit him."

"Power?" Joe asked. "Does he get some kind of authority by taking Nitalia to Mab? Or Titania?"

"The queens of the Fae do not let go of their authority easily," Tanara said. "I doubt that Goodfellow is so naive as to think that he would be seen with favor after such a trick."

"From the way he was acting when I left him, he just wanted to be left alone to canoodle with that cute Alethea chick," I said.

"The Princess Alethea?" Tamara asked. Her eyes were big. "Robin Goodfellow was romantic with the *Princess Alethea*?" The way she said it, you'd have thought I said that Neil Patrick Harris was sleeping with Lady Gaga.

"Yeah," I said. "Last time I saw them, they were romantic-ing all over the grass. I was a little scared she was romantic-ing the breath out of the poor little feller."

"Well," Tanara said, with a look at Mama. "That explains quite a bit."

"Indeed, it does," Mama said, a thoughtful look on her face.

"Maybe it explains a lot for the ones who grew up in a world of magic and munchkins, but it doesn't really do a thing for the rest of us," Amy said.

"Munchkins aren't real, dear," Mama said absently. "But Princess Alethea certainly is, and her father Alfont is very, *very* real. And very powerful."

"Lemme guess," I said. "He doesn't like Puck?"

Tanara laughed. "Your son has a gift of understatement, Ygraine!" She turned to me. "Aloft doesn't like anyone, and he despises anyone who can grant him no power or wealth. Goodfellow has unparalleled access to the kings and queens of Faerie and is allowed to pass freely between the courts, but he has no wealth to speak of. Or possessions, honestly. The Puck's trade has always been in secrets kept and given, and in power. He would never be able to pay a dowry of the type Alethea is sure to command."

"Unless he got a shitload of money in a hurry," I said.

"Like the kind of money a king or queen has access to," Skeeter added.

"Like the kind of money a king or queen would pay to get back their kidnapped daughter," Amy concluded.

"That's why she's the detective, ladies and gents," I said, bowing in my girlfriend's general direction.

"So, you think Puck took my daughter to be able to afford Princess Alethea's dowry?" Mama mused. "It makes sense, in a way. He has no conventional method of earning money, certainly not a sum so significant as to make Alfont consider him a worthy suitor for his daughter."

"So now we don't just need to find my sister, we need to find Puck a job so he can buy his wife, too? Is that what I'm hearing?" I asked. "This shit gets more difficult by the minute."

"Just wait until you have children, dear. Then you'll understand," Mama said, smiling at Amy. Amy blushed and looked at her feet, and I just shook my head. Babies weren't something we'd talked about, and I sure didn't want to have that conversation in the middle of a stranger's living room with Mama, Skeeter, and Father Joe taking part.

"Moving right along," I said to a collection of grins from my mother and my friends. "So we think we know why Puck took Nitalia, but we don't have any idea where he took her. Unless somebody's got an address for the wormy little bastard?"

"No one knows where Goodfellow keeps his residence. He lays his head wherever it is convenient, but he keeps his domicile very well-hidden," Tanara said.

"Okay, well, if we know anything, we know it's somewhere in Faerie," Skeeter said. "So that gives us our first step."

"Yeah," Amy agreed. "We need to get to Faerie."

"That's why we're here, right Joe?" I asked. "You said Roy had some kind of connections that could get us through to Fairyland."

"You did what, boy?" Roy popped up out of his recliner like his butt was spring-loaded, and he stomped across the room to stand over Joe. He had both hands clenched into fists at his sides, and I thought he was about to throw down with the much larger, and much younger, priest. I hopped up to try to get between them, but Amy put a hand on my belt and held me back. I reckon she figured that me stomping a muddle into our host would put a damper on our negotiations.

"I told them that you may know of a path to Faerie," Joe said. "And I think that secret was no longer very well-kept once we met your Fairy Princess wife." He pointed to Tanara for emphasis, and Roy looked a little embarrassed.

"Okay, I reckon that might be right. But you didn't know nothing about Tanny, so it still won't give you any kind of excuse for bringing strangers to my door. I told you when those sumbitches threw me out that I didn't want to ever see none of you collared assholes again." Roy seemed a little bit like the kind of guy who sometimes just wanted to pick a fight to get somebody to say he was right, and I didn't have time for that.

I stood up, my bulk displacing a lot of the air in the room. "Do we have a problem, Roy?" I asked. I intentionally kept my tone light, but there was no question that I wasn't in a mood to play. "Because we need to get passage to Faerie, and I don't really care how we do it. The fairy ring Mama came through the first time is under a movie theatre now, and the video game that sucked me in the last time got taken off the market on account of it being a tool Puck used to kidnap human kids."

"And I have no return trip in the charm I used to pass through the veil between worlds this time," Mama chimed in.

"So, if you've got a doorway to Fairyland sitting around here somewhere, I'd be much obliged if you'd put whatever shit you've got going with Joe and the Church aside long enough to open it."

"It's not Fairyland," Mama and Tanara said in unison.

"I guess they are sisters after all," Skeeter said, not near as quiet as he probably thought he did.

Roy glared at me, then back at Joe. "What do you think, honey?" he asked Tanara.

"We should help them," the woman said simply. "Children are rare among our kind, so every one is precious. Even a child of Winter."

"Thank you," Mama said.

"Don't thank us yet," Roy said. "It still ain't gonna be easy. There's two ways I know to get to Faerie around here. One is through the trunk of a giant live oak deep in the woods a day's hike from here. It's closer, and faster, but there's been reports of some kinda monster living in the woods near the tree."

"Monsters ain't usually much of a problem," I said. "In fact, monsters are kinda our thing."

"Alright," Roy said. "If you want to try to fight your way through to the tree, that's fine. The other way is a little farther away, but safer. At least, usually."

"What's that path?" Amy asked.

"Well, you go up on Lookout Mountain outside Chattanooga, and you go up to the caves at Ruby Falls. There's a troll in there, and under the floor of his lair is a passage to Faerie. He's usually pretty reasonable, but if you catch him in a bad mood, or you're rude to him..." He looked at me when he said that. I didn't understand why, so I just stared back. After a minute, he went on. "If you're rude to him, you'll probably have to fight him. If you do, bring fire. Trolls regenerate, and fire is one of the things that can stop them."

"So we traipse around in the woods around here looking for a mysterious monster to kill, or we go see Rock City and kill a troll in the caves outside Chattanooga. Is that about it?" I asked.

"Pretty much," Roy agreed.

"Sometimes I feel like my life is nothing more than a series of bad choices made between terrible options," I grumbled. I turned to the crew and asked, "What do y'all want to do?"

9

———————

Everybody pretty much wanted to try the closer option first, and I didn't blame them. It made the most sense, trying to get through to Faerie by the nearest route would be faster, and we didn't exactly have a surplus of time to work with.

We all went out to gear up while Mama got a map and some rough directions from Roy. I still didn't like the dude, but he seemed pretty trustworthy. At least as long as we did what we said we'd do and got the hell off his property soon.

"What did this guy do to get thrown out of the Church, anyway?" Skeeter asked as he opened the back hatch on the Groover and started putting on body armor. Skeeter ain't much good in a fight, but he's made a lot of money selling collectibles on eBay and doing free-lance IT work, so he can afford the best gear money can buy. He thinks it makes him look tougher, and I never have had the heart to tell him it makes it look like he's armor-plating a toothpick. Sure, he's a bigger badass than he used to be, but he still ain't putting any fear into the hearts of men. Or women. Or housecoats. Or schnauzers.

"It's a long story," Joe replied, strapping down a Colt 1911 pistol in a holster on his leg. Joe carried a Buck hunting knife and a Winchester 700 rifle with a scope and bipod, too. He wasn't the best of us close in, but the preacher could shoot Washington's eye out of a quarter from a hundred yards.

"We got time," I said. I had Bertha in a shoulder rig, a couple extra magazines under my right arm, and my caestus on my hands. The metal-clad spiked gloves made me feel even more badass than they looked. I didn't go in much for long guns. Bertha was usually all the firearm I needed. I slung Grandpappy's sword over my head in a scabbard that left the handle sticking up over my left shoulder and practiced drawing it a couple of times. I'd gotten better with the sword as time went by, but I was always going to be more of a punch and shoot things kinda guy.

"Roy was excommunicated for falling in love with his work," Joe said.

A lightbulb went off for me, and from the way Amy's head snapped up, it did for her, too. She paused in checking her weapon, a H&K MP-5 submachine gun, and asked, "So that woman in there, she's the reason Roy was fired from the church?"

"If I get fired for a woman, I hope she's at least that pretty," I muttered.

"She is," Amy said. I blushed and nodded at her, and she gave me a grin that let me know she was almost joking.

"Yeah, Roy and his Hunter ran across her out west somewhere, and she glamoured the crap out of the Hunter. I don't know if she was going to kill him or what, but apparently when Roy got there, the Hunter was tied to a spit over a huge fire. He shot the fairy, she kicked the crap out of him for it, and eventually they got tired of trying to murder one another and started talking."

"Turns out the whole fight was a misunderstanding. Seems Darryl, the Hunter, had come upon Tanara while she was taking a bath and made a lewd suggestion or two. She took offense and beat his ass."

"I don't blame her," Amy said. "Some of these Hunters need some sense beaten into them every once in a while. Or every day."

I didn't take the bait. I thought I was doing real good by ignoring that obvious shot at my behavior and proving the lack of truth in her words by not responding. That's what I was telling myself, instead of admitting I didn't have anything sufficiently smart-assed to say in response.

"Anyway," Joe continued. "Roy talked Tanara into not having broiled redneck for dinner, and they started living together. The Church takes a dim view of priests breaking their vows of celibacy, so they kicked him out."

"Three or four times a day," Roy said from the porch. We all turned around, with varying degrees of embarrassment at him finding us listening to him.

"What was that, Roy?" I asked.

"They didn't like me breaking my vow of celibacy three or four times a day," Roy said with a grin. "Of course, they never met Tanny. If they had, they'd understand."

I didn't high-five the crotchety old fart. I really didn't. But I damn sure wanted to. Instead, I looked at Mama, who had come out onto the porch with Roy and Tanara. "You ready to go?" I asked.

"I am. Are all of you prepared?" Everybody nodded, then Mama turned to Tanara. "Thank you for your hospitality. I hope you remain well and that no harm comes to your home or family."

"And yours as well," Tanara replied. The two women inclined their heads formally, and Mama came down the steps to where I waited. "Robbie, did I see a Mossberg twelve-gauge in your truck earlier?"

"You did," I said. "You want it?"

"I believe it might prove useful." I opened the back door of the truck and opened the gun case built under the back seat. I pulled out the shotgun and handed it to her, along with a bandolier of shells.

"The ones with blue paint are cold iron shot," I said. She shuddered at the mention of the deadly fairy-killing metal. "The white ones are holy water, the reds are mixed with white phosphorous, and the one with silver paint...well, I reckon you can figure that one out."

She loaded the Mossberg with alternating phosphorous and silver rounds, then slung it over her shoulder. "Let's go," she said.

"You heard the lady," I said with a slam of the truck door. "Let's go find the door to Fairyland and get my sister home safe!"

Seven hours later, I was a lot less chipper about the whole idea. Seven hours later, we were ass-deep in wilderness, gathered around a campfire and being real thankful that it wasn't cold out since we didn't bring cold weather gear. Even living on top of a mountain, I still live in Georgia, so I don't own what normal people would consider cold weather gear.

I reached into my backpack and pulled out a quart jar of moonshine. Mama looked at me, then sighed.

"You are absolutely your father's son, aren't you?" she said, shaking your head.

"As long as old man Peabody still makes apple pie, I'm not going on a road trip without a jar in the truck somewhere." I took a long pull of the sweet white liquor and passed the jar to Joe. He took a good, long pull and passed it along. Sobriety was not a vow the Church made him take when he slapped on that collar.

The jar made it to Mama, and she dipped two fingers into the liquid, flicking it into the fire. It blazed up a little at the splash, and she smiled up at the sky. "For the ones we've lost," she said, and took a long sip.

She handed me back the jar, and asked, "Are we camping here tonight, then?"

"We might as well," Amy said. "This clearing is on high ground, so we're good if an unexpected rain comes up, and we've got a stream right here for running water. We're not likely to find a better spot before sunset."

"You ain't wrong," Skeeter said, unzipping his backpack and pulling out a ball of string.

"What's that, Skeeter?" Joe asked.

"You ain't never been camping with me, have you?" Skeeter said.

"No, but I don't think that's a tent."

"Not even close," Skeeter said. "This is how me and Bubba have camped ever since tenth grade." He dug around in the bottom of his bag until he found a pair of carabiners, then unrolled the ball of string on the ground between two trees. He wrapped one end of the long rope around a tree trunk, over a couple of low-hanging branches, and secured it with the carabiner. Then he did the same thing with the other end, spread the strands apart, and sat down in his very portable, very collapsible, pretty darn comfortable, nylon hammock.

Skeeter swung back and forth a couple of times, kicking his feet like a little kid on the playground. "This is living. All I got to do is wrap up in my sleeping bag, and it's like I'm lying on air. Because I am."

"That looks better than this ground mat I brought along, but I guess I'll live," Joe said, a little crestfallen at the comfort Skeeter was obviously enjoying.

"You know I wouldn't do that to you, Joe," Skeeter said. "There's two more in my bag. I brought one for Mrs. Brabham, too."

"You may call me Ygraine, Skeeter."

"No, ma'am, that wouldn't be respectful," Skeeter demurred. "But I appreciate it."

Mama smiled at him. "I haven't been Mrs. Brabham for a long time. I have missed it."

I turned away from them, digging through my own pack for the pair of hammocks I had stowed there, and rigged up sleeping arrangements for me and Amy while she went down to the creek and filled up a couple of jugs of water for everyone. A couple of purification tabs later, and we didn't have to worry about anybody contracting a bad case of the trots off anything that might have crept into the water.

"I'll take first watch," I said. "I ain't even close to sleepy."

"I'll stay up with you," said Joe. "We should watch in pairs since we have enough people."

"Fair enough, Padre," I agreed. I took up a post with my back to a big elm poplar tree, putting the fire behind me so I'd be in shadow and anything coming toward me would be illuminated.

Everybody turned in not too long after that, and I settled in to keep an eye out for bears and cougars, way more likely to cause trouble in the hills of Tennessee than my usual prey. Nothing showed up, and about four hours later, Mama came over and sat down next to me with her Mossberg across her lap.

"Are we okay, Robbie?" she asked. "You still haven't really talked to me about all this, not one-on-one."

"I haven't really had a lot of time to figure everything out, Mama," I said, letting out a long breath and watching it cloud up in the cool air. It was still warm enough for just a sleeping bag, but the temperature had certainly dropped as night went along.

"I understand that," she said. "It's a lot to take in."

"Hell, part of me was convinced that seeing you back in Athens was a hallucination," I said. "There was so much going on, what with Jason being crazy and wanting to kill me and all, I just kinda put you out of my mind most of the time."

"I don't blame you. But you understand now why I had to go, at least?"

"Yeah, I understand. I reckon. But what I don't understand is why you didn't feel like you could talk to me, or to Pop, or even Jason about it. You could have told us what you are."

"Could I?" she asked. I turned and looked at her, but she looked me right in the eye. "Could you honestly say that twenty-two years ago you were as accepting of other species as you are now? And your father? I daresay he never got over that particular blind spot."

"Well, he kinda got over hating lycanthropes, on account of turning into one," I joked. Neither of us laughed. Pop's death was still fresh to her, only learning about it the day before, and that brought it back for me. I thought for a second and then nodded, not that she could see it. "You're right. He never would have been okay with it. He would have called you a liar and a monster, or worse. And that would have made me and Jase think less of you, and that wouldn't have been no good neither."

"Your grammar has gotten atrocious since I've been away," Mama said.

"Ignore him when he talks like a moron, Mother," Amy said from the shadows. "He knows better, he's just lazy."

"Always has been, dear."

"You don't mind if I call you Mother, do you? Ygraine seems too casual, and Mrs. Brabham seems too formal."

"You may certainly call me Mother, dear. It seems to fit me, I think."

"Well, if you two are gonna sit out here and talk about my grammar, I reckon I'll just drag my ignorant behind to bed," I said, standing up and walking toward my hammock. I gave Amy a kiss and threw a couple more pieces of wood on the fire, then settled in to sleep, with the low hum of the two most important women in my life talking in the shadows.

10

"Great God Almighty, Bubba, you have got to do something about that snoring!" Being awakened by Skeeter bitching is not on the top ten list of my favorite ways to wake up. The only reason I didn't kill him with my bare hands is I had to pee too bad to run him down.

I rolled out of the hammock into a standing position, then pushed my way through some underbrush to find a quiet place to take a leak. I finished my business, then turned to see a giant fist filling my field of vision. I had just enough time to turn my head a little, so I took the punch on my cheekbone instead of flush on the nose, but it was still enough to knock me flat on my ass, right in the puddle of pee I'd just created. Now I was pissed, in more ways than one.

I looked up and saw a giant muscled beast standing over me, its shoulders shaking like it was laughing. Then I heard the *huff-huff* coming from it, and I knew it was laughing. At me. At me, knocked on my ass in a puddle of piss. This was not the kind of morning I had in mind when I rolled out of my hammock.

I sprang to my feet and charged the thing, lowering a shoulder to ram right into its stone-gray stomach. Its very hard, unyielding, and fur-covered stomach. I hit the thing at a dead run, but it didn't even budge an inch. It just slammed an elbow down between my shoulder blades and sent me to the ground again. At least this time I wasn't lying in pee.

I rolled over, and the thing was just standing there chuckling at me again. It looked down, its yellow eyes almost buried in the folds of its face, and grinned. Well, I couldn't really tell if it was grinning or just snarling like it was going to eat me. All I knew was that I could see a lot more teeth than just the two curved tusks protruding from its lower jaw, and it looked like it was still laughing at me.

But this wasn't the first time I'd tangled with a critter way bigger and stronger than me. It also wasn't the first time one of those critters had knocked me flat to the ground without even breaking a sweat. And it sure as hell wasn't the first time I'd had to come up with some way to level the playing field against a monster bigger, meaner, and tougher than me.

So, I got up on one knee and punched that gray bastard right in the balls. I swung an uppercut into its jewel sack with everything I had, and I swear I thought I felt something rupture under my knuckles. The creature stopped smiling as it tried real hard to keep its eyes from popping out of its skull, and it dropped to its knees just inches in front of me. It wobbled there, clutching its crotch, eyes wide and mouth open in a silent "o" of absolute agony, so I decided to put something hard in its mouth.

I rested the barrel of my Judge revolver on the teeth between those curved mini-tusks and cocked the hammer. "You so much as blink wrong, and I will send double-ought buckshot crashing right through the back of your skull, do you understand me?"

The thing started to speak, but I held up a hand. "Blink once for yes. Do you understand me?"

Blink.

"Good. Now we're going to go back to my camp, real slow. I'm not going to take this gun out of your mouth, and if you try anything stupid, I will decorate the forest with your brains. Are we clear?"

Blink.

"Excellent," I said. Then I looked around and realized I had no way to get back to camp because I couldn't get up without taking the gun out of the monster's mouth. Then it couldn't stand up with my pistol in its mouth, and we sure as shit couldn't walk through the woods that way.

"Stand up," I said, taking the gun out of its mouth and clambering to my feet as quick as I could. I managed it a lot faster than my granite-faced friend, but that's probably because nobody had played Whack-A-Mole with my marble bag lately. He got up, and I pointed the gun at his dick.

"You think your shit hurts now?" I said, waving the gun. "Just imagine what happens if you piss me off. Now let's go."

We managed a weird kind of shuffle through the woods back to camp, with the monster walking sideways and me getting smacked in the face with a shit ton of branches because I kept watching the monster's crotch instead of watching where I was going.

We stepped into the clearing, and the low hum of conversation halted the second folks got a look at us.

"Robbie, what the hell are you doing with that ogre?" Mama asked.

"Bubba, why does it smell like pee all of a sudden?" Skeeter asked almost simultaneously.

"This is an ogre?" I asked Mama. "Shut up," I said to Skeeter.

"That is indeed an ogre. But what is wrong with it? Is there something wrong with its face?"

I looked at its face and couldn't see anything wrong with it. But I didn't know what an ogre was supposed to look like. This one looked like somebody took the Gray Hulk, gave it tusks like an Arkansas Razorback, put it in a pair of cutoff overalls and the biggest damn pair of Birkenstocks I'd ever seen, and then set it loose to wander around in the woods for a couple years. *Birkenstocks? What the hell kind of monster can afford overpriced flip-flops? My life is weird some days.*

"I don't know about its face, but there's something wrong with its balls. As in I punched it in them. But I'm fine, thanks for asking."

"Of course you are," Mama said. "Ogres are peaceful creatures. I don't know why you felt the need to strike one in the first place."

"Thank you, my lady. I am Gr'kang'thun'xanlaxitan. But most species with malformed mouths such as yours choose to call me Greg." His speech sounded a lot like somebody grinding rocks together in his mouth, but I could understand him pretty well.

"I am Ygraine, Daughter of Winter. This is my son, Robert, and his friends Amy, Skeeter, and Joe. We are pleased to meet you and offer sincerest apologies for any misunderstandings that arose upon our initial contact."

I turned to the big gray bastard, who cocked his head at me. "I'm pretty sure there ain't no misunderstanding when a damn eight-foot gargoyle sucker-punches the shit out of you." I wasn't quite ready to forgive and forget, no matter how peaceable Mama said this granite-faced shithead was.

The ogre looked at me, cocking his head to one side and then the other like a curious bulldog. "I am sorry I hit you, human. But you were urinating on my rosemary."

"Who's Rosemary? I didn't see anybody."

"My herb garden. Rosemary is an herb." He turned to Mama. "Are all the humans in this world stupid? I have encountered few of their kind, and they have not been impressive overall."

"Not all of them, but my son is exceptional in many ways," she said, her lips pursed in that disapproving way that only mothers can really manage.

"I'm going to pretend that I'm either too stupid to be insulted, or that you aren't insulting me, and let's just move on the part where we beat this monster's ass and clear the path to the tree with the portal in it."

"Portal?" the ogre said. "What portal are you talking about?"

"We have to get to Fairyland, and the word we got was that there's a portal in a big-ass oak tree back here, but we'd probably have to kill you to get to it," I said. "Sorry about that, but we're kinda on a mission."

"That asshole Roy sent you, didn't he?" The ogre's face went a little red, and I started to think that maybe telling the giant monster my entire plan wasn't the best move I could have made.

"We talked with Roy, yes," Joe said, stepping forward, his empty hands held in front of him to make him look totally non-threatening. I don't know what universe a two-hundred-pound human is going to look threatening to a four-hundred-pound ogre with fists the size of Honeybaked hams, but I'm sure the gesture was appreciated. "Do you have a problem with him? Is that why he told us you were dangerous?"

"I am dangerous...to Roy. That douchecanoe trapped me here when he and his idiot wife destroyed the portal." The ogre leaned on a nearby tree, which creaked in terror under the strain.

"Douchecanoe?" Mama repeated. "I don't think I'm familiar with that term."

"It means butthole," I said, trying to keep my language clean, or at least clean-ish around my mother. I knew it was gonna be a losing battle, but I thought she might appreciate the thought. "I ain't quite sure how the Jolly Gray Giant here heard it, but whatever."

"I get the internet, human. I read The Bloggess. I'm cultured. Unlike some people." I was pretty sure I wanted to punch him in the nuts again, but it seemed like a poor choice.

"That's neither here nor there," Amy said. "What do you mean, Roy and his wife destroyed the portal?"

"The last time they passed from Faerie into this world, they were being pursued. I was part of that pursuit, and as they entered this world, they triggered a spell on the tree that closed the portal and destroyed any link between this place and Faerie, cutting off pursuit and trapping me here, away from my family and all that I have known."

"Why were you chasing them?" I asked.

"Excuse me?"

"You said you were part of the pursuit, so why were you chasing them? If you're such an injured party here, why were you chasing Roy and Tanara in the first place?" I holstered my pistol and crossed my arms in front of my chest. He seemed like he didn't want to throw down, and I felt like even if he did, the pile of us could take him, so the odds of me having to shoot him in the junk were pretty low.

"Roy stole something from my father. I was trying to get it back."

"What did he steal?" Skeeter asked. I looked over at him and could almost see the glint of fairy gold in my best friend's eyes. He was a huge fantasy literature nerd, so in his head there was no chance that Roy didn't have a magic ring tucked away somewhere, or at least a goose that shit gold bricks or something like that.

"Pumpkin seeds," the ogre said.

"What?" Skeeter asked, his voice going up a full octave from his normal irritating high-pitched tone. "You mean, like magical fairy pumpkin seeds that grow pumpkin stalks up into the clouds where giants have gold-pooping geese or something like that, right?"

The ogre looked at him, and for somebody with a face like the University of Georgia mascot, only with a worse underbite, he managed to convey a whole lot of "you're a dumbass" with one look. "No. They are just pumpkin seeds. They are of Faerie, so they would grow larger than normal in mundane soil, at least for one generation."

"If all they stole were pumpkin seeds, why even chase them?" Joe asked. "The last time I checked, seeds were something pumpkins produced in abundance." He wasn't wrong, either. We all got drunk one Halloween carving pumpkins on my back deck and throwing the seeds over the rail down the side of the mountain. The next time I turned around, the hillside below my house was full of damn wild pumpkins.

"My father's pumpkins were widely regarded as the best-tasting in all of the Summer Court. He held the seeds of the best fruit from each harvest back for planting the next season. Those are the seeds that Roy and Tanara stole."

"Why?" Amy asked.

"Because were gonna use them to make a new portal back to Faerie," came a grouchy voice from the woods. "And we would have had it, too."

"If it hadn't been for you meddling kids," Me, Skeeter, and Joe all said in unison as Roy stepped into the clearing holding a shotgun, followed by Tanara carrying a lever-action .30-.30 Winchester.

11

___

"Put down your weapons," Roy said. "And Greg, go get them damn seeds." He and Tanara spread out so that one shot from my Judge couldn't take them both out, not that I thought too seriously about that. Much. Okay, maybe for a few seconds, but not more than ten.

"What the hell are you doing, Roy?" Joe asked, stepping forward. Roy and his wife both trained their weapons on him, and Joe froze in place. I could feel my face getting a little red. I really don't like people pointing guns at my friends. Especially Joe, who's one of the kindest people who's ever been willing to put up with me.

"You need to put those peashooters down before somebody gets hurt. Somebody that looks a lot like you," I said, my voice a low growl.

"You think I'm scared of you and your big pistol, boy? I know better. I'll cut you in half with a load of double-ought buck before you can say boo. Then me and Tanny will take care of your friends and this dumb gray bastard, and I'll finally get my hands on them seeds."

"Seriously?" Amy asked, stepping forward a little. "This is about pumpkin seeds? What the ever-loving hell is so special about these seeds?"

"The pumpkins are really big," Greg said. "That's all."

"That ain't all, you jackass," Roy almost yelled at the ogre. "Those seeds don't just make big-ass pumpkins, although they do that, too. They take root here and in Faerie at the same time."

"So they make magical big-ass pumpkins. Big deal," I said, taking a step forward to make a solid line beside Amy and Joe, blocking Skeeter from the gun-toting redneck's view. I didn't know what he was going to do, but I figured if Joe and Amy both wanted him to be able to do it without being seen, it was probably a good idea.

"It ain't just the pumpkins, you stupid hick," Roy said, his shotgun pointing at the ground as he smacked himself in the forehead at my stupidity. "The vines can be used to weave a doorway to Faerie along the root system of the pumpkins. As long as the fruits exist in both realms at the same time, we can use them to travel between this pit of idiocy and Faerie whenever we choose."

"Don't call my boy stupid, human," Mama said, taking a step toward him. Roy and Tanara both leveled their guns at her, and I saw a little smile flicker across her face.

"Now!" she yelled, and clapped her hands over her ears. I caught on right away, and I dropped to one knee, closing my eyes tight and covering my ears. Amy and Joe did the same thing as Skeeter tossed a flash-bang right in front of Roy and his fairy wife.

The stun grenade went off with a thunderous boom and a flash of light that made spots in my vision through closed eyelids. I heard a second boom go off right behind it and opened my eyes to see Roy spinning around, his shotgun waving wildly through the air, smoke pouring out of the barrel. I stood up and yanked the gun out of his hands, then clubbed him to the ground with a big right cross.

I turned to Tanara, but she was already on the ground at Amy's feet, her gun lying in the dirt beside her and blood streaming from between her fingertips as she clutched her face.

"By dose!" she said, her speech distorted by her fingers and her broken nose. "Doo bitch, too boke by dose!"

"Shut up, Tanny," Mama said, stepping forward. Her shirt had a bunch of new holes in it, and she looked *pissed*. "I liked this shirt, and your jackass husband had to go shoot it. Now quit your sniveling and be glad we're letting you keep breathing."

"I haven't decided on that yet," I said, shaking my head to cut the ringing in my ears a little. "I just got back on speaking terms with my mother, and I don't take kindly to assholes shooting her. Now what about this portal you sent us here to find? Is that all bullshit?"

Roy looked like he was about to pee himself, and I'm not completely sure he could hear everything I was saying, so I prodded him in the side, not exactly gently, with one foot and yelled, "WHERE'S THE PORTAL, DICKHEAD?"

"WHAT?" he hollered back.

"POR-TAL?"

"Oh," he looked even more scared. "I mighta lied." He was still talking loud, but he wasn't yelling anymore at least.

"What are you saying, asshole?" I poked him in the side with my foot again, if we're being real generous with the definition of "poke." He rolled around for a second or two, but stopped and waved his hands to stop me when I drew back for another kick.

"There's no portal here! Just don't kick me again, dammit!"

"Sonofa*bitch*!" I turned and stomped off to keep myself from putting my foot through Roy's lying-ass face.

Joe knelt next to the man and said, "What are you saying, Roy?"

"The ogre's telling you the truth. We closed the portal behind us when we came through. He squeezed through just before it shut, and we ain't been able to open it since. Tanny was hell-bent on her old nurse delivering her baby, so we had to get them seeds, get them planted, and get the portal set up before we could get to the business of procreating," Roy said.

I stopped pacing as the pieces all fell into place like a *Tetris* game. I turned around and looked at Roy, knowing full well my eyes were big as damn dinner plates. "You mean this whole thing was on account of you wanting to get laid?"

He didn't speak for a second, then he looked over at Tanara, then back at me, and said, "Well, can you blame me?"

I thought for a second, took a look at Tanara, or at least as much of her as I could see since she still had both hands clapped over her face and a little bit of blood on her chin. She was a damn good-looking woman, what I would typically say was way out of Roy's league, him being a skinny bandy-legged dude of around fifty, and her looking like a twenty-something supermodel. But then I glanced over at Amy's smoking hot body and realized that there truly is absolutely no accounting for taste.

"Nah, I reckon I can't blame you on that one, son," I said. "But it don't forgive you trying to rob us or you shooting my mama. I'm still pissed about that one."

"Well, what are we gonna do?" Skeeter asked. "We still need to get through to Faerie, and now we've wasted a whole day on this asshole's lies."

"He ain't wrong. I reckon the best thing for us to do is get out of here and head to Chattanooga, unless that was all bullshit, too." I looked down at Roy and used my pistol to make it real clear how happy I was going to be if he was lying about the Ruby Falls portal.

"There is a portal in Chattanooga," Greg said. "It is reportedly somewhere in the caves at Ruby Falls."

"Sounds good," I said. "Let's go." I turned to go, then thought better of it. I picked up Roy and Tanara's guns and handed them to the ogre. "I reckon you can do something with these?"

He grinned a husky grin and nodded. "Indeed I can." The jolly gray giant put one hand on the end of the barrel of each gun, one hand on the stock, and flexed his shoulders. The guns twisted together with a loud *screeeeech*, and in a few seconds, Greg was holding a nice steel pretzel with engraved wooden stocks. He dropped the mangled guns in the dirt at Roy's feet and snarled down at the man.

"Stay out of my woods, and stay away from my pumpkin seeds," the ogre said. "I have resigned myself to never seeing my family again, but if you continue to attempt to use my father's legacy for your personal gains, I will not even shed a tear over your graves as I dig them."

Roy looked scared, but Tanara just looked pissed. I wasn't sure what was up with her running from Fairyland, but I didn't believe she was just gonna live and let live with Greg after a stern talking-to.

I sighed. "I can't believe I'm saying this..."

"Oh, tell me you ain't gonna say what I think you're gonna say," Skeeter said.

"I completely agree," Joe said quickly. "Anything else would be unacceptable."

"What are you talking about?" Greg asked.

"You should come to Chattanooga with us," I said. "We gotta get to Fairyland anyway, and it sounds like you don't really want to stick around here."

"Not to mention that we don't trust these two assclowns not to keep bothering you for your seed," Amy said.

I laughed out loud. I didn't even try to hold it back. She glared at me. "Sorry, but that one caught me as funny."

"We'll see how funny it is when you room with the ogre tonight," she shot back. I closed my mouth with a snap.

"Anyway," I said, turning back to Greg. "For all those reasons, and the fact that we might need a little more muscle than we have with us right now, if you want to come with us to find this cave portal and go back home, I reckon we could make room in the truck for you. In the back, I mean. There ain't no way you're fitting inside." He was damn near eight feet tall, and even with a full-size truck, I barely fit in it. An ogre was just stretching Ford engineering a little bit too far.

Greg scrunched up his face like he was thinking real hard, then finally, he nodded his head. "I will accompany you to the portal in the caves. As much as I dislike caverns, it is the best chance I have at returning home. It will also keep my father's seeds from falling into the hands of thieves such as these." He glared at Roy and Tanara, who both scooted backward a little on their butts in the dirt.

"It's settled, then," I said. "Let's get marching back to Roy's house, then we can get on the road to Chattanooga." I turned and started packing up camp.

"What about these two?" Joe asked, standing over Roy. "We can't take them with us, but I don't feel right just leaving them out here with no consequences for their actions."

"Kill 'em," I said. "I don't care what you do with 'em." I walked off and started loading my pack, leaving a couple of shit-scared asshats sitting in the dirt with my family and best friends, who would no more likely kill two unarmed people than I would buy Duran Duran's Greatest Hits album. About fifteen seconds later, I saw Roy and Tanara haul ass through our campsite back toward their house like their asses were on fire.

Everybody else came back to the camp and started packing their shit. Mama looked over at me. "That wasn't very nice, Robbie."

"I didn't mean to be nice, Mama. I meant to scare the shit out of them. Did it work?"

"It did, indeed," she replied. "We should leave as soon as Greg returns. It will take us several hours to hike back to Roy's house, and there is no telling what he will have done to our vehicles by then."

"I'm pretty sure he won't do anything to our cars, especially since he thinks Bubba might kill him and eat him if he does," Skeeter said.

"Please do not try to eat Roy," Greg said, stepping out of the woods with a small pack over one shoulder. "Human is disgusting enough when fresh, and I am certain that any dish made with Roy would be starting from rotted stock."

"Good to know," I said. "Don't eat rotten humans. Words to live by. Let's get you back to Fairyland before I have to ask why you know this."

12

———

As predicted, our vehicles were untouched when we got back to them. In the case of my truck, I would believe it was fear. In the case of Skeeter's Groover, it might also have something to do with the high-voltage car alarm he wired to it. Anybody touching his wheels without his permission was in for a nasty, nasty shock.

"Let's roll," I said, opening the back door of the truck and throwing my pack inside.

"Slow down, Bubba," Amy said. "I've got to use the bathroom, and we might take advantage of Roy's absence to get a quick shower in. Chattanooga's only a couple hours away; we can get there before they close with no problem."

"She's got a point," Mama said. "Bad enough we wasted a day and night while Nitalia is still trapped in Faerie, but I could live without riding in an enclosed space with ripe Hunter for several hours."

"Yeah, I reckon I'm probably a little ripe. But you don't think Roy left his door unlocked, do you?" I asked.

"He lied to us, ambushed us, and probably would have killed us. I don't really care if his door is locked or not," Amy said. She drew her pistol and shot out the deadbolt in Roy's door, then planted a kick right above the knob. The doorjamb splintered, and she stepped across the threshold as we watched. "Dibs on the shower!" she called over her shoulder.

"You know there ain't gonna be a drop of hot water after that, right?" I asked.

"I'm made of magic," Mama said. "I can heat my own water."

I grumbled, resigning myself to a cold shower and a long car ride with a wet ponytail. I walked around to the back of the truck and dropped the tailgate, sitting down and motioning Greg over to sit next to me. The shocks on the truck protested a little at having both me and an ogre all on one axle, but I didn't listen. I knew from experience that DEMON could reimburse me for trucks I destroyed in the line of duty, even if the Church had gotten a little stingy with their vehicle allowances.

"So, you're raring to get back to Fairyland?" I asked.

"Yes, I am very much desiring to return home," the ogre said.

"You got a lady ogre back there you wanting to get back to?"

He blushed a little bit. The big gray bastard actually turned a little bit pink around the edges. "Yes, I do have an ogress I am very fond of and would very much like to see again."

"What's her name?"

"It is largely unpronounceable to humans, but you would probably call her Kate."

"That's a good name." We sat there in silence for a few minutes, then Joe came over.

"How's it going, Bubba?" he asked.

"I'm making it. How about you?" I replied.

"I'm fine. But I'm not the one dealing with finding out that his long-lost mother isn't just back in the picture, but she's also a fairy princess. That's a lot to process at one time."

"That's true," I allowed. "But it don't really matter how much it is to process, it ain't on the list of stuff I can deal with right now."

"So you're just going to ignore it, pretend it's not really a thing?" Joe asked. "I can't think that's healthy, Bubba."

"Is it more or less healthy than ignoring the fact that I've sworn a vow of celibacy and still reconnected with an old girlfriend on a case and now have to re-evaluate the last couple decades of my life?" I fired back. Joe didn't say a word, just turned around and walked off to sit on the porch steps next to Skeeter.

"You have sworn an oath of celibacy?" Greg asked. "But you and the blonde woman seem very close."

"Not me, dude," I said. "I've sworn a lot in my life, and even sworn a couple oaths, but none of them involved celibacy. No, I was talking like I was Joe, on account of he just did all that."

"So you have not sworn an oath of celibacy?" The ogre looked confused, and when a critter that looks like a hunk of granite mated with a bulldog looks confused, it is a damn sight to behold.

"No, I have not." I decided to just keep it simple.

"Good," he said. "Even though you urinated on my herbs, I did not think you were truly stupid."

"So you think celibacy is stupid?" I asked. "'Cause I sure do."

"It may not be stupid," the ogre said. "But it is not smart, either." We both laughed, then Amy came out on the porch looking all clean and damp from the shower, and I was real happy I hadn't sworn any oaths of celibacy.

"My turn," Mama said, and walked into the house.

"I'm fixing some lunch," Amy said. "Come in here and help me, Skeeter. They have a microwave that's got more buttons than my computer. I might need some tech support."

An hour later, we were all fed and clean, and Roy's kitchen was sorely depleted. We left the dishes for him, proving that we were either the worst houseguests in the world, or just vindictive assholes towards people who pointed guns at us. I know I'm both.

We put the cars in the wind and pulled into the parking lot for Ruby Falls about an hour before closing time. That felt just about perfect to us since we wanted to get started on the tour and then manage to get "lost" long enough to find the portal.

But plans being what they are, as soon as I stepped out of the truck, half a dozen people ran screaming out of the ticket shack like their hair was on fire. I just leaned forward, put my head on the hood, and bounced it off the truck three or four times.

"What's wrong, Bubba?" Amy asked, closing her door. I pointed to the chaos up at the entrance, and she sighed.

"Some days you just have the best damn timing," she said. "Okay, everybody, gear up. Looks like we're going in official."

I walked around to the back of the truck and opened the door. Mama was already out on the other side, so I flipped the whole back seat up to get to the gun case under the seat. First thing I did while Amy was grabbing her Kevlar vest was to grab Bertha's shoulder rig off the back of the front seat where I always keep her draped if I'm gonna be driving more than half an hour or so and strap on the big Desert Eagle over my XXXL Ultimate Warrior t-shirt. Then I grabbed a big flannel shirt from the gun case and threw on a long-sleeve shirt. No need for everybody in the world to see the cannon I was toting around.

I picked up a black web belt with a Buck hunting knife on one side and a flashlight on the other, and strapped that on. Then I clipped my Judge onto the belt under my shirt and picked up my caestus. The metal-clad gauntlets that Amy gave for Christmas last year had threaded holes in the knuckles, and knowing where we were going, I added a cold iron stud about a quarter-inch long into each hole. Any fairy that wanted to throw down with me, I was gonna be ready. The belt had pouches for four spare magazines, so I filled them with loaded cold iron mags, too. The shoulder holster carried two mags, so I slid on iron mag and one white phosphorous mag in there. I might not be able to kill a fairy setting it on fire, but it would damn sure make it uncomfortable. I left the regular hollow points in Bertha, my Fairyland equivalent of a less-lethal load. I slipped some spare .45 long bullets and some extra .410 shells for the Judge in the pockets of my cargo pants, slipped a SOG knife with a paracord-wrapped handle into my boot, and I was ready to go.

Skeeter, Joe, and Amy all had on their Kevlar by now, and I knew their vests were lined with ceramic plates to stop blades as well as bullets. Good thing since I had been carrying the only guns I saw in Fairyland on my last trip, and I didn't think they'd gotten real interested in gunpowder since then. Skeeter and Mama both had Mossberg 12-gauges, Joe had his Remington rifle, and Amy had her Sig, plus an MP-5 strapped across her chest. We were loaded for bear, with guns, knives, flares, a couple more flash-bangs, and enough ammunition to star in *The Expendables 18*.

"Are we ready?" I asked.

"Are we going to investigate a cave or invade Nicaragua?" Skeeter asked.

"Maybe both," Joe said. "I've got the first aid kit in my pack. Let's go see what's going on up there."

Amy led the way, "FBI" emblazoned on her vest in big white letters. I asked her once why she picked that agency to impersonate, and she told me it was more about getting people to listen to her immediately, and it raised way too many questions to run into a crowd of people with "DEMON" on her chest in three-inch high letters. Made a lot of sense to me.

We followed her up the hill, me running second, Mama and Skeeter after me, and Joe bringing up the rear. We left Greg in the truck for the moment, because an ogre running with a bunch of *federales* was more than even I could bullshit my way through. Amy pushed through the steady stream of panicked people like a salmon swimming upstream until one big old fat hillbilly came barreling down the sidewalk and almost knocked her flat. I caught Amy, then gave the redneck a shove to the side. He popped up on his feet and bowed up like he wanted to come at me, until he realized that he was about to throw down with a heavily armed grizzly bear that looked like it had no time for bullshit.

He made the right decision and took a shortcut across the grass down to the parking lot. "Nice deterrent, Bubba," Joe said with a chuckle.

"I didn't do nothing but look at him," I said.

"Yeah, and sometimes you looking at somebody is scarier than half the monsters we've chased," Skeeter said, slapping me on the shoulder.

"Mama, they're making fun of me!" I mock-protested.

"It just means they like you, dear. Remember back in elementary school when you used to push Melissa McKnight down on the playground? It's the same thing," she said.

"How did you know I liked Melissa?"

"Robbie, you are my son, and I love you, but subtle you are not," Mama said with a kind smile. All my friends nodded and chuckled. Even I had to grin at that. She wasn't wrong, my mother.

By the time we stepped into the lobby, the stream of people had slowed to a trickle, and there wasn't anybody there but one frazzled ticket-taker and a fat old security guard waving his arms at us like he was directing an airplane.

"We're closed," he said, coming over to us. "Sorry folks, emergency closing. Y'all gonna have to come back tomorrow."

I stopped cold in the middle of the room and stared at him. "Dude, can you not see? Look at us. Do we look like tourists? Shit, son, I'd about lay even money on us being scarier than whatever you got down there."

Amy stepped forward and said the single funniest thing I've ever heard come out of her mouth. With a completely straight face, she looked at that security guard and said, "Sir, please step aside. We're from the government. We're here to help."

13

───────────

I managed to not pee my pants at Amy's unintended joke, and instead, I stepped over to the confused guard and said, "What's down there, pal?"

"What do you mean?" the old dude asked. He was round little guy, with tufts of white hair sprouting out all around his head in a crown. He might have been five-eight, with spindly little arms and a belt stretched almost to its breaking point by his girth.

"I mean, what's down there making people run out screaming?" I pointed toward the entrance to the caverns.

"I don't know, I've been up here trying to keep folks from running over one another. Aaron went down there a few minutes ago to find out what was going on, though. Let me try to get him on the radio." He put a walkie-talkie to his mouth and pressed the button. "Aaron, this is base camp. What do you see down there?"

No response from the radio. He tried hailing his buddy a couple more times, but there was nothing.

I put a hand on his shoulder. "You stay up here. Get this woman out safely, then wait here for any stragglers. Make sure they stay calm and don't break their necks running down the sidewalk or something stupid like that. We're going down there to take a look, and if we can find Aaron, we'll send him up."

"What do you mean, if?" the old man asked.

"Well, boss, whatever's down there is probably pretty nasty, if we can judge anything from these people all hauling ass out like they are. So, if it got ahold of your boy, he might be...hurt pretty bad."

"Son, I know I'm old and fat now, but I still know the smell of bullshit when somebody shovels it on my shoes. You think Aaron's dead, don't you?"

"I honestly don't know," I said. "But if he ain't, we'll get him back."

"And if he is," Skeeter said as he stepped forward. "We'll deal with whatever killed him."

I just love it when Skeeter's mouth writes checks that my ass has to cash.

We walked through the turnstile and headed down into the caves, Amy in the lead, then me, since I could shoot over her head pretty easy, and if I went first, I'd be blocking the view of everybody behind me. Mama followed me, then Skeeter, then Joe covered our tails.

The caves were huge, a winding network of water-carved caverns that extended for miles in every direction. The lights were set up pretty regular, but it wasn't long before we got to a place where a trail of blood led off to the right, away from the regular tourist sections and into the unlit portions of the mountain.

"We gotta go down there," Skeeter said. "That dude Aaron could be down there hurt."

"Or he could be a whole lotta dead," I said. "But we gotta go anyway." I pulled my flashlight and aimed the beam down the tunnel ahead of me. The light got soaked up by the blackness like it was a living, hungry thing. The others fired up their flashlights, except for Mama. She picked up a rock, closed her eyes for a moment, and wrapped her hands around the stone like it was a baby bird or a firefly she'd caught and was taking it back to show somebody.

That metaphor proved to be more appropriate than I expected when she opened her hands. The rock in her palm glowed with a soft blue-white light, giving off enough illumination to see a good fifteen feet in all directions. She held the rock over her head, a glowing miniature sun barely three inches around.

"I think this might be better than your flashlights," she said.

We all just stared at her.

"What is it?" she asked. "I told you I am a Daughter of Winter, of the Royal Court of the Fae. No matter how long it has been since I have taken part in the politics of the ruling class, I remain a creature of magic, and I always will."

"I heard you," I said. "I just..."

"I think he means that this is really the first time we're understanding exactly what that means," Amy added.

"Can I do that stuff?" I asked. I was thinking that being able to cast magical spells would be pretty handy, especially if I could make stuff glow in the dark. I looked at Amy and started to get all kinds of interesting thoughts about the kinds of things I could make glow.

"I'm sorry, Robbie, but no. You are only partly Fae and have not spent any time learning how to use any gifts you may have inherited from me. Even if you had the innate ability, it would be far too late in life to begin training it now."

"Can Nitalia?" Joe asked.

"She has some magic, but it is not nearly as strong as mine," Mama said. "Her father was not a noble, so his ties to Faerie are less strong. Her gifts will fade and eventually disappear altogether if not used regularly, where mine will not."

"Wow," I said. "Okay, Mama, you just got bumped up the line." I put my flashlight back in its holster and moved Mama in front of me so my big ass wasn't blocking too much of the glow from her magical rock. "Let's move and see if we can find this Aaron dude and get him home before Gollum bites his finger off and throws him into the fires of Saruman."

Amy stared down the new tunnel, and we all followed. We hadn't even gone three steps before Skeeter pulled on my sleeve. "You know that's not even close to how all that happened in the books, right?"

"Yeah, I know, but I wanted to see if you could go a whole minute without correcting me about it," I replied.

"That was a no, by the way," I said to Joe. I extended my left hand back over Skeeter's head. "Pay up."

"Pay up? Y'all made a bet on whether I was going to correct Bubba or not?" Skeeter's tone was almost indignant. It was kinda funny, actually.

"Oh, it was nothing like that," Joe said. "We knew you'd correct him. We just bet on how long it would take you. I took the over. Poor choice, it turns out."

"What was the line?" Skeeter asked.

"Three minutes," Amy said from the front.

"You didn't think I could go three minutes without correcting Bubba?" Skeeter asked. Now he really sounded indignant.

"If I screwed up something from *Lord of the Rings*?" I said. "Yeah, I knew you couldn't. For the record, I was wrong."

"Exactly," Skeeter said, his voice all smug.

"Yeah, you couldn't last one minute, much less three. Now pay up." Skeeter pursed his lips like he was sucking on a lemon, and Joe slapped a five-dollar bill in my hand. Then we got back to the business of trying to save a dude's life.

The caves were beautiful in spots, where we could see the stalactite and stalagmite formations, and the awesome power of the water carving out sections of rock for millions of years. This was marred every so often by a dark brown smear on the wall or floor, showing us that something had been hunting in these caves for a long time. Then we came upon a pool of fresh crimson stretching almost the full width of the cavern floor, and I knew before I saw the nametag that we had found Aaron's final resting place.

"That's a lot of blood," Skeeter said. "It looks like the kind of mess you usually leave, Bubba."

"Not funny, Skeeter," I said. "This dude just showed up for work this morning like every other day. He didn't deserve this crap."

"No, he didn't," Skeeter said. "So let's figure out what did it, kill it, then find the portal to Faerie so you can take your bad mood out on somebody else." I looked over and could see by the way he had that little line between his eyebrows that he was pretty pissed at me.

"I'm sorry, buddy," I said. "You're right. I'm pissed that Roy sent us on that snipe hunt through the woods so he could try and steal some damn pumpkin seeds. I can't help but think if we'd gotten here last night instead of losing all yesterday and half of today dealing with that prick, that we might coulda stopped whatever was gonna happen here."

"Yeah, you got a point," Skeeter said. "But that ain't gonna help us hunt down whatever did this."

"You mean whoever," Amy said. I looked over to find her kneeling by the pool of blood. "There's a footprint here. It's half in the blood, and half out, and it leads farther down into the cave."

"Is it human?" I asked.

"Looks like it."

"That's not good," I replied.

"Why not?" Mama asked. "Humans are much easier to deal with than many other species we could be facing."

"Humans, yeah," I said. "But vampires aren't. Ghouls or ghosts aren't, and there are a bunch of other things that walk around like men and aren't. I don't expect it to be a vampire because it left behind way too much blood. But that still leaves a whole lot of unpleasant options."

"I don't expect it to be a ghost or a ghoul," Joe chimed. "The attack site is too neat. There's a lot of blood here, but no flesh, and nothing looks like something tried to eat this man. The undead, excepting vampires, aren't very concerned with discretion."

"So that leaves humans, or fairies, since there is supposedly a doorway to Faerie down here somewhere," Skeeter said.

"Or something we haven't thought of yet," I added. "Either way, we need to step lively and be alert. Mama, can you magic up another one of them glow-rocks?" I asked.

"I can," she said. She picked up a stone from the cave floor, held it in her hands for a few seconds, then handed it to me. I almost dropped it in surprise. It was freezing cold to the touch.

"Damn, that's cold!" I said.

"What did you expect, dear?" Mama asked, her tone mild but still with a hint of "my son is an idiot" in there. "I am a Daughter of Winter, after all."

"I reckon I expected a frostbite warning from my own mother," I grumbled.

"I suppose I expected my big bad monster-hunting son to be less of a baby about the cold," she said, handing her rock to Joe. "You take this one. I see perfectly well in the dark. Be careful, apparently the stones are very cold."

I just shook my head. She hadn't been in my life for a long time, but I remembered how it was pretty much impossible to get the last word on my Mama in any argument. "When were you gonna tell us you could see in the dark?" I asked.

"When it became relevant," she replied. I swear, talking to women is like trying to get a damn housecat to do what you want. They just sit, stare at you, and say "no" in a way that convinces you that's what you really wanted all along.

"Is there anything else you can do that you need to tell us?" I asked, fully aware that all my friends were grinning like fools at this woman twisting me up in verbal knots. I didn't much care. Even down in a cave, under tons of rock, with my sister's life in jeopardy in another dimension, getting ready to go fight something we had no idea if we could beat, I still felt better surrounded by this family than I had in a long time.

"Nothing relevant," Mama said. "Now, don't we have a monster to hunt?"

I started to say something smartass in response, but a very human scream echoed off the walls of the cave and let me know that now was not the time to make jokes, now was the time to whoop ass.

14

————

"Do you have any idea where that came from?" I asked Amy.

"None," she said. "Sound does stupid things in a network of caves like this. Whoever that was could be right around the next bend, or they could be all the way back up at the entrance."

"I'll take care of the finding," Mama said. "But this is going to take a lot out of me, so you four will have to handle the rescuing."

I didn't bother telling her that I figured I'd be doing most of the rescuing in the first place. No point in being insulting. Plus, we had an ogre with me, so maybe I wouldn't have to do all the heavy lifting. She got down on both knees in the floor of the cave and put her hands together in front of her chest like she was praying or something. After a few seconds, a tiny speck of red light appeared over her head. The speck spun and wobbled through the air, getting bigger all the time until it grew into a baseball-sized orb floating over Mama's noggin.

She opened her eyes, and Joe stepped forward to catch her shoulders before she toppled over. "Are you alright, Mrs. Brabham?"

She looked at Joe and smiled, patting him on one arm. "Joe, you're either going to have to call me Mama or Ygraine. I am not going to call you Father, so we should dispense with any formalities altogether. I'm fine, I just need a little hand getting up. As I said, that spell takes a lot out of me." She waved her right hand at the ball of light, and it flew off down the tunnel ahead of us.

"We should follow it. I tuned the spell to the scream, and to the blood. Wherever either the person who screamed or anything that has touched this blood is, the light will lead us there."

"Nice one, Mama," I said. "Toss me another glow-stone, and let's roll. You and Skeeter stay back here with your other light rock, and we'll come get you when we're done."

"Yeah, not so much," Skeeter said. "One thing, you ain't leaving the black dude alone with the old lady, no offense, in the scary cave. This ain't my first horror movie. I know who dies first in this scenario. Second thing, you ain't coming back, dumbass. You're going down there to find and save whoever's screaming, if they're still alive after whatever made them holler like that. Then you're gonna keep going and find the door to Faerie. And your mama is probably the only one of us that can recognize it, or open it. So we're going."

"Okay, then you two bring up the rear. Joe, cover them. Amy and I will go first and take care of any threats we find." For once, nobody wanted to argue with me, and we started down the corridor after our bouncing ball of red light.

We followed the orb several hundred yards, making a couple of sharp turns down barely-seen side tunnels, until the tunnel opened into a giant cavern, complete with underground waterfall and soft illumination coming from a stream flowing through the center of the cave.

"Wow," Amy said, looking around. "That's amazing." She wasn't wrong.

The chamber we were in was easily half a football field in all directions, and two or three stories high inside. The waterfall was lit from behind by some kind of glowing moss or lichens, and dots of light danced in the stream, phosphorescent fish I guessed. Stalagmites taller than basketball goals reached up to stalactites like giant teeth hanging ten or fifteen feet from the ceiling. The walls were splashed with all kinds of color, striations of minerals shooting through the rock at different levels telling the story of the cave's formation.

The most interesting thing in the cave, and the thing that had us drop to the ground and scoot back into the tunnel out of sight, was the group of men sitting around a cookfire on the banks of the underground stream. There were about eight of them, all dressed like rejects from *The Hobbit* central casting. Except full-sized. They wore leather armor, with furs over their shoulders and fur bits around their wrists and feet. They all wore long hair, tied back or worn loose over their shoulders, but more than one of them had their ponytails tied back to reveal the distinct points on the tops of their ears.

Every one of them were fairies. Not particularly nice fairies, judging by the condition of the woman they had bound hand and foot lying on her stomach at the edge of their circle.

"Raiders," Mama whispered, venom pouring through her voice as though the word was a synonym for "asshole." Which, maybe to her, it was. I cocked an eyebrow at her, and she sighed. "Female Fae do not breed often. It is very difficult for us to become pregnant, and when it happens, it is a cause for great rejoicing. That is one reason our numbers are few."

"You didn't seem to have a whole lot of trouble with it," I said. "You had me, then Jase, then you went back to Fairyland and had Nitalia."

"I was fortunate," she said with a little blush. "And your father was...remarkable in many ways."

I turned to Amy. I'm sure the horror was evident on my face as I said, "Does DEMON have any of those little mind-wipe things like in *Men in Black*? Because I really need some brain bleach right now."

"Sorry, Bubba, you're gonna have to live with that one," she said, her tone saying she was anything but sorry. I swear, the women in my life exist only to torment me. She looked at Mama. "What does the infertility of Fae women have to do with that girl down there?"

"Some of the less scrupulous men of Faerie have, at times, enlisted the help of bandits and raiders to pass through the veil and...

procure wives for them that would have a greater potential for producing offspring."

"Holy shit," I said.

"That's disgusting," Skeeter said. "You mean those guys down there are like Fae sex traffickers?"

"Unfortunately, that is exactly what I mean," Mama said.

"Well, there's some good news," I said, drawing Bertha and swapping out for a cold iron magazine.

"What's that, Bubba?" Amy asked. Her eyes were cold, and I could feel the rage rolling off her.

"If these assholes are here to take the girl back to Fairyland and sell her as a wife to some horny fairy, then the portal must be around here somewhere. And that ain't all," I continued with a grin.

"What else?" Skeeter asked, still a little wary of the grin I was wearing.

"We know these guys are the worst kind of scum, so I can shoot them all I want without feeling bad."

"Try to keep at least one of them alive, Bubba," Amy said, keeping her voice low.

"Why? You want to make sure you get to kill one of them yourself?" I asked.

"No. Well, I do, but that's not the reason. I want to make sure you don't kill them all so we can get information. There might be a whole ring of them, and if so, we want to do everything we can to stop them all, not just one small group." She made a lot of sense. But that's kinda our deal—Amy thinks things through, I blow things up.

"Okay, here's the plan," I said. "I'm going to go shoot a bunch of assholes. Y'all come in behind me and clean up the pieces."

"Is that what passes for a plan in your life, Robbie?" Mama asked.

"Oh, Mama B, you don't even know," Skeeter replied as I just stared at them. "That is probably the most complex, well-developed plan Bubba has come up with in the last three years. You know how I know this? Because there was something after the part about him shooting something. Most of his plans start and end right there."

I didn't bother sticking around to be insulted. If they wanted to make jokes at my expense, and I'm sure they did, they could wait until we were done rescuing damsels in distress. I walked to the end of the tunnel and stepped out into the cave. I had Bertha in one hand and a caestus with iron studs on the knuckles on my left hand.

I got to within about fifteen yards of the fairies before they noticed me, but when they did, it was like I kicked over a hornet's nest full of dickheads. They all jumped to their feet and pulled swords, except for the two that grabbed up bows from the ground and started scrambling around for quivers. I put a bullet in the first archer before he ever found his arrows, and fifty calibers of iron does a lot of bad things to a hundred-fifty-pound fairy. I left him lying on the ground with a hole in his chest you could put a normal person's fist through and drew down on the second archer.

He flopped over backward, kicking up a puff of dust from the cave floor when he fell, lifeless to the ground. I turned the see Joe prone in the mouth of the tunnel, his rifle stretched out in front of him with a little wisp of smoke coming from the barrel.

"Well, that's two down. How many—never mind," I started to say something clever, but three fairies ran at me with swords, and I was busy shooting assholes for a minute. The Desert Eagle is, as Ray Wylie Hubbard said, "a great big 'ol pistol," and it made a great big hole in two of the ones rushing me. They dropped like sacks of really bloody potatoes, a whole lot of their insides suddenly turned to outsides.

I let the third one get closer while I holstered Bertha, keeping Amy's reminder in my head to let one of them live. I blocked his sword stroke with my metal-clad fist, which wasn't the best idea I've ever head. Even wrapped in a steel-plated gauntlet, that shit *hurt*. The fairy drew back for another slice, and I planted a size-sixteen boot in his gut. He folded over like a cheap suit, and I clocked him on the back of the head with my caestus.

"I got your prisoner," I said to Amy as she stepped up to my side, her Sig tracking another fairy running in our direction. She dropped him with two shots to the chest, then put another two in the face of the one right behind him.

Amy knelt by the fairy on the ground, then glared up at me. "You suck at prisoners, Bubba. This guy's deader than a doornail."

"All I did was punch him in the head," I protested. I held my fist up to show her, then pulled Bertha and blew the leg off an oncoming fairy. This one held an axe. Well, at least until I shot his leg off. He dropped the axe after that.

"Maybe I can save that one," Amy said, rushing to the downed fairy.

"Wouldn't hold my breath," I said. I looked at the dude spurting blood all over the cave floor. It was going to take a hell of a tourniquet to keep him from bleeding out. I did mention it was a great big pistol, right? Well, it didn't quite blow the guy's leg off. It was still hanging on by a couple strands of flesh and muscle, but it was coming off eventually. If he lived.

I looked down at the one I punched and poked him with the toe of my boot. Nothing. I leaned down and slammed my fist into his skull, popping his head like a cantaloupe and smearing brains all over the ground.

"What the hell was that for?" Skeeter asked. He was sweeping his shotgun back and forth across the cave, but it looked like between my bloodbath and Joe taking out two more assholes with his rifle, Skeeter was woefully short on targets.

"Amy said he was dead, but I wanted to make sure. Don't need him spontaneously regenerating behind us," I said.

"What a load of crap," Skeeter said. "You just wanted to see if you could hit him hard enough to crush his skull, didn't you?"

I wasn't quite ready to admit just how right Skeeter was. "There might have been some of that in my decision-making process," I said.

"Don't try to sound like a corporate drone, Bubba. It makes me think everything in the world has gone upside down."

I grinned down at Skeeter, then looked around. "Hey, where's Amy?"

"She's right here, human," said a fairy who stepped out of a pocket of shadow just past the bound woman on the cavern floor. He was tall and bigger than the other fairies I'd just killed. He also had a knife pressed to Amy's throat and was using her as a human shield. "She doesn't have much to say right now, but I think she'd like for you to put down your weapons and step forward so that I can bind your hands. There isn't as much market for male humans in Faerie as females, but you all look strong enough. I think you'll make fine slaves."

15

———————

ontrary to all expectations, I was not the one who lost my
mind at the fairy's words. Skeeter, on the other hand,
exploded in a fit of fury that can only be unleashed by a
gay black man. "Slave?" he asked, his already high voice going up a
full octave. "*Slave*?!? Oh, *hell* no! I did not grow up black and gay in
Georgia, fight my whole damn life to make something of myself in a
world that doesn't know what to make of any bit of me, just to have
some assclown with pointy ears take me back a couple hundred years
to when my people were locked in cargo holds and trucked across the
ocean against their will!"

He stomped right across the cave to where the fairy stood, his arm
wrapped around Amy's neck and a dagger pressed to her throat. The
bad guy just stared at the fury he had unleashed, his eyes darting
around the cave like he thought somebody might be coming to his
rescue. He was going to be mighty disappointed on that front since
we'd killed every other bad guy in the place. Even the guy I shot in
the leg was done for, having bled out just after the head asshole
appeared.

"Stay back!" He gestured to Skeeter with the knife, and that was
all she wrote. Amy grabbed the wrist of his knife hand with both of

her hands and stretched that arm all the way out straight. Then she snapped the arm straight down over her shoulder, and I could hear the *pop* as his elbow dislocated.

The knife clattered to the cavern floor, and Amy spun from the fairy's grasp. She stepped back, still holding his wrist in one hand, and nailed him in the temple with a vicious side kick. He staggered but didn't fall, so she pulled him toward her and buried a knee in his midsection. He doubled over, and Amy let go of his arm. She twined both hands in his hair and slammed his face downward as she brought her knee up to meet him. A *crack* echoed through the cave as his nose basically turned to Jell-O, and Amy let him drop to the ground.

Skeeter stepped forward and kicked the downed fairy in the ribs. I heard another *crack* and figured it was a rib this time. Skeeter drew back for another punt, but I put a hand on his shoulder.

"He's down, Skeet."

"I don't care," my enraged little buddy said.

"Yeah, but remember, Amy wanted one left alive."

"Still not caring," Skeeter said, but he also wasn't still kicking the guy.

"You okay?" I asked Amy.

"I'm fine, just pissed that he got the drop on me."

"How did that even happen?" I asked. "I looked away for a second, then the next thing I knew, that asshole had his arm around your neck."

"That's about how it worked for me, too. I went to see about the one you shot in the leg, then I heard something off behind a stalagmite. I went over to investigate, and this dick jumped me."

"Well, I'm just glad you're alright," I said.

"Thanks. I'm glad we were able to capture him. We need him to find the portal."

A groan from the ground drew my attention back to the fallen fairy. He rolled around but froze when I stepped over him and aimed Bertha down at his face. "This is a Desert Eagle pistol. I know y'all don't know a lot about guns over in Fairyland, so let me explain what that means. It fires a bullet that has enough force to blow your leg off from fifty yards away. Imagine what that will do to your face from three feet."

He stopped moving, his eyes locked on the end of Bertha's barrel. I kept talking. "Yes, that is a very big barrel. It takes a big barrel to fire a big bullet. Bertha only fires big bullets. She's picky like that. Now, you're going to stand up, put your hands behind your back, and we're going to tie you up. Then you're going to lead us to the passage back to Fairyland, where we'll figure out whether or not we're going to kill you. I'm leaning toward yes, just in case you were wondering."

I stepped back to give him a little space. "Now get up," I said.

He just lay there, looking daggers at me. "Go to hell, human trash."

I poked him in the ribs with the toe of my boot. I might not have been as gentle as I could have, and I might have put extra pressure on the spot where I knew Skeeter had broken a rib, but I didn't kick him real hard. He rolled over a time or two and got to his feet.

"Put your hands behind your back," I said.

"Go to hell," he repeated.

"You are starting to sound like a broken record," I replied. I stepped in and backhanded him with my left hand. The iron studs on my knuckles left burns on his cheek where they touched him, and he dropped to one knee. He got back to both feet, then turned around and stuck his hands out behind him.

"Very good," I said. "Amy, you do have something we can use to tie this asshole up, don't you?"

She just grinned and slapped a pair of handcuffs on the fairy. I didn't even see where they came from, but it was definitely something I filed away for future use.

Just then Mama held up a hand, and we all fell silent. "I think I heard something. Has anyone seen the girl?"

We all shook our heads, and Mama walked off to a darkened section of the cave, Joe following close behind. A few seconds later, they came back with a battered and dirty, but mostly unharmed, human woman of about twenty. She was wearing jeans, a University of Tennessee hoodie, and no shoes. She looked pretty shaken up and dirty, but she walked fine, and she had enough presence of mind to walk right up to the handcuffed fairy and plant a knee in his nuts.

The fairy dropped to his knees, and she looked around at us. "Thanks."

"Are you okay?" Amy asked, stepping forward to put an arm around the girl's shoulders.

"Yeah, I'm fine. Just a little bruised. They said they were taking me back with them to..."

"It's okay," Amy said. "We know. That's not going to happen. Not to you, not to anybody."

The girl looked around at the fairy corpses. "I guess not. Why didn't you kill this asshole?"

"We need him to lead us to the portal," I said. I didn't think we needed to go too far into the whole "portal to where" concept, so I just left that part out.

"Is that the glowing hole in the cave wall?" she asked. "It's right over there." She pointed down one of the many side tunnels branching off from the main cavern. I couldn't see anything, but Mama nodded.

"I can see a glow coming from that direction. It's quite likely that she is correct," Mama said.

"So, do we just go through?" I asked, starting in that direction.

"Slow down there, big fella," Amy said, grabbing my arm. "We have to get..." She looked at the girl with one eyebrow raised.

"Cheryl," the girl said.

"Cheryl," Amy went on with a nod. "Back up to the surface so she can go home, and we should probably get our packs, and retrieve the ogre we left hanging out in the car. Plus, I wouldn't mind having a little food and a tent at hand if we're going to go be strangers in a strange land for a while."

"Makes sense," I agreed. "But what do we do with Prince Charmless here?" I asked.

Mama pulled a knife from her belt and slit the bound fairy's throat from ear to ear. Amy and I jumped back as blood fountained from his neck, and he collapsed to one side. Mama wiped her knife on the corpse's pants and tucked it back where she found it.

"Problem solved," she said. I gawked at her, as did everyone else in the cave. "What?" she said. "We were going to kill him. I just didn't waste time arguing about it. He couldn't be allowed to roam free in this world, and if we took him back to Faerie, we ran the risk of him alerting his confederates. Not to mention the fact that he was a sex trafficker, one of the lowest forms of life in this or any other dimension. So, I killed him. Now let's get you back upstairs and you can get home where you'll be safe." She directed this last bit to the girl, who took an involuntary step back as Mama's gaze fell on her. I didn't blame her. She kinda scared me, too.

Mama started across the cave toward the tunnel we came in from, and after looking at each other for a few seconds, the rest of us followed. We had all just reached the mouth of the tunnel leading out when the girl spoke again.

"Who's Oberon?" she asked.

Mama froze, then slowly turned to look at Cheryl. "Where did you hear that name?"

"The guys that took me said it a couple of times. They said that once they sold me to...Ray-something, I can't remember the name, that was all they needed to do before they got in touch with their contact and took out Oberon. I was just wondering who Oberon is. I think I've heard the name before somewhere..."

"Yeah, probably in school," Joe said.

"Oberon is my father," Mama said. "Let's hurry this up, Robbie. We have to get this girl to the surface so we can come back down here. Apparently, we have to save your sister's and your grandfather's lives."

EPILOGUE

I went through the portal first, my fists wrapped in cold iron and leather as I stepped into the shimmering blue light. I felt a disconcerting sensation of *nothing*, then I was wrapped in freezing air and felt snow crunch under my feet.

Aw, shit, I thought. *This portal comes out in the Winter Court.* I stepped forward to make sure nobody was going to land on me, then started to look around. There was snow everywhere, and I kept looking for an old British lamppost, but never saw one.

One by one, the others came through, Mama coming across last. She threw open her arms and took a deep breath, sucking in the frigid air like she was coming home from a long trip. Which I guess she was, in a way.

"Quickly," she said. "We must not stay here. My mother will be able to sense my presence within the Winter Court, and she will send soldiers to intercept us. We must get to a neutral or unclaimed territory as soon as possible. If her men find us, there's no telling what she will do."

"I'll tell you what I will do," said an impossibly tall woman who stepped out from behind a tree. "I will throw your treacherous little behind in my deepest dungeon and let you rot there with all your little mortal friends to keep you company."

"Hello, Mother," Mama said, looking at the newcomer. I could see the resemblance. This woman, Mab I assumed, looked like Mama with the knob turned up to eleven. She was tall with cold, chiseled features and eyes like chips of ice. Her skin was flawless and pale as the finest china. Her long fingers tapped out a slow rhythm on her folded arms, and blood-red nails tipped each one.

She wore a gown of pale blue, trimmed with white fur, and her jet-black hair looked all the more stark for the contrast. Everything about her screamed power, and dignity, and cruelty. My first look at my grandmother was not exactly milk and cookies.

I stepped forward and held out my giant hand. "Hey there, Grandma," I said, thickening up my Georgia twang even more than normal. "I'm Bubba. I'm your grandson."

Mab stared at me for a minute, then looked at Mama, then back at me, then back at Mama before finally settling on me. She snapped her fingers, and a dozen heavily-armed fairies came out of the woods. "Take them to my dungeon," she said. "Tell the torturer he is having guests."

Barely the beginning.

PART II

COLD AS ICE

1

I woke up to the sound of screaming. At least it wasn't mine this time. I lay still for a minute with my eyes closed before I asked, "Who is it this time?"

"Joe." Skeeter's cracked voice came from across the room. I shook my head, guilt washing over me at the thought of Joe being tortured on my account.

The screaming continued, off and on, for an hour or two. I honestly lost track of time for a while and just lay there listening to one of my best friends in the world being tortured out of his mind at the hands of a nasty-ass fairy. I swore to myself, just like I did every time the bastards came into our cell and took somebody out for Head Torturer Brandis's daily "entertainment."

But finally the horror movie soundtrack stopped. This time it cut off abruptly, so I knew Joe had passed out from the pain. *Brandis must be off his game today*, I thought. On a good day, he usually managed to get one of us to scream ourselves completely hoarse before he let us pass out, but Joe still had a lot of voice going when his howls of pain cut off like a switch was thrown.

A few minutes later, the guards dragged Joe's limp body back into the cell and dumped him on a pallet of straw in the corner. Skeeter made as if to rise and go check on him, but the point of a guard's sword drew him up short. I didn't move. I didn't bother. I knew he wasn't dead; they wouldn't kill him. They wouldn't kill any of us, no matter how much they might like to. No, we were being kept alive so Queen Mab, my grandmother, could get her rocks off daily listening to my friends shriek in unbelievable agony.

Then every night, after torturing my people all day, she sent in the healers to undo all the damage Brandis inflicted so he could start the next morning with a clean slate.

Not to put too fine a point on it, my granny was batshit nuts.

After the guards locked the cell door behind them, Skeeter and I crawled along the floor to check on Joe. The cell was barely more than four feet high, so neither of us could stand up in it, keeping us crouched and off-balance at all times.

"Joe, you okay?" I asked, shaking his shoulder. He moaned a little but didn't open his eyes.

"Come on, Uncle Joe, what did they do this time?" Skeeter took our bucket of drinking water and dipped his shirttail in it, dabbing it across Joe's forehead and washing off a little of the blood. Really, he was just smearing the old dirt and blood around, but it made him feel better, so I didn't bother saying anything. Besides, we didn't have to worry about infections; the magical fairy healer asshole would be by in a few hours to put Joe right as rain so he could get another dose tomorrow.

"Is he okay?" Amy's voice came from the next cell over.

"Yeah, just passed out, I think," Skeeter said.

"I'm fine," Joe croaked. "I was faking." I looked down at him and saw the hint of a grin under the blood and muck caking his face. He looked like ten miles of bad road. If he was faking that, he deserved an Oscar.

"Oh, thank God," Skeeter said, rocking back to sit cross-legged on the straw. "I thought this time they'd gone too far and killed you."

"They won't kill us," I said. "We're too useful as bargaining chips."

"Speak for yourself," Skeeter said. "You're Mab and Oberon's grandson. I'm a gay black human trapped in Fairyland, which is way less fabulous than all those picture books made it out to be. There's not a rave or a disco anywhere."

"You hate disco, Skeeter," I reminded him.

"I hate dungeons more!"

"Fair enough," I said. I sat back against the wall and looked at Joe. "Anything new this time?"

"Yeah, there was," he said. "That's why I decided to pass out. I thought this might be important. While they were burning all my hair off with long kitchen matches, one of the guards from somewhere else in the castle came in and told them to cancel tomorrow's sessions."

"Why?" Amy's disembodied voice asked. I had no idea how long we'd spent trapped in the dungeon, so I couldn't tell how much time had passed since I laid eyes on my girlfriend, but I knew it was too damn long.

"They said something about distinguished guests and not wanting them to be disturbed if they heard us screaming. I might have said something about them not hitting hard enough to make a puppy scream, and that's when Brandis decided to pierce my nipples again. So, I passed out."

"Huh," I said, wondering what kind of guests the Queen of Winter receives, and who existed that she gave a damn about.

"So, no torture tomorrow," Skeeter said, laying back on the straw. "Kinda makes this feel like Christmas Eve."

"I fought a magically summoned giant elf knight last Christmas," I reminded him. "And the Christmas before that, you were hunting a ghost. Christmas usually sucks for us."

"Let me dream, Bubba," Skeeter grumbled at me. "Let me dream."

"Instead of dreaming, how about some planning?" Amy asked from next door. "Any disruption in the normal rhythm of this place should give us some opportunities."

"You thinking about busting out of here, sweet cheeks?" I asked.

"Always," she replied. "And if you promise to never call me sweet cheeks again, I might even take you with me."

"Deal," Skeeter, Joe, and I all said at the same time.

I heard Amy scooch closer to the bars of her cell. Her next words came across in barely a whisper. "Okay, so when the healer comes tonight, here's the plan..."

The healer came in with our dinner, if you want to call a loaf of not-quite stale bread and a bucket of warm water dinner. As usual, there were two guards with the healer, one with his sword out and the other carrying dinner.

The healer ducked into the cell and knelt by Joe's pallet, peeling the loose shirt off his body with ruthless efficiency. I heard the ripping sound as the cloth pulled away from the flesh it stuck to with dried blood, and Joe cried out in pain. Even if he wasn't trying to make sure the guards were watching him, he probably would have yelled.

The healer started his work, his hands glowing pale yellow with magic as he eased Joe's agony. Healing reverses the damage done to a body but hurts almost as bad while it's being done as the original injuries. Joe was playing up the pain even more, making a real show out of it tonight. Within moments, the dungeon echoed with his cries of pain as the healer's hands pressed hit cuts and burns. The guards stood just inside the cell, grinning and watching the show as Joe writhed at the man's touch.

"Hey, you gonna put that food down, or am I gonna have to arm wrestle you for it, Larry?" I asked the chunky guard carrying the food. His real name was something lyrical with a lot of apostrophes, but I just gave all the guards names from classic literature. This one was Larry, and his bald buddy with the sword was Curly. I didn't see Shemp or Moe tonight, so I figured they were probably already drunk in the barracks. At least I hoped so.

Larry knelt in one of the front corners to set the food down, and Skeeter swarmed him. He skittered along the ground like Gollum on speed, wrapping both hands around the loaf of bread and shoving his face into it. He started chewing noisily, and I came right in after him.

"Let go of that, you little shit!" I yelled. "That's gotta last all three of us 'til morning, and you know Joe needs to eat after a healing!" I ducked between Larry's legs, which at my size put him way off balance.

"Back up, fool!" Curly bellowed from his spot by the cell door. Curly never came all the way into the cell. Like me, he was a tall guy and getting hunched down into our cell was difficult for him. When he showed up tonight, I knew we had caught our first lucky break since landing in Fairyland.

I did as I was told—I backed up. Of course, that wedged Larry's shins right into my armpits, so when I straightened up onto my knees, the already off-balance guard went down in a heap. The second his feet left the ground, I sprang for the door, and Skeeter leapt for Larry. He planted both knees in the guard's chest and leaned his forearm into the stunned man's throat.

I didn't have the explosion out of my stance I used to, but I still got off the blocks pretty well for a fat old guy with bad knees. I was fast enough to knock Curly's sword aside and slam a shoulder into his gut before he got the door closed, anyway. We tumbled out into the hall past the cell, and I planted a knee in his balls to take him out of the fight for a minute.

I looked back into the cell to see how the others were doing and was impressed. Skeeter had Larry choked out and was pressing a sword to the healer's stomach. Joe sat up on his pallet and held the guard's dagger in one hand. I saw they had their side of things well covered, so I yanked Curly's keys from his belt and tossed them to Amy. Then I knelt down beside Curly and drew his dagger.

"Curly, old pal, let me explain your situation to you. There's two ways this can go. We can take all your shit and lock y'all up in them cells where Moe and Shemp will find you when they bring breakfast. That's not going to go well with my Granny, but you'll at least be able to tell your side of the story. Or you can object to that plan, and I can carve a zipper from your nuts to your nose right here and leave you staring at your own guts and trying to figure out what goes where. What's it gonna be?"

"Only cold iron can harm the Fae, you fool. And we are not so stupid as to carry cold iron in the keep. You can no more cut me with that blade than you could fly."

"Plan C it is, then," I said. I reversed my grip on the dagger and slammed the pommel right between his eyes. I heard a *crack* as his skull fractured, and he slumped lifeless to the floor. I turned back to the others. "Hurry it up. He won't stay out long."

"Try these," Amy said from beside me. I looked up, and she held out a set of leg and arm shackles to me.

"I'm not really into that, but I've got some silk scarves at home I've been meaning to talk to you about," I said with a smile. She shook the cuffs at me, and I rolled Curly over and hog-tied him. I threw him into her cell and shoved a rag in his mouth while she got more restraints for Larry and the healer. There were several empty cells in the dungeon, so after we forced the healer to patch Joe up, everybody got their own private room. We even left them their underwear, which I thought was awfully kind of us.

Once our captors were imprisoned, we took stock of our meager weapons. Two swords, three daggers, and one satchel of various herbs and salves. Joe and Skeeter put on the guards' armor, and Amy threw the healer's robes over the rags she was wearing. Our own clothes were long gone, confiscated upon our arrival, and the tunics we'd been stuck in since stunk to high heaven. So did we, frankly, but there was nothing we could do about that until we got out of the castle. And we couldn't get out of the castle until we found my mother, who was Mab's prisoner somewhere else in the keep.

"What are we going to do to disguise you?" Skeeter asked. "I hate to point this out, but you're almost as conspicuous as me, and you know exactly how many brothers you've seen on *Game of Thrones*."

"Well, I guess we'll have to get lucky and hope nobody notices us," I said.

"Hope nobody notices the only black dude in all of Fairyland walking alongside Hagrid from Harry friggin' Potter, with a chick healer and some random guard?" Skeeter raised an eyebrow at me. "This might be your worst plan ever, Bubba."

"Well, as long as I'm always raising the bar," I said. "Come on, let's go save my mama from my crazy-ass granny before she gets turned into a toad or something."

2

We climbed the winding stairs from the dungeon, stopping at every landing to listen above and below for sounds that somebody had raised an alarm. Everything was quiet when we pushed the door open and stepped out into a wide hallway. I recognized nothing from when we were brought in, but that might be due to the burlap sack that covered my head from the moment Granny caught us stepping through a portal into her kingdom.

I cleared the door and looked right and left. We were alone, for the moment at least. Everybody gathered around, and Joe looked to me. "Where now, Bubba?"

"Shit, I don't know," I replied. "I was bagged and tagged when they carried me in here. What about y'all?"

"I could see a little," Amy said. "I twisted the hood around over my face and got an idea of where we were going. I think the exit is this way." She turned to head down the hall, but I grabbed her elbow.

"Hold up, hon. We can't leave yet," I said.

"Bubba, did that guard hit you in the head? What the hell are you talking about, we can't leave yet?" Skeeter asked.

"We gotta rescue Mama. She's somewhere in this castle, and we gotta save her. Plus, these bastards got Bertha hid somewhere in this joint. No way am I leaving Granny Batshit's castle without two of my favorite girls."

"Good phrasing," Amy said with a little smile.

"I'm big, but I ain't completely stupid," I said, winking.

"That remains to be seen," Skeeter shot back. "Alright, which way to get your mama?"

"Well, if the exit is that way," Joe said, pointing in one direction. "Then it stands to reason that we should go the opposite way to go farther into the castle. Although I do want to point out that it might not be our best idea. That healer took care of the worst of my injuries, and I think I've regrown all my teeth and toenails, but I'm still pretty beat up."

"Who needs toenails, anyway?" I said. "You just have to cut 'em all the time. And it ain't like I've ever been known for good decision-making. So let's go save Mama." I started down the hall that we assumed led into the castle, not waiting to see if they followed. They were my best friends; of course they'd follow.

Amy said, "He has a point. If he started making good decisions now, we'd think he was replaced by an imposter." The others nodded, and they followed me down the hall.

We walked about thirty yards before the hallway ended in a right turn. I figured we'd reached the far wall of the castle, and now we were going to continue circling the keep. I played enough dungeon crawl video games to know how these things lay out.

Of course, I've played enough dungeon video games to not be surprised when I turned the corner and came face to face with a faerie, too. This one wasn't a guard, but she looked to be a maid or some other servant. She was a slight, short woman—maybe five feet tall and a hundred pounds soaking wet. Her eyes went wide when she saw a giant human walking around not in chains, and she opened her mouth to scream. I wrapped my hand around her face, almost completely engulfing her head in my palm, and leaned down to her.

"Please don't do that," I whispered. "I'm trying very hard to be quiet, and I really don't want to hurt you. I will if I have to, and that will make this unpleasant for everyone. Especially you. Now, can you keep quiet?"

She nodded, her eyes watering a little. I wasn't sure if it was fear or stink, but my money was on terror. I mean, we smelled pretty ripe after being in a dungeon for a couple weeks, but she looked really scared. I took my hand off her mouth and stood up.

Amy stepped forward, holding out her hands so the little faerie could see she was unarmed. "Now, we're not going to hurt you, okay?"

The serving woman nodded again.

"What's your name?"

"Elisa."

"That's a pretty name. Elisa, do you know where the queen's daughter is?"

Elisa looked around, fear blossoming back in her face. "I can't talk about the princess. Her Majesty will be very cross with me if I speak out of turn."

"We promise not to tell," Amy said. I just leaned against the wall and cracked my knuckles. It doesn't take much for me to look intimidating, so I just behaved naturally.

It worked. Elisa's eyes went wide, and she pointed behind her down the hall. "She's in the second room down there, right past the wardroom."

"What's a wardroom?" Skeeter asked.

"In modern military parlance, a wardroom is a place where officers eat or just hang out," Joe said. "I assume it means something similar here, although it's typically used in reference to a ship."

That's when the three faeries in armor bearing swords stepped out of the first door down the hall, proving that the wardroom in this castle was pretty much like a wardroom on a ship, only with more swords and nobody dressed like The Village People.

I shoved Elisa to the side and rushed the soldiers, bowling all three of them over with a running clothesline. They fell to the stone hall with a clatter, and I turned and tossed one of them through the open door, taking down another pair of faeries.

"A little help?" I called, bulling my way into the room, dragging the other two struggling officers. Fighting a bunch of armed knights in close quarters would be bad enough, but doing it out in the open would be even worse. I had a size advantage on pretty much everybody, but I had no interest in duking it out with every faerie in the joint.

Joe and Amy ran into the room after me, Joe sliding to the right and Amy moving left to form a triangle blocking the door. Skeeter staggered in a second later, Elisa thrown over one shoulder, kicking and scratching the whole way.

"What the hell did you bring her for?" I asked.

"I couldn't leave her out there to raise the alarm," Skeeter said.

"Good point," I admitted. Then I reached out and thumped the girl on top of one of her pointy ears. "Stop that shit, or I'm going to hit you. If you sit down and shut up, nobody will hurt you. I promise."

She stopped moving in an instant, and Skeeter dumped her on her butt, then closed the door and wedged it shut. I turned back to the room to see exactly what kind of mess I'd run headlong into this time.

It wasn't too bad, as Bubba decisions go. There were about ten faeries in the room, and the quarters were so close their swords were useless. That meant that the ones we stole from the dungeon guards were useless, too, though. And all of these guys had daggers. Which they promptly drew.

"Well, this is gonna suck," I said. Then I took a deep breath and let out a huge roar. I charged the nearest faerie, slamming him into the guy behind him and driving us all into the floor. He was too stunned by my idiotic frontal assault to do anything but drop his knife and fall down, sandwiched between my bulk and the armored officer beneath him. I heard a few things crack as we hit the floor, and the bottom guy's breath *whooshed* out of him.

I sprang to my feet, my knees popping like a .22 pistol as I did. The rest of the knights looked at me, their eyes wide as they wondered what the psychotic giant was going to do next. That was exactly the reaction I was looking for, so I gave them what they wanted—something stupid. I bent down and picked up the guy that I'd made into the meat in a Bubba/floor sandwich by his breastplate. I hauled him up in front of my chest and ran forward again, this time using the armored faerie as a battering ram. I slammed his back plate into one dude's face, crushing his nose and sending him to the floor in a heap. Then I spun to the left, using my cargo's feet to kick another guy in the face. I spun back around, missed the nearest soldier, and tossed my now-unconscious bludgeon into a pair of faeries drawing their daggers and coming at me from my right side.

Joe and Amy joined the fray, throwing kicks and punches and generally fighting like normal people, instead of like a crazed redneck pro wrestler. Skeeter stayed back, keeping an eye on Elisa and his back pressed to the door. After my initial onslaught, it took less than two minutes to subdue or knock out ten faerie knights, which either said something about the power of humanity, or the fact that no matter how much training you have, you just can't fight crazy. Take your pick.

We used belts and tore up tabards to tie them all up, and bound Elisa as well. Once we had everybody all tied up and relieved of their weapons, Amy took over.

"Who's the ranking officer here?" she asked. No answer. She stepped up to one particularly young faerie and sliced off his left ear with a purloined dagger.

"I repeat, who's the ranking officer here?" Nothing. She stepped down the line to another baby-faced solider, and seconds later, tossed another severed ear over her shoulder. To their credit, the men she cut parts off of didn't cry out, but the third one did faint when she slapped him in the face with his own pointy ear.

Amy knelt down beside a fourth elf and pressed her blade to the side of his face, but froze when a voice called out, "I am Captain Falarun. I am the senior officer present. Do what you will to me, but harm my men no further."

Amy wiped her bloody dagger on the man's leggings and stood, walking over to the guy who called himself Captain Falarun. "You're in charge?"

He glared up at her, a haughty sneer on his face. "I am."

"Then why does this guy have more stripes on his shoulder than you?" she asked, kneeling by a man sitting next to Falarun.

Falarun's eyes widened, and his mouth worked as he tried to speak.

Amy just shook her head at him. "Never mind. That's what I needed to know." She grabbed the man with all the stripes on his armor and pulled him to his feet. She yanked him over to a nearby table, and Joe set a chair in front of it. They put the man in the chair, untied his arms, then tied him to the chair.

Amy and I pulled chairs up to the table opposite the prisoner and sat down. "Hi there," I said. "My name's Bubba. I think you know my granny, Mab. She's kinda your boss, right?"

The man nodded, but didn't say a word.

"Good. Now you're going to tell me everything about this castle's defenses, and I'm going to restrain Amy here from cutting off any more pieces of your men. You understand me?"

"I will never speak to you, human filth," the faerie said, then spit in my face.

I didn't bother to point out the contradiction in him speaking to me to tell me he wasn't going to speak to me. I just grabbed the top of his head and slammed his face into the table, shattering his nose and sending a spray of blood several feet to either side.

Joe stepped up and pulled the woozy man upright in his chair.

"Now," I said. "I think we should try that again. Maybe without the spitting."

3

———————

Half an hour later, I had sore knuckles and a lot more information about the layout of the castle. General Pranthis had a broken nose, two split lips, a black eye, the respect of his men, and quite possibly a ruptured testicle. It was that last gift that made him give up any semblance of resistance and tell us everything we ever wanted to know about Queen Mab's castle, its inhabitants, and its defenses. All in all, I considered it a fair trade.

"Bubba, that was...extreme," Skeeter said, stepping up to walk beside me as we headed toward the hidden staircase Pranthis swore led to my mother's chambers in the keep's western tower.

"You think that was extreme? Damn, son, don't you remember what they did to us in the dungeon? I'm pretty sure at least three of those boys in that room helped torture us."

"Yeah, but they sent in the healer every night," Skeeter protested.

"Who gives a damn? Knowing we were gonna get healed was just another part of the torture. Every time that healer showed up, it meant we weren't getting any real time off, we were all just gonna be right back in the shit the next morning. Besides, I didn't do anything to that dude that I haven't seen on *24* at least twice."

"You know that's a TV show, right?"

"You know we're in Fairyland, right? How the hell is that different?"

"I kinda gotta give you that one." He shut up.

We turned a corner, and I held up a hand to slow everybody down. There was a pair of guards walking about ten yards in front of us, heading in the same direction we were. They were talking amongst themselves, and I was pretty sure they hadn't heard us, but that could change with one wrong step.

"What's the plan?" Amy whispered in my ear.

"Beat their asses?" I replied.

"Good plan." She slapped me on the shoulder, and I charged the pair. They heard me, of course—even barefoot running with no armor I still made *some* noise—but they couldn't get turned around, process what was happening, and get their weapons drawn before I could cover the distance between us. Like most of the Fae, they were way smaller than me, so when I barreled into them, they went down in a clatter of armor and bruises. I didn't stop, just went through them and turned around a couple feet past the downed guards.

Amy and Joe were hot on my heels, quickly knocking the men unconscious and stripping them of their weapons and sword belts. "Now what?" Amy asked.

"Huh," I said. "Yeah, I guess we can't just leave them out in the hallway, can we?" I turned to the interior wall and tried the nearest door. The knob turned, and the door swung open, revealing a half-dressed faerie woman pulling a dress on over her head.

"Oops," I said, stepping into the room. I strode across the floor and pushed her down onto the bed, pressing my hand over her mouth. "Bring them in here," I called out to the others.

Amy shook her head at me as she dragged the first guard into the room. "Why does it not surprise me that you found the one room in the castle with a topless woman in it, Bubba?"

"What can I say? I've always been lucky," I replied with a grin. I pulled enough of the woman's dress down to give her some semblance of modesty, but I didn't let her off the bed or take my hand off her mouth long enough for her to scream.

Skeeter followed Amy and Joe into the room, carrying the guards' equipment, and pulled the door closed. I took my hand off the woman's mouth, and took a step back. "I'm really sorry," I said. "But we're going to have to tie all of you up and gag you. We're kinda escaping from my granny's dungeon, and I think it would go badly for us if we just let y'all run around. So...sorry."

The woman opened her mouth wide like she was about to scream, and Amy stepped forward, slapping her across the face with a loud *crack*. All the air rushed from the woman's lungs, and she gaped at Amy, her eyes like saucers.

"Did you miss the part where the really big guy said we were escaped prisoners?"

The woman shook her head, silent.

"Does that make you think that we're nice people?"

Another head shake.

"Do you see that we're all carrying swords and knives?"

A nod this time.

"Do you think for one second that I won't cut you into little pieces?"

Back to a head shake.

"Good. Now sit there and keep your damn mouth shut while we tie these men up and throw them into your closet. Then I'll tie you up on the bed and make sure you're relatively comfortable while we go about our business. Is that clear?"

Nod.

"Excellent." Amy stepped away, then turned back to the terrified faerie. "But if you make so much as a sound, I will cut your throat from ear to ear. So sit there and keep your damn mouth shut."

I moved over to help her finish tying up the guards. "Damn," I whispered. "How much of that was for real?"

"Enough that I'm pretty sure she doesn't want to test me. Get me out of this castle, Bubba, before I kill somebody. I'm hungry, I'm dirty, and I'm tired of being locked up. Let's find your mom and get the hell out of here."

"We still have to find my sister," I said.

"I know," Amy said. "But I am not going back to that dungeon. Do you hear me?"

"Loud and clear."

"How far are we from the entrance to the tower?" Joe asked.

"I think it's supposed to be around the next corner," Skeeter replied. I nodded. That fit with my memory of the general's mumbled directions. Mumbled because I might have knocked out a couple of teeth during our "conversation."

Joe put on his "take charge" voice, and laid out a plan. "I'm going to go ahead and scout. Bubba, you and Skeeter wait here while Amy and I go check it out. If we run into any guards, one of us will come back to get you."

"Or you could just deal with it while we wait here in perfect comfort and safety," Skeeter said. I looked over at him, and he was settled into a plush armchair in the corner of the room with a decanter of wine on one knee and a plate of fruit and cheese on a table beside the chair. He looked like a skinny black kid had been dropped into a painting of the French nobility or something. I had to laugh.

"Don't get drunk on faerie wine, Skeeter. We might still need your ferocious combat skills before the day is through."

"Bubba, you know I'm a lover, not a fighter."

"Exactly. I might have you proposition the next armed guard we come to. The way your love life goes, he'll run screaming into the night rather than date you." Skeeter didn't reply, just drank wine straight from the decanter while flipping me the bird with his other hand.

I turned back to Joe, but Amy was pulling the door closed behind them as they crept out into the hall. With nothing else to do, I sat down on the edge of the bed and looked over at Skeeter. "You think we'll find her?" I asked.

"Your mom or your sister?"

"Mom. Nitalia. Both. Either. Shit, Skeet, I don't know. Hell, until a couple months ago, I didn't know I *had* a sister, now I've traveled to a friggin' magical dimension to save her. Let me correct that—I've traveled to a magical dimension *again* to try and save her. Shit, I didn't like this place the first time I came here, and now I'm back. If I never see another faerie as long as I live, it'll be too soon, much less another damn Fairyland dungeon."

"Another dungeon?" Skeeter asked. "You mean you got locked up the last time you were over here, too?"

I might have glossed over some of the high points of my last trip through the looking glass when I told Skeeter about it. I nodded. "Yeah. I met Titania last time I was here. I kinda shot her cousin; then I killed him in a duel. There was some dungeon time involved in all that."

"Before or after you killed him?"

"Well…a little of both. I was in the dungeon before I killed him, then I broke back into the dungeon after I killed him to rescue the humans Titania was holding there and free Puck's girlfriend so they could get married."

"Bubba," Skeeter said, setting the decanter of wine down on the table by his fruit tray. "One of these days we're going to talk about communication and how I need to know what happens when you're out of my sight."

I opened my mouth to reply, but the sound of boots running in the hall outside brought me to my feet. The door flung open, and Amy appeared. "Haul ass," she panted. "We found the stairwell, but the guards found us. Joe's holding them off, but I don't know how long that's gonna last." She turned and sprinted away, me and Skeeter hot on her heels.

I overtook Amy in a few long strides, then turned the corner and ducked a wild backswing of Joe's sword. "Whoa, padre!" I yelled.

He faced a pair of guards with daggers, but Joe was holding them off pretty well with his sword. I crouched down on one knee and yelled back to Skeeter, "Ramp it, spider monkey!"

My little buddy rounded the corner at a dead run, took two long, gangly steps, then planted a foot in the middle of my shoulders. I stood up, Skeeter dove forward over Joe's head in the vaulted hallway, and flew into the guards with a clatter of armor and elbows. Skeeter rolled free, leaving a pair of dazed faeries lying in the middle of the floor.

I pushed past the stunned Joe and stepped up to the first guard. I reached down, grabbed the front of his tabard with my left hand, and pulled him up. Three quick punches to the face and his eyes rolled back in his head. I repeated the process with the second guard, and a few seconds later, the fight was over.

Amy caught up with us just as Skeeter got to his feet. "What the hell happened? That ruckus must have woken all the dead in the Winter Kingdom."

"I kinda threw Skeeter at the bad guys," I said. "But he knew it was coming."

"It was something we practiced back in high school. You see, there was this still Bubba wanted to steal liquor from, but there was a fence around it."

"An electric fence," I said. "I learned that the hard way."

"He peed on it," Skeeter said.

"Turned my pecker blue for a week," I agreed.

"So we figured out how to use Bubba as a ramp to get me over the fence. When he said that, and I saw him kneeling there, I figured that's kinda what we were gonna do."

"Glad you didn't land on a knife," Amy said.

Skeeter turned ashen with the thought. "I...never thought of that."

"Shit," I said. "Me neither. Might not want to try that against armed opponents."

"You think?" Amy said, smacking me upside the back of the head. "Where are these stairs?"

"I assume they're near this section of wall," Joe said, walking about ten feet down the hallway and pointing. "That's where the guards were standing."

"So Mab went to all the trouble of creating an invisible door; then she posted guards outside it so everyone could see where it is?" Joe asked.

"Did I mention my granny's a little nuts?" I walked over to the section of wall he was staring at. It didn't look any different from the rock around it, but when I put my hand out, it went straight through. "Huh. That's different."

I stepped through the wall, which was just an illusion, and started up the narrow staircase behind it. The others followed after a few seconds, and we wound our way up the spiral stone steps for several minutes before we reached a small landing with a door.

I knocked and pushed open the door into a lavish apartment. The room was decked out like you'd expect royal chambers to be, with a lush sitting room, complete with sofa and several armchairs in front of a roaring fireplace. There were doors on either side of the room, so I assumed at least one of them led off into my mother's bedchamber.

My mother stood in front of the fireplace, staring into the flames, a glass of wine in her hand. She spun around as we stepped into the room, smiling broadly. She might have been the best-dressed prisoner I'd ever seen. She was clean, dressed in a glorious deep blue gown, with her hair cascading down her shoulders in curls adorned with diamond hair clips.

"Robbie, my love!" she exclaimed, grinning from ear to ear. "So glad you could make it. Are you here to escort me to the ball?"

4

I looked at my mother, decked out in an amazing gown of what looked like blue velvet, with white fur trim and diamonds all over the place. She had a neckline that plunged *waaaaaay* farther than I ever wanted to see on my mom, estranged or not, and a sparkling necklace of sapphires, diamonds, and rubies that looked like it was worth more than my house. Or maybe even Skeeter's computer. She didn't look much like a prisoner, and her quarters were definitely a step or two above the cramped dungeon cell we just escaped from.

"Mama?" I didn't know where to start. There were so many questions and so few words.

"We have to get out of here," Amy said. She stepped forward and grabbed my mother's wrist. "Mrs. Brabham, do you have traveling clothes?"

"And maybe a snack?" Skeeter added, hunger making him sound kinda like a gay Oliver Twist. When we were kids, the level of food at our houses was something almost legendary. Some days, I wondered if our mamas were competing with each other to see who could make the best supper and get us to want to eat at her house. We finally came up with a rotating schedule. My house Mondays and Wednesdays, Skeeter's house Tuesdays and Thursdays. Friday night supper was always in town before the football game, and Sunday dinner was at your own house, unless there was a meal at church. Saturdays we were pretty casual since our mamas were already working on Sunday dinner, so we just grabbed a sandwich or something.

"Oh, Skeeter, you always were the hungriest thing!" She walked— no, *glided*—over to Skeeter and pinched his cheeks. It was like watching a weird episode of Donna Reed at the Ren Faire.

Skeeter blushed and ducked his head like some demented Eddie Haskell while Mama led him over to an overstuffed chair and sat him down, clucking over him the whole time. Amy, Joe, and I exchanged confused looks.

"Ummm...Mrs. Brabham? We really need to get out of here," Amy reiterated.

Mama spun around on her heel, a scowl across her face. "Young lady, I am not letting this child leave my home hungry. Now you can come over here and get a snack yourself, or you can sit there and be quiet, but we are not leaving this house until everybody has had a proper meal. Do you understand me?" I stood up a little straighter at the whip-crack of her voice. I remembered that Mama, too. That was the one who told me in no uncertain terms what would happen to my rear end if she ever caught me trying to teach my little brother to pee on the electric fence again, or throwing rocks at wasps' nests, or throwing wasps' nests at my sixth-grade teacher's house, or any of a hundred harmless pranks I pulled when I was a kid.

Amy's jaw snapped shut so fast I could hear the *click* from ten feet away. She shut up but still walked over to where Mama was setting up a damn gourmet spread in front of Skeeter.

"Oh, are the rest of y'all hungry, too? Well, Robbie, don't be rude, bring some chairs over here. No wait, Skeeter, sit down on the floor. Yes, honey, right there on the rug. We're going to have a picnic!" Mama clapped her hands and grinned her demented Suzy Home-maker grin, and that was all I could take.

"No, Mama. We're not hungry. Well, we are, but we're going to take our picnic to go. We are getting the hell out of here, right damn now, and you are coming with us. I don't know what Granny Frostbite has done to your brain, but this ain't you talking. Now get changed into something you can run and ride in because we're leaving." I'd never talked to my mother like that. She came back to Faerie before we had too many of the normal teenage blowups, so I think my tone took her by surprise. That was fine by me, as long as she wasn't stunned into immobility.

Her eyes went cold, and I could have sworn the temperature in the room dropped. When I was a kid, I used to think that getting chills for my mother looking at me hard was just me being silly, but now that I knew who and what she was, I thought it might be a real thing. "Robert Edward Brabham, you do not speak to me in that tone. I am your mother, and you will respect me. I know that we've had our difficulties, but—"

"Mab's glamoured you, Mrs. B.," Skeeter said from the chair. "As much as it hurts me to say it, Bubba's right. We've got to go, and you've got to get changed. Your mama's done cast a spell on you to make you think you want to be here, but you don't. You only came back to find your daughter. Remember Nitalia? Your little girl? Mab kidnapped her, and we came here to get her loose."

Mama's eyes got a faraway look in them, like she was trying to listen to Skeeter through a fog, then she shook her head. "Mother would never harm my baby girl. She loves me and loves my babies. Isn't that right, Robbie?"

"I don't know, Mom. The first time I met Granny, she threw me in the dungeon."

"Where you will be returning if you continue to annoy me, grandson." I *thought* the room got a little chilly when Mama got mad. When Mab spoke, there was no damn question. A thin layer of frost ran across the floor and crept up the walls.

I watched my breath appear in front of me as I whispered, "Shit." I turned around, and there stood my grandmother. Not some portly white-haired woman in an apron with a tray of cookies in one hand and a pitcher of lemonade in the other. Nope, my dear, sweet granny was Queen Mab, insane ruler of the Winter Court of Faerie, and she was sporting her full ceremonial garb.

Mab stood ramrod-straight, white hair cascading down her shoulders, shot through with streaks of blue that seemed to shimmer through her locks like light shining through the frozen surface of a lake. Her skin was flawless, pale as milk, with high cheekbones sharp as razors and eyes so blue that they could only be created with magic or Photoshop. She wore a long gown in a pale blue trimmed in white, the pastel blue of wave tops or a cloudless sky. Mama's gown was the blue of midnight, making the white trim stand out and contrast her dark hair, while Mab's trim of silver almost bled into the color of her gown, which almost faded into the white of her skin, making you have to stare to see where the dress stopped and her flesh began.

And stare we did, because in addition to being beautiful, she looked *dangerous*, like a museum-quality dagger carved of diamonds. She stood in the room, letting us soak in her presence for a moment before speaking again. When she opened her mouth, she gave a chilly smile that didn't even reach the same zip code as her eyes.

"Robert, my dear, I am sorry that you were kept in such rough accommodations for the initial portion of your visit. I do hope that you and your friends can find it in your hearts to forgive me. I have taken the liberty of expanding your mother's apartments here in the tower to accommodate you all." She waved a hand, and a door appeared in the wall by the fireplace. "Down that hallway you will find fresh clothing and a bathing room for each of you. Please avail yourselves of it before the ball this evening. I hate to be so gauche as to point it out, but you stink, dear."

"Sorry, Gran," I said, folding my arms across my chest. "I ain't figured out how to shit in a bucket without getting a little funky."

"Besides, all the cutting and beatings your pals downstairs handed out made us a little sweaty and bloody," Joe said with a growl.

"Again, my apologies to you all, and I do hope that I can make amends by inviting you to the ball this evening. I am certain that you will enjoy the entertainment."

"What kind of entertainment?" Amy asked. "Are you going to have us drawn and quartered for the amusement of your court?"

Mab blinked rapidly, as if surprised by something. "I hadn't considered that. My goodness, I wish I had met you earlier, my dear. I would have been able to rearrange the schedule and accommodate you. But no, you will be able to witness the tournament."

"Oooh! A tournament! I love tournaments!" Mama actually clapped her hands like a schoolgirl. I looked over at her, and she had a vacant grin on her face like she was some idiot teenager, not a woman with a thirty-five-year-old son.

"What kind of tournament?" I asked.

"Oh, don't worry your pretty little head about that, Robert," Mab said, gliding over to pat me on the shoulder. Seriously, do any of the women in Fairyland ever *walk*? Maybe it's just something with the long gowns. "Now, all of you go get cleaned up, and your escorts will take you to the Great Hall in two hours. Don't dawdle. It will take some time to get the bloodstains out of your cuticles. I know from experience."

Her voice went hard, and when she spoke again, it wasn't the airy, faux-gracious tone she'd been using with us. This wasn't dear sweet Granny telling me to go wash my hands before she gave me a cookie. This was Queen Friggin' Mab, the ultimate ruler of the Winter Court and everything in it. Which included us. "Appropriate clothing will be provided for you. Leave the purloined weapons here. You will neither need them nor be allowed to carry them in my presence. Test me at your peril."

Then, quicker than a blink, the dancing fairy-granny was back. I got a good look in her eyes, and she was as batshit crazy as Skeeter's mama that time we threw mud pies at the sheets she had hanging out to dry on the clothesline. Except Skeeter's mama just beat our asses so bad we ate standing up for a week. Mab looked like she would happily use our intestines for Christmas tinsel if we did anything to piss her off.

I did what I always do when faced with an absolutely insane

woman at close range. I agreed with her. "Yes, ma'am. We'll go get cleaned up and be ready to go to the ball in a couple hours."

"Grand decision, Robert. I look forward to seeing you in your formal garb." She turned to go but turned back to me when I cleared my throat. As much as I wanted her the hell away from me, there was one more thing that I needed to know.

"Was there something else, dear?" she asked, one narrow, manicured eyebrow clawing its way to the ceiling.

"Um...yes ma'am. You said something about a tournament. What are they gonna be fighting for?"

"Oh, didn't I mention the prize? I have invited sixteen of the most valiant warriors from throughout the Winter Court to join us this evening and face each other in single combat. They are battling for the richest prize in Faerie—my daughter's hand in matrimony." With that, she turned and swept out the door, which vanished behind her, leaving just blank stone where the exit used to be.

"Did you hear that, Robbie?" Mama squealed, clapping again. I was really going to have to do something to get her out of Mab's spell soon. This enthusiasm was murder on my eardrums.

"Yeah, I heard it," I said, trying to figure out what I was going to *do* about it.

"Isn't it wonderful!" Mama said, her voice almost high enough to make dogs whimper. "I'm going to be married again. They say the third time's the charm!"

She turned and walked off through the door that I assumed led to her room, holding her hands in front of her like she had a bouquet and humming "The Wedding March."

I looked around at my friends, who all looked at least as confused as I felt. "Well," I said. "Let's go get cleaned up. Sounds like we've got a wedding to spoil."

5

———————

An hour later, we were all scrubbed and standing in Mama's parlor, waiting on Amy to emerge from her room. "I probably shouldn't make any jokes about waiting on her, should I?" I asked Skeeter.

"That depends, Bubba. Do you ever want to see her naked again?" Despite being queer as a golf helmet, Skeeter has always had an uncanny level of insight into the way women think. Or maybe it's because he's not spending most of his time around a woman thinking about getting her to sleep with him that he's got a line into how she thinks. One of those. Either way, I just nodded and kept my mouth shut.

Until Amy stepped into the room, whereupon my mouth dropped open and my tongue rolled out, down my jaw, and across the floor like a cartoon wolf. I let out a low whistle, and Skeeter just nodded.

"I hate to break it to you, Bubba, but I think I'm switching teams," Skeeter said.

"Get in line, skinny man," Joe said. "I have a vow of celibacy to throw away." We both stared at him, and he shrugged. "I'm a priest. I'm not dead."

I just shook my head at my friends, closed my gaping mouth, and walked over to the most beautiful woman I'd ever seen, who also happened to be my girlfriend.

Amy was decked out in an emerald green gown that plunged to a neckline trimmed in diamonds that looked like frost. A snowflake pendant hung with its long point right above her cleavage, not that she needed any help drawing attention to her boobs, which looked like little clouds of happiness floating along under her dress.

Her hair was pulled partway up with silver-and-diamond hair clips, then let loose to cascade down her back in golden curls. Diamond earrings matched her necklace, and at the end of her long sleeves, a pair of diamond bracelets glittered. I walked up to her and kissed her on the cheek.

"You look absolutely stunning, darling. I don't think I've seen you look prettier since the last time I almost died and you were the first thing I saw when I woke up in the hospital."

"Bubba, from any other human being, that would sound completely stupid. But from you, it is the sweetest thing I think I've ever heard. Now kiss me like you mean it, you giant hunk of handsome man-meat." She wrapped her long arms around my neck and pulled me down to her. Our lips pressed together, then opened, and I kissed her for a lot longer than I should have felt comfortable kissing anybody in front of my mama. But I enjoyed it so much I just didn't care.

She pulled back and said, "Now let me see how they cleaned you up."

I grimaced, but stepped back so she could take in the whole picture. It wasn't a pretty picture, but it didn't look any more ridiculous than any of the other men would look. I hoped. My hair was washed and pulled back into a neat braid, with silver and blue wire running through the braid to give it the hint of Winter Court that apparently Granny Mab decreed. My beard was likewise braided, but in multiple segments, with crystals woven into the ends of each braid. I didn't quite jingle when I walked, but I did feel an awful lot like I had a wind chime hanging on my face.

But that wasn't the worst part. The worst part was the clothes. I left my room to take a bath, which took place in a huge communal bathing room with pools of water that started out hotter than hell, with jets of steam bubbling up to make magical fairy hot tubs, then gradually cooled down as you moved through the pools. But while I was gone, somebody stole my clothes and replaced them with some crap that looked like it was straight out of *Lord of the Rings IV* or something. I almost barged out in the hall in nothing but a towel, but everything laying on my bed looked a lot like the same crap the guards wore, so I figured it was just what people wore in Fairyland. Only bigger.

I was wearing a tunic, at least I reckon that's what it was called, some kind of long nightshirt that hung halfway down to my knees. It was blue, of course, a light blue that reminded me of a Volkswagen Beetle a girl I'd wanted to sleep with in high school drove. It was almost impossible for me to fool around in a Beetle, even at fifteen. I had garters on my sleeves to hold them up, and the whole thing kinda felt like I was wearing a circus tent. The tabard over it was a deep blue that kinda matched Mama's gown, trimmed in silver fur that I was pretty sure didn't come from any animal I'd ever seen.

And there were hose. I was wearing leggings. Thick pantyhose that were almost impossible to pull up over my thighs, but after a solid five minutes of wrestling, flopping on the bed with my legs in the air, and hopping around the room like a jackass, I managed to get them up over my ass and get Little Bubba tucked down my left leg so I was pretty sure I wouldn't terrify any small children. I really hoped I didn't have to pee while I was wearing this crap. Or worse. So I stood in Mama's parlor in front of my girlfriend, my mother, and my two best friends looking like a Sasquatch escaped from a Renaissance Faire, dressed in blue from the ties in my hair to the soft leather boots on my feet. I didn't have a gun or a knife anywhere, nor anywhere to tuck one if I had it, and my pantyhose were riding up something fierce. I was becoming more of a feminist by the second and gaining a new appreciation for kilts at the same time.

Amy tried hard not to laugh, but she couldn't manage to keep a smile off her face. "I think you look very handsome, Bubba."

"Thank you," I said. I looked at Skeeter and Joe, but they were both wise enough to put their hands up and take a step back, saying nothing. I wouldn't murder my best pals for giving me crap about my clothes, but I was not at all above punching them.

"Well, I think he looks absolutely *darling*," Mama said. She swooped over and took my left arm, waving at Amy to grab my right. "And now he can escort the two belles of the ball to my engagement party!"

"You seem awfully happy about this, Mama," I said. "Aren't you still worried about finding Nitalia?"

"She's a grown woman, Robbie, just like you're a grown man. I have all the confidence in the world that she's just fine. Now let's make our way to the festival!"

"The festival?" I asked.

"The festival!" Mama repeated.

"The festival," Skeeter sighed.

"I'm going to shoot the first person who says 'home before dark,'" Amy said with a sharp look around. "I like some Sondheim, but *Into the Woods* is overdone. Give me *Assassins* any day."

"Be careful what you wish for," Joe said, stepping past us and pulling open the door. The two guards in the hall looked at us, then nodded to Mama and started off down the stairs ahead of us. I let Mama and Amy go ahead of me, since spiral staircases are pretty much a single-file thing, and I hung back a few steps to whisper to Skeeter and Joe.

"Look," I said. "I don't know what the hell is going on with Mama, but we are *not* letting her get married. Especially not to somebody Mab likes."

"And exactly how do you plan to stop her?" Skeeter asked.

"I don't know yet, but I'm thinking there's got to be some way to wreck this tournament. Maybe we can knock out all the competitors, or just the two finalists, or something. But my mother is not getting married to anybody that my granny decides is suitable. That's for damn sure."

"Okay, we're with you, Bubba, but you'd better come up with

something pretty quick because from the sounds of the hallway, there's a heck of a crowd waiting for us," Joe said.

He wasn't wrong, either. We stepped out of the hidden door into a hallway packed with people all dressed in their finest gowns and what I reckoned was formal wear for dudes in Fairyland. I was glad to see everybody was pretty much wearing the whole tunic and hose thing, so even though I looked stupid, I didn't look any more stupid than everybody else. I expected it to take us forever to get through the crowd, but we picked up two more guards at the secret door, and the armored dudes with swords made a pretty good path.

Mama held out her arm again, and I stepped forward to take it, waving Amy up to my other side. Hell, as long as Mama said we should enter together, I was down with that. We came to a huge double door at the end of the long hallway, and I let go of Amy's arm to reach for the handle. A hiss from Mama froze me in place, and two of the guards stepped in front of us to open the doors. They yanked them open simultaneously, and a little man in a tailcoat and a top hat hollered out, "The Honored Princess Ygraine, her son Robert Edward Brabham, his Consort Amanda Hall, Squire William James MacIntyre Kwame Jones III, and their sage Joseph MacIntyre."

I'd never been announced when I entered a room before, not even when I ran onto the field at UGA. Every head in the room turned to stare at us, but it was obvious they weren't interested in looking at me. Mama and Amy held the eye of every man and most of the women in the room. I was just the giant idiot between the two beauties. I only existed to make them look even prettier by comparison, not that they needed any help.

The crowd parted, and a long red carpet led from the doors to a dais where Mab sat, looking regal and gorgeous and somehow dangerous, all at the same time, all without moving or speaking. She just radiated danger, like a coiled rattlesnake. Only this one wouldn't give you the courtesy of a warning noise before she struck. Mab sat on a throne of crystal, a giant thing that looked uncomfortable as hell. To her right sat an empty smaller version with a dark blue cushion on it. There was another empty crystal chair on her left, with three smaller chairs beside it.

"Is the one on her left for me?" I asked.

"Very good, Robbie," Mama said, her lips never wavering from the smile she'd plastered on her face the second the doors opened. "Yes, you are to sit to the left of the queen, as her defender. Your woman, the squire, and sage shall all sit on the dais below you."

"Squire?" I heard Skeeter mutter behind me. "Yeah, I know what that really means. That word stars with 's' too, but it sounds a lot different."

"Skeeter," Mama said. "If you speak in the queen's presence without her asking you a direct question, she may very well seal your mouth shut permanently." Mama always did know how to shut Skeeter up, even when we was in school.

"Whatever, Mrs. B. All I know is I didn't come all the way to Fairy-land to star in some medieval remake of *The Help*."

We made it to the front of the room and all bowed to Granny, then took our seats. Mab stood, clapped her hands, and said in a loud voice, "Thank you all for coming. Not that I gave you a choice. We are here to celebrate the pending engagement of my lovely daughter Ygraine, finally to someone who I deem worthy. Sixteen of the greatest champions from throughout the Winter Court are here tonight to duel for her hand in marriage. Many will fall, some may die, but in the end, my loving daughter shall finally ascend her proper place as my heir, with a suitable spouse at her side."

I wasn't sure what made me want to puke more, the words my grandmother was saying, or the smile on my mother's face as she heard them. We didn't just have to stop this farce of an engagement, we had to break whatever brainwashing Mab had done to Mama, too.

"Now, ladies, gentlemen, and distinguished guests, enjoy the music and the food. Once we have dined and drank, let the games begin!"

6

W e ate, and I have to admit, Granny Mab knows how to throw down a feast. There was about half a dozen courses, every one better than the one that came before. We were all seated at the head table, with Mama to one of Granny's elbows and me to the other. Amy sat next to me, with Joe on the other side of her. Skeeter was pointed to a position behind the table with the other squires, but when somebody mentioned him serving our food, he almost fell over laughing. Joe stepped in, spoke to the trim faerie dressed in the deepest navy blue trimmed with silver, somebody Mama identified as the Master of Ceremonies, and said a few quiet words. Seconds later, the man appeared with a chair for Skeeter next to Joe.

"What did you say to him?" I asked.

"I explained that squires into our world serve different duties there and are frequently used as food tasters and trusted advisors more than servants."

"Good thing, too," Skeeter said. "I'm pretty sure we ain't ready to commence with the killing yet, but the first time you look at me to cut your steak for you, the only thing I slice will be your fat neck."

I covered my laugh with a wine glass and took a long sip. The sparkling fruit juice was delicious, felt a lot like drinking sunlight, but didn't have much of a kick to it. "When's the hooch come out, Granno?" I whispered to Mab.

She turned to me, a frosty smile on her lips. "My dearest Robert, we do not imbibe at meals in the royal dining hall. Should any of my subjects become unruly or inappropriate, I would be forced to take action, and that would disturb my enjoyment of my meal. We wouldn't want that, would we?" The look she gave me sat over a smile, but I swear I felt a lot like a mouse staring up at a cobra.

"No, ma'am," I said after taking another long swallow of fruit juice. "Besides, this is delicious. What is it?" I figured it was some sort of exotic fruit that only grew in Fairyland. It tasted kinda like apple juice mixed with sparkling pear something.

"It is the fruit of a pear tree blended with sweet apple juice, with a dash of dryad tears to make the bubbles. I have my alchemists brew it especially for me."

"Dryad tears?" I asked. "How to you harvest those?"

"I find that cutting off their fingers is the best method. It allows them to weep, while keeping them conscious much longer than flaying. Serious beatings tend to render the dryads comatose and unable to cry, and flogging jars them too much. The tears just fly everywhere when the whip strikes. Plus, a few days in rich soil and they'll regrow all their fingers, so we can harvest them weekly. Drink up, we can make plenty more." She waved a careless hand at a servant behind us, who stepped forward to refill my glass.

Despite the desert that appeared out of nowhere in my mouth, I set the glass down on the table and pushed it away. "I think I'll switch to water. I want to make sure I keep my head clear for the entertainment, after all."

"Of course you do," Mab replied. "After all, you want to see who your new father will be."

I tried to hold my tongue, but that always makes me look stupid, so I just let fly. "I know who my father was, and it don't matter who you stick my mama with, they won't ever take his place." I left out the fact about my brother turning Pop into a werewolf and me killing him myself, but the look in Granny Psycho's eyes told me she knew exactly what buttons she was pushing.

After the meal, all the lower tables were cleared to the walls, making a big open space in front of us. A small band of men with what looked like round-bottom guitars stepped forward and started to play, and a couple of drummers started to beat out a merry rhythm. Mab clapped her hands three times, and faeries from all around the room moved onto the floor in couples, moving in beautiful patterns just like they'd rehearsed it all.

I watched the dancing for about as long as I could stand without getting bored, which amounted to about fifteen seconds, then leaned over to Amy and started to make wisecracks about the dudes in pantyhose dancing like pansies. Of course, that's when Mab turned to me with another one of those devious little smiles on her lips.

"Would you like to show us some of the dances of your land, Robert?"

"Nah, Granny, I'm good."

"I'm sure I insist."

"Nah, I really can't. I don't want to embarrass any of your boys out there. Besides, I've got this bum knee. Old football injury, you know?"

"No, I don't know. And understand before you respond, grandson, that no one denies me three times in my own hall. So, I ask once more, would you like to dance, Robert?" Her eyebrows climbed so far that I thought they were making a break for it, but I finally settled on the right answer.

"Of course, Granny. I'd love to dance for your amusement. Come on, Amy." I stood up and started walking behind the table.

"Why do I have to be humiliated just because you pissed off your grandmother?" Amy asked.

"Because you'd rather not see me die. At least, most days."

"Oh don't worry, Bubba. If anybody ever kills you, it'll be me," Amy said, pushing her chair out and following me.

I stopped and bent down between Joe and Skeeter. "Y'all gotta go take care of making the boogie happen."

"What do you want us to play?" Joe asked.

"I don't care, just something with a beat to it that I can maybe shake my groove thing to a little bit. I figure if I humiliate myself for a few minutes, Granny will let me sit back down, and we can get on with the figuring out how to keep my mama from marrying some jackass faerie."

"And the whole finding your sister part of the trip," Skeeter said.

"Yeah, that too," I agreed. "But that's back-burnered until we can deprogram Mama and get the hell out of this castle. I'm pretty sure Nitalia isn't here, and that means she's still in danger, wherever she is."

"Yeah, because she'd be so safe here," Amy muttered. I couldn't disagree with her. After all, I was pretty sure I was about to do a Fairyland dance-off to keep my sociopathic magical grandmother from murdering us all and serving redneck spleen for dessert.

I took Amy by the hand and stepped to the middle of the floor. The dancers and musicians cleared a space for us, and I took a bow. "Hey y'all. I reckon most of y'all know who I am. I'm Queen Mab's grandson Robert, but y'all can call me Bubba. Granny asked me to give y'all an example of how we cut a rug back in my part of the world, and my lovely assistant Amy has volunteered to help out." I gestured over to where Amy stood, all decked out in her green gown with those glorious boobies pushed up to say hello to the whole room. She curtsied, and I realized that the curtsey was probably invented right along with the corset, or the medieval equivalent to the push-up bra. Because one bow in that dress and Amy might put out her own eye.

"So my buddy Skeeter and his uncle, Father Joe, are gonna provide some musical accompaniment. Hit it, boys." I waved to our impromptu backing band, and Skeeter started pounding out a rhythm on the drum he'd confiscated from a very confused faerie musician.

Now let's be clear. I ain't a dancer. I ain't even as much a dancer as Robert Earl Keen, and he put out an album called *No Kind of Dancer*. But I can shake my big fat ass enough to keep from getting murdered in my granny's ballroom. So that's what I did. Skeeter and Joe started off with a simple two-step, and I managed to parade Amy around the floor without stepping on her feet more than a couple times. With a nod to Skeeter, they switched to a slower waltz rhythm, and we 1-2-3'd a few more laps.

Then Granny decided that I was not being appropriately humiliated and hollered out, "This is boring, grandson. Entertain me or I shall start lopping off fingers from your squire."

Skeeter, his being the fingers in jeopardy, didn't even miss a beat. He gave me a three-second drumroll, then broke into the pounding beat of that classic hit "Macarena." I shot him a dirty look, but slapped my hands to my hips and Macarena'd the best I could remember for about twelve bars. Then Skeeter changed up the beat again, and it got real *Soul Train*, real fast.

Amy stepped up beside me, and right after my last hip thrust in my third time through the Macarena, she tagged herself in and started doing the Running Man to Skeeter's half-assed backbeat. Joe handed his weird guitar off to a faerie musician and walked out to the floor. He walked right up to Amy's face, like we were in *Step Off Vol. 17* or something, and started doing the weird-ass sprinkler dance where he put one hand behind his head and stuck the other arm straight out in front of his face, then spun around jerking like an idiot. Mab was grinning at us acting stupid, and the faeries were getting into it, so I figured the dumber we looked, the less likely we were to get murdered.

Looking dumb is not a challenge for me, especially when there's music. It works better with tequila, but I reckon dryad tears and apple juice can get me there, too. I got a running start, slid up to Amy on my knees yelling out, "HEEEEEEYYYYYY, Sexy Lady!" Then I hopped to my feet, ignored the shotgun pops that came from my kneecaps, and started dancing Gangnam Style, complete with the crazy cowboy dance spanking my own ass.

Not to be outdone, Joe (the Catholic priest and Knight Templar, Holy Avenger and Enforcer of God's Will on Earth, remember?) sprinted to the far end of the hall, hollered out, "Nobody puts Baby in a corner!" and came at me in a dead run. Well, I've seen *Dirty*

Dancing, so I knew what was up. He took a flying leap, and I played Patrick Swayze to his Jennifer Grey, catching him around the waist and hoisting him high over my head and spinning around with my arms fully extended.

"This ain't as easy as it looks," I grunted through clenched teeth as I held his two hundred twenty pounds over my head.

"Neither is this," Joe whispered. "You're pushing on my belly, and I've really got to fart."

Then he did, and my head was enveloped in the most noxious damn green cloud I've smelled since my last serious beer hangover. I'm pretty sure half my damn beard fell out, and I threw Joe up into the air and ran out from under him. I kinda hoped he'd land on his feet, but after the bomb he just laid on my face, I also kinda didn't care.

But he stuck the landing and held out his hands to me and Amy. We stepped forward and bowed to the cheering, clapping faeries on all four sides, then made one last bow back to Granny Mab, who stood from her throne to give us polite applause. I reckon the sight of two idiot men throwing each other around like demented pro wrestlers was good enough to spare us from execution.

Mab held up her hands, and the room fell silent, just like flipping a switch. "Thank you, Robert, for that...lovely demonstration. Truly, the dances of your homeland are...impressive. But now, it is time for the evening's true entertainment. Let the tournament to find a suitable husband for my daughter begin!"

I looked around to my friends and saw the same thought reflected in their eyes. *Well...shit. Now what?*

7

____

Mab gestured to the Master of Ceremonies, who stepped to the center of the room. "Our entertainment for the evening shall be a trial by combat for the hand of the lovely Princess Ygraine." He gestured one slim hand to Mama, who stood up and curtsied. Polite applause filled the room. Granny leaned over to me and said, "I know you believe that I am being capricious and cruel, bespelling your mother to find this all a wonderful idea. Understand that nothing could be further from the truth. I know how much she cared for both of her husbands and would never force her into an arranged marriage. I am cold, but I am not often cruel."

I didn't bother to remind her of my time in her torture chambers. If she was finally being nice to me and not threatening to throw me back in the dungeon, I figured I'd let it ride. But of course, I couldn't *completely* let it go. "So what's the plan, Gran? Sounds like you've definitely got one. Wanna share it with your boy here?"

"I have a plan, grandson. It is a very simple plan. I shall hold a tournament, and my daughter will marry the winner. Look at these competitors. Do they not all appear to be worthy fathers for you?" She waved her arm, and I looked out over the bunch of dudes and critters lined up in front of me. There were half a dozen faerie knights

—tall, thin, stupidly handsome guys with swords and shields and gleaming armor. There were a couple of random humans in the mix —big ugly mothers who looked like they bench-pressed Buicks in their free time. But the half dozen or so that worried me were the monsters. I recognized the troll, a huge gray beast with ridiculously long arms ending in jagged claws. And I figured the hairy bastard that looked to be about nine feet tall with a jutting lower jaw and a pair of curved tusks jutting out from his mouth was probably an ogre. But I didn't have any idea what the wiry little gray-skinned guy with the red baseball cap was supposed to be, besides creepy. He just stood there smiling and showing off double rows of pointed teeth, like somebody shoved a shark's mouth in a midget's face. There was a vampire, and what looked like some kind of fish/man, and one shadowy looking *something* that I never could really focus my eyes on.

"What the hell, Granny? Not all of those things are faeries," I protested.

"No," Mab replied, and I could almost smell the disdain dripping from her words. "There are quite a few humans in the mix as well."

"And monsters!" I almost shouted, but managed to keep my voice down. After all, some of those monsters were real close, and I didn't have any of my guns.

"Yes, as I said, there are humans and other lesser beings. Hopefully none of them will emerge victorious." Mab didn't bother to look at me, but I could see the corner of her mouth turn up a little. I got the impression that she'd like nothing better than for the troll to win and Mama to have to marry the slimy bastard. Well, that wasn't going to happen. I motioned for Joe to scoot over, and he came and knelt beside my chair.

"You gotta enter this thing, pal," I said, keeping my voice low. I knew Mab could hear me, just like I knew this was part of her plan all along. She was the frigging Winter Queen, after all. There was no way she wasn't thinking three steps ahead of me.

"What are you talking about, Bubba? I can't enter the tournament. I'm a Catholic priest. I can't marry your mother! Besides, most of those things look like they'll tear me apart."

"Yeah, but most of them look like I could take 'em," I said with a lot more confidence than I felt. Joe obviously smelled bullshit but held his tongue.

"So what, I'm going to enter, then sprain my ankle and tag you in?"

"That's pretty much what I had planned on, yeah. Then while I'm fighting the tournament to keep Mama from marrying a troll, Skeeter and Amy can turn this place upside down to find Nitalia."

"You really think she's here?" Amy whispered.

"Not really, but I think she *was* here. If y'all can find any clue to who took her, that'll be a big help when we get out of here and start looking."

"Damn, Bubba," Amy said. "That's almost a real plan. It's kinda like I'm rubbing off on you."

"Well, I think I did still volunteer Joe to fight a troll, so don't go signing me up for MENSA just yet," I said.

"Yeah, no kidding," Joe agreed. "And by the way, how do you expect me to get into the tournament? There's sixteen dudes standing there. I doubt Mab is going to just let me jump right in and screw up her tournament brackets."

"You let me worry about that," I said. I pushed my chair back from the table and stood up. "Granny, I'd like to inspect the competitors before our entertainment begins. Would all the humans please step forward?"

Five guys moved up. One of them was a monster of muscle and bad tattoos, not anybody I wanted to think about my mother sleeping with, but nobody I wanted to screw with either. Two more were big dudes, looked like they could handle themselves in a scrap, but nothing too impressive. I guessed they were cannon fodder for the troll—just there to make shit interesting for the court. One guy was skinny as a rail and had more knives strapped to him than I had hair on my arms. The last guy was pretty boring, just an average-looking guy who kept glancing at the ogre and the other monsters around him like he was trying not to shit himself right there in front of the queen. That was my guy.

I stepped up to Joe Average and looked him up and down. He was about five-eight, maybe a hundred seventy pounds. "You don't want to be here, do you?" I asked.

"No, sir." His voice shook when he looked up to speak to me.

"Why don't you run away now?"

"Queen Mab said she would flay my entire family while I watched if I didn't take part in the tournament."

"That's too bad," I said. Then I turned back to my grandmother, who watched me intently. "Granny, this man can't fight for Mama's hand in marriage. He's injured."

"I see no injuries, Robert. What is wrong with him?"

"Sorry," I whispered. Then I swung around, threw an uppercut with all my weight behind it, and slammed my fist into the little dude's jaw. I heard a *crack*, then a *thump*, followed by another *crack* as his head hit the floor. "He has a broken jaw and a concussion. He cannot compete. But fear not for the integrity of your tournament, Grandmother. I have a champion to put forth. I present to you, Joseph the Elf-Bane!" I swept my arm toward the head table, and Joe stood up, giving us a little wave.

"Hi," he said, completely deflating my big buildup. So much for a theatrical entrance.

Mab sighed. "Take your place among the competitors," she said to Joe. "Let's not delay this any further."

Joe jogged around to stand in the spot vacated by the little guy I decked. "Try not to get dead," I said, turning to go back to my seat.

Mab scowled at me as I sat down, and I looked to my left to see that Amy and Skeeter were gone. They used the hubbub created by me decking one of the entrants to slip out of the hall unnoticed, at least by me, and unhindered by the guards. Hopefully they could come up with something that would point to my sister's whereabouts while Joe and I tried to keep Mama from marrying an ogre. Or anybody, really. I was way too old to have to go shoot another father. That's the kind of shit that wears on a man, I swear.

The tournament started off without any real surprises. The troll ripped his opponent limb from limb, despite the Master of Ceremonies announcing that all preliminary bouts were to be fought until a competitor was unconscious or surrendered. I mean, I reckon the human that fought the troll was unconscious pretty soon after he got bitch-slapped with his own left leg, but I couldn't really tell from where I was sitting. Dude's eyes were definitely closed when the troll held up his severed head and drank blood from his throat before wiping his ass with the guy's hair and dropping the head to the polished marble floor.

"I reckon I'm glad I'm not the fella that has to clean that up," I said.

"Be more thankful you aren't the man who was just slaughtered by a troll, grandson," Mab muttered back to me. Then she waved a hand through the air in front of her, and all the blood, limbs, and entrails vanished into a puff of snowy air.

"Can you teach me that trick?" I asked. "I have the worst time getting blood out of my leather jacket. And my leather boots. And my blue jeans. I usually just assume my t-shirts are a goner after every fight, but if your magic works on cotton, too, then we might have us a party." Granny looked over at me, and the glare on her face dropped the temperature in the room ten degrees. Usually that's a metaphor, but when your grandmother is the Queen of Winter, it's legit. I could see the breath in front of my face as I turned back to the action just in time to see a pair of faerie knights finishing up their duel. Spoiler alert: the faerie won.

Another human got taken out by the skinny thing in the red hat that looked like a psychotic middle schooler. It swarmed up the tall dude like a spider monkey and choked him out in about eight seconds flat. Then it casually walked off to the side and sat down again, not even breathing hard or breaking a sweat. A pair of guards hauled the unconscious human off, and the ogre took the floor.

Another one of the faerie knights stepped up, his helmet tucked under his arm. He bowed to the head table, bowed to the crowd, then bowed to the ogre. He slipped the helmet on over his auburn hair and drew his sword. The ogre didn't bother with any of that chivalry nonsense; he just took one step forward and slammed his arms straight down, trying to shatter his opponent's head with his fists. Problem was, there was no head there to shatter. The knight stepped a foot to the right and neatly hamstrung the huge monster with one stroke of his blade. I heard the tendons behind the ogre's knee snap like a bowstring, and the monster dropped to its knees. Raising its head to the sky, the ogre opened its mouth to let out a shriek of pain, but no sound came out save a slight gurgling hiss as the blade slipped through the ogre's neck and severed its head from its shoulders. The head was the size of a beach ball, but without anywhere near the bounce as it dropped to the spotless ice-blue carpet, turning quickly to purple as the ogre's crimson blood fountained from the stump of its neck.

The knight stepped up to the dead ogre, wiped his sword clean on the beastie's pants, and kicked the corpse over to land on its side. Then he turned back to Mab, bowed again, and walked over to sit next to the other winning faerie. Granny magicked away the remains again, and the last remaining knight stepped into the clear space. He looked around for his opponent, and Joe got a shocked look on his face when he realized that he was the last one standing for Round One.

"Couldn't be anything simple, like the ogre, could it?" he called to me.

"Kick his ass, padre!" I hollered back.

"He's got a sword, Bubba. I've got a crucifix and a prayer!"

I hated to disagree, but I was pretty sure he only had a crucifix.

8

I had a sudden thought. "Hey Granny," I said, leaning over to Mab. "What if nobody acceptable to you as Mama's husband wins the tournament?"

Mab looked over at me, suspicion arching higher than her eyebrows. "What do you mean by that, Robert?"

"Well, it occurs to me that there are some people here that you wouldn't let Mama marry no matter what, so I was wondering what happens if one of them wins the whole shebang?"

"I suppose if there are no winners that I consider suitable matches for my daughter, then she would be free to remain a spinster, should she so desire. But I must say, I consider all of the entrants to be perfectly suitable mates for Ygraine."

"Even the troll or the ogre?"

"They are no less deserving of love than the human swine she married when she ran away from me," Mab said, a cruel smile twisting up one corner of her mouth.

I managed to hold back the angry words that leapt to my tongue, but just barely. "But I wouldn't be acceptable, would I? I mean, I know we ain't in the US of A, but some things are pretty universal, ain't they?"

Mab looked like I was something the cat puked up in her favorite pair of shoes. "No, Robert, you are the furthest thing from an acceptable match. Even if you were not a blood relation, I would never allow anyone of my line to mate with...you."

Damn. Granny was *harsh*. But she told me what I needed to hear. "Joe!" I hollered, standing up. "Get up here!"

Joe looked from me to the faerie knight standing across the floor from him and held up one finger. "Excuse me just a second." Joe ran over to stand in front of the table. "What do you want, Bubba? I'm busy figuring out how to beat this guy's ass right now, so unless you've got Bertha hidden under the table, maybe you oughta let me get back to it."

"Yeah, you just got replaced on the card, pal," I said. I raised my voice so everybody in the hall could hear me. "By my right as a member of the royal family, I am entering this tournament. I do not consider any of these men or beings a fair match for my mother, the Princess Ygraine, so I shall win this contest and her freedom to choose her own husband. I shall cut through these foes like a scythe through wheat, leaving none standing in my wake."

Joe looked at me, appreciation on his face. "That wasn't bad, Bubba."

"I've been reading a bunch of old *Conan* books. I just tried to talk like those dudes." I came around the table and nodded to the knight, who looked bored. At least, as much as anybody could look anything when their whole face was wrapped in metal.

"Begin!" the Master of Ceremonies shouted, and the knight whipped his sword up and came at me. He moved pretty damn quick for a guy wrapped in steel, and I barely got out of his way. But I did, spinning to the right and planting my foot right in his ass. He sprawled face-first on the stone floor with a clatter but rolled over and sprang to his feet a lot faster and nimbler than anybody in plate armor ever should. Magical assholes, every one of them.

He advanced on me a lot more slowly this time, swinging his sword side to side like a viper moving across the sand. It was almost hypnotic, if I could forget for a second that he wanted to open my guts up like a stripper's miniskirt in the VIP room. I didn't forget. I just kept backing away until I bumped into one of the guards in the crowd ringing the fight. The guard shoved me in the back, but I turned around and grabbed him by both wrists, pulling him into the fighting circle. He struggled, then pulled away from me, but not before I spun him around and yanked the big two-handed sword out of the holder on his back. He glared at me, but I was armed now, so I didn't much care.

Sword fighting wasn't much on my curriculum at the University of Georgia, but ever since getting Great-Grandpappy Beauregard's sword back from Jason, I'd spent some time studying it. This claymore was bigger than Grandpappy's sword, but the principles were the same. The knight charged me, stabbing with the point of his sword, looking to make Bubba-kabobs, but I sidestepped his thrust and knocked the blade aside. I spun my sword around in a cut to the man's neck, forcing him to bring his sword up fast to keep me from ending the fight in spectacular fashion real fast. Sparks flew as our blades crashed together, and I used the force of the rebound to spin me around and slash at his knees. A six-foot sword has a hell of a lot of momentum, so even though he caught the slice on his metal greaves, it still crashed into his leg and knocked him to the ground. I gave up on any kind of reasonable sword fighting when he went down and chopped at him like I was going after a copperhead in the front yard with an axe. My sword clanged again and again off the stone floor as he rolled away from me. After three huge swings, I had to step back for a breather, and he slowly staggered to his feet.

I'd only landed one decent shot to his shin, but rolling over and over in full armor left him bruised all over like he'd just rolled down a big hill in a tire. He sucked in a deep breath and came at me again, his sword held low and pointed straight at my belly. He was barely ten feet away when he lunged for me, so instead of trying to do anything fancy, I just flung the sword at him.

He was too close to stop or duck, so the hilt of the big claymore caught him right in the faceplate. His feet went out from under him like I'd clotheslined him, and he sprawled flat on his back. His sword skittered across the marble tiles, and his head hit the floor with a metallic crash. I took two quick steps to him and stripped the helmet from his head.

"Do you give up?" I asked. He didn't answer, just slammed a gauntleted fist into my ribs. Okay, so I reckon that was kind of an answer, just not the one I wanted. I crumpled to the side and rolled to my feet, one hand wrapped around my bruised ribs. The knight got to his feet, too, but at least this time he had to work at it a little and didn't just pop up to his feet like a damn mutant ninja faerie or something.

We squared off against each other again, this time without swords and him without his helmet. I was still in the stupid double and hose I'd been wearing all night, so I was at a pretty sizable disadvantage as far as defense was concerned. He crept forward, throwing little jabs with his metal-clad fists like he was trying to rope-a-dope me or something. I took a step back, then another, then another, then felt a bar across my back as the guard with the big axe on a pole pushed against me.

"That's far enough, human," the guard growled in my ear. I looked over my shoulder at him, hoping that my opponent would take the bait. He did, taking two big steps forward and swinging at my head with a huge right hook that would have broken my skull if it had landed.

I didn't let it land, though. I spun around, grabbed the guard's pole arm in both hands, and kept right on spinning. I let go of the guard just as I got turned back around toward the knight, and the guard staggered backward right into the path of the punch meant for me. Metal fist met metal helmet, and the resulting *CLANG* sounded like a church bell on Sunday morning. The guard clapped both hands to his head, which meant that there was a six-foot stick with an axe blade on it just falling to the floor in front of me. I grabbed it, snapped the head of the halberd off across my knee, and spun the stick over my head like a really fat Jackie Chan.

The guard dropped to his knees, snatching his helmet off and clapping his hands to the side of his head. My opponent took a couple of wobbly steps back, cradling his now-broken hand against his chest and saying things that I assumed were faerie curses and not insults about my mother, given that she was sitting right there next to *her* mother, the Winter Queen. I didn't bother to ask. I just slammed the pole into the knight's right arm, then swung around to tag his left knee, then I spun the pole around and jabbed him in the gut.

That move works a lot better when the jab-ee isn't wearing an overpriced tin can around his middle. My poke didn't have any more effect than if I'd reached out and thumped the tip of one of his pointy ears, and by then, the knight had knelt down and drawn the dazed guard's sword. He came at me, but his swings were clumsy in his left hand. I blocked one, then tagged him on the side of the head with my stick. That was a lot more effective, making him step back and shake the stars from his vision. While he did that, I smacked his wrist with the pole, sending his sword tumbling to the floor. Then I reversed my grip on the pole, putting the jagged end that used to hold an axe blade up against his now-exposed throat.

"I don't want to kill you," I said. "This is supposed to be until a knock-out surrender. So surrender, and I won't have to see how much blood you have to lose to be knocked out."

The faerie knight glared at me, but said nothing. I pulled the pole back and rapped him on the top of the head with it. "Don't be a dumbass. You got no outs here. Just tap out and I won't have to do any permanent damage."

"You couldn't if you tried, human."

"Yeah, ask Titania's cousin Chauvan. He's in a hole in the ground now because he didn't think I could hurt him. Now yield, dipshit." I snarled at him and saw his eyes go a little wide. Good to know my exploits in the Summerlands from last year weren't a complete waste of time.

The knight dropped to one knee and held up both hands. "I yield. I am vanquished."

I took a step back, watching him to make sure he wasn't going to try anything funny. I didn't know just how much knights in Fairyland were like Knights of the Round Table, as far as chivalry and not cheating and stuff went.

Apparently not too far, since one of his knight buddies stepped up beside him and lopped off his head with one stroke of his sword.

"What the hell did you do that for?" I hollered.

"Knights of the Fae do not yield. We fight, and die, for our queen. The only way we may be vanquished is in death. If you do not have the honor to take his life, I do." The taller knight glared at me, and I recognized him as the one that killed the ogre earlier. I had a bad feeling that this dude might turn out to be a problem later.

Granny stood up and clapped, magicking away the dead knight and repairing the guard's halberd.

I handed him his axe-on-a-stick, then walked back to the table and got a drink of fruit juice. "What's next, Granny?" I asked with a grin.

"You will rest through the early portions of the second round, which is good. For in the second round, you face Ulfthren, the Troll Prince," Mab said with a chilly smile.

I looked over at the slimy dude with razor-sharp claws at the end of each finger. He grinned at me, then picked something from between his teeth. It took me a second, then I realized that it was a piece of arm from his first-round opponent. Great, my opponent in the next round literally *ate* the last person to battle him. That's when I really started to regret not getting that accounting degree.

9

Amy ducked her head and gave a tiny curtsy as she passed the guard on the way out of the Great Hall. Skeeter did the same, complete with curtsy. "We gotta go pee," he said. "Which way to the royal loo?"

The guard looked confused, then chuckled. "To the right, then around the corner. Second door will get you into the kitchens, then there's a privy in there."

"Thanks, mate," Skeeter said, tipping an imaginary cap to the man and walking off down the hall in the direction the guard indicated.

"I couldn't tell if that was a horrible Crocodile Dundee impression or if you sounded like Dick Van Dyke in *Mary Poppins* after nine shots of whiskey," Amy said.

"Take your pick. We're out of there. Now we just need to make sure that Bubba's sister isn't here, find some clue to where she might be, and find something to break whatever spell Granny Psychopath has cast on Mrs. B. And I really do have to pee," Skeeter replied.

They walked down the stone hallway and turned into the door to the kitchen. Their senses were assaulted by a myriad of smells, every one of them delicious, and the bustling sounds of a dozen people all moving around quickly in a small space. Amy's mouth gaped as she watched half a dozen near-collisions, avoided only by last-second spins, turns, and course adjustments, all by women carrying trays laden with steaming bowls of soup, trenchers of meat and gravy, platters of vegetables in all the colors of the rainbow, and trays of mugs filled to the rim with sparkling juices and ciders. In the center of the maelstrom of activity, a rotund faerie woman with a red face and frizzy red hair sticking out every which way under a grease-spattered mob cap whirled in circles like a faerie Tasmanian Devil, pointing at minions and shouting instructions, corrections, additions to pots on stoves, and finally, after the pair of newcomers stood there for a long moment watching the insanity, yelled to them, "What do you two want? I don't have time for noble looky-loos, so if you came to filch an extra dessert, tell Mab's overstuffed grand-ape that he needs to go on a diet anyway!"

"Um...we just want to know where Princess Ygraine's daughter is taking her meals tonight since she wasn't in the Great Hall with the rest of us," Amy asked.

Every person in the kitchen froze, one woman stopping so abruptly in front of Skeeter that a huge gout of soup splashed from a silver tureen right onto his chest. There was a loud clatter as a spoon dropped to the floor, and the cook spun back to Amy with a look of pure horror on her face. "The Princess Nitalia? Is she *here*?" She spun back to her subordinates, fury turning her face splotchy and red. She snatched up a wooden spoon and began to lay about her like a knight surrounded by enemies. "Which one of you," *whack,* "idiots knew the Princess was here," *whack,* "and neglected to tell me?" *Whack whack whack,* each delivered to the head of a nearby kitchen helper with the flick of a wrist, leaving minions rubbing their scalps and wincing.

"Wait, ma'am, wait!" Amy called. "We aren't sure the Lady Nitalia is even here, but we are here to find her if she is. Would you please stop hitting people and listen to me?"

"Yeah, she's banging on them heads like she's leading a steel drum band," Skeeter muttered.

The woman stopped hitting her assistants and waved them out of the kitchen. "Leave us. Take those dishes to the Hall. We'll be finished by the time you're back." A stream of faeries and humans bee-lined for the doors, leaving a trail of delicious scents behind. She stepped over to Amy and Skeeter, spoon still held like a sword. "Now, what is this about looking for the princess?"

"We came to your land in search of her. Her mother is very worried about her."

"Oh, aye," the cook nodded. "I could see her practically dripping with concern as she appraised the looks of her suitors tonight."

"She's under a spell, you bitch," Skeeter growled.

Cook spun on him, swinging the spoon around in a looping arc to catch him square atop his head. "Call me that again, little human. I have many recipes for human idiot, and I've not had stock to test them in a century. Of course Mab bespelled her daughter, you fool. She ran away once. You can't imagine the Queen of Winter would allow a slight like that to happen twice. Or go unanswered should the opportunity arise, which it did the moment you band of merry jack-asses stepped into her domain. Why would you come here in the first place?"

"Our transportation wasn't the most reliable," Amy replied. "But you said that Nitalia isn't here? Do you know where she might be?"

"The princess was here," the cook admitted. "And she was a delight. Loved my cooking, didn't beat the serving wenches if the food wasn't piping hot when it arrived. Do you have any idea how hard it is to keep food even a little warm in the Court of Winter? There are random snowdrifts in every hall! But no, Lady Nitalia vanished from here months ago. No one has heard from her since. The queen is near-frantic with worry, not that she would ever admit to it. She fears the princess has been taken by her grandfather and is now a captive of the Summerlands."

"Would that be all that bad?" Amy asked. "Is Titania any more nuts than Mab?"

The cook's eyes went wide, and she laid the spoon across Amy's lips. "Don't speak that name here! If the queen hears you, she'll have you beheaded for a certainty! And yes, the Queen of Summer is every bit as insane as our beloved queen, but even more cruel."

"Somehow I find that hard to believe," Skeeter muttered.

"What did I tell you about interrupting your betters, human?" Cook snapped at him, thwacking him on the forehead with her spoon.

"You didn't...never mind," Skeeter started to protest, then gave up as he saw the spoon coming his way again.

"Would you mind pointing us in the direction of the princess's chambers so that we may look for any hints her abductors may have left behind? We are unfamiliar with the Summer Court, so any information we can uncover will be exceeding helpful," Amy asked, a deferent look on her face.

The cook preened a little to have a lady of such apparent high station asking her help and admitting her ignorance, which was exactly what Amy hoped for. "Of course, dearie. You just come over here and take this tray. The men never question a woman laden down with foodstuffs, no matter how fine her clothes." She handed Amy a tray, then put an empty plate on it, and covered the whole thing with a huge silver domed lid. Amy hefted the mock dinner to her shoulder and listened intently as the cook gave her directions to the princess's tower.

Seconds later, they were back out in the hall, Skeeter leading the way as Amy followed with her "burden." "That was pretty good back there," Skeeter said. "I'm glad you could talk to her. Everything I said just seemed to piss her off."

"My mother worked as a sous chef for a caterer when I was in high school. I picked up extra money running food on some of their parties. I learned real fast that anyone who is in charge of a kitchen is the king or queen of that little domain, and you'd better show the proper deference. Those lessons came in handy when I started working in D.C."

"I bet. Only none of the old men in DEMON will hit you in the head with a spoon if you interrupt them."

"No, but there are a couple of senior field supervisors with enough magic to make your mouth disappear. One of them did just that to a guy I dated my first year in the agency. He was a little bit of a loudmouth—cocky, with an inflated sense of his importance to the organization. He looked pretty ridiculous walking around for three days with no mouth."

Skeeter gawked at her. "How did he not die? You need to at least be able to drink something!"

"No, you need to be able to ingest fluids," Amy corrected. "He had to have an IV until he wrote out a three-page apology that he promised to read in front of our morning briefing as soon as his face was put back together."

"Did he?"

"Oh yeah. There was about a zero percent chance he was going to screw with the guy who could make his mouth disappear. Especially not on Salisbury steak day in the cafeteria. We broke up after that. I realized that I really liked him a lot when he couldn't speak, so it probably wasn't going to work out now that he had his voice back."

"Then you met Bubba."

"Oh, no. This was better than ten years ago. There were a lot more mistakes between that guy and Bubba. But there's not enough tequila in the world to get me to tell you some of *those* stories. Now, pay attention. The princess's door should be hidden in that section of wall right...oh shit."

"What is it? Oh shit." Skeeter followed her gaze to the man standing guard duty in front of what appeared to be a blank stretch of wall. It was Captain Falarun, one of the officers they'd fought, and beaten, when they first escaped the dungeon. He turned to the pair, smiling as he saw the tray of food.

"Oh, good, Cookie did save me a tray from the feast...wait, I know you..." He opened his mouth wide to shout an alarm, and Skeeter ran forward. The skinny man reared back and punted the faerie knight between the legs with all his might, only to immediately fall over, clutching his toes.

"Kicking the man in armor while wearing slippers is not the

smartest way to begin a fight, human," Falarun said with a smile. "The big one was annoying, but at least he wasn't stupid."

"You talk too much," Amy said. The knight's head whipped around to focus on her, and he caught the tray Amy swung full in the face. His head slammed into the stone wall with a sickening *crunch*, and his eyes went vacant. He slid to the floor in a clatter, and Skeeter dragged himself to his feet.

"I don't know what's worse about that," Skeeter said, flexing his toes and grimacing in pain. "Breaking all my toes, or having somebody think that Bubba's the brains of the operation."

"Oh, definitely the second," Amy said, stepping through the illusionary wall behind Falarun and leaning back out to grab the unconscious man's shoulders. "Now grab his legs, and let's get him hidden before somebody comes to investigate that racket."

They wrestled the guard through the illusion, then Skeeter limped back out and gathered up the discarded plate, tray cover, and badly dented tray. "You really knocked the shit out of him, you know that?"

"Well, I wasn't trying to make him faint from laughing, like some people I won't mention."

"That's cold, Amy. Cold. Now, where's the princess's bedroom?" He looked around the open space tucked away in the wall, then looked back at Amy. "This doesn't look like a princess's bedroom."

"Have you ever been in a princess's bedroom, Skeeter?"

"No, I gotta admit that. I've been to bed with a few queens, but no princesses."

"Oh, good lord. Maybe I hit the wrong one with the tray," Amy groaned. They were in a large room filled with half a dozen pools, each around eight feet in diameter and filled with water. Steam rose from several, but they seemed to cool as they got farther from the doorway. The arrangement looked familiar, more so when Skeeter caught sight of the shelf laden with towels along a nearby wall.

"Are we...?" he started to ask.

"Yes, Skeeter, we're in the royal bathroom, not the royal bedroom.

The cook lied to us, and by now has, no doubt, alerted every guard in the castle that we're poking around where we're not supposed to."

"Well, I'm glad to see that we can screw up just as bad without Bubba around as we can with him. What next?"

Amy looked down at the unconscious Falarun. "Well, I am an employee of a shadowy branch of the United States government, and we happen to have a man right here who probably has information we want. Tell me, Skeeter. Have you ever heard of waterboarding?"

10

I had a little time to rest up while I watched the other bouts of Round Two, and I needed it. There were three of the faerie knights still in the running. I was the lone human, or mostly human. I figured I was going to have to learn about being part faerie at some point, see if it got me any kind of magic powers. I mean, if close to forty years of living and almost twenty of hunting monsters hadn't shown 'em to me, I didn't have real high hopes, but you never know.

The other half of the new competitors were one vampire, a troll, some kind of shadowy figure that my eyes wouldn't focus on no matter how hard I tried, and the skinny kid with the red ball cap. Two of the faerie knights met up first, and they obviously knew each other and respected one another. They saluted with their swords, then set to whalin' on each other like two gorillas fighting over the lone female ape in the zoo. Reminded me of a story I heard about this monster hunter chick in Cleveland one time. Sounded like a badass. But I digress. After a solid five minutes of beating the tar out of each other, one faerie stumbled, and the other one caught him right upside the helmet with the flat of his sword. The now-concussed faerie spun around and collapsed flat on his back. The other dude raised his hands over his head, celebrated for a few seconds, then went to check on his fallen buddy. I was impressed with his sportsmanship, and thought if Mama had to marry any of these assholes, he'd be my pick.

There was no such sportsmanship or kind feelings in the next match. The vampire squared off against the last faerie knight and beat his ass from pillar to post. The knight took one swing at the vamp, who just leaned out of the way of the blow, then stepped behind his armored opponent and punched him in the back of the head. His helmet rang with the impact, and he dropped to one knee. The vamp grabbed the knight's non-sword arm, planted a foot in the guy's armpit, and yanked the arm clean off, armor coming with it. Then he swung the arm like a steel-clad baseball bat into the knight's face. The faerie lay on his back, blood pouring from his shoulder, as the vampire legitimately ripped his arm off and beat him half to death with it. He kept the whooping going long after the faerie stopped moving, then stuck his face in one end of the severed limb and sucked it dry. He dropped the desiccated arm onto the unconscious knight's chest and turned his blood-soaked face to Granny, who nodded at him and waved away the remains of his fallen opponent. I reckon that's another way to score a decisive victory.

The skinny dude in the red hat and the shadowy guy squared off next, and I was pretty interested in watching this match, frankly. Mostly because I didn't know what either one of these things were, but also in part because I might have to tangle with one of them before my day was done, and I needed to know what, if anything, would hurt 'em. Their match started off kinda tentative, with them circling around each other, trying to get a sense of what the other one was doing. The shadow-thing glided more than walked, but maybe that was just a side effect of me not being able to really focus on seeing its feet, or really any other part of it. The skinny dude just circled, his eyes never leaving his opponent.

The shade flew into motion quicker than a hiccup, crossing the distance between them in the blink of an eye. He had his hands pressed to each side of Red Hat's face, and I couldn't tell if he was trying to squish his head like a grape or pull him in for a kiss. It didn't much matter in the long run because as soon as he got that close, Red Hat drew a pair of long, narrow knives from under his short brown jacket and stabbed the shadow. He stabbed that shadow-dude musta been fifty times in a split second, then started to carving. There was no blood, but flecks of shadow drifted to the floor like it was meat off a prime rib at a carving station. With every flick of Red Hat's wrist, more of the shadow guy's substance flew away. After half a minute or so of them squeezing heads and cutting down opponents, the shadow guy let go of Red Hat's gourd, spun around like a tornado made of smoke, and shot straight up through the ceiling. Red Hat turned to Mab, his hands suddenly empty, and gave a grand bow, whipping off his red ball cap and sweeping it to the ground in front of him. I noticed when he stood up, his hat left a smear of blood across the white marble where it dragged.

Me and the troll were the last match, and I needed it. Joe had been rubbing my shoulders, trying to get me back in fighting shape, but I'd had less than half an hour to recuperate from going one-on-one with an armored faerie knight, and now I had to wrassle a troll. The more I think about the dumb shit I've done in my life, the dumber it all seems. This time it wasn't just me, for a change. It took two generations of bad decision-making for me to end up in unarmed hand-to-hand combat against a damn troll in Fairyland.

I nodded to Granny and stepped into the cleared circle in the middle of the crowd. I might have been imagining it, but it sure felt like there were a lot more people watching than in the first round. It was like everybody in the Winter Court wanted to see the mostly human get his guts ripped out by a troll. For me, I wasn't so much looking forward to that part.

"Stick and move, Bubba!" Joe hollered as I stared at the troll. This was an ugly son of a bitch, no question about it. It would probably be a solid nine feet tall if it stood upright, but it walked all kinds of hunched over in this weird loping stride. It wore a loincloth, which was a blessing because as ugly as the rest of it was, I didn't even want to know what troll junk looked like. It was covered in grayish-brown skin that glistened like it was oiled up, only the oil was like congealed pig fat or something because it was covered in this yellow slime that looked like nothing so much as if the universe had hocked a huge loogie on the thing, and it was covered in nasty yellow phlegm to go with its nasty gray-brown skin.

If its overall appearance wasn't bad enough, it had long arms that dragged the ground and would probably have scraped the floor even if the thing stood up straight. It looked to have at least a ten-foot wingspan, and every foot-long finger was tipped with a grotesque hooked claw, also dripping with yellow sludge. I looked in its beady red eyes, and it grinned at me, showing off a jagged smile missing a few pointed teeth but with still more than enough shredding capacity to tear off big hunks of Bubba-flesh and shove them in its greedy maw. It probably wasn't the nastiest thing I've ever seen. I mean, I did play Division I football. But this was damn close.

I got ready to rumble with the troll, wishing the whole time I had Bertha. Hell, at that point, I'd have probably used *Skeeter* as a weapon if he'd been handy. Just before the Master of Ceremonies announced us as the final bout for round two, I heard somebody behind me clear his throat. I turned, and the guard whose halberd I snatched in round one stood about three feet away. He extended his arm, big damn axe leaning down to me.

"I think you may need this," he said.

I took the pole arm with a nod and twirled it around over my head like the little dudes in those kung fu movies. Or I tried to, but I gave up after I almost sent the axe swinging into the crowd. I just held it with both hands and pointed the business end toward the slimy monster.

The troll chuffed out what I guess passed for a laugh in Troll-ese and charged me. It ran in this weird kinda double-jointed lope, but it covered a shitload of ground, getting to me in just two steps. I swung at its side with the halberd, but it stepped inside the axe's path and blocked with one gangly arm. I ducked as the other arm buzzed over my head, claws whistling through the air. A little bit of the yellow slime dripped onto the back of my neck and damn if it didn't start to burn my skin!

"Are you freaking kidding me?" I said. "You're big, strong, ugly with razor claws, *and* you sweat acid! That ain't even fair." I swung the pole around to crack a rib or two, but the troll just snatched the halberd, snapped the long handle over its knee, and flung the pieces aside.

I bull-rushed the ugly bastard while it focused on my weapon, slamming a shoulder into its chest. The troll toppled over, and I kept right on moving, stomping one foot into its stomach and the other in its upper chest as I went over it. This time I did hear some ribs crack —three hundred fifty pounds of rampaging redneck are a lot for one sternum to handle. Didn't help much, though, since by the time I got myself a little bit of breathing room and turned back around, the troll was already on his feet and running for me. I snatched the pole arm out of the hands of another guard, this time setting it for the troll's charge like a pikeman against cavalry.

Leave me alone, I've watched movies. I know what a pikeman does.

What a pikeman doesn't do is deal well with trolls because this one just stopped and reached forward, leaning over the huge axe blade and snatching another halberd out of my hands with its ridiculously long arms.

But I was ready this time. I planned ahead, and when I ran over the troll, I stopped right about where it tossed the last axe it broke. So when Slimy McAcidface jerked this one out of my hands, I bent over and picked up the remnants of the last weapon it broke. I grabbed the broken shaft first, picking up a three-foot pole about two inches around. I tapped the splintered end on the ground twice, squared my feet, and teed off with that stick like I was Jack Nicklaus at Pebble Beach. Now I ain't never played gold, they don't hardly make courses that'll let me on in my work boots and blue jeans, but I have bashed a bunch of monsters in the balls with sticks. And that's what I did this time. I hollered "Fore!" at the top of my lungs and cracked that troll square in the nuts with the busted end of a medieval weapon of war.

Now getting hit in the balls hurts. Getting hit in the balls with a stick hurts worse. But I have to assume that getting hit in the balls by a fat hillbilly who thinks he's gonna die if he doesn't whoop your ass right that second has got to hurt worst of all. And the worst part of it would be the splinters in your nutsack when it was over.

Judging by the look on that troll's face, which looked like a cross between Fat Bastard from that *Austin Powers* movie and a Hungry Hungry Hippo with an air hose shoved up its ass, it hurt a hell of a lot. The big gray bastard clutched its jewel purse with both clawed hands, dropped to its knees, and opened its mouth to let out a screech of the most abject agony.

That's when I picked up the other half of the broken halberd and chopped the poor bastard's head clean off. It spewed eggplant-purple blood every which way as it rolled across the marble floor, leaving streaks of yellow acidic slime mixing with purple blood all over the place. Granny was gonna be real glad she ScotchGuarded the rugs with magic after this fight.

I looked up at Mab, sitting on her throne of ice all stone-faced and pissed-off looking, twirled the axe around a little, spraying the front row of bystanders with troll blood, tossed my weapon to the floor in a huge clatter, and said, "I think I win. Again. Who's next Grann-o? You set 'em up; I'll knock 'em down!"

Someday I'm gonna learn not to let my big stupid mouth write checks my ass can't cash.

11

———

"Well, if Falarun wasn't lying, the entrance to the princess's tower should be behind one of the next two doors," Amy said.

"If he was lying, he's got a lot more willpower than I do. I can't believe you actually *did* that to him," Skeeter walked with both hands over his crotch, wincing at the memory.

"He could have talked at any point, Skeeter. We're on a schedule, and he had information we needed."

"Was this a 'what would Jack Bauer do' moment for you, Amy?"

"More like a 'what can I do to a guy that would give Bubba nightmares' moment."

"Well, I'm pretty sure you got there. I know I ain't gonna sleep anywhere around you without wearing a plate mail chastity belt, that's for damn sure. Is it this door or the next?"

"I'm not sure," Amy said, putting her ear to the dark wooden door. "I couldn't understand everything he said through the screaming."

"Yeah, especially when it got real high-pitched." Skeeter turned the knob. "This ain't locked."

Amy pushed the door open, and the pair slipped inside. They stepped into a large room full of books. Shelves lined every wall from floor to ceiling, and the smell of old paper and leather book bindings wrapped them up like a warm cocoon. Six long tables sat in the center of the room, each with eight padded chairs and lamps for reading. A pair of ladders hung on tracks that ringed the room to reach the top shelves, some fifteen feet off the floor. Moonlight cascaded in through huge skylights, bathing the deep wood tones in cool blue illumination.

Glowing orbs of yellow hung in midair, suspended and lit by some type of magic, floating lamps to provide general lighting in addition to the table lamps and skylights. The overall feeling of the room was peaceful, a marked contrast to the edginess throughout the rest of the castle.

"Wow, look at some of these titles," Skeeter said, running his finger across the spines on one shelf. "*Care and Feeding of Chimeras, Gryphon Breeding for Humans and Other Idiots, History of the Mongrelization of the Fae*...wait a minute!"

"What, you thought racism was just a human thing?" Amy asked.

"No, but this is kind of like finding a copy of *Birth of a Nation* in the White House. I just didn't expect it to be all out in the open like this."

"You've seen the way Mab looks at Bubba. I don't think she's happy to have a half-human grandson."

"Well, be honest. If Bubba walked into your dining room and announced to all your friends that he was your long-lost relative..."

Amy laughed. "Yeah, it might take some adjustment."

"Is that why he hasn't met your family?"

Amy's eyes turned cold as she whirled on Skeeter. "I don't have any family. And it's *not* something I talk about. Ever."

"Seriously?" Skeeter didn't quite hold back the snort. "Do you remember who you're talking to? Amy, my adopted mama threw a 'Kwame' into the middle of my name so I wouldn't forget I was black! I grew up in Dalton frigging Georgia! Do you think there was ever a single second that I forgot I was *the* black kid in my class? And look at Bubba. We are in Fairyland looking for his kidnapped half-sister because his mother comes back after twenty years and announces,

'Hi honey, I'm the Heir to the Winter Court of Faerie. And that's not even getting to the fact that he killed his daddy *and* his kid brother, both of them werewolves! If you've got something that can beat that, I'll give you a pass. But otherwise, spill it, girl." Skeeter stood there, arms folded, jaw set, staring at Amy until she let out a huge sigh.

"Okay, fine. But you are *not* telling Bubba this. I'll tell him. In my own time. Which might be never. He does not need to meet my family, and they do not need to meet them. Frankly, I don't ever need to see most of them again. When I left home, I swore the only way I'd ever come back was in a tank, guns blazing."

"Sweet Jesus, girl, who are you kin to?" Skeeter asked.

Amy didn't speak for a long time, just walked back and forth between two of the tables, chewing on a thumbnail. Finally, she stopped and turned to Skeeter. "No laughing. No questions. And *no* telling Bubba. Deal?"

Skeeter mimed taking a key out of his pocket, locking his lips, and tossing the key over his shoulder. Then he crossed his heart and nodded.

"Okay. My father...is Franklin Hargroves." She said the last in a rush, like she wanted to get the words out before they could linger on her lips.

"The televangelist?"

Amy nodded.

"The 'God will destroy America because gay people can get married' guy?"

Another nod.

"The dude that protests the funerals of American soldiers holding up signs that the deceased is going to burn in Hell for supporting the liberal gay agenda in America?"

"Yup, that's dad. The most famous asshole in America. My father."

"Well, there's still Rush Limbaugh. I think he's more famous. But your pop's right up there."

"Thanks. That's the little ray of sunshine I was looking for."

"Whatever," Skeeter said. "Let's go find the princess's bedroom.

She obviously ain't in here, and if she shares much DNA with Bubba, she likely ain't ever set foot in a library." He turned and started for the door, but Amy reached out and grabbed his arm.

"Wait, that's it?" she asked.

"That's what? Your dad's an asshole. I wouldn't piss in his mouth if his guts was on fire. If he was piloting the last lifeboat on the *Titanic*, I'd rather drown with Leo than get in a boat with that douchenozzle. If I had to choose between a root canal without Novocain or a twenty-minute car ride with your daddy, I'm be in the dentist's chair faster than you can say 'homophobic shitnugget.' But that ain't got a damn thing to do with you."

"But he's my *father*. And he's said and done all these terrible things."

Skeeter's usually smiling face went solemn, and he looked in her eyes. "Amy, I have no idea who my birth family even is. All I know is my mama gave me up for adoption because she couldn't afford to give me the kind of life she wanted for her child. I never looked for her, and never will. What I got instead was a bunch of straight white rednecks that couldn't possibly be any more different from me. I've got an uncle that never spoke to my mama again after she brought home a black baby and a cousin who's a Pentecostal preacher that can't be in the same room with me at a reunion for more than five minutes without going on about praying for me to change my sinful ways and hoping Jesus will show me the right path. We all got assholes in our relations; that's why we build our own families when we grow up. That dickhead that donated some of your chromosomes ain't no more your daddy than Mab really is Bubba's granny. That's just blood. You, me, Bubba, Joe—we're *family*. And that counts for a whole lot more than some accident of birth. Now can we get to looking for some clues before Bubba screws up and wins this tournament? I know we're southern, but marrying your mama is a little backwoods even for our people."

Amy let out a relieved laugh and scanned the room for something that might give an indication about Nitalia's location. "What's this?" she asked, walking over to a book sitting alone on a pedestal at the front of the room. It was a small book, no bigger than a drugstore paperback, but bound in blue leather and trimmed in the whitest silver. Amy picked it up, and a spark crackled from her fingertips.

"Ow!" She dropped the book but picked it back up immediately. "This is not normal, Skeeter."

"Did you miss the glowing portal we stepped through to get here and all the dudes with pointy ears?" Skeeter walked over to stand beside her.

She slapped him on the arm. "Smartass."

"You know it. Now what's that?"

"It's called a book, Skeeter. It's where people stored information before the internet."

"Now who's a smartass?"

"Turnabout's fair play." Her face turned serious. "I don't know. I can't read the words on the cover, and it shocked me when I picked it up."

"So why did you pick it up again?"

"I guess I've been hanging around Bubba too long. Come on, we need to find the princess's chambers. Let's get out of here."

"You still have the book in your hand," Skeeter said.

Amy looked down at her right hand, and sure enough, there was the book, still right there. "Huh. That's odd." She set the book down on the pedestal and stepped away. After three strides, Skeeter spoke up.

"Amy..." Skeeter said.

"Yeah, Skeeter?"

"Look down."

The book was back in her hand. Amy flung it across the library this time, and both of them ran for the door. They sprinted across the dark wooden floor and out into the hall, slamming the heavy oak door behind them. "Okay," Amy said, her back to the door. "That was weird. Now let's find Bubba's sister, or at least some clue as to where she might be, and figure out how we're getting her out of here."

"I think we might need to find something else first," Skeeter said.

"Yeah, what?"

"An exorcist. Look in your hand."

Amy looked down, and there was the little blue-and-silver volume, nestled in her grip. "Son of a *bitch!*" she shouted. "I guess now we're looking for a librarian to tell us about this stupid book. Crap. Why did I touch this thing in the first place?"

"It probably has some kind of spell on it to make people pick it up. But I'm all about finding a librarian. I got dibs on Christian Kane. I've had a crush on him ever since *Angel.*"

"I don't know, Skeeter. I have to admit, I'm kinda into John Laroquette," Amy said.

"The dude from *Night Court*? The old guy on *The Librarians*?"

"What can I say? I dig the distinguished look."

As they walked down the hall in search of Princes Nitalia's room and a librarian, Skeeter idly mused, "I wonder how Bubba's doing?"

12

───────

I stood there trying to decide whether to cuss, puke, or just bleed. My right forearm felt like I'd shoved it into a running garbage disposal, and there was so much red dripping down my face it looked more like I was an old-school pro wrestler than the grandson of a Faerie Queen trying to win his mother's honor and freedom back. Admittedly, at that point, I was mostly trying to win my life, but the skinny bastard across the floor from me was trying to win an opportunity to find out if Georgia Bulldog was dish best served raw.

The fight started off pretty simple. I even went into this one with a plan, before it all went to shit. The little dude didn't look like much standing still. He was pretty much humanoid, except he had gray skin and huge black eyes. Like, no pupil, black. I didn't notice anything different about his mouth until he opened it to smile at me when I stepped up to start the fight; then I remembered the triple row of pointed teeth. He rocked his head from side to side, loosening up, then opened his mouth in a huge yawn. I swear, the little bugger either could unhinge his jaw like a boa constrictor.

Either way, I wasn't too worried about it. I saw his first couple of matches, and while he was a legit badass, I figured I knew his tricks by now. He'd wait until I threw the first haymaker, then use his speed and those gangly arms to swarm me and try to rip out my carotid. I knew how to deal with that—cheat. So I waited until he thought I was overextended, and when he went to clamber up me and take a bite out of my throat, I dropped down to one knee and slammed my arm into the stone floor, hoping to smear the little dude across the marble like a cockroach.

Except he was even faster than I thought, so all I ended up doing was punching the shit out of the floor while he wrapped his arms and legs around my neck and middle and reared back to chomp me like Pac-Man. I figured that no matter how tough I am, getting half my throat chewed out in the middle of the floor was going to be more than Granny could fix, even if she wasn't a psychopath. Which she was. So no guarantees she'd even try. So I spun around and slammed my back into the floor, aiming to pin the squirrelly little bugger between me and the stone.

I said he was fast, right? Good, because that whole reverse belly-flop thing didn't work out so good, either. I mean, it was okay for the skinny asshole, who just swung himself around me so he was sitting on my chest while I slammed into the floor. All the breath went out of me in a *whoosh* and a "Dammit!" and the gray-skinned buttmunch kept on riding me like an over-furred bronco. At one point, he even used my damn beard for a handhold and bucked like we was either in a rodeo or dating. I wasn't much interested in either one.

I laid on the floor, all my breath spent and new bruises growing on top of old ones, and I looked up at the little guy riding me like an afternoon shift lap dancer, and I began to seriously reconsider my career choices. I mean, seriously, what did I really care if my mama married a garden gnome or a bridge troll, or maybe even a faerie prince? She ran out on me two decades ago. I didn't owe her shit. It ain't like the rest of my family interactions ever made the pages of *Southern Living*, or even *Garden & Gun*. I killed my daddy and my brother, and now I was stuck in Fairyland with a psychotic gremlin on my chest trying to rip my guts out. Maybe I'd be better off just surrendering, letting Mama marry whoever won this damn tournament, and hauling my fat ass back to the land of cold beer and hot fried pickles.

I looked over at Mama, sitting next to Mab in all their finery, and that sealed the deal right there. Not Mama. No, she sat there grinning like an idiot at the spectacle we put on thanks to the spell Mab put on her. No, it was the look on my granny's face that sealed the deal. That bitch sat up at the head table smiling like the cat with a belly full of canary, and I knew right then I wasn't gonna just beat this red-hatted little shitbird, I was gonna whoop the ass of every faerie in the Great Hall.

Laying there and seeing that look on Granny's face, that cruel self-satisfied smirk took me back to high school when I got shot down by every cheerleader for a Homecoming date because they didn't date fat football players. It was that kind of superior, smug look that all the smart kids in class wore whenever I got up to stumble through some kind of presentation in English. It was the sneer that my college conditioning coach wore when he told me I'd wash out of UGA before the first semester was over. It was the look that was supposed to put me in my place, remind me of my station, and send me back to the mountain to plow a rocky field every day and make cheap moonshine at night. It was the look that said, "You ain't good enough to be here, so go the hell home."

It pissed me off.

The skinny dude reared his head back to bite my throat out and came down at me with every pointy tooth in his damn head gleaming. So I did exactly what any sane man would do when confronted by a mouth full of razor-sharp faerie teeth: I stuck my fist in it. I shoved my hand straight in the little bastard's mouth, trying to play Mike Tyson on his epiglottis. I got my whole hand in his mouth, and his eyes bugged out as his jaws slammed shut by reflex. That hurt. A lot. But he loosened his grip on my tunic, and I was able to roll over and push myself up to my knees.

The toothy little bastard with a mouthful of redneck fist just went with it, not thinking to open his mouth enough to let my hand out. No, he just chomped down hard, again and again, tearing my forearm and wrist to shreds with them teeth, but I figured that was better than him chewing on my neck. I dragged my beaten carcass to my feet, still hauling five and a half feet of faerie on the end of my right arm.

"Let go of me, you little shithead," I grumbled. He shook his head, ripping even further into the meat of my arm, and I opened my hand inside his mouth. I twisted my arm around, cutting myself even more in the process. I twisted around enough to reach his tongue, and I wrapped my fingers around the thick, wet muscle and *pulled.*

Flashbacks of a naked sasquatch duel shot through my head, and I decided it was just way better not to ever think about where my hands have been. I twined my fingers around the faerie's tongue and yanked it up, doing my level best to rip it out by the roots. The little dude opened his mouth to scream, and I jerked my hand free, shaking about a pint of blood and spit to the floor. My opponent stood there glaring at me for a split second; then he flung himself at me again. I was ready for him this time, though, and I caught him by the throat and slammed him to the floor like an Undertaker choke slam.

Then a wave of dizziness and pain hit me, and I struggled to my feet. I looked down at my mangled right arm, covered in my blood, shredded tattoos, slobber, and a little bit of yellow stuff that I couldn't identify, and the pain got the better of me. I puked up fruit juice and faerie feast right on the little dude's face.

"Damn," I muttered. "That's nasty. Even for me. Sorry little guy," I mumbled as I staggered back to the edge of the clear space, looking for Joe.

I found him holding out a cloth to me. It looked like it used to be one of Granny's tablecloths, but I didn't care. I tore it into strips and told Joe, "Keep an eye on him while I sit here for a second and try not to pass out." I dropped to one knee and wiped my hand and arm off the best I could, then bound it up in tablecloth scraps. It looked pretty bad, and I couldn't move two fingers, but I was still alive, and that's what mattered.

"Here he comes," Joe said, and I dragged myself to my feet.

"Any idea what this bastard is?" I asked.

"I think he's a redcap."

"I can see he's got a red cap, jackass. I don't need no master's degree for that."

"No, he *is* a redcap. He's basically a faerie version of Jeffrey Dahmer. They exist only to kill, usually in the most painful ways possible. The nobility of Faerie uses them as assassins when they want to send a message."

"Well, message received," I said, turning back to face the little gray asshole. So I stood there trying to decide whether to cuss, puke, or just bleed. Of course, there wasn't anything left to puke up, and if I bled too much more, I was going to pass out, so I went with Option A.

"Come get some, you son of a bitch!" I hollered, and charged at the redcap.

That was obviously about the last damn thing he expected because he just stood there as I barreled into him like he was a Vanderbilt quarterback and I was back in the SEC. I heaved him up on my shoulder and never slowed down. I just kept on charging, and the circle of spectators opened to let me through. I carried the redcap with my shoulder buried in his gut all the way to the wall of the overgrown dining room and slammed him into the unforgiving stones. He hit the wall like a June bug on a windshield, and I heard his ribs crack of the scream of pain echoing through my ear.

I backed up, and the redcap slumped against the wall. He held up a hand. "Mercy," the little dude croaked.

"Do you yield?" I asked, loud enough for the whole room to hear. Out of the corner of my eye, I saw Mab stand up and fold her arms across her chest.

The faerie assassin cut a glance over to my granny, then back to me. "I cannot yield. You must fall."

"Not gonna happen," I growled. I reached out and palmed his forehead like it was a basketball. I slammed his head into the stone wall, then let go to check his eyes. He was still conscious, so I did it again. And again. And again. I beat his skull into that stone wall until his eyes rolled back in his head and he slumped to the ground. My opponent unconscious, I turned to Mab and started walking toward her table, ready to declare myself the victor.

It was the smile that gave it away. If Mab was as slick as she thought she was, I'da been dead on the floor. But the second I saw the corner of her mouth twitch up, I knew there was trouble coming. I spun around, dropping to one knee as I turned to see the redcap coming at me with razor-sharp blades in both hands. I stood as he got to me, wrapping my arms around him and slamming the faerie to the ground in a thunderous crash. One blade went spinning off to the side, disappearing into the crowd. He buried the other one in my thigh, still valiantly fighting for Mama's hand. I snatched the knife out of my leg and flung it aside, then struggled to my feet, one arm still wrapped around the redcap. I hefted him into the air, then brought him back down to the floor with my full weight atop him. His ribcage sounded like breakfast cereal with all the snapping and crackling coming from it, and when he tried to scream, it just came out a spatter of spit and frothy lung blood.

I stood up, leaving the broken redcap on the floor, and glared at Mab. "You told him he had to kill me or die, didn't you?"

The corner of her mouth twitched again. "I did. You are not worthy to bear my blood, mongrel."

"Well, here you go, Granny. Here's some pure faerie blood for you." I picked up the redcap's body, still barely breathing, and slammed it onto the table right in front of her. Then I snatched up a gleaming knife from beside my plate and shoved it into the dying faerie's chest. A little spurt of blood shot from the redcap's mouth, leaving a line of crimson across Mab's glorious blue dress.

I turned to look at the stunned spectators, covered in a mix of blood from me and the redcap, looking like something out of a damn Francis Bacon painting. I looked around the gathered throng and gave them my best psychotic grin. "Okay, bitches, who's next?"

13

─────────

Amy rounded a corner, putting them right back along the same corridor where they first exited the Great Hall to go snoop around and look for Bubba's sister. The second she spotted the two royal guards standing at attention beside the door, she spun and quick-walked back the way she came, pushing Skeeter ahead of her. "Not that way."

Skeeter craned his neck to see past her, moving backward with her assistance. "What? What is it?"

"We're right back where we started. That asshole Falarun gave us a load of crap about a secret door. We're no closer to finding Bubba's sister than we were when we left him there to handle the tournament all alone. And I'm stuck with a magic book that I can't put down. Dammit!" She kicked nearby door, frustration boiling over. Then she leaned against the wall, rubbing her bruised toes.

"You have definitely been hanging around Bubba too long."

"Or not long enough. He only kicks doors when he's wearing steel toes," Amy said with a rueful grin. "At least I managed to get the book to let me tuck it into the belt of the gown instead of carrying it everywhere."

"Yeah, that's something, I reckon. Alright, let's figure out a plan.

We've poked around in every secret room we could find, and none of them had a tower attached to them."

Amy's eyes widened at his words. "Except the one we never went back to."

Skeeter gave her a puzzled look. "What are you talking about? And before you go any further, let me be real damn clear here—I am *not* going back into that dungeon. Bubba's sister can rot before I poop in a bucket again."

"Could have gone my whole life without that visual, thanks," Amy replied. "But that wasn't what I meant. Bubba's mother was in a tower, wasn't she?"

"Yeah, what about it?" His eyes widened, and he smacked himself on the forehead. "Dammit!"

"Yeah, exactly. If you have two members of the royal family that you wanted to keep prisoner, but you had to keep them in gilded cages, wouldn't you put the cages right next to each other?"

"You think his sister's in the same tower as his mama?"

"We never searched it. We just took his mother at her word that the entire tower was hers."

"I didn't think faeries could tell a lie? Pretty sure I read that somewhere."

"I don't remember her ever telling us directly that it was only her apartments, just that there wasn't anyone else there. Holding back information isn't the same thing as telling a lie, and the Fae have had centuries to learn how to parse the truth and split hairs."

"Now I *know* you've been around Bubba too long. Your moral compass is starting to point a lot more south than it used to."

"Skeeter, I work for the federal government. Moral compass-ectomy is a minor surgery that all recruits undergo their first week on the job. Let's go." She stepped past Skeeter and started back down the hall, running her fingers along the outer wall, looking for the secret entrance to the tower.

The search went quicker the second time, even without guards posted at the entrance. Five minutes later, the pair of them slipped through the illusory wall and ascended the spiral staircase to

Ygraine's rooms and hopefully to some clue about where Nitalia was, or at least where she might have been. Skeeter's eyes were fixed on his feet as he walked up the narrow passageway, so when Amy stopped short in front of him, he ran headfirst into her, his forehead slamming into her butt as she stood on the stairs.

"What the hell?" she hissed at him.

"Sorry. Why'd you stop?" he replied, lowering his voice to match her whisper.

"Guard," she whispered, then her tone brightened as she spoke to someone out of sight around the curve of the tower steps. "Oh, hello there. The Lady Ygraine sent us to fetch her daughter for the final rounds of the tournament."

A gruff voice drifted down past her to Skeeter's ears. "Huh? Princess Nitalia isn't up here anymore. Everybody knows that...shit, you're with that ugly human grandson of the queen, aren't you? Hey!" Skeeter heard the *thunk* of unprotected flesh meeting armor.

"Dammit!" Amy's voice came down in a muttered murmur, followed by the clatter of more armor banging against wood and stone. "Out of the way, Skeeter!"

Skeeter pressed himself flat against the wall as a guard in full armor tumbled down the steps in front of him, rolling all the way down and through the fake stoned wall in a thunderous clatter of metal and profanity. "Um...Amy? Everything okay up there?"

"Yeah, come on," came the growled reply.

Skeeter followed her up the stairs at an increased distance, both to keep his nose out of her butt cheeks and to avoid being brained with falling faeries. Seconds later, they stepped together into the parlor of Ygraine's tower apartment. Amy limped back to the door and dropped a heavy wooden bar into brackets on either side of it. Then she turned and limped over to sit on an overstuffed chair and started to rub her right foot, wincing at the touch.

"You wanna tell me what happened?" Skeeter asked.

"Not really." Amy glowered at him.

"I don't think I care."

"I kicked the guard. It didn't go as planned."

"Want to elaborate?"

"Is saying no an option?"

"Not really, no."

"He got suspicious, so I kicked him in the balls. Except plate armor includes a plate codpiece to protect against just that kind of attack. Kicking a man in armor in the balls is not a good idea when you're wearing these stupid slippers they forced me into."

"I thought you would have learned not to kick things after your little argument with the door."

"Well, like you keep saying, I've spent way too much time with Bubba lately."

"He's been my best friend for decades, but he is not what I would ever call a good influence," Skeeter said with a nod. He looked around the room. "We know Bubba's mama's room is over there," he said, pointing off to the right. "But I reckon we've got no clue what's through that door." He pointed to a door opposite the one they assumed was Princess Nitalia's bedchamber.

"Then that's probably where we want to start looking," Amy said, not moving from her chair.

"That your way of saying 'get on that, Skeeter'?"

"I'm injured."

Skeeter glared at her without saying a word, then turned and walked over to the door. He put a hand on it, feeling the surface for heat, or traps, or anything else that he wouldn't like. Feeling nothing, he turned the knob and pushed the door open. "Umm, Amy? I think you want to come over here and look at this," he said, not stepping across the threshold.

Amy limped over to his side, stopping cold at his elbow. "Shit. That's a lot of flowers."

"Yeah," Skeeter agreed. They stepped into the room, and Skeeter took a long look around. The room was simply furnished, but well-appointed. Tapestries covered the exterior walls, huge woven depictions of grand battles. Faerie knights riding dragons battled giants, ogres, and trolls in one. Another showed varying scenes of Mab throwing bolts of raw magical power against a hideously deformed woman in green robes and a crown, flanked by men and women adorned in similar colors, all scattered dead on the ground. Yet another was a life-size portrait of Mab woven into a giant wall hanging, enchanted with an illusion of snow falling in background of the tapestry.

"Nothing like a modest ruler," Amy said.

"Yeah, and Mab is nothing like modest," Skeeter agreed.

The tapestries covered every inch of bare wall between the two large wardrobes and the door, stopping only at the edges of the huge canopy bed that dominated the center of one wall. Skeeter stepped into the room and pulled back the drapes surrounding the bed, and flowers spilled off the bed to join the carpet of lilies, tulips, roses, and other varieties that covered every inch of the floor from wall to wall.

"Huh," Skeeter said. "More flowers. What do you think it means?"

"Well, Skeet," Amy said. "Flowers don't really grow in winter, do they?"

"Nope."

"My guess is they were left here as a message to someone."

"Us?"

"I doubt it. Nobody knew we were coming to get Nitalia. No, this looks like a more political statement to me. Kind of a big middle finger to Mab."

"The kind of thing you'd say to somebody you used to be married to?"

"Maybe, or maybe something you'd say to somebody who used to be married to your current husband?"

"You think this was Titania?" Skeeter looked around before he said the name, like he was afraid the Summer Queen would step out of a wardrobe and attack at the mention of her name.

"Kinda makes sense, doesn't it? She gets her granddaughter and gives the finger to Mab at the same time."

Skeeter thought for a moment, picking up a rose and smelling it while he pondered Amy's suggestion. "Yeah, this looks like the kind of petty bullshit that blows these people's skirts up. So now what?"

"Now we go downstairs and tell Bubba not to worry about the

tourney, 'cause we know where Nitalia is." She turned and stepped into the parlor.

"What about his mama? Don't we still need to keep her from marrying a troll?" Skeeter said, following her. He, once again, wasn't watching too closely where he was going, so when Amy stopped in front of him, he walked right into her back again, making them both stagger forward. "What the shit, Amy?" He stepped to the right to see around her. "Oh."

"Yes, human," General Falarun said from the parlor. The battered faerie guardsman stood with three grim-faced men in full armor holding halberds. "Oh, indeed. You didn't seriously believe that you could assault a member of Her Majesty's personal Honor Guard with no consequence, did you?"

"Well...kinda," Skeeter said.

"I have heard the torturer misses his playthings. He will quite enjoy having you returned to him. Get them!" He swept an arm toward the humans, and his men moved into the room, two going for Skeeter and one for Amy.

Amy looked at the division of the soldiers and smiled. "Just one for the girl? Yeah, that's going to end badly." She stepped up to the knight, spun around the head of his halberd to get inside the radius of his swing, and grabbed the shaft of the long weapon. Instead of wrestling with the bigger, stronger man for the weapon, she just held on with both hands and dropped straight down onto her back. As the halberd levered the knight up off his feet, she planted both of hers in the man's armored belly, flexing her knees then snapping her legs straight. The faerie vaulted right over her backward, slamming into the doorframe of the bedroom in a crash of armor and flesh. Amy came to her feet, picking up the discarded polearm from the downed guard.

"Skeeter, duck!" Amy yelled, and the thin man dropped to the deck. She swung the halberd in a huge arc, crashing into the pair of guards that were advancing on her friend. The big axe slammed into the first guard, knocking him into the second and sending them down in a tangle of metal-clad faerie. Skeeter sprang to his feet, grabbing a sword one of the men dropped and started flailing at their helmeted skulls with it like a percussionist in a steel drum band.

Amy turned the halberd onto Falarun, jabbing his mailed stomach with the point of the axe. "You can surrender, or I can really start to use this oversized can opener on your gut. Your call."

Falarun stood staring at her for a long moment, then Amy saw his eyes widen just a touch. That was the cue she was waiting for. She slid her hands up on the haft of the halberd, jabbing the butt end of the axe back under one arm, right into the gut of the first guard she clobbered. She whirled on him, clanging the butt of the axe into his helmet with a bell-like ring. Then she spun back to the dispirited faerie, a smile stretching from ear to ear.

"Now, Captain, about that surrender?"

14

———————

I didn't watch the other fight in the third round. I was a little busy getting Joe to bandage me up so I could quit bleeding all over Granny's tablecloths. Not that she cared, since anytime a drop got too close to her, she just waved a hand and magicked it away. I was sitting on the floor in front of Mab's table, listening to my bones try to knit and groaning every once in a while when I saw Joe sit up a little straighter.

"Hey, that's not fair," he said, then he stood up and looked at Mab. "He can't do that, can he?"

"Do what, human?" I heard Granny speak over my head, and the way she said "human" you woulda thought it was the nastiest slur she could think of. I had to face facts: my grandmother was a racist. Or a speciesist, I reckon, since I'd seen faeries of all different colors running around and she didn't seem to hate them. Maybe it was dimension-ist, since by all appearances she liked the trolls and ogres better than she liked humans. Yeah, that's it. My grandmother was a dimension-ist. Family—can't live with 'em. Pass the beer nuts.

"He's got that other faerie healing him! That won't make for a fair fight. Not to mention the fact that he's in full armor, and Bubba's been fighting in a doublet and hose this whole time!" Joe protested.

"Not much to worry about there, padre," I said. "I got a run in my stockings in that last fight, so if I can manage to get my leg high enough to kick this dude, I'm gonna pretty much be fighting commando under this serapé."

Joe looked down at me. "That is very high on the list of things I never, ever want to think about, thank you."

"Rule number one—don't visualize. We are in a dangerous line of work, Joe, and some things just can't be unseen."

Granny's voice cut through my witty banter. "You are welcome to use whatever weapons or armor you choose, and you may utilize any healing magics that you have open to you. There is nothing in the rules against that. It is not my fault that you have chosen to battle through this contest without fully exploring the rules."

"But your men confiscated all our weapons and gear. We don't have any of it!" Joe yelled. I tugged on his pant leg, planning to remind him that yelling at the psychotic faerie queen in her own castle probably wasn't the smartest thing he could do, but then I gave up. He works with me; smart is right off the table.

I heard a bell-like tone ring through the air, and there in front of me was all our shit. My pants, my boots, my 3XL Black Badge Division t-shirt that I ordered off the *Wynonna Earp* TV show website, and maybe most importantly, my underwear. I ain't particularly bashful, but I didn't relish the idea of Granny's entire court getting acquainted with Bubba Jr. Laying atop the pile of clothes was the most beautiful sight in all of Fairyland: Bertha. My beautiful Desert Eagle pistol in her shoulder holster gleamed at me just like a drunken sorority girl winking at a pledge right after the last keg ran dry.

I hauled myself to my feet, trying not to drip too much blood everywhere, and limped over to the pile of clothes and gear. I reached up under the doublet, ripped the overgrown pantyhose off without bothering to take them down slipped my drawers on, then stripped the rest of that frou-frou crap off right in the middle of the Great Hall, to no small number of gasps from the assembled faeries and other magical critters. I looked around and growled a little. "What? Ain't y'all ever seen a man with tattoos before?"

"I'm not sure they have seen one quite so large, grandson," Mab said.

"Well, let 'em get a good look," I grumbled, pulling on my jeans. "Hey, Granny, before I go getting my favorite t-shirt all bloodied up, you wanna send a healer over her to patch me up a little?" I figured as long as she was being magnanimous enough to give me back my guns, I might as well ask for the whole world.

"I don't think that would be quite fair. I do not wish to show favoritism to any one competitor, after all." I figured she'd say something like that. But it wasn't the first time I'd heard "no" from a woman, and I figured it wouldn't be the last. Oh, well.

Apparently, his vow of celibacy kept Joe from getting quite so sanguine about rejection because he pressed the issue. "I don't think it would be a question of favoritism, Your Majesty. After all, you wish to provide as great a spectacle for your audience as possible. Up to this point, all the duels have been well-fought contests. It would be a shame to have the final bout be so one-sided as to bore those assembled for your tournament."

That was pretty good, I thought. Appealing to her pride and making it seem like it was about her. Maybe dealing with church politics had taught Joe a thing or two. Mab considered his words, then spoke. "Your words have merit. Healer!" She waved a hand, and the little faerie that healed us every night after the torturer got finished with us appeared in a flash of light.

The little dude looked up, startled, like he'd been in the middle of something important when Mab teleported him. "Oh! You again. My goodness, what have you gotten yourself into this time? Even Brandis of the Long Blades has never done work this rough."

"Well, there was a troll," I said. The little dude's eyes went wide. "But I killed him. Then there was a redcap." His eyes bugged out even more. "And I killed him. But now I gotta face this faerie over yonder wearing the tin can." I pointed at the knight across the room. "And I gotta kill him. But standing is kinda hard. So if you could patch me up so I can go whoop this guy's ass, I'd really appreciate it."

He looked at me, then at the knight, then at me, then at Mab, the whole time more and more sweat just beading up on his little bald head. Finally, I reached out with the shredded remains of my pantyhose and rubbed his forehead dry. "Dude! Get your shit together and heal me. I got some faerie ass to kick."

He jerked and shot one last look at Mab. When she nodded, he stepped closer to me and held up his hands. His palms glowed with a soft yellow light, and as it reached out to envelop me, I felt my wounds start to close. One rib snapped into place with a *crack*, and I yelped. I didn't wince manfully or grit my teeth; I yelped like a stray dog run over by a pickup truck. That shit *hurt*. But most of it was fine, and after a couple minutes of getting magicked on, I was fit as a fiddle.

And hungry as hell. I threw on my t-shirt, strapped on Bertha, my Judge revolver, Great-Grandpappy Beauregard's sword, and hooked my caestae to my belt. The metal-and-leather spiked gloves were my favorite Christmas gift ever from Amy, and before getting to Fairyland, I'd replaced the spikes with cold iron studs so I could actually hurt these bastards if I ended up scrapping.

Who was I even kidding? I knew I was gonna end up punching the shit out of somebody, so I made sure it would hurt as much as I could. I patted the little healer faerie on the shoulder and stepped over to Mab's head table. "Thanks for the gear and the mojo, Granny. I promise to put on a good show for you."

"Just try to last long enough to make it entertaining. None of Sir Null's previous opponents have lasted more than a minute."

Well, that didn't sound good. I leaned over the table and grabbed a hunk of something that looked like a roasted turkey leg off my plate. Healing and getting healed takes a bunch of energy, so while my little medic was about to fall over, I was just hungry as hell. I wolfed down the "turkey leg," which was probably some magical creature that I'd never heard of, and washed it down with some of the fruit juice Mab had in our glasses. I would have preferred a Guinness to carb up, but apparently the magic of Fairyland doesn't extend to making good beer.

"That was yummy, Grann-o. What was it? Baby dragon? Phoenix? A goose that laid golden eggs?"

"Turkey."

"What?"

"Turkey. It's a large, stupid bird, but the meat is delicious."

I'll admit, I was disappointed. Not just that it was turkey, but it wasn't even like some kind of magical turkey. Just regular old dumb-as-a-rock turkey. Oh well, still yummy. Properly fortified, I turned to my opponent. "Let's do this," I said over my shoulder.

Mab stood up, and the murmur of conversation in the room shut off like somebody flipped a switch. She raised her hands and said, "Ladies, Gentlemen, and Beasts of all races, I thank you for attending my feast and tournament!"

I really wanted to mutter something about them probably having less of a choice than I did but decided this would be a bad time to provoke the psychotic magical faerie queen. And Skeeter says I never learn anything.

"We have now moved into the final round of our contest, pitting my grandson, Bubba—" Wow, I never heard anybody sneer my name before. I didn't particularly enjoy it. "Versus Sir Null, a valiant Knight of the Fae. Will the competitors please step forward?"

I walked to middle of the room, standing across from the last of the faerie knights. Six of these dudes started the tournament, all in gleaming armor covered in curlicues and decorations. Except this dude. His armor was jet black and completely unadorned. His helmet was smooth, with a visor that looked more like a smoked glass motorcycle helmet than a suit of armor. His features were completely obscured, but I remembered from watching him fight in the first couple of rounds that he moved like he was wearing regular clothes, not like he was wrapped in steel with his visibility hampered. Mab wasn't joking; he really had cut down all his opponents in less than a minute. But he'd never run into anything like me.

He was slender, even in armor, and only came up to about my chin. He had a long sword strapped across his back, and I'd seen him wield it one- and two-handed. He didn't have a shield, so I didn't have that to worry about, but I wasn't real sure how tough that armor was. *Whatever*, I thought, *if it gets to be too much of a pain in my ass, I'll just crack him out of that shit like a lobster*. He stepped up to me and gave me a nod. I nodded back, and Mab clapped her hands twice.

"Duelists, remember the rules of the tournament. There are none. You shall battle until one of you concedes or is rendered unconscious. Should death occur, it will be a regrettable, but unavoidable, accident." The way she said that last bit let me know exactly how much she would regret me having a fatal accident on the end of this dude's sword. "Now, for the hand of my daughter, either in marriage or freedom—begin!"

The knight drew his sword, the raspy *hiss* echoing through the Great Hall. He spun the blade in great arcs around his head and in front of him, advancing on me cautiously, one foot in front of the other as he glided forward. One step. Two steps. Three steps. With the fourth step, halfway to me already, he raised his sword above his head and charged.

So I drew Bertha and put three fifty-caliber rounds right in his chest. He went down like somebody hit him in the chest with a sledgehammer, which I reckon wasn't too far off the mark. His sword skittered across the stones unheard over the clatter of his armor crashing to the floor, and he slid backward several feet before the momentum of the bullets dissipated. I blew off the end of my pistol and holstered Bertha, mugging for the crowd a little. They looked at me in stunned silence, as if they couldn't believe I took out the badass with the blade in ten seconds.

Or like they couldn't believe what a colossal dumbass I was to turn my back on an opponent without making sure he was dead. I barely had time to register the sound of metal-clad feet rushing at my back before the son of a bitch put his shoulder in my spine and tackled me to the floor.

I guess faeries are pretty tough, after all. Shit.

15

———

"Well, that didn't go as planned," I said to Joe.

"That's good to hear," he replied. "Because if you planned to do nothing with that hand cannon besides piss off the little man with the big sword, I would have to call you an idiot."

"You call me an idiot all the time."

"Good point. You should move now."

I did. I dove to my right, tumbling across the stone floor in an awkward roll, but getting enough separation from Sir Null to avoid being cut in half. Sir Null? What the hell kind of name is Sir Null anyway? He's probably some kind of faerie douchebag whose real name is Chad, uses mustache wax, and won't shut up about CrossFit.

I didn't have too much time to dwell on the douchiness of my opponent because he kept trying to cut my head off. After dodging for a minute didn't seem to be doing the job of tiring him out nearly as well as it was tiring me out, I figured I'd better fight fire with fire, so to speak. I would have rather fought fire with fire, *literally*, but I didn't own a flamethrower. Making a mental note to see if Amy could get me a government surplus flamethrower if we ever got back to our dimension, I drew Great-Grandpappy's sword and turned to face the knight.

Great-Grandpappy's sword had an overlong hilt, kinda like Null's, but his was shaped a lot like a big femur. I never knew Great-Grandpappy, but from the stories I heard, he was a tough old sumbitch. Wouldn't surprise me a bit if he killed a damn grizzly bear with his bare hands and built the sword out of its leg bone. I didn't take too much time thinking about my sword's provenance since I needed to get it up and in the way of Null swinging for my neck. The blades met with a clang and shower of blue-white sparks, and I felt myself driven back from his power.

"Damn," I growled. "You're a strong little bastard."

"And you are unworthy of the royal blood that courses through your veins, you mongrel dog."

"You know that's redundant, right? I mean, I ain't the most educated man in the room, and I know that's redundant." I parried his next stroke and slashed out with a low slice aimed at his knees. Of course, the nimble shit just jumped straight up and over my blade, so I didn't just miss, I looked stupid doing it. That was fine. I let go of the sword with my right hand, letting it carry over past my body with my left. Then I balled up my big right fist and nailed him on the point of his helmeted chin with a huge uppercut.

Right on his steel-clad chin. I rang his bell pretty good, and he staggered back, shaking his head like he saw a whole bunch of tweety birds flying around, but I let out a scream fit to rattle the windows as I felt two knuckles shatter on his helmet. I looked down at my fist, which was already starting to swell, and let out a string of profanity that impressed even me. I'm pretty sure I didn't even know what all those words meant, and Joe turned downright pale at the cussing.

I sheathed my sword, ripping the caestae off my belt. If I had any chance of using my right hand again, I had to get it bound up before it swelled to the size of a basketball. I jammed the leather-and-metal glove down over my broken fist, letting out another scream of agony as I forced my fingers into the confines of the glove. I let out a long breath as the support of the caestus muffled the pain a little bit and slipped the other glove on. I looked up to see where my opponent was, and of course, he recovered faster from getting punched in his armor than I did from punching said armor, and he was charging back at me, swinging his razor-sharp blade down at my head.

I crossed my wrists together over my head, trapping his blade in the steel-wrapped gauntlets. I slid to the right and twisted my hands around, getting a good grip on his blade with my gloves and yanking forward. He didn't let go of his sword, and his momentum pulled him right into my knee strike. Which again slammed into his damn full plate armor. I saw what was happening and pulled my strike at the last second, so I just banged my knee instead of shattering my patella, but it still didn't tickle. I let go of his sword and slammed both fists into the back of his head in a big hammer blow. My knuckles howled at the treatment, but the caestae kept me from further injuring myself.

Null didn't fare so well this time, as the heavy gloves did way more damage than just my bare hand. I saw a couple of serious dents appear in his helm and figured he was probably at least concussed. My thoughts were confirmed when he dropped his sword, yanked off his helmet, and threw up all over the white marble. Good, now we were both hurting. I took one step forward and slammed my steel-toe boot into his gut, for once managing to not injure myself when I landed a decent shot. Null rolled over onto his back, and I bent down beside him, grabbed his helmet in my left hand, and cracked it across his face. His nose pulped and blood streamed down his face. He got his hands up to block the next blow, and I pitched the helmet off into the crowd. The last thing I needed was for him to get his noggin' wrapped in steel again just when I finally managed to hurt his sorry ass.

I yanked him to his feet and pulled back my fist, ready to knock him into the middle of next week. Then I felt a burning in my gut and looked down. The son of a bitch had his hand pressed against my belly, with the hilt of a knife barely showing. The sneaky little shit stabbed me!

I staggered back, letting go of the knight and yanking the blade out of my gut. It hurt a lot more coming out than it had going in, and I dropped to one knee. Sir Null, asshole sneaky stabber that he was, didn't give me even a second to recover, stepping up and planting one armored foot right in my newly-perforated gut. It wasn't the worst pain I'd ever felt, that was a cross between having my brother run me through with Great-Grandpappy's sword and having an Auburn right tackle step on my balls in a football game, but it was sure as hell on the Top Ten list. I didn't even have the power to roll over and do anything cool—I just flopped down on my belly and bled on the floor for a second or two.

Null pressed his advantage, stomping a mudhole in my ass and trying his level best to walk it dry. He put one heel in my kidney and his other foot on my shoulders and stood on me, presumably proclaiming his triumph to the room. I couldn't hear what he was saying over the sound of my blood rushing out of my body. I didn't bother trying to push myself up onto my feet; I just rolled over enough to topple Sir Dickhead to the floor in a clatter of armor and very un-knightlike swearing. I dragged myself over to his side and started to rain blows down on his unprotected head with my caestus. I didn't get much leverage and hardly any real strength behind my punches, but the cold iron studs I screwed into my gloves before leaving home did some damage regardless.

My chickenshit opponent pulled away from me, scrambling to his feet and raising his sword high overhead. I managed to get all the way back up to my knees, just high enough to look up into his bloodied face as he prepared to bring that gleaming hunk of steel down on my face and end me once and for all.

"You simpering fool," he snarled at me. I have to say, with all that blood pouring out of his nose and that real nasty grimace on his face, he didn't look like much of a knight. Even if I wasn't opposed to Mama remarrying on principle, I don't think I would have approved of this douchenozzle being my father-in-law. Good thing it would only happen over my dead body. Too bad that was looking like more and more of a literal statement.

"This should have been so simple. I win this idiotic contest, take the Princess Ygraine back to my Queen Titania, and cast her down at the feet of her father, Oberon. Then we would have Mad Queen Mab's daughter and her granddaughter, enough leverage to send her completely over the edge when we forced her to watch their execution. But you had to interfere, and now I am revealed as a knight of Summer in the very heart of mine enemies."

I looked around, and it did seem that people were pointing at him and scowling a lot more than they had any of the other fights. I reckoned it was just because I had the fans on my side, but him being the sworn enemy of everything in the Winter Court did make a lot more sense. I spit a big blood-loogie on the floor and grinned up at him. "So you're saying you would have gotten away with it, if it hadn't been for those meddling kids?" I laughed, which turned into a bloody coughing fit, and that sent me off into a cussing fit, which led to more coughing. This was going nowhere fast. "What are you gonna do, now that your plan's screwed, Summer's Eve?"

I didn't expect him to recognize the brand name of a feminine hygiene product, but I knew I'd just called him a douche, and that was enough for me. When you're bleeding out from a punctured something really important on your grandmother's marble floor in Fairyland, you take what little victories you can get.

"I plan to carry your head back to my queen as a soup tureen, then ship your sister's corpse to her mother one piece at a time." He raised the sword over his head, and I slumped to my side on the floor. I couldn't hold myself upright with just the one hand, and I needed my right to reach around behind my back and draw my little Judge revolver from the paddle holster at the small of my back. I squeezed the trigger on the pistol three times and emptied three .410 shells of double-ought buckshot right into Sir Dickweasel's chest and face. The pellets bounced off his armor, and only a couple of them actually hit flesh, but the cold iron loads I'd put in the little gun before leaving home did the work of ten bullets, tearing through Sir Null's face and skull.

He screamed in agony and dropped his sword, falling to his knees and clawing at the bloody holes in his head. The little pellets didn't make it through his skull, so I hadn't landed a killing shot, but it looked like it hurt. A lot. He writhed in pain while I crawled over to him, leaving a smear of blood across the white stone floor behind me. I pulled myself up to his side, wrapping my iron-clad caestus around his throat. "You ready to die, shithead?" I gasped into his ear.

"Your puny weapon cannot even penetrate my armor, fool," he said, spitting blood out of his mouth.

"Yeah, that's something you oughta know about the Judge," I said, cocking the hammer back on the little pistol. "It shoots shotgun shells, which is what put all those pellets in your ugly face. But it also shoots a forty-five-caliber bullet, same as the Colt Peacemaker, the most famous damn pistol in the world. It'll punch through that tin can you're wrapped in like it's tissue paper. I just wanted you to know that before I shot your arrogant ass." I pulled the trigger on the pistol, sending a round through his breastplate and right into his black little heart. Then I pressed the gun to his temple and put the last shot in his head, just for good measure.

I rolled over, looking up at the ceiling as my toes started to get cold from blood loss. "Hey Granny, I won. Can I borrow that healer again?" I croaked, then my vision went dark.

EPILOGUE

I woke up in a bed. Not my bed, but a bed, which was a hell of an improvement over every other time I'd woken up in Fairyland. There were pillows and a blanket, and I was even clean. *I could get used to this* was my first thought.

My second thought was, *Shit. Am I dead?*

Then I moved, and I heard Amy's voice, and I figured if I was dead, then I made it to Heaven, so it's fine. But Skeeter spoke next, so I knew I wasn't dead. I love the boy, but my Heaven does not involve him anywhere where I'm lying in a bed with my girlfriend.

"He's awake," Amy said, relief in her voice.

"Bubba?" Skeeter said. "You really ain't dead! Good." That's my best friend. Grasp of the obvious like nobody's business.

"I ain't dead," I agreed. I opened my eyes and looked around. I was still somewhere in the Winter Court Palace, but I was in a room I'd never seen before. It was full of damn flowers, all kinds of roses and lilies and other crap I couldn't name if you put a gun to my head. "Where the hell am I?"

"You're in your sister's room," Mama said. I pushed myself up in bed and took a good look around. Mama was sitting in an armchair in one corner of the room, just watching me. Skeeter and Joe were in chairs pulled up next to the big four-poster bed, and Amy was sitting on the foot of the bed beside my legs. She looked worried. I reached out and patted her foot.

"I'm fine," I said. Then I took a quick mental inventory to make sure I wasn't lying. I felt okay, and I couldn't see no blood on the bed, so I musta been fine. "Did Granny send the healer?" I asked.

"No, Robert, I healed you myself after I disposed of Sir Null's remains," Mab said from behind me. I turned, and she was in a chair in the opposite corner from Mama. The two faerie women glared at each other like a pair of pissed-off old tomcats, and I figured Mama's spell either got broke or wore off. She looked pissed as hell at Granny. I remembered what Mama looked like when she was that kind of pissed, usually at me for whooping Jason's ass over something when we was kids. Granny didn't seem fazed by it, but she was about as far from Mama as she could get and still be in the same room.

"I appreciate that, Grann-o. Now if you'll excuse us, we've got to get to the Summer Court and whoop somebody's ass." I swung my legs over to the side of the bed and froze. "Ummm...where's my clothes?" I ain't usually the most bashful type, but walking around in front of everybody wearing nothing but tattoos and butt hair was a little much, even for me.

"We'll wait in the sitting room while you get dressed," Mama said, standing up and walking to the door. Joe and Skeeter followed, with Granny waiting until they'd cleared the door to stand up.

"I'll wait here to make sure he doesn't fall over," Amy said. I raised an eyebrow at her, and she gave me an "I'll explain in a minute" look.

When the door closed behind Granny, I stood up and walked over to the wash stand with my clothes on it and started to get dressed. I noticed as I pulled my t-shirt on that Mab had not only cleaned the blood out of my shirt, but she'd fixed the hole Sir Douche had left in it when he stabbed me. Maybe Granny wasn't a complete psycho after all.

Nah, she's a total psycho.

"So what's the deal?" I asked Amy.

"Mab released the spell on your mother as soon as you killed

Null, who was actually Sir Kairn, a high-ranking knight in Titania's court. He was sent here to win your mother's hand, giving Titania control of Mab's daughter and granddaughter. If he could make sure you didn't live through the tournament, all the better."

"How did they come up with that? I wasn't even supposed to be in the tournament!"

"Apparently Titania knows you, or at least knows of you. She knew you wouldn't be able to resist sticking your nose in."

"Yeah, we met the last time I was here. I broke out of her dungeon, too."

"You know, if you stop getting thrown in dungeons, you don't have to break out of them."

I didn't dignify that with a response, just moved on. "So Mama's not head-screwed by Granny anymore, and now she's pissed."

"Yeah, pretty much."

"And we've got to invade a hostile chunk of Fairyland to go rescue my sister."

"Yep."

"And they've already sent assassins to kill me."

"You nailed it."

"Must be Tuesday," I said, lacing up my last boot and walking to the door. I slipped into Bertha's shoulder rig, then stepped out into the sitting room. "Alright," I said. "What's the deal? Why is everybody so damn interested in my sister? There's something y'all ain't telling me, and it almost got me killed once. I ain't doing another damn thing until somebody tells me what's really going on."

Mab and Mama looked at each other, then Mama spoke. "You know that it is very rare for the Fae to have children."

"I've heard something like that." I moved to sit in an armchair opposite the couch Mama was on. Skeeter was sitting next to her, and Mab was in an armchair beside the one I was in. Joe stood behind Mama, and Amy perched on the arm of my chair. I wasn't too keen on sitting next to my murderous grandmother, but I was a little weak on my feet from the fighting, the almost dying, and the healing, so I had to sit somewhere.

"It is even more rare for one of the royal family to have more than one child. In fact, it hasn't happened for five thousand years," Mama said.

"Wow. So sis is some kinda miracle baby?"

"You both are," Mab chimed in. "Many among us believe that you are the fulfillment of an ancient prophesy, one which foretells a ruler that will emerge, one of a pair of siblings of royal blood that will unite Winter and Summer in eons of harmony, bringing peace to the land and shattering the enmity of millennia."

I thought about that for a second. "So you're saying that me and my sister are supposed to bring the Winter and Summer Courts of Faerie together and make y'all not hate each other anymore?"

"That is what the prophecy says." Mab nodded.

"That is why I strove for so long to keep Nitalia's existence a secret, and to keep you from having anything to do with the Fae, or the supernatural at all," Mama said. I remembered her not liking Pop being a Hunter, and not wanting me and Jase to follow in his footsteps. But then her magic made her come back home, and all bets were off as far as that went.

"So, if we're supposed to end all this fighting and hating, why are people trying to kidnap Sis and kill me?" I asked.

"For the peace to come about, the current power must shift," Mab said simply.

"She means that if this happens, her and Titania won't be queens anymore," Skeeter chimed in, earning himself a glare from my grandmother. He ignored it. He knew Mama loved his ass and wouldn't let psycho Granny eat him.

"Your rude friend is correct," Mab said. "And the lure of power is strong, the desire to keep power even more so. There are many within the Courts who would not like to see a shift in the balance of power."

"Like you and Titania," I said.

"Among many others, yes."

"Well...shit," I said. "So we've got to go into a magic kingdom where everybody there wants to kill me, rescue my sister that I've never seen before, and probably fight a faerie queen with incredible power, all because I'm supposed to be some kind of redneck Harry Potter and overthrow the friggin' universe?"

"I think it's more a Luke and Leia thing," Amy said. "Since there are two of you, and you're brother and sister."

"Not twins, though," Joe pointed out.

"And none of the creepy incest stuff that always squicks me out when I watch the first movie now," I said.

"Does this mean I get to be Han Solo?" Joe asked.

"Oh yeah, because Skeeter's totally C-3PO," I replied. I glanced up at Amy, who held up both hands.

"Don't even look at me like that! I am *not* wearing a slave Leia costume."

"You're all insane," Mama said. She turned to Mab. "Insane, I tell you. Can we please go rescue my daughter now?"

I stood up and took Amy's hand, then looked at Mama and the rest of my band of merry idiots. "Yes, Mommy-wan-kenobi. Let's go kick some summer sausage."

T o Be Continued

PART III

HOT BLOODED

1

"I gotta say, I'm getting real damn tired of Fairyland dungeons," I said, my butt going numb from the cold flagstones I sat on. I probably would have paced, but the damn cell was too short. I knew this because I'd seen this cell before, a few months back, the *first* time I was thrown in a dungeon in Fairyland.

"Well, there's a pretty damn easy solution for that, Bubba," Skeeter griped from the opposite wall. "Just quit pissing off faeries that can throw your ass in dungeons!"

"Easier said than done," Amy chimed in. She was on a bunk, at least, if by "bunk" we mean a few four-by-four timbers holding up a woven net of rope with a pallet of straw on it. But it was better than the cold, stone floor. Well, maybe. She kept slapping at her legs like something was biting her. There weren't any bedbugs on the floor, at least not that I could see. Or maybe they were just afraid of me.

"Look, y'all wanted to whoop that dude's ass as much as I did. How was I supposed to know he was one of the damn Royal Guard?"

Three Days Earlier

After finding out that my kidnapped half-sister Nitalia wasn't, in fact, being held in the palace of the Winter Court by my psychotic grandmother Mab, and after I fought a bunch of faerie knights, magical monsters, and one really hungry troll to make sure my Mama didn't have to marry any of those people, we took some of Granny Mab's best horses and struck out for the Summer Court. Mama knew the way, being brought up in Fairyland, and with borrowed clothes mostly hiding our outlander status, we headed down the road.

"You know this ain't gonna work, right?" Skeeter said, pulling his horse alongside mine. It wasn't hard, given that my poor horse was panting from hauling my big ass already, and it wasn't even lunchtime yet. I was glad we brought extra mounts because it was starting to look like I'd only get about half a day out of each one. I reckon when you're used to hauling around faerie knights, who probably weigh like a buck-sixty even all armored up, throwing a three-hundred-pound redneck on your back seems like punishment detail.

"What ain't gonna work, Skeeter?" I asked. I looked around, but nobody else was close enough to hear what we said. Good thing, too. I didn't want anybody having second thoughts about the plan. It wasn't much of a plan, but it was the closest thing to one we'd had since we struck out after Nitalia in the first place.

"This disguise. I look more like a damn Klingon than a faerie."

"Well, then we better just hope we don't run into any Roman faeries out here in the woods. Give it a chance, Skeeter. Mama says you look way different to somebody who doesn't know it's you. But since we know you, the glamour don't work on us. I don't know shit about magic, so I gotta trust her."

"Just remember, I've seen enough horror movies to know what happens to the one black dude. If shit goes down, I am not sticking around to see if it's true. I will be LL Cool J hiding in the oven with my damn parrot quicker than you can blink."

I looked at him a little cockeyed. "Did you just make a *Deep Blue Sea* reference in the middle of an honest-to-god Fairyland quest?"

"Don't judge me. That movie's a classic. Besides, you can quote every line of *Sharknado*."

"I gotta give you that one," I agreed. "Just try to stay in the middle of the pack, and stay down if any shit starts flying."

"Bubba, we been friends more than twenty years. Around you, shit *always* starts flying." He dropped his horse back to ride alongside Father Joe, leaving me to my thoughts. I was in the lead, with Skeeter and Joe behind me, and Mama and Amy bringing up the rear. I didn't think much about the two of them getting all buddy-buddy and sharing secrets, or worse, baby pictures of me, but I did like the idea of Amy covering our rear. She was the best shot amongst us, and I knew she still had her backup .380 in her boot, even if we packed away her service weapon when Mab made us promise not to ride through her realm with our "mortal weapons" visible. That meant Bertha was tucked into a saddlebag, but I made sure I could get to her quick if I needed to.

I rounded a bend in the road, and the dirt track opened up into a wide clearing in front of the gates of a small town. A pair of faerie guards stood at the gate, but their weapons were at rest. We looked like just normal travelers, even if I looked like a half-giant. Apparently, that was a thing that happened sometimes, like with the half-ogre guard I met last time I was in Fairyland. I pulled Blue, the name I'd given my overworked horse, off to the side of the road and waited for the others to catch up.

It took just a couple of minutes for everybody to gather around, then I asked, "Do y'all want to go into town? We could eat lunch, water the horses, and take a break, then hit it hard in the afternoon."

"My ass loves that idea," Amy said, standing up in the saddle and rubbing her butt.

"I could do that for you," I volunteered.

Mama reached out and slapped my shoulder. "Don't be impertinent, Robbie."

"I wasn't being impertinent. I was trying to be helpful, just in case there was a spot she couldn't reach," I protested. "And y'all shut up." I glared at Joe and Skeeter, who tried without success to hide grins behind their hands.

"We should go into town," Mama said. "This is Wellspring, a town I remember. The inn here has always had a reputation for good food at fair prices, and the stable hands can check the horses and care for them while we eat." She didn't even wait for anybody else to say anything, just flicked her reins and started toward the gates.

I looked at her back for a few seconds, then turned to everybody else. "I reckon we're going into town. Try not to start any fights you can't finish."

"Like we're the ones that have been barred from every strip club in Tennessee, Arkansas, and West Virginia," Skeeter said as he rode past me.

"West Virginia, Bubba?" Joe said. "That's impressive."

"It was mistaken identity," I protested to Amy's disapproving glare. "I ain't never even been to a West Virginia strip club!" She ignored me, just rode on up to the gates.

An officious little faerie with a plume in his helmet stepped forward as we got to the entrance to town. "Halt!" he barked, even though we were already stopped. "Dismount and lead your horses over to the inspection area." He waved his arm to a patch of grass off to the right where two more guards stood around looking bored. They looked a little less bored when we walked over, but it seemed to be a mix between staring at Amy, staring at me, and trying to figure out what Skeeter was. Maybe his disguise wasn't holding up quite as good as we'd hoped.

Skeeter was right about one thing—though faeries came in all shapes, sizes, and colorations, none of them looked anything like an African-American human. And every human settlement I'd seen in my two trips to Fairyland looked whiter than a Ralph Lauren commercial, so he stuck out a little. To combat this, Mama had stuck fake pointy faerie ears on him, put a long white wig on his head, and cast a glamour to make him look like an old faerie wizard with bluish skin and white hair. She said this look was popular among the magic-wielding Fae, but I thought that sounded like just the best pile of crap she could come up with at the time.

"Open your packs for inspection and taxation," the little dude with the feather announced, striding over to us.

"There are no local taxes in the Winter Court," Mama said, looking down her nose at him. When we were back on Earth, she was my normal mama, but it seemed like the longer we traveled through Fairyland, the more she remembered that she was a princess of the Fae, and everything that meant.

"There are now," Feather-Head said, putting his hand on his sword. "Or is that a problem?" The way he leaned on the word "problem" and the way the two guards around us suddenly turned into six told me that we were going to have a serious problem, and soon.

"Of course that is a problem, you thieving little bootlick," Mama sneered at the man, whose head jerked back at the insult. "You dare attempt to extort money from a member of the royal family as though I were a common traveler?" Completely ignoring the fact that we went to great lengths to look *exactly* like common travelers, Mama went full Mab's daughter on the little guard, and I have to admit, I enjoyed watching his feather twitch in fear.

"Royal family?" one of the guards muttered to another. "Then what is she doing with a couple of humans and a Klingon wizard?"

"My dear lady," Feather-Head said, his tone dripping sarcasm, "you are no more a royal than that hulking oaf with you is anything more than a drooling half-ogre half-wit. Now open your saddlebags or I will have you arrested!" He yelled that last bit loud enough that his heavily-waxed mustache quivered, and I couldn't hold back a laugh.

"What is so funny, you giant moron?" Feather-Head asked me, his face stopping somewhere around the top of my belly.

"I'm sorry, I can't hear you. Let me get closer." I got down on my knees, which put us more or less face to face. "Now, what was that you were saying, little buddy?"

The little faerie's face went all the way past red to purple, and he drew the rapier at his side, whipping it around to slash across my chest. Except I expected this from the moment Mama started acting all royal with him, so I blocked his slash with the caestus I had slipped onto my left hand. The thin blade of the rapier hit the steel-lined gauntlet with a tinny *clink*, and I reached around and clobbered him with my right hand. I didn't have my caestus on that hand, so I didn't kill him by burying the cold iron studs into his skull, but I did ring his bell pretty good.

He spun one full revolution around, and his plumed helmet went another half-lap around his head, so by the time he managed to focus his eyes on me again, I was standing, his sword lay in the grass a few feet away, and his helmet was on sideways. "You shall die for that, beast!" he shrieked, drawing a dagger and rushing me.

That ended about as well as you'd expect—with him flat on his back on the grass and my footprint in the center of his breastplate. "Now don't get up, little fella, but let me be real clear. That woman over there, she's my mama. And Queen Mab is her mama. So that makes me Queen Mab's grandson. Now if you want to be the one to throw down with a couple of members of the royal family and their friends, that's fine, but I want you to know exactly what you're getting into before you do."

Feather-Head smiled up at me, then slowly got to his feet. "I am so grateful to you for pointing out your relationship to the Winter Queen, Your Highness. It will help keep everything perfectly clear in the days to come. Now, there is one thing I feel that I should point out to you."

"What's that, little buddy?" I asked. I probably could have left off the "little" comment, but...nah, I really couldn't.

"You left the lands of the Winter Court some hours back along the road. This town, Wellspring, has long been disputed territory between Mab and Titania, but finally a rotation of ownership was agreed upon some two decades ago. Mab agreed to ceded control of the town to Summer for a century, after which it would pass to Winter. Which means, of course..."

"That we ain't in the Winter Court," I said, a chill creeping into my bones despite the fact that we were in the Summerlands.

"That is correct, you great buffoon. You are in the lands of Titania and her Consort, Lord Oberon, and you have assaulted one of her Royal Guard in the course of his official duties. You shall hang for this, but not before I return you to Tisa'ron to collect my reward. Men, seize them all! And confiscate all their belongings for the glory of Her Majesty, Queen Titania of the Summer Court!"

And that's how we ended up in a Fairyland dungeon. This time.

2

____

"It might have been the right thing to do, Bubba, but that don't change the fact that we're in another damn Fairyland dungeon," Skeeter grumbled.

"I don't know what you're all complaining about," Mama said from her bunk. "I find the novelty of this entire adventure quite thrilling." She sat cross-legged on her bunk, a placid smile on her face and no evidence of creepy-crawlies or bitey little critters anywhere around her. I guess Summer Court bugs don't like Winter Court flesh. Nah, that don't hold water. Mama's half Summer Fae.

"Mrs.—Sorry, Ygraine—I think you might be forgetting that when you were living in the lap of brainwashed luxury back at Mab's palace, we were in the dungeon there, too." Joe paced the front of our cell, occasionally shoving his face up against the bars to see where the guards were. "I think they've left us alone for the moment. What's the plan, Bubba?" Joe turned back to me with a look of such hope on his face it was almost heartbreaking. I swear, he looked like a kid just getting out of bed on Christmas morning before he runs into the living room and sees that Santa Claus brought socks and underwear. Again.

"Plan?" I repeated. "Shit, Joe, I ain't got a plan. My plan ran out of planning right about the time we got tossed into the damn dungeon. I mean, shit, I done broke out of this joint once, and the dungeon in the Winter Court, too. I figure that's about two more dungeons than any one redneck oughta have to bust out of in a lifetime, so I am plumb out of ideas."

Joe gaped at me for a full minute before he realized I was serious, then he slid down the bars to sit on the floor with me and Skeeter "Then what are we going to do?" he asked.

"Well, we got a couple of choices," I said. "We can either try to come up with a way to bust out of here, which is gonna be tougher than usual on account of my already having done it once."

"Or?" Amy asked, slapping her leg and muttering something under her breath about letting bugs run around in a castle.

"I haven't quite figured out what the other option is yet," I admitted after a pause.

"Perhaps I could be of assistance, then," Mama said, standing up from her bunk and walking over to the door. She grabbed hold of the bars and gave them a good tug. She wasn't screaming, and it didn't look like her hands were on fire, so I reckoned the bars weren't made of iron. She leaned into it, and I saw her shoulders tense up, and after a few seconds, her face turned red, and the veins started to pop out on her forehead. She looked about like she was going to blow a gasket, then she relaxed and slumped forward. "Perhaps I am not as strong as I once was," she said, panting a little as she leaned against the bars. "In my youth, these would have proven no challenge at all to a royal daughter of the Sidhe. Of course, in my youth, I wasn't wearing this, either." She held up her right arm to show a band of metal encircling her bicep. The iron cuff was lined with silk to keep it from burning her skin, but it looked like it sapped her strength something fierce.

"That thing's why you can't just wiggle your fingers and magic us out of here, isn't it?" I asked.

"Yes, Robbie, the iron blocks my magic, so while I can wiggle my fingers to my heart's content, it accomplishes nothing." She walked back over to the bunk, her shoulders slumped.

"Well, maybe I can yank it off of you," I said, standing up. Well, mostly standing up, anyway. The ceilings in the dungeon were high enough, but the cells were cut a little short for my size. I crouch-walked over to where Mama sat on the bed and looked at the cuff the soldiers put on her arm when we were arrested.

"Huh," I said. "That don't look good." Whoever made this thing knew what they were doing. A set of small spikes pointed in and down along the bottom of the cuff. As long as Mama didn't try to wiggle out of it, she wouldn't have any problems. But if she pulled the cuff down on her arm, a pretty serious chunk of her skin and muscle was liable to come with it. "Well, shit. I'm sorry, Mama. I can't get that thing off you. It's gonna take a key."

"It's okay, Robbie. You tried." She patted me on the head like she used to when I was little and she wanted to let me know I was still her favorite, even now that Jason was around. Looking at how things turned out, I reckon she had pretty good taste in that regard.

I turned to the rest of the team, putting on my best "we're down two scores at halftime against a team that we should be wiping the floor with" coaching vibe. I clapped my hands and said, "Alright, let's all put our heads together and make a plan." Then I stood up straight and promptly almost gave myself a concussion smacking my melon into the ceiling. I sat all the way down on my ass on the cold, and very hard, stone floor and let out a grunt.

"I don't think that went quite to plan," Joe said, never moving to even see if I was okay.

"But the sentiment was right," Amy said, standing and walking over to me. "You okay?"

It was good to know *somebody* gave a shit. "Yeah, I'm fine. Ain't like it's the first time I've been conked in the noggin."

"Or likely to be the last," Mama said from beside Amy. "But you're both right. We cannot find Nitalia while trapped here, and we don't yet know if she is even in the Summer Court. So, we must escape our confinement, post-haste."

"I should have known you weren't from Georgia," Skeeter said. "Ain't nobody anywhere near where me and Bubba grew up ever used the term 'post-haste' in a sentence correctly. Okay, how we getting out of here?"

"Well, we can't exactly use the same ruse I used last time," I said. "Because that time I just broke in dressed as a guard and whooped everybody's ass on my way out. It's a lot harder starting behind a locked door."

"What about luring a guard in and overpowering him, like we did in Mab's dungeon?" Joe asked.

"They were pretty good about putting enough guards on us to keep us in line when they dumped us in here," I said, not really thinking much of that idea.

"That's it!" Skeeter jumped to his feet. I was really starting to envy all my under-six-foot friends. They could stand up straight even in the cell.

"What's it, Skeet?" I asked, shoving my jealousy aside for a moment.

"Poop."

"Huh? What's wrong? You just said it was a good idea, now it's poop?"

"No, Bubba, the *idea* is poop."

"Well, why don't you tell us about it, and we can decide if it's a shitty idea or not? Or maybe we can polish the turd a little bit." I wasn't really sure why Skeeter hated his idea all of a sudden, but if it let me make poop jokes and Amy didn't slap me for it, I was gonna go as far as they'd let me.

"Oh, trust me, it's a shitty idea," Skeeter said. "Just not how you think. Mrs. B., call the guard. Tell him you need the facilities."

Mama's face lit up like a three-week-old Christmas tree falling on a lit match and she walked over to the door. "Guard! Guard! I require assistance!" She put on her snooty court voice, like she used when we were at Mab's psychotic dinner party.

I leaned down to Skeeter. "I don't get it."

Skeeter grinned up at me. "Your mother has to use the bathroom."

"What's that got to do with us getting out of here?"

"The guards will have to let her out of the cell to go to a bathroom befitting her status as the daughter of the Consort, Oberon."

"You mean king," I said.

"No, he means Consort," Mama said from the door. "The Fae are always ruled by queens. We are a matriarchy."

"Does that mean that male faeries can't get their birth control covered by insurance and all the women leaders write laws about how they have to handle their reproductive organs?" Amy said with a smirk.

Mama laughed. "No, it means that silliness like that is completely ignored. We have more pressing things to do than measure our genitalia. Besides, it's hard to whip out your vagina and lay it on a table for comparison."

Amy laughed too, and I was about to say something to defend my gender when a guard came to the door and saved me from getting my ass kicked by my mother *and* my girlfriend.

"What do you want?" the guard growled. I noticed that he stayed well out of arm's reach on the other side of the door.

"I require use of a water closet," Mama said, keeping that imperious tone to her voice.

"I left you a bucket."

"That is what you brought our food in. It is also the only bucket we have to drink out of."

"It's a dungeon, not an inn. Maybe think about your preference in accommodations before you commit treason next time."

I saw Mama's back stiffen. "That would be challenging since we have not committed treason this time, much less any other time. Now get this door open and take me to the facilities! And I do not expect to use the commoners' toilets. Take me to the bath chambers befitting the daughter of Oberon himself!"

Even from the middle of the cell where I was, I could see the shock on the face of the guard. He snapped to attention, like he'd suddenly remembered who he was dealing with, and snatched up a ring of keys from a nearby table. He switched into full-grovel mode as he fumbled with the keys and opened the door, leading Mama out into the main room of the dungeon. "My apologies, Your Highness, I...I forgot myself. I will escort you to the facilities myself...I mean, I will...I mean—"

His fumbling for words cut off with a *clang* as Mama grabbed the front of his tunic and slammed his face into the bars of the cell door. He slumped to the ground, and Mama snatched his sword free as the other guard started in her direction, confusion all over his face.

"I thought you had to go..." the guard said, then shut up as he looked down at the sword point at his throat.

"They don't put the top of the intellectual heap on guard duty down here, do they?" Amy asked, pushing the cell door open. "Grab your buddy, drag him into the cell, then hand me your sword."

The guard did as he was told, except I took his sword and sword belt from him as I exited the cell. Me, Skeeter, and Joe stood along one wall watching as the ladies did all the heavy lifting. Mama locked the cell doors, then snapped the key off in the lock. "That is for speaking rudely to a member of the royal family. Enjoy your bucket, asshole."

It amazed me how quick Mama could flip-flop from faerie princess to redneck mother in her dialogue, but thinking more on it, she had always been a remarkable woman. We turned to head up the stairs, Amy in the lead with the sword she claimed from me, and me bringing up the rear because nobody'd be able to see around me on the winding staircase up to the main floor anyway. We crept up the stone steps, worn smooth from centuries of booted feet, and Amy pushed open the heavy wooden door at the top of the stairs.

Then she froze as half a dozen guards leveled halberds at her. She called over her shoulder, "I think they were expecting us..."

3

––––––––

"I wish I could say that I didn't believe you capable of such behavior, but you were always a willful child," Oberon said, pacing the dais in front of the royal audience chamber. I was a little uncomfortable, not just because we were all lined up kneeling on a cold stone floor and my knees ain't what they used to be. Nah, part of it was memory. The last time I was in this room, Titania sentenced me to fight her cousin, an asshole faerie bandit I called Scar, to the death.

It worked out okay since I shot his ass deader than hell and rescued the kidnapped human girls I went to Fairyland to rescue, but it was still not my favorite moment to dwell on. At least that time, Oberon had been on my side, sorta. This time I wasn't sure where he stood. I mean, he stood on a raised platform about ten feet in front of me, but I didn't know what he wanted out of our meeting. I pretty much just wanted to either sit down or stand up.

"Screw this," I said, getting to my feet. One of the faeries knights came over and pointed his pike at me, so I took it away from him, snapped it over my knee, and tossed it to the ground. "Kiss my ass, Peaseblossom," I said, stopping him dead in his tracks with a glare. "I'm too old and too fat for this kneeling shit. My knees hurt, and I gotta pee. Now you can either escort me to the facilities, or I can snatch that stupid helmet off your head and fill it full of homemade Mountain Dew, if you know what I mean."

I could tell by the look on his face that he had absolutely no idea what I meant. I reckon there ain't many Pepsi distributors in Fairyland. "I mean, I'm gonna piss in your hat if you don't show me where the crapper is." I let out a sigh. Metaphorical threats lose a lot of their oomph when you gotta explain them.

The knight looked to Oberon, then back to me, then back to Oberon, then back to me. I decided to step in before the little idiot gave himself whiplash. "Oberon, quit jerking him around and tell the little goober to take me to the can." Oberon waved a hand, and the knight made a "follow me" gesture. I stepped through a little door in the far wall, took care of business, and double-checked that I still had my Judge revolver in a holster tucked into the back of my belt. I loaded it with .45 long rounds for this trip, all cast in cold iron just for this occurrence. I tucked the little gun back under the tail of my long-sleeved shirt and stepped out of the potty.

There was a line waiting for me when I opened the door, every last one of them dancing like they had ants in their underwear. I reckon when I stood up and demanded bathroom privileges, it opened the floodgates, so to speak. A dispirited Oberon sat on one of the thrones on the dais, his intimidating appearance completely wasted on a bunch of humans who all had to pee too bad to notice him being all threatening and shit. Plus, let's face it, I've dealt with a lot worse things than a pissed-off faerie king. I've fought trolls, vampire ballerinas, naked sasquatches, and seen Amy before her morning coffee. I ain't easily intimidated anymore.

While the rest of the crew took care of business in the well-appointed washroom, I walked over to where Oberon sat looking all glum. "So, I reckon you're my grandpa," I said, looking him up and down.

He turned to me and gave me a once-over. It ain't like he'd never seen me before. Hell, when he was disguised as Oakroot, we traveled halfway across the Summer Court together. But this was the first time both of us knew what we really were to one another. Or, I reckon, the first chance we had to try and figure out what we were to one another. "I suppose I am your grandfather. Had I known that when we first met, things may have gone differently."

"I doubt it," I said. His eyebrows went up, but I went on. "From what I've seen in my time in Fairyland, and everything I've read about y'all over the years, you're a bunch of tricksters who can't resist getting one over on somebody, no matter what it costs. So I reckon you still would have played the harmless old merchant. Sure, maybe you would have stepped in earlier when I was dealing with Scar, but I kinda doubt it. If Mab's attitudes toward humans are anything like the way the rest of y'all feel, that is."

Oberon smiled, a kinda wistful thing that only touched his eyes from a distance. "My former wife's views on humans and dalliances with them are one of the reasons I left the Winter Court. She became increasingly jealous of the few human maids we had, convinced they were trying to lure my eye from her. She even went so far as to have one girl flogged for flirting with me, when all she did was bring the clean laundry to my quarters."

"Well?" I asked, giving him the "don't bullshit a bullshitter" look. I had little confidence in the fidelity of a man who left one faerie queen to go marry another faerie queen. Gramps was a good-looking dude, too. He had "player" written all over him.

"I had no interaction with the child, other than to take laundry from her, I swear! There may have been one or two...or more... serving women in the palace that I had relations with, but that poor child was not one of them. Mab had her flogged for a conversation about a tear in my tunic, nothing more!"

"Yeah, Granny's crazier than a shithouse rat. I found that out first-hand." I told him about the dance-off, and the tournament to keep Mama from marrying some jackhole, and everything else that we'd dealt with since we traveled to Faerie. "And now we get here and we end up tossed in the dungeon. I got to tell you, Gramps, I'm damn tired of Fairyland jail cells."

"Then perhaps, Grandson, you should stop antagonizing people with the authority to throw you in jail," he said.

"Easier said than done," I replied, with a pretty solid sense of deja vú. "Now what?" I asked once everybody gathered back in front of the dais. "We ain't going back to that dungeon without a fight, and I can damn sure guarantee that your boys here don't want to throw down with us. We might just be a bunch of humans—" Mama cleared her throat, and I gave her a little nod. "We might just be *mostly* a bunch of humans, but we will take a toll on your little cluster of guards here, and I don't think you've got all that many of them to spare."

"What makes you say that, Bubba?" Oberon asked.

"It's been a few months since I was here, but I recognize at least half these boys as asses I whooped on my last trip through. If you have plenty of guards, anybody who got the shit kicked out of them by a human would be long gone. So, since they're still here, I reckon there's a soldier shortage in the Summer Court. So, you ain't gonna be as likely to throw them away as you might have been once upon a time."

"Nice," Amy said with a smirk.

"I gotta get the jokes in when I can," I muttered.

Oberon stroked his chin, which I realized looked a lot more thoughtful when he did it, despite him not having a single hair on his face, and me having a beard worthy of ZZ Top. He just looked more prone to deep thinking, I reckon. After a few seconds, he nodded. "You are correct, Bubba. We do not have a surplus of guards, and thus we are loathe to throw them away upon a useless endeavor. You would certainly fall to their greater numbers, but there would be little to win, and much to lose even in a minor scuffle with such as your-selves. So you shall be assigned guest quarters here in the castle of the day, and at tonight's reception honoring our daughter, we shall bestow upon you a great boon." He looked up at the guard standing behind me, holding his broken spear in two hands. "Corporal Mathis, please escort my daughter, my grandson, and their companions to the guest quarters in the East Wing."

"Your Majesty? I'm a sergeant," the faerie stammered.

"No, Mathis. You *were* a sergeant. Then my grandson disarmed you without so much as breaking a sweat. Now you are a corporal." Mathis shrunk in on himself a little and waved toward the door in the back of the hall.

"And Bubba?" Oberon called as we turned to go.

"Yeah, Gramps?"

"Clothes will be laid out for you. Feel free not to bring the gun in your belt to dinner. Here we consider it rude to bring weapons to the table."

I turned away, a little surprised that he noticed. Maybe Gramps was a little more on the ball than I thought. "Where I come from, we consider it just paying attention," I said.

"What do you expect to happen at a state dinner and reception, Robbie?" Mama asked.

"Well, last time I went to dinner at one of my faerie grandparent's house, I ended up fighting for my life against a troll. Whatever Titania has planned, it can't be any worse than that, right?"

I knew the second the words passed my lips that we were all so incredibly screwed.

4

————

The "guest quarters" we moved to after our little chat with Oberon had about as much in common with a normal spare bedroom as a Motel 6 has with the Ritz. I walked into a huge parlor, with doors leading off to four bedchambers, one for Mama, one for Amy and me, one for Joe, and one for Skeeter.

Skeeter took one look in his room, picked up his pack and the clothes laid out on his bed, and promptly moved all his crap into the room with Joe. "I don't care if he's your good fairy godfather, Bubba, I don't trust that man. Hell, I don't trust anybody here in Fairyland. I feel like Malcolm X at a Klan rally already in this lily-white hellhole, and you can't tell me that there's ever been a horror movie where the black dude doesn't die first."

"*Deep Blue Sea*," I said, naming the movie that seemed to be the theme of my week.

"Samuel L. Jackson gets eaten by a damn shark, Bubba!" Skeeter shot back.

"Yeah, but LL Cool J lives," Joe pointed out.

"You ain't helping. Whose damn uncle are you, anyway?"

"Well, honestly Skeeter, with as many times as your mama said she was going to adopt Bubba, I think..." Joe let his words trail off.

Skeeter let out a *humph* that only a mid-thirties Southern black gay man can produce and stomped off to change for supper.

The last thing I heard from him before he slammed the door was "And I ain't wearing these damn pantyhose! They bind up my balls!"

I had to agree with him there, and my leg hair got all caught up in the hose, too. So I skipped the hose and the slippers for this welcoming ball, as did Joe and Skeeter. Amy and Mama decked themselves out in full faerie princess regalia, complete with fresh flowers in their hair. Amy looked spectacular out in a yellow and green gown that complemented her skin tone and blond hair, making her even more gorgeous than usual. I almost didn't notice the knife tucked into her corset when I hugged her.

"That's new," I said.

"Our last formal dining experience in this world was a little more adventurous than I expected."

"Adventurous?" I chuckled. "Baby, Thai food is adventurous. A tournament to the death against trolls and goblins is downright exciting."

"Well, I think having a cold iron blade at hand might come in handy."

Mama looked fantastic, but still somehow colder, in her rich gown of green and amber. Maybe it was her dark hair, with a few white streaks running through the black, or maybe it was something about her makeup, but even in all her Summer finery, there was a distinct touch of Winter chill about her ensemble. "Mama, you look fantastic, but I think you might have a little Mab showing," I said.

"I intend to, Robbie," Mama said with a smile. "It is important for me to show the Summer Court that I am not intimidated by their magic or their strength, even here in their center of power."

"And here I thought I was being a smartass wearing jeans instead of pantyhose to the dinner. Y'all are making all kind of political state-ments, and I'm just trying to find a place to hide my gun where Oberon won't find it."

"That's easy, Bubba," Joe said. "Give it to your mother. Oberon won't dare touch her without her permission, and he'll be honor-bound to gut anyone else who does. She could hide almost anything in those skirts, too." He wasn't wrong. Mama's dress billowed out around her legs in a mile or more of fabric hanging in folds that looked like the fronds of a weeping willow tree. I thought about it for a second, then went back into my room and grabbed the Judge.

"Here, Mama. Can you tuck this under your dress? I'd give you Bertha, but she's liable to make you walk funny."

"Thank you, Robbie. I do think that a ten-pound handgun might be a little much to strap to my leg, but this should be fine." She disappeared into her bedroom for a minute, and when she came back, the gun was nowhere to be seen. I figured it was kinda like asking how a woman fit so much crap into a purse—just way safer never to ask.

Once we were all dressed and all our weapons hidden, I opened the door and told Corporal Mathis we were ready for our next torture session. I mean, formal dinner. Same thing.

A state dinner in the Summer Court wasn't all that different from a state dinner in the Winter Court. Dozens of dishes I didn't recognize littered the table, there was no meat anywhere, no booze, and I was pretty sure everybody there wanted to murder me. So...it sucked.

I sat next to Mama at the high table, while Skeeter, Amy, and Joe were tucked away at one of the lower tables near the back of the hall. I felt pretty sure they still had a clear line of sight in case I did something stupid, or maybe just for *when* I did something stupid. The plate in front of me was loaded with a bunch of different kinds of fruit and berries, and some leaves of something that looked enough like poison ivy that I was pretty sure I didn't want to eat it. I moved food around on my plate while everybody else ate, until finally Mama leaned over to me.

"What's wrong, Robbie? Do you not like the food?"

"The salad's fine, Mama, but are they bringing out the main course anytime soon?"

"Of course, it should be out shortly. I believe the servers are simply waiting for you to put down your fork to indicate that you are ready for the meat."

"There's meat?"

"Of course there's meat. We're faeries, not elves. We eat meat, and I believe Oberon had a pig slaughtered just for this occasion."

Hearing that we were at a Fairyland pig pickin' sent my salad fork to the table with a clatter as I sat back, hoping for some serious barbecue. I wasn't disappointed, because the second the skinny waiter behind me whisked my plate away, a pair of huge hairy bastards hauled a whole damn table out and set it down on the floor in front of our table. Titania stood up and didn't even have to clink her fork on her glass to get the room to fall silent. I reckon that's what real authority looks like.

"Friends, family, and honored guests," she said, looking around the room, but conveniently never letting her gaze fall on Mama or me. "We are pleased tonight to have with us Prince Consort Oberon's daughter from a...previous alliance, Princess Ygraine. She has brought her...son and his boon companions with her into our lands on a great quest, and we wish them all the best in their endeavors. We understand that Ygraine's daughter has vanished and that she has traveled far and wide to find her and bring her home safely."

I felt Mama stiffen beside me, and I put a hand on top of hers, trying to keep her from jumping up and doing something rash. Surprised the hell out of me since I'm usually the one doing the something rash, not counseling against it, but I reckon after all these years hanging around Skeeter, I must have picked up something. She glared at me, and I squeezed her hand a little.

"This ain't the time, Mama," I said. "You know she's just trying to bait you."

Titania turned to me. "Is there something you wish to add, Bubba? I seem to recall from your last trip into our lands that you are far from shy." She smiled at me, and Summer Queen or not, her smile was downright arctic.

I stood up. "I merely wanted to make sure my mother understood what a great boon you were doing for us by lending your resources to our trip through the Summerlands to search for my sister. We have both been very distressed since we learned that she was not, in fact, being held by the mad Queen Mab of the Winter Court. Our greatest hope in discovering her whereabouts are here in the realm of Summer, so we are grateful for the assistance that you are providing."

"It seems that someone has taught this monkey to dance since the last time he dared trespass in the realm of Summer," Titania said with a grin.

"I've always been an excellent dance partner. Your cousin Chauvin could certainly speak to that, were he able to speak at all," I replied with a smile. I was doing so good, too. I kept Mama from putting her foot in her mouth, only to stick mine in all the way up to the kneecap.

Titania's grin froze on her face, and she turned to me with glittering eyes. "Yes, we recall how you handled the transgressions of *our royal cousin*. You shot him in cold blood."

"I believe I was forced to duel him to the death. I decided it wasn't in my best interest to trade punches with the little shitball, so I shot him. My blood didn't feel cold, it felt just fine. His was pretty much spilling all over the dirt, though. But hey, let's not let this pig die for nothing. Not like your jackass cousin. At least we can eat the pig, so we'll get some value out of him."

"Of course, Bubba," Titania said, and the smile she gave me made my blood run cold. This woman had a plan, and I didn't know what it was, but I could tell that it wasn't going to end well for me. She clapped her hands, and serving faeries jumped on that pig like a dog on a bone. I sat down, and the waiter-faerie put a heaping plate of pig and potatoes and other things that I mostly recognized, or at least passed for stuff that I recognized, down in front of me. I shoved the cold feeling in my gut aside and ate while I tried to figure out Titania's next move.

I didn't have to wait long. The other shoe dropped even before I got to the dessert course.

I managed to down my last swallow of sweet white wine before

Titania was back on her feet, but just barely. "Now that we all have dined, my dearest Prince Consort has a boon to bestow upon his living daughter and his most...undaunted grandson." She gestured to Oberon, who looked an awful lot like a man walking to a firing squad when he stood up and walked around in front of the table.

"As many of you know, my daughter has spent most of her life separated from me. Due to the vagaries of our life with the Winter Queen, we were separated many years ago, and I was unable to guide her in her life as a father should."

Nothing about this sounded like the way a good talk started. From the way Mama was white-knuckling her napkin, it all sounded pretty crappy to her, too.

"Therefore, I was unaware of my relationship to...Bubba on his first trip through our lands. This ignorance on my part led to many misunderstandings in our earliest meetings, and for that, my grandson, I most humbly apologize." He turned to me and bowed like he was on the damn Shakespearean stage or something. I swear to God his forehead almost bumped into the floor, he bowed so low. When he stood up, the look on his face was anything but contrite. Grandpa Oberon was *pissed*, and I couldn't tell if it was at Titania for making him do whatever he was about to do, or at me for just being born. I figured it was a little bit of column A, a little bit of Column B.

"Therefore, I would like to offer this boon to my grandson as an act of contrition. I will assist his band of...mortals in finding his missing sister and give him an opportunity to be heralded as a legend among Summer Court heroes, a truly epic adventurer, a hero whose name will never leave the lips of the citizens of Faerie from this day forth."

"Oh shit," Mama muttered.

"What?" I whispered.

"That horrible bitch Titania is going to get us all killed."

5

———————

Oberon walked around the open area in front of the wreckage of the dinner pig like an actor playing Hamlet, chewing on every piece of scenery in the place. "Dear friends, you all are no doubt aware that the Western communities and farms have been ravaged by a great threat these past many years. This horrific beast has murdered villagers, burned crops to charcoal, demolished entire towns, all without recourse. We have been far too occupied with defending our lands from the omnipresent threat of an incursion from the Winter Court to reach out a hand to do more than succor the victims after the fact, doing nothing to prevent future attacks."

He turned and pointed to me like he was Matlock and I was the guilty dude sitting in the courtroom. "But now, my people, the Great Mother herself has seen fit to provide us with an answer to our prayers. We no longer have to make the impossible choice between leaving our Eastern border exposed to the raids and horrible depredations of the Winter Fae or ignoring the suffering of our Western-most citizens. Now, with the arrival of my grandson, soon to be regarded as the greatest Monster Hunter in the history of Faerie, we have a solution to all our problems!"

I leaned over to Mama. "Your pops kinda likes to lay it on thick, doesn't he?"

"He isn't often allowed to speak in public, serving as Consort to both Mab and Titania. He makes the most of every opportunity he is granted. Unfortunately, this time we are the worse for his grandiose proclamation."

"What the hell is he talking about?" I asked.

"I don't know yet, but he looks like he's building to a big finish. I'd say we're about to find out how screwed we really are in a few seconds."

I turned my attention back to Oberon in time to hear him come to the punchline. "...swooping down from the sky, its fire blasting all in its path to cinders. But now, thanks to my grandson, we will be rid of the great dragon Xythigax once and for all!" Granddaddy Oberon waved to the crowd, who erupted in cheering and applause. They were on the verge of breaking out into a roaring chorus of "Bub-ba, Bub-ba," when a shrill voice cut through the din.

"Are y'all out of your goddamn mind?!?" Silence crashed down like throwing a switch, and every head in the room turned to stare at the speaker. For his part, Skeeter seemed not a bit concerned that he had the undivided attention of every faerie from the guards to the queen herself. He stood up, his chair screeching across the stone, and stomped up to Oberon.

He came face to chest with the towering Prince Consort, who didn't look any too happy at the interruption. Honestly, Granddaddy Oberon was looking at Skeeter the way Skeeter usually looks at me, kinda like he'd slap the taste out of his mouth if he thought it would do any good. "May I help you, human?"

"Skeeter."

"Excuse me?"

"My name is Skeeter, and I am your grandson's technical assistant and best friend. And I am one of the people you just enlisted to kill a damn dragon, which we are *not* going to do. What we are going to do is find Bubba's sister, make sure she's safe, and then get the hell out of your kingdom and never come back. We're not going to fight any tournaments, we're not going back to any dungeons, we're not fighting any dragons, and nobody is marrying anybody they don't want to marry. Is that absolutely damn clear?"

"What is clear, little human, is that my grandson has taste in friends that rivals his taste in clothing, which is to say deplorable. You overreach in spectacular fashion, little man, and—"

"If you call me little anything one more time, I'm gonna slap the points off your damn ears. Now you might think you know something about humans, but let me explain to you the species known as *Homo Bitchus*, which is to say a gay man that has had enough of your shit. Now I am going to go sit down at my table, knock back the last of the wine, then I'm going to snap my fingers at one of your overdressed waiters until he brings me even more wine, and maybe some dessert. And you are going to figure out some better way to apologize to your grandson than sending him, and more importantly me, off to fight a damn dragon."

I managed to stop myself from standing up and cheering Skeeter on, and I didn't even laugh at the look on Oberon's face, which was somewhere between somebody who just saw his parents having sex and a guy who got hit in the nuts with a fastball. Skeeter turned and started to walk off, but Oberon reached out and clapped a hand on his shoulder, effectively stopping him in his tracks.

"I don't believe I gave you leave to sit," Oberon said, and his voice was deadly calm. He turned Skeeter around, then shifted his grip to the front of his tunic and pulled him back until my buddy was only a few inches away from Oberon's chest. The tall faerie then bent at the knees, placed his hand in the general vicinity of Skeeter's belt buckle, and straightened up. Skeeter's feet rose up off the floor a couple of inches, then more as Oberon lifted him until they were face to face.

"Now, *little human*, let me be very clear in what I am saying to you. Though your friend is my grandson, I was completely unaware of his very existence until a very short time ago. I remained unaware of his relationship to me until I saw his mother in our Court several days ago. So if you think being my grandson's friend gives you any hold on my goodwill, you should think again. I am the Prince Consort, not the king, so you need not refer to me as Majesty. But you *will* speak to me with a civil tongue in your head, or I will rip out your uncivil one and wear it around my neck on a golden chain."

He dropped Skeeter, then leaned down so they stayed face to face. "My grandson *will* face the dragon Xythigax, and if you choose to accompany him in that quest, you may. He may die, or he may vanquish the beast. Either outcome is equally palatable to me. Do we understand each other?"

"I understand one damn thing, Grandpa," I said, looking at him over the barrel of my Judge revolver. "I understand that a regular bullet won't kill you, but if you don't step the hell away from my best friend right now, we're going to find out how cold iron shot feels sprayed all over your face."

"You dare bring a mortal weapon into my presence?" Titania asked from her dais.

"I'm a daring sonofabitch, sweetheart. Now please shut the hell up. You make me nervous, and I don't think this is a time anybody wants me getting twitchy." I never took my eyes off Oberon. This was a gamble, but I knew he was a showman and liked the brazen shit I pulled last time I was in Fairyland. Maybe if I got a little lucky, I could get out of this without anybody I liked ending up dead.

Oberon turned to glare at me, moving slowly and keeping both hands visible. He'd seen what my guns can do, and he knew I was a pretty good shot. I was counting on him not knowing that the accuracy on a .410 shotgun shell fired from a pistol at fifty feet left something to be desired. The Judge is a great little gun, but it's a close quarters gun, to be damn sure. My fairy grandfather stood up and took one big step back from Skeeter, who moved around to stand beside Joe. All my people were on their feet now, with their hands on whatever weapons they had tucked away in their clothes or managed to scrounge from the dinner table.

"What do you want, grandson?" Oberon asked.

"I just wanted to convince you not to turn Skeeter into a toad, or his namesake, or something," I said, lowering the weapon. "Y'all want a dragon killed, I'll kill a dragon. Y'all want somebody to fight a monster? Hell, that's my whole gig. All you gotta do is ask, Pops. But don't threaten my friends. It makes me grumpy."

"Well, we certainly wouldn't want that, would we?" Titania asked. "Or am I still not allowed to speak in *my own hall*?" The temperature in the room rose with her words, and I remembered that while Mab might control the Winter, Titania's power over Summer and all its aspects would be at least as absolute. She could make things a little hot for me if she wanted to.

"My sincerest apologies, Your Majesty," Mama said from right beside me. "My son is not accustomed to court and its code of conduct."

"I would say that he is almost unaccustomed to the code of conduct of beasts, but I would fear I was insulting the beasts." The Summer Queen glared at me.

I just kept my mouth shut. I drew down on her man in the middle of her castle. I had no moral high ground.

"While that is often true, he means well. Mostly." Mama gave me a dirty look, and I tried my best to look ashamed of myself. I probably sucked at it, especially since I wasn't the least bit ashamed of myself.

"I have been insulted in my own home, Daughter of Mab. How will Winter make reparations for this affront?" Titania folded her slender arms across her not-so-slender chest and looked down her nose at Mama.

Mama opened her mouth, but I decided to stick my foot in mine instead. "How about I kill your damn dragon, like I just said I would. For shit's sake, y'all, can we just get to dessert already? If I'm going out tomorrow to hunt a dragon and probably get turned into barbecued Bubba bites, I'd at least like to finish up with a nice piece of cheesecake or something."

Mama whirled around, her eyes huge. Titania shot me a look that would have terrified a smarter man, and Amy slapped me on the arm in that way that women hit you when they can't believe you did the same stupid thing you've done every single day since they met you. With every eye on me, I stood there, shrugged, and said, "What? I got a sweet tooth."

"Guards!" Titania had evidently reached the saturation point on my bullshit because with a wave of her hand, we were rounded up and led out of the ballroom without even getting a chance to look at the dessert. I had to look on the bright side, though. At least they weren't taking us back to the dungeon.

6

The next morning, armed guards rousted me from my bed
with the dawn. I kinda figured there would be something
like that coming, so I slept in my travel clothes and
managed to restrain myself from beating all their asses. Okay, I beat
one of their asses, but I really just punched him a couple of times and
maybe stepped on his nuts when I walked over him to get my
shoulder holster with Bertha. Everybody was pretty much in the
same state of readiness, so five minutes after they came beating on
the door, we were standing in the courtyard surrounded by horses
and faerie knights with swords, pikes, and crossbows.

I think they decided they wanted me to leave.

We got into the saddles, Mama having talked one of the guards
into grabbing us a basket of bread and meats from the kitchen, and
were just about to roll out when Oberon made his grand entrance.
We were already starting to sweat a little in the warm morning sun, a
helluva contrast from Mab's Court, and Oberon came swooping down
a grand staircase on the outside of the battlements like he'd been
overseeing the keep's defenses or something stupid like that. I was
about ninety percent sure he'd just been waiting on us all to get on
our horses so there was no way we could miss seeing him.

"Ah, my dear grandson and soon to be national hero! I am so pleased that I was able to catch you before you embarked on your perilous journey."

"I'm pretty sure I liked you better when you were talking in a stupid accent and driving a cart," I grumbled.

"I have gifts that will aid you in your journey," Oberon said, passing a medallion on a leather cord up to me. I took it, turning it over in my hands. "It is a magical compass that will lead you to the dragon's lair."

"Just what I always wanted," I said.

"I thought you always wanted a beer fountain in your living room and a stripper pole in the bedroom," Skeeter chimed in from behind me.

"Well, yeah, I want that, too."

"You've got a lot better chance with the beer fountain," Amy said, surprising no one.

Oberon handed a shield to Amy. "This will protect you and any nearby from a dragon's breath. It is resistant to fire, frost, lightning, acid, and noxious gases."

"You're gonna want to keep that handy," Skeeter said. "There's sausage in the basket, and you know how it makes Bubba fart."

"I seem to recall somebody else getting a little gassy at our last stop in Fairyland," I shot back, looking at Joe. The priest had the good grace to look embarrassed, but I still hadn't forgiven him for farting in my face at Mab's Court. He damn near made my beard fall out.

"This will transport you back to this keep, but only once it is immersed in dragon's blood to activate it," Oberon said, handing a clear crystal on a gold chain to Mama. "The crystal will glow red when it has been exposed to enough dragon blood. Then just say my name three times, and you will return to us."

"I kinda wish we could get one of those for my car keys. I always lose those damn things," Amy said with a smirk.

"Do you people take nothing seriously?" Oberon finally snapped, whirling around and glaring at all of us. "I am trying to grant you boons that will help you in this quest, and possibly keep you alive, and all you do is make jokes! Is life always like this with you people?"

Skeeter glared at him. "Don't even start 'you people-ing' me. I will get all kinds of ethnic on your pointy-eared ass."

Oberon looked confused. I leaned over to Skeeter and, in a loud whisper, said, "I think he means humans."

"Oh. That makes sense, I reckon." He waved a finger at the faerie prince. "But the point still stands. Humans are people, too, dammit."

"I swear to God, Skeeter, if you say Human Lives Matter, I am going to pound you into the ground like a tent stake," I said.

"Well, they do."

"Yes, they do. Also not the point."

Oberon cleared his throat. I turned away from Skeeter to look at my irritated fairy grandfather. "Oh, you ain't done? Skeeter and I was just amusing ourselves while you finished up."

Pops handed spears to Skeeter and Joe. "These spearheads are made of enchanted silver and will pierce the dragon's hide, hopefully from a safe distance."

Joe looked at Skeeter, then laughed a little. "If I make one spear-chucker joke, you're going to stab me, aren't you?"

"Nah, you're family," Skeeter replied, then whirled on him. "Of course I'm gonna stab you, cracker! Uncle or not, you right here carrying a damn spear next to me, so who's the spear-chucker now?"

"Joe," I said firmly. Everybody turned to stare at me. "What? Joe threw javelin in track when he went to high school. He won the State Championship! Skeeter ain't never thrown nothing but shade in his damn life."

My best friend shot me a dirty look, but he knew it was true. After a resigned shake of the head from Oberon, we loaded into a couple of wagons and were on our way. Amy rode point on a white horse with a silver mane, I took the lead wagon with Mama, and Skeeter and Joe took up the rear in a second wagon. A quick look through the cargo showed that regardless of whether or not she actually wanted us to return, Titania outfitted us well for a journey. There was plenty of food, bedrolls, and a couple bows with several arrows. I didn't bother telling anybody there that I was pretty sure our whole party flunked archery in summer camp. Besides, we had guns.

We rode out of the gates of the keep, then down the main thoroughfare of the city to the southern gate. A pair of guardsmen escorted us to the outer walls of the capital, then turned around and went back. We rode for an hour southward, then I pulled the wagon off to the side of the road and called Amy to circle back to us.

"What's up, Bubba?" she asked as I got down from the wagon.

"Well," I said. "Anybody got a plan to find my sister and get the hell out of Fairyland?"

"Aren't we hunting a dragon?" Amy asked.

"Not if we don't have to," I replied. "Now I don't know anything about dragons except what I learned from *Skyrim* and Anne McCaffrey novels, but those all told me they're big mean sonsabitches that breathe fire and eat people. Neither of those are things that make me want to go screwing with them. What about you?"

"Me neither," she said. "But if Oberon has your sister, he's not going to let her go until we kill the dragon, is he?"

"Nitalia was not in that palace," Mama said.

Every head turned to her. "How can you be so sure?" Joe asked.

"I cast a spell the first night we were in the dungeon. She was in Tisa'ron, but not for some time."

"Don't you think that goes on the list of shit we ought to know?" I asked.

"I only learned this after we were imprisoned in the dungeon. As soon as we got out of the dungeon, you got us into an almost certainly fatal quest. It's not like I've had an abundance of time, Robbie."

She might have been absent for a couple decades, but she was still my mama, and she still knew how to put me right in my damn place. I just nodded.

"Well, Mrs. B., do you have any idea where your daughter might be?" Skeeter asked.

"I do not, but if I am given a little time, I can likely repurpose Robbie's dragon-finding compass to locate Nitalia. No doubt that was my father's intent when he gave it to us."

"You got a lot of faith in a dude who sent us on a quest that will probably kill us," I said.

"Oberon's quest will only pose a threat to us if we undertake it. If we ignore it completely and continue on our true mission to find my daughter, then all in the Summer Court will merely assume we are dead."

"Faeries are sneaky," Amy said. "I like it."

"You would, Miss Black Helicopter," I grumbled.

"You're just mad you won't get to fight a dragon," Amy said. She wasn't wrong. She turned to Mama. "What do you need to cast the spell?"

"Usually I would need something that belonged to the person I am trying to track, but since we have two relatives here, a small sample of blood from myself and Robbie should allow me to craft the spell. Then I will need a few plants that should be easy to acquire in these woods, a scrap of moss, and a flat circle to cast in."

"Wait a second, can we back up to the part where you need my bloo—OW!" I yelped and jerked my arm away from Amy, who stood next to me with her dagger out.

She held the blade out to Mama, a few drops of my blood on the tip. "Will this be enough, or should I stick him again?"

Mama grinned and took the blade, drawing it across the back of her forearm, mingling our blood on it. "This should be sufficient. Thank you, dear. Now, Robbie, will you come with me into the woods?"

"Didn't a whole bunch of bad musical theatre come out of those three words?" I asked, following her off the path. I turned back to the others. "Y'all try to set up some defenses and don't get dead before we come back." Joe snapped off a sarcastic salute, Amy ignored me, and Skeeter shot me the bird. About the response I expected. I followed Mama through the underbrush, digging a bandana out of my pocket to tie around my bleeding forearm.

We walked for a hundred yards or so, until the road was way out of sight, then Mama stopped in a little clearing surrounded by massive oak trees. She walked around the clearing three times clockwise, then three times counterclockwise, then looked up at the sky with her eyes closed. She took a deep breath, held her hands straight out from her sides, and just stood there, meditating or praying, I reckon. I got bored after a few seconds and sat down on the ground with my back to a tree. The Judge was digging into my back, so I pulled the holstered pistol out from the waistband of my jeans and put it on the ground beside me. Mama stood stock-still for a long time, long enough for me to wonder how she was holding her arms out like that for so long.

After what felt like half an hour, but was probably less than five minutes, she let out a deep breath and relaxed. She looked over at me, and her eyes looked different. Where before they had been ice blue, now they were a brilliant green with bright flecks of gold that I could see from ten feet away. "That's better," she said, and I noticed that her hair didn't look the same, either. When we left the road, white streaks shot through her dark hair, proclaiming loudly both her age and her membership in the Winter Court. Now those same white streaks were blond and red, and the jet-black hair was more a dark auburn.

"Um, Mama?" I said, patting the ground next to me for the butt of my gun.

"Yes, dear?" she asked, turning to me with a gentle smile. Her eyes flashed gold, and I felt a wave of comfort wash over me. What was I worried about? This was my mama, who loved me more than anything. My mama, who would never hurt me— I gave my head a hard shake and scooted away from her on my butt.

"What the hell is going on, Mama? Why are your eyes funny?"

"Oh, that? I'm sorry, Robbie." She shook her head, and the glow in her eyes faded, along with the warm fuzzy feeling I had. It was good to be back to my grumpy-ass self. "I had to delve deeply into the Summer magic to be able to cast here. As a child of the Prince Consort and the Queen of Winter, the land will allow me to work magic in either realm, but while I am within one kingdom's borders, I must adhere to its rules and whims. Summer magic wants to be warm and comforting, promoting light and life and warmth. Thus, the minor changes in my appearance while I am here. I assure you, I will return to my normal appearance when we return to the mundane world."

"Yeah, but what about me feeling so...strange?" I asked.

"You are of my blood, even if the magic was never brought to life within you. The land recognized you and wanted you to feel good."

"Why?" I asked.

"I'm sorry?" She tilted her head to the side, like a dog that caught the car it was chasing and now had no idea what to do with it.

"Why did Fairyland give a shit if I was happy?"

"Because if you're happy, I'll be more likely to stay. The lands of Winter and Summer are as much in contest as their rulers, and if Summer thought it could persuade me to stay by making you happy, it would certainly attempt to do that."

A wave of bitterness roiled up from my gut, and I scowled down at the dirt. "Shows what this stupid Fairyland knows. I couldn't keep you anywhere, no matter how I felt about it."

I heard the sharp gasp and looked up. The hurt on her face looked like I'd slapped her, and I thought I saw tears welling up in her eyes. I couldn't make myself care. Twenty years might have passed, and it might have been a life or death situation for her, but I still hadn't managed to forgive her for running out on me and Jason way back then. I sat back down, positioning my pistol within easy arm's reach. "You gonna cast your spell, or do I have to get stabbed again?"

Her eyes flashed, but she dipped her head as if to say *I deserved that.*

I didn't disagree.

"I'll begin. Please remain alert. This is a relatively minor working, but I am tampering with a spell laid on the gem by the Summer Queen herself. I would not put it past Titania to have taken precautions against my tampering."

"What does that mean?" I asked, sitting up straighter.

"Basically, if anything horrible runs into the clearing...kill it."

7

———————

Mama used her knife to carve a rough circle into the dirt, then reached into a pouch on her belt and sprinkled something I couldn't really see into the air. She started muttering in a language I couldn't understand, and my interest in spells went from minimal to zero in a big hurry. That left me on the outside of a magical casting circle, watching a woman I barely knew cast a spell I didn't understand, all the while stuck in a forest in a magical dimension where just about everything wanted to kill me. All in the hopes of finding a sister that I'd never laid eyes on.

And there was a dragon out there somewhere.

My life is weird enough on a good day, but this shit took the absolute cake. I leaned back against a tree and closed my eyes, thinking back on happier days, like the last time I went fishing.

Never mind, that got interrupted by Skeeter calling about a case.

Then there was the time we went out in Nashville and we all got drunk.

Skip that one. We ended up going to damn Alabama. There was a demon in that mess.

Then there was...nope. Well, maybe...nope. What about...not a chance.

After a few minutes of digging around in my memories looking for something good to dwell on so I wouldn't think so much about being stuck in Fairyland with a mother I hadn't really forgiven for abandoning me twenty years ago and coming up empty, I decided I needed to do some walking around. I stood up, my knees popping like a .22, and slipped the Judge back into the small of my back. I looked over to Mama, but she was kneeling on the ground, sitting back on her heels, with her face turned up to the sky. I thought about calling out to her, but her eyes were closed and there was a soft golden glow around her, so I figured she was fine. Anyway, I couldn't see anything around us, so she oughta be fine while I stretched my legs for a minute. Maybe I'd even find something worth eating while I was out there. There was some jerky in the provisions Mama got us from Oberon's place, but fresh beats dried any day of the week.

It was a really pretty forest, all thick old-growth oaks and maple, with the occasional spruce and pine mixed in with the hardwoods. Moss carpeted the ground, muffling my steps and making it a little tough to tell where I'd been. I tried to keep Mama in sight while I wandered, but it didn't take long for me to lose sight of her between the trees. I was pretty confident that I could find her, even in an unfamiliar forest. Besides, if I got into any real trouble, Bertha could shout loud enough for the gang to find me anywhere.

"Hey," I said a while later. "What's that?" Nobody answered, of course, but it didn't make it any less a good question. Something blinked between the trees, like a lantern. That's when I noticed that it was dark all of a sudden. *Damn magical forests. It was just after lunch when I left Mama, and I ain't been walking more than half an hour.* "Mama? Is that you?" I called in the direction of the lantern. I reckoned she knew what was going on with it getting dark so fast, so I oughta head over to where she was. Hell, she might have even come looking for me. She still wasn't going to win any Mother of the Year awards, but with Mab as an example, it ain't like she had much to learn from.

I walked toward the lantern, but it ducked behind a tree, and I lost it. I caught sight of it a minute later, even deeper in the forest.

"Hey, Mama! I'm back here!" I hollered, but the light just kept moving away from me. "Alright, dammit, I'm sorry. I was a dick. Now slow down a little bit and let me catch up." The lantern paused, then moved again, but slower this time. *Okay, well, she might still be pissed, but at least she's gonna let me catch up before we bust out of the woods and the whole crew sees us fighting.*

Except I didn't catch up. I lost sight of her for just a second, then came around a tree, and there was her damn lantern, bobbing along in the now full-on dark, maybe fifty yards away. I couldn't see nothing of her but her lantern light, but I just put my head down and stumbled and bumbled my way through the underbrush after her. Branches and vines that seemed to almost bend out of my way a little while earlier in the light of day now reached out to trip me, snag my shirt and shoulder holster, or tangle in my braided hair as I shoved my way after Mama and her bobbing, weaving, irritating damn lantern.

Finally, after what felt like an hour fighting through the foliage, I burst out onto what I expected to be the side of the road where our wagons and my friends waited for us. Except I wasn't anywhere like that. Nowhere like that at all.

No, I was in the middle of a ring of glowing toadstools at least twenty feet across, with a carpet of green moss underfoot. The clearing was immaculate, without even a branch or a sprig of grass to be seen. There was just a smooth carpet of moss, me, a floating ball of yellow light, and one of the most gorgeous women I'd ever seen.

"Welcome," she said, and her voice sounded like a symphony, the softest lover's whisper, and a dinner bell all rolled into one. She was tall, almost as tall as me, with long arms, long legs, and long blond hair tinged with green. I couldn't tell if her hair was really green, or if that was something coming off the mushrooms.

"Uh...hi," I said with a stupid little wave like I was some teenage boy looking at his first hot girl, instead of a grown-ass man.

"I am Vlanriel, and these are my woods."

"I'm Bubba. I'm just passing through."

"Are you?"

"Well, yeah, I wasn't planning on sticking around. We've got to..." All of a sudden, I couldn't remember what I was supposed to be in such a hurry to do, or who I was supposed to be doing it with. It couldn't be all that important, could it?

"Who is we, Bubba?" she purred into my ear. When did she get that close to me? I never even saw her move. And how come she was holding my shoulder holster? "What is this?" she asked, turning the pistol over in her hands.

"That's Bertha," I said. "She's one badass Israeli fifty-caliber bitch, and if she decides to holler, it's a bad day for everybody." I puffed out my chest. That had to impress her, right? I mean, fifty caliber is a big...um...a big something, anyway.

"Well, we don't want any bad days, do we, Bubba?" She breathed into my other ear, and all the hair on my arms stood up at once. That's a *lot* of hair.

"No, I reckon we don't want bad days." I giggled when I said it. From somewhere deep in the back of my head, I heard a howl of righteous anger at the mere concept of me giggling, but it happened. God help us all, it happened.

"Good, then we'll just send your badass Israeli bitch on her way, won't we?" She flung Bertha and her shoulder holster off into the trees. Her other arm snaked around my waist, then stopped when she found the Judge. "What's this, Bubba?"

Her voice was sad, kinda disappointed, and I felt just awful for making her feel bad. I didn't want her to be disappointed, so I just reached around behind my back and flung that nasty old pistol off into the woods. Who needs a gun anyway? As long as I was with Vlanriel, everything would be fine, right?

"That's good, Bubba, that's very good. Whatever that thing was, it felt dirty. It felt dirty, and cold, and hurtful. We don't need anything like that here, do we?"

"No, we don't need nothing like that," I agreed.

"Are you tired, Bubba?" I hadn't been, not too bad, but as soon as she asked, I did feel a heaviness in my legs.

"Yeah, I kinda am."

"You look tired. Why don't you come over here and lie down?" She led me to the center of the ring of toadstools, to right where the little glowing ball floated, and gestured for me to lay down on the carpet of moss.

I looked at the orb of yellow light. "Hey," I said to it, barely recognizing my own voice for the dreamy quality. "You ain't a lantern. You ain't Mama at all."

"Mama?" Vlanriel asked, her voice a lot less dreamy and sweet all of a sudden. "You aren't here alone?"

"Nah," I said, waving a hand at the floating ball of light. "Mama and me came out into the woods so she could cast a spell to find my sister. I saw your little glowing buddy here and thought it was her. But it ain't. Hey little buddy," I said, reaching out to try and pet the thing, but my hand passed right through it. My fingers tingled, like when I put my tongue on a nine-volt battery, but I couldn't pet the thing.

"Who is your mother, Bubba?" Vlanriel was real concerned about Mama all of a sudden, and when I turned to look at her, she wasn't smiling at all.

"Well, she's Mama," I said. "You know, Princess Ygraine, daughter of Oberon and Queen Mab, so step-daughter of Titania, I reckon."

"Are you saying that you...*you* are Titania's grandson?" She floated back from me, and that was the first time I noticed how her feet never touched the ground. That explained how she was able to look right in my face. Most of the folks I'd run into in Fairyland were short, but Vlanriel was right there at my eye level. Except now she floated away and looked all worried.

"Well, I reckon I'm her step-grandson, if we wanted to get all technical. But I don't think she likes me very much. Not as much as Mab does, anyhow."

"M-m-*Mab*? The Queen of Winter?"

"Yeah, but I call her Granny. Only if she ain't around to hear me though. I don't think she likes it much."

"You are the grandchild of both houses of the Fae?" She was flitting around the clearing now like a pinball on cocaine, and her little glowy ball was doing the same thing. I was starting to think they didn't like Granny Mab or Oberon, but that was silly. Vlanriel was a nice person. I reckoned she liked everybody.

"We have to flee," she said to the glow-ball.

"Where we going?" I asked. "I got a couple wagons back at the road with the rest of the gang. It'll be kinda crowded, but I'm sure we can make room for you. And your little glow-buddy can just float along with us. Ain't that right, Lightnin'? I'm gonna call you Lightnin', on account of you look just like a firefly's butt, and we call fireflies lightning bugs. But I don't mean to say you look like a butt, that ain't nice. I just mean that you light up just like a firefly's butt does, so I oughta call you Lightnin'."

"Shut up, you imbecile!" Vlanriel snapped, wheeling on me with her eyes aflame. She was a lot less pretty than she was a few minutes ago. "*We* are leaving. *You* are staying, right here in this mushroom ring, where you won't be able to tell Mab *or* Titania that I've been hunting in the Summer Forest again. Neither one of them would like that."

"No, they wouldn't, Vlanriel. They banished you to the Lands Without Season many years ago. They would be very displeased to hear of your return." I turned, and Mama stood just on the other side of the ring of toadstools. Her hands were glowing with amber light, and her hair kinda floated all around her head, yellow and red light crackling on the ends. She didn't look happy to see Vlanriel.

"Hey Mama!" I waved and shouted. "This is my new friend Vlanriel, and her little buddy Lightnin'. We're going on a trip, but I don't know where."

"No, Robbie, I don't think so." Mama waved her hand, and an orb of mixed green and amber light flew out from her fingers to smack into my face. Vlanriel flew to the center of the circle, but not before some of Mama's magic splashed all over her.

As the magic exploded around me, everything changed. The clearing didn't look beautiful anymore; it looked dead. All the trees were gnarled and twisted, and the ground was nothing but churned earth. The toadstools were black and green-speckled things, huge, horrible fungi that pulsed with a wicked green light. And Vlanriel? Well, let's just say that she was what ugly witch stories sprang from, and the stories didn't do her level of ugly justice.

I looked at her, then looked over at Mama standing outside the ring of toadstools. "My guns are all outside the circle, ain't they?"

"Yes, they are, Robbie."

"And you can't do much more than blow up a glamour when you're outside the circle and we're inside, can you?"

"No, that is about the limit of my abilities."

"Well then, I reckon we're going old-school," I said. I reached over my shoulder and drew Great-Grandpappy Beauregard's sword from its scabbard with a steely *hiss*.

"Vlanriel," I said, giving her one last chance to run like hell. "You can drop this circle right now, and I won't chop you into sushi."

"Or I can destroy Mab's daughter, trap you in the mushroom ring for all time, and no one will ever learn of my transgressions."

"Yeah, I figured you'd say something like that." I put both hands on the hilt of my sword, and charged.

It was on.

8

———

I ran at the hunched, twisted image of what seconds before was possibly the most beautiful woman I'd ever seen. Vlanriel dove to one side, and I slammed into the boundary of the circle at full speed. Rather than bursting through the magical barrier in a blaze of glory, like happened in the action movie in my head, I slammed into something that felt like a cross between a cinderblock wall and an electric fence. I smacked into the circle, and everything locked up. I twitched in some kind of super-sized St. Vitus Dance while the magic coursed through my body. I might have drooled just a tiny bit.

After several excruciating seconds, I forced enough strength into my arms to peel myself off the barrier and slump to the ground. Lightnin', no longer looking like a firefly but in his full will-o'-the-wisp visage, leaned over me. "Did that hurt?" the disembodied head asked. "It really looked like it hurt."

I struggled to my feet and glared at the floating skull, glowing with a sickly green light. He looked like a cross between Ghost Rider and one of those fish you see pictures of at the bottom of the ocean. Lightnin' was now just a head floating over an emaciated body wrapped in a grave shroud. I liked him a lot better when he looked like a firefly's ass.

He reached out a hand to steady me, but Mama yelled, "Don't let it touch you!"

I dodged to the left, not exactly smoothly, but just enough not to let the wisp get his fingers on me. "Why not?" I hollered.

"Wisps lure unsuspecting travelers deep into the woods and drain their life essence. If it touches you, it can siphon your life force!"

"Shit," I muttered. "Like a vampire."

"Without the biting, but yes."

"I hate vampires," I said, bringing my sword up. The tip wobbled thanks to the aftershocks running down all my muscles. The aftershocks of that circle felt a lot like the time I peed on an electric fence back in ninth grade. I had weird boners for a month after that, just popping up out of nowhere. Or maybe that was just from being fourteen. Hard to tell.

"I'm not a vampire, Bubba," the wisp said, sliding forward. I couldn't get a good handle on how it was moving. Its feet didn't really touch the ground, and I started to wonder if its body was just for show. Everything I'd ever read about will-o'-the-wisps said they were just disembodied lights, but this one seemed real attached to his body. I slashed with my sword, and it ducked backward, just like a real boy. I advanced on the thing, slashing with the blade right around the creature's middle.

"Come on, Bubba," it whined, ducking and dodging and slip-sliding backward every time I took a shot. "I don't want to hurt you. You're my friend, remember? That's why I brought you out here into this awesome wilderness, because that's what friends do. They take friends to cool places."

"So they can suck their life out of them and leave them stranded in a magic circle? I don't think so. You can only run so far, Lightnin'. You're stuck in here with me."

"And with me," Vlanriel snarled, coming at me from my left side. She would have buried her little dagger into my side if I hadn't been watching out for her. But I used to play hide and seek with my brother Jason, who was a sneaky bastard even before he got turned into an evil werewolf and tried to take over the world. So Vlanriel didn't have a single chance of sneaking up on me. I just stuck out my fist, and she obligingly ran her face into it. Then she fell down into a heap of ill-fitting, dirty rags with a bloodied nose.

With the hag out of the fray for a few seconds, I turned all my attention to Lightnin'. "What the hell are you doing with that chick, anyway? Can't you get your fill of souls or whatever on your own?"

"I was banished to the Lands Without Season, trapped with no ready food supply. Titania and Mab conspired to starve me. When Vlanriel offered me the opportunity to come back here and feast, I took it."

"How did you get back?" Mama asked from outside the circle. "A banishment decree is usually more difficult to circumvent, particularly if levied by both monarchs."

"Let me live and I'll tell you," the wisp said, diving to the ground to avoid my blade.

"Deal," Mama said.

"Hey!" I protested. "I'm the one doing the killing or not killing here. I get to decide if I'm going to perforate this assclown. And I'm still leaning toward perforating." The assclown in question was backed up almost to the edge of the circle, its orb-head swinging from side to side as it looked for somewhere to run. I had it pretty well hemmed in and was just about ready to skewer me some lightning bug when Mama's next words stopped me cold.

"Please, Robbie. I need him."

Well, shit. Even as pissed as I still was at her, she was still my mama. I couldn't very well just say no. But I didn't want to say yes, either. "Fine. I won't kill him until he gives us everything he knows. But if it's bullshit, I'm going to split his nonexistent head with this sword and use his glowing blood to make flashlights."

"I don't have blood," the orb said.

"I can make light any time, Bubba. We don't need flashlights," Mama chimed in.

"I was just making a poetic-type threat, like you're supposed to do in a damn sword fight. I mean, shit, ain't neither one of y'all seen *A Knight's Tale*? It's all about the patter. Chaucer taught us that!"

"What's a Chaucer?" Lightnin' asked.

"I was trapped in Faerie for twenty years, Robbie. I missed a lot. Apparently, *A Knight's Tale* was on the list."

Well, double shit. I sheathed my blade. "Well, we gotta put that shit on the 'Must Watch' list. We can make it a whole family thing. Amy loves that movie." *Heh heh. Amy hates that movie, but it'll be hilarious anyway.*

"Does this mean you aren't going to kill me?" the wisp asked.

"As long as your information doesn't suck, and you don't attack me, I won't kill you," I said.

"Good," the wisp replied. "We were able to get back into the Summerlands with—" The orb exploded, showering me with yellow luminescent glitter. It reminded me of the time I got drunk on cheap tequila and ended up at Glow Jell-O Wrestling Night at Boob-a-palooza in Tampa. That shit took weeks to wear off. I think parts of my beard still glow in the dark.

"Silence is golden," Vlanriel said, her hands pulsing with an ominous red light.

"Well, now *everything* is golden, since you just painted the inside of the circle with will-o'-the-wisp guts!" I hollered, trying to wipe Lightnin' out of my eyes.

"Don't worry, half-breed. Soon everything will be red. That's the color you humans bleed, isn't it?" She let fly a bolt of crimson light, and I dove to one side as it scorched the earth I stood on. I belly-flopped onto the turf, skidding a little and getting grass buried in places I really didn't want grass.

"Ow, shit!" I hollered, scrambling to my feet and drawing my sword.

Vlanriel didn't say a word, just flung another bolt of red lightning at me almost before I had my blade out. But then something weird happened. Yeah, something weirder than me standing in the middle of a mushroom ring in Fairyland fighting a wicked witch while covered in will-o'-the-wisp guts. My bar for "weird" is pretty high, after all.

As the bolt of power streaked right toward Bubba Jr., I swung Great-Grandpappy Beauregard's sword down to block, hoping to deflect the power enough to keep me from getting completely nut-cut by the witch's magic. But it didn't deflect anything; it *absorbed* it. The blade glowed crimson for a second, I felt the hilt get warm, and then it was just like nothing ever happened.

I'm not sure who was the most surprised between Vlanriel, me, and Mama, but I was sure as hell the one best suited to take advantage of it. Vlanriel stared down at her fingers like they'd malfunctioned or something, and I let out my very best barbaric yawp and charged her. This time I completely intended to run smack into the boundary of her magical circle, but I wanted to have her between me and it when I did.

So I buried my shoulder in her gut, right under the ribs, and I just kept on trucking. I lifted up a hair, and the psychotic witch's feet popped up off the ground. Her added weight was less than carrying a passed-out Skeeter, and I've done that more times than I can count. I picked up speed, hitting maximum Bubba velocity just before I ran into the circle's walls, thinking I'd smear her all over the magical barricade like a roach on a bathroom tile.

Except it didn't work anything like that. When I rammed Vlanriel into the circle, it *popped* out of existence without so much as a token resistance. One second it was there, glowing faintly in my peripheral vision, then the next second, it blew up like a piece of Bubble Yum stretched past its outer limits. I stomped on a couple of the toadstools as I went over but didn't break stride. I veered to the left a little and drew a bead on my new target. Half a dozen steps later, I rammed the wicked witch's spine into the trunk of a giant oak tree so hard I knocked down a shitload of leaves, three dozen acorns, and one pissed-off squirrel.

Vlanriel's ribcage made noises like a bowl of Rice Krispies, and she screamed like a Clemson sorority girl finding out the keg was empty. My head slammed into the trunk of the tree, too, and I flopped back onto the turf, my bell well and truly rung. I thought for a second about getting up and trying to finish the fight, but I rolled over and puked instead. Concussions suck.

I dragged my dizzy ass over to lean up against another tree, and through the stars and tweety birds filling my vision, I saw Mama coming across the clearing like a lion after a wounded gazelle. Her hands glowed yellow, and the same golden light streaked from her eyes. Her strides were measured and slow, and she never took her eyes off the fallen Vlanriel. The broken witch writhed on the carpet of moss, trying to drag herself into the cover of the forest, but Mama would not be denied.

My mother held out one hand, wiggled her fingers at the fleeing witch. A vine split the moss and twined itself around Vlanriel's foot, holding her fast. When the witch rolled over to try and fight her way free, Mama gestured again, and another vine popped out of the ground and held her other leg fast. "Don't leave so soon, Vlanriel. We're just getting started." We might have been in the Summer Court, but Mama's voice sure had one hell of a chill to it.

Vlanriel looked up at Mama's face, and she started to scream, then cry, then beg, alternating between English and two or three other languages that I didn't recognize. Mama just scowled at her and brought her other hand up. A few curt gestures, and vines snaked out of the ground and pulled the shrieking witch down flat on her back. Vlanriel struggled, but no amount of thrashing would free her from the plants Mama called to do her bidding. A few more steps, and Mama stood over the fallen woman. I couldn't see her face anymore, but her hair was floating in the air like in the movies when somebody does a shit-ton of magic, and there were gold and green and orange sparks flitting around her head. What-ever Mama had planned for her fallen foe, it wasn't going to be nice.

"Vlanriel, witch of the bogs, you were banished to the Lands Without Season, never to return to the Winter or Summer Courts. As a child of both Courts, I hereby find you guilty of breaking your banishment. There is only one punishment for this crime, not to mention the crime of attempting to harm one of royal blood. For those crimes, I sentence you to death."

I drew a breath to argue, but Mama threw a look over her shoulder that shut me up cold. I'd survived one fight against a powerful faerie witch today. I didn't need to take any chances with another one. Especially when her eyes glowed orange and lightning flashed at her fingertips.

Mama held her hands above her head, and a beam of green light streamed from her palms down to where Vlanriel lay screaming in the grip of the summoned vines. More vines sprang from the ground all around her, wrapping around her brow and slamming her head back into the ground. A vine no bigger around than my pinky finger snaked its way around her face and shoved itself between her teeth, wedging her mouth open. I grimaced as the vine ran into her mouth, and her screams became more and more strangled. Mama opened her hands to the sky, and yellow light streaked down to wrap her in a saffron glow. She clapped her hands together, and the light coming out of her hands flashed to red. At least a dozen vines, all thicker than my wrist, shot out of the ground all around Vlanriel, then arced over the terrified woman's body, spiking their tips through her legs, her chest, her stomach, her throat. More and more vines shot up, then arced over to pierce the witch and pin her to the ground until finally there wasn't a visible inch of skin left, just a lumpy mound of vines with blood and skin oozing from it.

Mama turned to me, and I found myself bathed in that same orange light. I tried to scurry away, but the second the magic hit me, I stopped wanting to flee. My concussion faded, all my sore muscles vanished, and even lingering soreness from my old college knee injury vanished. I wasn't just healed from this fight, I was *healed*. Of everything.

I looked up at Mama, and her eyes no longer flashed yellow or orange. Her hair didn't spark, and as the last of my old injuries healed, the light around her dimmed until it was just normal sunlight backlighting her as she stood in the clearing. "Thanks, Mama," I said, standing.

"You're welcome, Robbie. Can we rejoin the others now?"

"I think we probably should. Do we need to...do anything about them?" I gestured at the splattered remains of the will-o'-the-wisp and the lump that used to be a witch. I walked around the clearing picking up my guns and shoulder rig as Mama looked down at her handiwork.

"No, the forest will reclaim them. I daresay Vlanriel will be more useful as fertilizer than she has been for a thousand years."

"I don't doubt it." We walked in silence for a few minutes before I spoke again. "I'm sorry I ran off. And I'm sorry I was a dick."

"I'm sorry *I* ran off. And I'm sorry I didn't send word."

"It's okay."

"No, it's not."

"No," I said. "I reckon it ain't. But I forgive you, and you're still my mama."

"I can live with that, then. Now let's find your sister. I'd like for you to meet her."

"I'd like that, too." Then we walked through the woods to where the rest of the team stood by the carts waiting for us.

"That was a long damn spell," Skeeter said as we came out of the forest. "Bubba, what is all over you?"

"Guts," I said. They all gaped at me. "Long story. Let's get the hell out of these woods so I can find a beer. Mama, which way are we heading?"

"Well, I have good news and bad news," she said. "The good news is that the spell worked. I have a strong sense of which direction to travel to find Nitalia."

"That's great," Amy said.

"What's the bad news?" I asked.

"We still have to go south. According to the spell, Nitalia is either with, or is very close to, the dragon Oberon sent us after."

In a repeat of what felt like my phrase of the day, I just looked at Mama and shook my head. "Well, shit."

9

The light was fading by the time we got all the crap loaded onto the wagons and back on the road. Amy rode ahead looking for a village or anything with an inn, but I wasn't real hopeful. If we'd made decent time, we probably would reach a safe place to stop for the night, but since we spent hours casting a spell and then fighting a faerie witch in a ring of mushrooms that wouldn't even get me stoned, it was probably gonna be a night of sleeping on the ground for my heroes.

"Are you okay, Robbie?" Mama asked after we'd been rolling for about half an hour. "You seem very quiet."

"I'm alright," I said. "A little pissed that I fell for the will-o'-the-wisp, but I'm okay."

"Why would you be upset about that? The wisps have lured travelers to their death for centuries. They are very good at it."

"Yeah, but I'm a monster hunter, remember? I been doing this a while, and I've fought some serious shit."

"I remember. I was there for some of that serious shit." My mind flashed back to Mama tied to a stake, about to be burned alive, and me killing my kid brother to save her life, and the lives of pretty much everybody on the east coast. She had seen some shit, indeed.

"Yeah, so you know what I mean. This is what I do. This is who I am. I shouldn't get lured into the woods like some dumbass in a fairytale!"

"Robbie, my love, you *are* in a fairytale. My entire life is a fairytale, and not a particularly happy one. I have an insane mother, a power-hungry heartless father, two dead husbands, one dead son, a kidnapped daughter, and one remaining son who wavers between loving me and wanting to kill me. If that doesn't sound like a tragedy straight out of the tales, I don't know what does."

"I never waver," I said, staring at the reins in my hands and the brown rumps of the horses in front of me.

"Excuse me? You never waver? You haven't been able to decide whether to shoot me or hug me since I walked into that recording studio in Alabama."

"That ain't the point. I love you, Mama. I never stopped loving you, not even when you left and went back to Fairyland. I ain't saying I haven't wanted to strangle you more than once, but I can think two things at once. I mean, hell, I love Pop. I never didn't love Pop, not even when he..."

"When he murdered your first love." Mama finished the sentence for me, because all of a sudden there was something in my throat and I couldn't talk.

I got my shit under control and went on. "I loved Jason every minute of every day, even when I shoved three feet of steel through his chest. I love him every minute today. So I love you, Mama, and after tonight, I'm almost over being mad at you. Not quite, but almost."

"Well, thank you for that."

"Don't thank me yet," I said. "We got to fight a damn dragon, and that means I gotta be more of a Hunter than I ever have been. So I love you, but I gotta get back on my game. I can't be 'working through shit' with you, or dealing with any of my feelings about you leaving and coming back, or not telling me that you ain't human, or not telling me that *I* ain't human for that matter."

"You *are* human, Robbie. Mostly."

"Yeah, but not completely. I'm part faerie, and I don't even know what that means, if it means anything. Is that why I heal fast? Is that why I move a little faster than most people? Is it why I'm strong?"

"No," Mama said, her voice firm, like back when I was little and asking for the hundredth time if I could open a Christmas present on Christmas Eve. "Half-fae are not magical by nature, although they may have an affinity for magic that, if trained, could blossom into some ability. You are strong because you work out, just like any other man. You are fast because you train constantly, probably in a vain effort to keep up with that lovely girlfriend of yours, who is more capable than almost any human I've ever seen."

"Yeah, me too," I agreed, peering through the darkness ahead to see if I could get a glimpse of Amy's blond hair or her white horse. No such luck.

"Healing? That may come from me. It is almost impossible to kill a faerie."

"I noticed," I said. "I've had to do it a few times, and it ain't easy. Cold iron will get you there, but about anything else is useless. No, wait, fire works too, but you gotta get 'em really good."

Mama's face went pale, and I could almost see the memory of being tied to a stake and threatened with burning a year ago. "Yes, we can be killed by immolation or cold iron. Decapitation or crushing will also get the job done."

"Maybe that's why Jason couldn't kill me with Great-Grandpappy's sword," I said, having an unpleasant flashback of my brother. The more I remembered Jason, the better I felt about killing his ass.

"No," Mama said. "You killed him with the same sword, remember? And I think there may be more to that blade than we understand, so that's not it. You likely survived because your brother either didn't want to kill you, or he was very bad with a blade. But your faerie blood will aid in your healing, make you more resilient and resistant to things like poison and disease."

"I'll have to write that on my character sheet," I muttered.

"What?"

"Sorry," I said. "It was getting a little D&D up in here for a minute.

So that's it? I'm half faerie, and all it does is keep me from getting a cold?"

"There are other benefits, but unless you plan on learning to walk across dimensions, they are largely irrelevant to you."

"Once I get the hell back to my world, it's going to take dynamite to get me out of Georgia, much less into another dimension again. But just out of curiosity…" My words trailed off as Amy rode up.

I reined in the horses and drew Bertha as Amy came alongside. "What's up?" I asked.

"There's a wide clearing beside the road in about half a mile. It looks like as good a place to make camp as anything I could think of, since I doubt we're going to make it to a town tonight."

"That sounds like a plan," I said. "Mama, that work for you?"

"It should be fine," she said. "Your compass no longer works exactly as designed, but the sense that I get from it is that there is still some distance before we approach the dragon's lair. We should be safe to make camp in the area Amy describes."

Wagons ain't the fastest mode of travel, but it was still less than ten minutes before we came around a bend in the road to the clearing Amy mentioned. It was a wide spot in the road, more than enough room for two carts to pass without any trouble, and there was a good thirty yards on either side of the road cleared of woods. I pulled my cart off to the right and climbed down, rubbing my sore back.

"You alright, Bubba?" Skeeter asked, hopping down out of his wagon without so much as a grunt. Must be nice, not being the one who turns into a punching bag for every damn monster in the free world.

"I'm sore as shit, Skeeter. I'm tired, my ass hurts from the wagon seat, my back hurts from fighting a faerie witch, my pride is bruised to hell from getting bamboozled by a will-o'-the-wisp, and my shoulder feels like I just got tackled by the entire Alabama offensive line. Again."

"That sucks. Want me to go look for water for the horses?"

"Yeah, but don't go too far into the woods. There's weird shit out there." Skeeter gave me a little mock salute, and I set to unharnessing the horses. Amy strung up a picket line between the two wagons, and Joe started unloading the tents and stuff. Mama waved her hands, and a glowing ball popped into the air about twenty feet up, bathing the clearing in a soft, golden light. Then she walked toward the edge of the campsite.

"Where you headed, Mrs. B.?" Amy called.

"I'm going to see to our perimeter," Mama replied. "I'll set a trip line around the clearing that will alert us if anything crosses into the circle."

"Good idea," I said to the horse in front of me. "I gotta admit, Horse, Mama's pretty smart."

"She has pretty good hearing, too, Robbie," Mama called from fifty feet away.

"Damn faeries and their pointy ears," I grumbled to the horse. He didn't care. I reckon he wasn't prejudiced against people with pointy ears, having lived his whole life in Fairyland and all.

A couple hours later, we all sat around a dwindling campfire, our bellies full of mediocre travel rations and our feet warmed by the fire. The Summerlands were pretty temperate, just like I imagined they would be, but there was just enough chill in the air to make the fire welcome.

"Do we need to set a watch, or will your wards be enough to wake us in case of danger?" Joe asked. He lay on his back, looking up at the stars.

"The barrier I set will reactivate my light spell at full intensity if anything other than one of us crosses it. That way we can still go into the forest for privacy if anyone needs to relieve themselves, but any creature larger than a field mouse will cause a miniature sun to pop into existence and wake up everyone within a mile or more."

"Good thing," I said. "Since we ain't been exactly secretive about being out here. Anything that wants to do us harm won't have any trouble finding us."

"Anything that wants to hurt us here is almost certainly magical in nature and could track us that way, Robbie," Mama said.

"Oh yeah. Good point. So we don't need to set a watch, then?"

"No, we should be fine. And it's a nice night, so we won't even need the tents," Mama said.

"Yeah, I figured you could have one wagon, Amy could have the other, and Joe and Skeeter can sleep under the wagons."

"Where will you sleep, then, Bubba?" Amy asked, her voice all sweetness and light.

"Well, I figured, um...well, I figured I'd share the wagon with you?" I felt my ears burn a little, even though it wasn't like me and Amy hadn't been sharing a bunk every night since we got to Fairyland. But it was a little different just coming right out there and saying it, what with my mama watching and all.

"I know, babe," she said, leaning into me. "I just want to mess with you a little bit. I love it when you blush."

"He's always been so easy to embarrass," Mama said. "Remind me when we get home, and I'll tell you some stories about when he was a little boy. He was the most modest child I'd ever seen!"

"Yeah, Bubba even hated to shower with the guys in gym class," Skeeter chimed in.

"Like you would know," I said. "You spent every day in gym class stuffed inside a locker." He shot me the bird, and I chucked a hunk of jerky at his head. For a little while, it was like we were all just out camping, shooting the shit and having a good time. It didn't feel like we were out in the middle of the woods in Fairyland hunting down a dragon and my missing sister. It just felt...natural, and fun, and safe. We sat around talking for a bit longer, then put the fire out and we all went to our respective beds. I drifted off feeling warm, safe, and content beside the woman I love.

Then we all got woke up by Mama's magical burglar alarm going off and I remembered that we were in a magic forest where literally everything wanted to kill us all.

10

"Um...hi?"

Those are not the first words I expect to hear from the monster that breached my security in the middle of the night in a magical dimension. Of course, I also don't expect anything that breaches my magical wards to look like Joel Grey in a strange, geriatric remake of *Men in Tights*, either. The wizened little man with big eyes and thin white hair was obviously Fae, but that was all I could see from where I stood in the back of the wagon, with him square in Bertha's sights.

"Amy, check him for weapons, cuff him, and bring him over here. Joe, you cover her from anything near the perimeter." I never let the barrel of the giant pistol wobble, not even the tiniest bit. A Desert Eagle is a big damn pistol, and heavy to hold on a target for any length of time, but I'm a big dude, and I've had lots of practice introducing Bertha to people we might not like.

"I assure you, I am alone, and I mean you no harm. I am but a weary traveler, looking for a refuge from the road for the night," the man called out as Amy approached. She came at him on a diagonal keeping out of my line of fire and moved slowly so that Joe could see anything coming in after her and shout a warning or take it out from a distance.

"That's fine, pal. We trust you one hundred percent," I shouted back. "But we're still going to check all that out before we turn our backs on you."

Mama hopped down from her wagon and made some gestures in the air. The light dimmed to something more like normal interior light and focused more on the wagons instead of lighting up all of creation. "There," she said. "That will also reset the trip line, so if he does have any friends out in the woods, we'll know about it before they get close enough to help him."

"Or hurt us," Amy said, hauling the little dude over by our wagon and guiding him to the ground gently. "I'm going to take these cuffs off. The iron content is hurting him."

"How can you tell?" Skeeter asked.

"I can see the blisters on his wrists. Besides, Bubba's got him covered, right Bubba?"

"He even looks at you wrong, I'll paint the grass in brains, darling," I said.

"You always say the sweetest things, Bubba," Amy replied.

"I'm a poet," I growled.

The little man said nothing, just sat cross-legged on the ground with a bemused smile on his face. Amy released his hands, then stepped back and took up a position behind him and off to one side. She was close enough to subdue him if she needed to, but out of the way in case I decided to give him an acute case of lead poisoning. I hopped down out of the wagon and dropped to one knee in front of the guy.

"Okay, pal. Who are you and what are you doing out here?" I asked after making sure that Joe and Mama were still watching the perimeter. Those two had the best long-range ability to take out an attacker, and I felt like Amy and me could handle the little guy if he got rowdy.

"My name is Taryllan, and I am just a traveler on the road. I went to visit my son and his wife in Tisa'ron, but I got a later start leaving than I wanted, so I was still on the road much later than I wanted to be. I had hoped to rest in Hamittown, where my cousin lives, but I grew tired. I spotted this clearing and thought to stop for the night. I heard your horses and decided to see if you would let me take shelter with you. Then your wards went off, and you woke up much more suddenly than I had expected." Nothing about him looked dangerous, which, of course, made me think he was probably even more dangerous than I expected. Spending so much time in Fairyland was making me downright untrusting.

"How much farther is it to Hamittown?" I asked.

"About three hours," the old man said. "That's assuming nothing tries to eat me on the road. There's a dragon near these parts, you know."

"Nothing's tried to eat you so far, and it's got to be close to midnight," I replied. I didn't have a real good sense of time, what with my cell phone not getting signal in another dimension.

"That means anything still out there hunting is going to be desperate enough to eat stringy old man meat!" he protested. I had to give him that point. He was the hunting equivalent of picking up a girl in the bar when the ugly lights come on. You just take from what's available, no matter if it ain't exactly prime pickings. "Please," he begged. "Just let me camp inside your circle. I won't even stay near you or your people. Then I'll be gone at first light."

I looked at Skeeter, who shrugged. "I ain't too worried about the old dude. I mean, I think even I could whoop his ass, and I ain't exactly the heavyweight around here."

"We can't just turn him out onto the road to be eaten, Bubba," Joe said.

"You can't," Amy said. "You're a priest. I work for a shadowy government agency that technically doesn't exist. I can totally send him out into the darkness to be eaten."

"Here," Mama said, stepping forward. She pulled the little man's sleeves down until they covered most of his hands, then turned to Amy. "Now put the handcuffs back on him. He should be fine as long as they don't touch his skin."

Amy did as Mama asked, cuffing the little dude's hands in front of his body. Then Mama helped him up and escorted him over to her wagon. She pointed to the ground by the wheel. "You sleep here. If you move from this spot, my son will shoot you in the leg. It won't kill you, but it won't feel very good. If you try to hurt anyone, *then* he'll kill you."

The little dude looked like he didn't know whether to thank her or run off into the woods, but he sat down and leaned his back against the wheel. "Thank you very much, ma'am. I appreciate the kindness."

"It's not kindness," Mama said. "I don't want you anywhere near us unless I can keep an eye on you. This seems like the best way to do that. In the morning, you will travel with us to Hamittown. There we part ways." She knelt by him and carved a half-circle around him in the grass with her knife. Then she wiggled her fingers, and sparkling dust fell from her hands onto the grass. "Now if you cross this circle, it will trigger the wards as surely as if something breached them from the outside. So don't."

"Yes, ma'am," he said.

The rest of us separated and went back to our sleeping spots, but sleep was a long time coming.

I have to admit, it was kinda nice waking up with the breeze on my face, birds chirping in the distance, Amy nestled up under one arm, Skeeter snoring like a buzzsaw from the other wagon. Okay, not so much with the last part, but the rest of it was nice. I slid my arm out from under Amy's head, trying not to wake her, and smiled as she opened her eyes.

"You're sweet, but I've been awake for a little while," she said.

"Good, because I've gotta pee like a racehorse." I rolled out of the wagon and stumbled off behind a tree to deal with morning necessities. On my way back, I noticed something odd on the ground beside Mama's wagon. Or, more to the point, I noticed that there was nothing on the ground by Mama's wagon. I drew Bertha and spun around, looking for a skinny old man who should have been stuck in an alarmed circle in the dirt.

"Hey, Mama?" I called out.

"Yes, Robbie?" Mama sat up straight in her wagon, looking like she'd been awake for an hour already. Was I going to be the only one who woke up with a string mop on my head and a Brillo pad on my chin? The more heads poked up, the more certain I was that everyone I traveled with looked better when they got out of bed than I did. Not that it was particularly high bar to get over.

"Where's your little old dude?" I asked Mama.

"He's right...sonofa*bitch*! Where did the little bastard go?"

I'll own it: I'm not at a point in my life yet where hearing my mama cuss doesn't amuse the shit out of me. "I don't know, Mama, that's why I'm asking," I hollered back.

I walked over to Mama's wagon, and Amy met me there. Joe crawled out from under our wagon, also looking pretty close to perfectly put together. At least his hair was mussed a little. "What's going on?" he asked.

"The little dude vanished," I said.

"Taryllan?"

"Did we have any other little dudes traveling with us?"

"Good point. When did he vanish?"

"Sometime in the night," Mama said, kneeling beside the wheel. "My wards are still intact. I don't have any idea how he could have escaped."

"Teleport spell?" Amy asked.

"We can't really do that," Mama replied.

"Maybe he turned himself into a frog and just hopped away," Skeeter said, walking up and rubbing sleep out of his eyes. He, at least, looked a little rumpled and had a little bit of drool dried on his chin.

"We can't really do that, either," Mama said, reaching out with a napkin to clean his chin. Some people will just always be mothers, no matter how old folks get.

"Well, what do we do?" Amy asked. "He didn't hurt anyone, although he certainly could have."

"I reckon we just move on," I said. Everybody turned to look at me like I was crazy, and I held up my hands. "Look, he didn't hurt nobody. It don't look like he stole nothing. So we might as well keep on trucking down to Hobbitton and get on about our business."

"Hamittown," Skeeter corrected. "Hobbitton was from *Lord of the Rings*."

"Whatever. Load up the wagons while I feed the horses. Mama and Joe can get some grub going, and we can be on our way pretty quick."

"Why do I have to cook?" Joe asked.

"Because I've eaten Skeeter's cooking and don't want to die today. Now get us something to eat, so we can go kick some ass."

11

I saw the smoke a good half hour before we got within sight of Hamittown. Amy saw it, too, and spurred her horse on ahead of us. A couple minutes later, she was back, her eyes wide. "You are *not* going to believe this shit!"

"I wrestled a naked sasquatch and recreated the big finish from *Dirty Dancing* in a no-shit fairy palace. Do you really think there's something left I don't believe in? Besides an honest politician, that is," I said.

"It's a dragon." She was a little pale, and a little out of breath with excitement, or fear, I couldn't really tell which. "Or, it was a dragon, at least."

"You're saying somebody already killed the dragon?" I asked.

"No." Her face fell. "I'm saying the dragon destroyed almost the entire town and flew away. It was still there when I rode up to the gates, but as soon as I got there, it took off. I didn't even get a shot at it."

"Holy shit," Skeeter said. "A real dragon? Like, flying, burning, teeth, the whole deal?"

"Well, I wasn't close enough to see teeth, but yeah, it was flying, and the whole damn town was on fire, so it was pretty much a dragon.

Long tail, wings the size of a jumbo jet, a body that looked like a barn —a dragon."

"Was anyone hurt?" Joe asked.

"I couldn't tell, but I'm guessing there's probably a lot of people injured there."

"Then we need to get there quickly. My magic may be of use," Mama said.

"Alright," I said. "Let's haul ass. Mama, you get on the back of Amy's horse. Amy, take Joe's rifle with you in case the dragon comes back. Y'all ride on ahead and start making with the healing, and we'll get there as fast as we can with these things."

They did as I asked and rode off toward Hamittown. "Well, this is gonna make going after the dragon even more a pain in the ass," I said.

"Why?" Skeeter asked, pulling his wagon alongside mine.

"We're going to have to split up. There's no way Mama is going to leave a bunch of hurt people if she can help."

"Neither will I," Joe said. "Sorry, it's part of the vows."

"Yeah, I kinda figured. That means two or three of us are gonna have to go dragon-hunting without Mama's magic. But we can't just let people die, and we can't leave the dragon alone, especially not after this shit. Let's get there and see what we can do." I snapped the reins, and we pushed the horses as much as we could for the next twenty minutes until the Hamittown walls came into view. Well, what was left of the Hamittown walls, anyway.

I'm betting it used to be a cute little town, even with the big wall of tree trunks surrounding it. But now, it just looked like a bunch of matchsticks scattered around what was left of a campfire, with a field hospital set up off to one side. The wall was destroyed, smashed to toothpicks by the dragon's giant legs, I reckoned. The fires were mostly out by the time we got there, but smoke still wafted up into the air from the burned-out husks of homes, shops, and one big central inn.

We parked the wagons outside what used to be the gate, and I left Skeeter to deal with the horses. Joe and I walked through the wreckage, the smell of smoke and burned flesh making it hard to breathe. Pigs, chickens, and dogs lay smoldering in the grass by the smoking buildings, but we didn't see any bodies. Yet. A line of weary men and women spread from the well in the center of the village to the last building still burning, a two-story structure that I figured used to be the inn.

"There's Mama," I said to Joe, pointing to a flash of golden light. Sure enough, Mama knelt beside a screaming woman, pressing her hands to the woman's face. That golden light flashed again, and the woman's screams stopped. As we got closer, I could see that she was asleep.

"She okay?" I asked.

"No," Mama said, her voice tight and curt. "She just lost everything and received horrible burns trying to pull her husband and daughter from the blaze that engulfed their home. I healed her physical wounds, but the pain she suffers will endure for a long time."

"Shit," I said. I reached down and helped Mama to her feet, but as soon as she was upright, she shook free of my grasp and made a beeline for a man writhing in pain on the ground. I looked to Joe, who nodded at me.

"I'll help her. I can do more good here than fighting a monster, anyway." He followed Mama and knelt by her side, taking the man's hand and murmuring encouragement as she healed.

I looked around, trying to find somebody in authority, but everyone around me was either screaming in pain or trying to help somebody who was screaming in pain. I walked back to the well and said, "Who's the mayor or whatever?"

A woman pulling a bucket from the well pointed to the flaming structure. "He'll be the one behind the bar in there. I don't think he feels much like talking, though, on account of being burnt to a cinder."

"Do you know where the dragon's lair is? And how long have y'all been living next to a dragon anyway? That kinda seems like something that would be an issue." I said.

She handed her bucket off to the man next to her and wiped her face. Soot left a black streak across her brow that would have been funny if the whole place didn't look like a damn war zone. "It's a cave maybe two hours farther west. He's been there for years, but never been a problem until recently. He'd take a cow every now and then, or a couple of sheep if he was feeling lazy and didn't want to hunt, but mostly, he left us alone. He'd never hurt anybody before Jacob, and even that was probably an accident. But Oberon got all bent out of shape and started sending expeditions out to hunt him, and now I guess he's decided that we have to be punished for Jacob's stupidity."

Amy and I shared a look. There was more going on here than we knew. Typical damn faeries, always working an angle. The pointy-eared bastards were worse than TV preachers and politicians rolled into one. I asked the question. I had to ask the question. "Who's Jacob and what did he do?"

The woman spat on the ground before she answered. "Jacob is… was the mayor's youngest son. Stupid shiftless, lazy, good-for-nothing little rat-faced prick that he was, he was still the mayor's son. Couple months ago, he took it upon himself to 'raid the dragon's lair' like he was some kind of hero out of legend. It's not the first time a local kid has done something stupid like that, of course. Happens a couple times every century. Some brat gets a wild hair and tries to go steal some of Xythigax's treasure. The really brave ones might make it back with a gem or a goblet. Most of them come back empty-handed, with melted swords and scorched pride. Xythigax is a patient dragon, not that I've known any other dragons, but he usually doesn't get too offended at the antics of the younglings."

"What made this time different?" Amy asked.

"Jacob didn't go in there trying to steal a trinket to impress a girl. No, that stupid bastard wanted to prove his worth as a warrior so his papa would send him to Tisa'ron to join the guard. Like standing by a city gate all day searching wagons was some great thing. But he wanted out of Hamittown so bad he could smell it, so he went in to slay the dragon."

"Oh, shit," I said.

"Yeah, exactly. The stupid boy must have snuck up on Xythigax and gotten a lucky shot in or something. Because he managed to piss the dragon off enough that he came back to town wrapped in a sheet. Xythigax flew right over the walls and dropped him on the steps of the inn. It was the first time most of us had ever seen him up close, and it was every bit as scary as you'd expect. I don't know if you saw him before you rode in here, but he's a big bastard. Bigger than the inn itself, even. He dropped that crispy boy's corpse on the steps of the inn and said that our truce was over, and if any of our people ever set foot in his cave again, he'd level the town."

"And the mayor got all pissed that his kid was barbecued and went in there," I said, shaking my head.

"If only it was that." The woman spat again, then stepped forward, lowering her voice. "The mayor's wife is some kind of distant cousin to Queen Titania. She might have three drops of royal blood, but that's enough for the queen to get all defensive about her nephew being killed by a dragon."

"Yeah, she gets kinda touchy when people hurt her relations," I replied, thinking about my first trip to a Fairyland dungeon thanks to beating the shit out of one of Titania's cousins. He also happened to be a bandit and an asshole, but neither of those things counted as much as being a royal cousin. I could definitely see the Summer Queen going postal on a dragon for hurting one of her relatives.

"So she ordered Oberon to put a price on the dragon's head. The kind of price that made people from all over come looking for a piece of fame and fortune. But all they found was fire. Well, the mayor's wife kept getting more and more furious that nobody was avenging her son, never mind that a dozen warriors had gone into that cave and come back on their shields. Literally, on their shields. Xythigax delivered them. Just the heads, though. He said he enjoyed the snacks, but getting them out of the shell was difficult, and could we please send some with more fat on them, it made the flavor better."

"Wow, Bubba, he's gonna love you," Amy said.

I looked down at my belly, a little aggrieved. Then I noticed that I still couldn't see my feet while standing, a challenge I've lived with since I was about twenty, and I had to admit she was right. "I just hope he doesn't get to find out how well-marbled my ass is," I said. Looking back at the woman, I asked, "Do you know anything that might help us get the drop on the dragon?"

She looked at me like I was stupid, and I realized that this wasn't a video game. Talking to the right random villager wasn't going to give me the clue that helped me avoid all the dragon's traps and weapons to kill it while it slept.

"You want my advice, human?" she asked.

Amy and I both nodded. "Run east. Or south, or north, or any direction that puts as much distance between you and Xythigax as possible. Because he's awake, he's pissed off, and he's starting to really like the taste of people."

So, of course, I completely ignored everything she told me and went charging into the dragon's cave with no more protection than the shirt on my back.

12

An hour later, Amy and I pulled our lathered horses to the side of the trail and tethered them loosely to a tree. She looked at me as she draped the reins over a low-hanging branch. "This is a little optimistic, don't you think?"

"What do you mean?"

"Tying up the horses like we think we're coming back out of this cave." For the first time since I'd known her, I saw real fear in her eyes. I mean, we'd been in some deep shit before, and I'd seen her scared. But that was always in the middle of a fight, when the shit was bouncing off the fan blades right into our faces. I'd never seen her scared *before* a fight.

I put a hand on her shoulder, turned her around, and pulled her in close. "We're gonna be fine."

"It's a *dragon*, Bubba. We've never fought anything like this before. Hell, I've never even seen anything like this before. I don't even know of anybody that's fought a dragon, much less fought one and lived."

"Well, I always have been original."

She laughed, and her breath felt warm against my chest. "That you are, you big dumb idiot. That you are." She looked up at me. "Are we really going to be okay?"

"Shit, Amy, I can't tell you that with any certainty. But I can tell you one thing: I've fought trolls, vampires, werewolves, zombies, and every other damn thing I've come across, and I'm still here. *We're* still here. Yeah, it's a dragon. You're scared. Hell, so am I. But just remember that no matter how big or bad this thing is, it ain't gonna be no worse than wrestling a butt-nekkid Sasquatch and grabbing its little Bigfoot."

She laughed again and pulled back. This time, when she looked up at me, at least a little bit of the confidence was back. "Yeah, I guess it won't be worse than a nest of vampires."

"Or a horde of zombies."

"Or a dimension-shifted elf."

"Or a bunch of horny old people possessed by Cupid."

She stared at me. "What the hell?"

"Oh yeah, that was before we met. I had to beat up a bunch of cupids that were screwing around with an old folks' home. It was like a geriatric swinger's party. I've never seen so many octogenarian boobs and butts in my life."

"Now *that's* scary," Amy said. She turned back to her horse and started to gear up. She got her shield down and looked over her shoulder at me. "Thank you, Bubba."

"Hey, what's a boyfriend for if not to hold his beautiful fiancée when she gets scared?"

She spun around, her hand on the butt of her pistol. "What. Did. You. Say?"

I took a step back, not that it would matter if she decided to shoot me, but more to get distance to do it right. I dropped to one knee and dug a thin silver band out of my pocket. The stone in it wasn't a diamond. In fact, I didn't know exactly what it was, and Mama wouldn't tell me, just smiled when she gave it to me. I held the ring up to her. "Amy Hall, I know this might be a stupid time to throw this out there, being as how we're in the wrong dimension about to go into a cave hunting a dragon that might very well burn us both to brisket and eat us, but I've never been known for my good timing. Amy, I love you. I know I should have come up with some kind of flowery shit to wrap around it, but that ain't who I am. I'm just big dumb redneck with more guns than some small countries and more beer than Milwaukee, but I love you. I promise, if we get out of this stupid Fairyland, that I will love, honor, cherish, and respect you for the rest of my life."

A tear rolled down her cheek, but by the smile that stretched across her face, I thought it might be a happy one, so I went ahead with it. "Amy, will you marry me?"

She didn't speak. She stood there beside her horse in the middle of Fairyland, with an enchanted shield in one hand and her service weapon in the other, tears rolling down her face as she nodded. Then she dropped her shit and tackled me, knocking me flat on my back in the dirt right outside a dragon's cave. She kissed me all over my face, then sat up with her knees on either side of my chest.

"Robert Brabham, you might have the worst timing in the history of marriage proposals, but yes, I will marry your big silly ass. I love you, you stupid lunk." Then she fell on top of me and started kissing me again. I just lay there enjoying the moment until she got all the kissing out of her system. After a few minutes she got up, then held out her left hand. I slipped the ring on her hand and she looked at it.

"It's a little—oh!" Her eyes widened as the ring flashed with blue light, then shrank down to fit her finger perfectly. "Wow. Um…did you just give me a magical engagement ring?"

I looked at her hand, where the strange white stone now pulsed with a warm yellow light. "I reckon I did. I didn't know it was magic, I promise."

Amy raised an eyebrow at me. "You didn't steal this from Mab, did you?"

"No!" I protested. "I wouldn't trust anything from that crazy woman's palace any farther than Skeeter can throw me!"

"And it isn't Titania's, either?"

"Amy, I did not steal your engagement ring. Mama gave it to me."

Her eyes got full again. "Your mother gave this to you?"

"Yeah," I said. "We were in the truck coming back from Muscle Shoals, and she took it off her hand and passed it over to me. She said

Pop gave it to her, that it had been passed down all the way from Great-Grandpappy Beauregard and his sister Tavvy. They were the first Hunters in our family, and I reckon he had it made for Great-Granny Ruth. But Mama didn't say nothing about it being magic. I hope it ain't stuck or nothing."

"Don't you worry about that, Bubba. It's never coming off, magic or no. Now let's go kill a dragon. We need to find your sister more than ever, now." She picked up her weapons and started toward the mouth of the cave.

"Why now?" I asked, following her.

She didn't even look back, just turned her head to the side to call over her shoulder, "Well, I'm going to have to have a maid of honor, silly! Now let's go kill a dragon and rescue your sister, because when we get home, we've got a wedding to plan!"

I was suddenly scared of a lot more than just the dragon waiting for me in the cave.

Half an hour later, I wasn't any less scared of what would be waiting for me on the other side of the dimensional portal home, but I was starting to feel really creeped out by the environment I was in. The entrance to the cave was little more than a narrow slab in the rocks, a crack barely big enough for me to squeeze through, even with sucking in my gut to the farthest point. I didn't quite get stuck going in, but I sure as hell hoped there was a back door, or a garage exit, or something. I let Amy take the lead, not just because I could shoot over her, but also because she had the shield. I didn't trust Oberon and his magic trinkets, but I wasn't going to just ignore the fact that we had a supposedly magical shield to protect us from dragon's breath. I had Skeeter's spear held out in front of me, but I couldn't figure out a good way to carry Bertha and the spear at the same time without having either the long pointy thing or the pistol in my left hand, and that seemed like a good way to either poke or shoot the wrong person, so my second-favorite girl nestled under my left arm, her weight a comfort against my side.

It was darker than the inside of an elephant's butthole, and the only light we had was Amy's cell phone. I was impressed by its ability to hold a charge the whole time we were in Fairyland until she told me that she turned it off as soon as we got here. Silly me, I killed the battery on mine the first couple of days playing Plants v. Zombies. But even Amy's good fortune had its limits, and within fifteen minutes of the entrance, her light went out, leaving us fumbling around in the pitch dark. I took advantage of the momentary disorientation to grab my girlfriend—*fiancée's* ass a couple times, but calmed down after she elbowed me. The third time. There would be plenty of time to fool around after we killed the dragon.

It took a few minutes of stumbling and fumbling around in the dark before my eyes began to adjust, or maybe it was just that some light was coming in from somewhere ahead of us. The floor of the cave was smooth, almost like it was manufactured, with no pebbles or stones scattered around. I ran my hand along the left-hand wall, and Amy kept a hand on the right, with her left on the haft of my spear in case the whole tunnel got wider suddenly. It didn't, just stayed a little wider than I could reach with my arms extended.

I suppose we walked for about ten or fifteen minutes before I noticed the tunnel becoming noticeably brighter. I whispered "stop" to Amy, and she came closer.

"What is it"

"I can see a little better. What about you?"

"Yeah, a little bit."

"It looks like it gets wider up ahead. Maybe we're coming up on an opening or the main body the lair. I should go on ahead."

"Are you on drugs, Bubba? You're as quiet as an avalanche and subtle as a hand grenade. Plus, I have the shield. Hold my rifle, I'm going to reconnoiter." She unslung the shield from across her shoulders, then handed me Joe's rifle. "Stay here, you big oaf," she whispered, then kissed me. She slipped away into the darkness, her form outlined against the obvious light coming from the far end of the tunnel. I put my back against the wall and slid down to sit and wait.

And wait. And wait.

I don't do so good with the waiting. I'm much better at the kicking doors in and beating the shit out of things part of the job. So after what felt like about a year and a half of waiting, but was probably something south of five minutes, I gave up. I got to my feet, picked up my spear, and started down the tunnel after Amy. The tunnel grew steadily brighter as I moved along until I could actually see where I was putting my feet, a welcome change.

That's when I realized why the floor was so smooth. This wasn't a natural cave. The tunnel I walked along had been carved out of the mountain, leaving a perfectly smooth and level floor. Hell, I lived in a house built with modern technology, and I didn't have a level floor! Whatever made this tunnel, and by extension the cave I walked toward, had some serious tech or some serious magical power. Neither of those things seemed good for me. But I still saw nothing of Amy, so I kept going.

I walked for a good fifteen minutes (a real fifteen minutes this time, not a sitting in the dark multiplying time by five because I was bored fifteen minutes) before I came to the mouth of the tunnel. There was absolutely nothing resembling cover at the cave end. No rocks, no stalagmites, not even any handy corpses of giant animals to duck behind. But the one thing I did find as I got to the end of the tunnel was unexpected: voices. I recognized Amy's immediately, and the other voice sounded familiar, but I couldn't place it.

I stepped into the cave, expecting to face a vicious dragon breathing fire. What I saw was even more outrageous than that.

"What the ever-loving shit are you doing in here?" I asked, completely baffled at the sight before me.

13

———

Sitting at a table serving Amy tea was Taryllan, the little old man who broke into our camp the night before, then mysteriously vanished before daybreak. He smiled when he caught sight of me, a grin splitting his face from ear to ear. "Oh, Bubba! I am so glad that you decided to join us. Your fiancée here was certain that you'd come looking for her, and I am thrilled to find that her faith in you was not misplaced. Congratulations, by the way, on your engagement. I think it was a lovely gesture to make your commitment to each other official before you dove into a potentially lethal situation. Well done."

I stood at the mouth of the tunnel, staring across at a room the size of a football field, or maybe a basketball arena. Either way, it was damn big, and damn tall, and there was gold, and jewels, and shining weapons, and armor scattered all around the corners. This was a dragon's lair straight out of a Peter Jackson movie. Except there was no dragon. There was a five-foot-tall faerie man with a skullett tied back into a long ponytail serving tea from a golden pot into a ceramic cup in front of my fiancée.

"What the ever-loving hell is going on here?" I asked, moving forward. They were sitting at a table smack dab in the center of the room, so I had a ways to go before I got to them. Even so, I moved the spear over to my left hand and popped the snap on Bertha's holster in case my girl needed to come out and play. I'd loaded her with cold iron rounds before we broke camp that morning, so any Fae I shot were in for a real bad day.

"We are having tea," Taryllan said. "I was under the impression that you had tea in your world as well. I'll admit that it is a little early by your standards, but I have a fondness for cucumber sandwiches, and it is never too early for cucumber sandwiches. Wouldn't you agree, Agent Hall?"

Amy didn't say anything, just sat there motionless. Her eyes were the only thing that moved, and they kept flicking back and forth, up and down, like she was trying to tell me something. There was a lot more going on with this little dude than I saw at first glance, and I proceeded with caution. "So, why didn't Amy come back looking for me?" I called out, still moving forward, but looking all around the lair for the dragon while I did. There wasn't another entrance, and I was pretty damn sure I hadn't passed a dragon in the narrow hallway coming in, so it had to still be in here somewhere. Maybe it teleported out for a snack or something?

"She said she would rather wait here for you. Now come along, the tea is getting cold. And if you walk any slower, the cucumber sandwiches will get soggy. I hate soggy cucumber sandwiches." The little man's voice grew sharp, and I could tell that he was used to having his orders obeyed. Seemed like everybody I'd met in Fairyland felt justified in telling me what to do, and it was getting old.

"Well, I ain't much of a fan of cucumber," I said. "Gives me the farts. So I reckon me and Amy will just be heading out. But I appreciate the offer of tea."

"Sit." He didn't raise his voice, didn't make any kind of threatening moves, but something in his voice told me that if I didn't sit down, right that second, that some shit was going to go down. I crossed the last few feet to the table and sat down beside Amy. I leaned my spear on the table, but Taryllan flicked his hand, and it flew across the room, clattering on the stone floor as it landed thirty yards away.

"No polearms at the table. You may keep your guns because it would take you longer to disarm than it will take us to enjoy a nice tea." For the first time, I noticed that a cup sat on the table in front of me. There was no cup there when I sat down. Whatever the hell this little dude was, he had some serious juice.

"Cucumber sandwich?" He held out a little plate with tiny finger sandwiches on it. The crusts were cut off, even. I'm not what you would call a fan of cucumber, I wasn't BSing him there, but since I was now sitting across from a telekinetic midget faerie who could made teacups appear out of thin air, I thought it would be less than prudent to refuse.

"Thanks," I said, and put a couple of sandwiches on the plate that miraculously appeared in front of me when I wasn't looking. I held the plate out to Amy. "You want any?"

She shook her head again, but Taryllan spoke again. "You may speak now, dear. I just didn't want you shouting at your beau and spoiling my surprise. You will find that you now have control of your limbs."

Amy glared at the little man and reached for the plate. "Thanks, Bubba. Sorry about this. He's got a lot more mojo than I expected."

"You'd be amazed how often that happens," the little wizard said, taking the plate, which still had the same number of sandwiches on it as it ever had, despite me taking half a dozen of the little white triangles for me and Amy. I didn't think I'd be surprised at all. It looked an awful lot like this little bastard worked real hard at being underestimated.

"So what's the deal, Taryllan?" I asked around a mouthful of cucumber. I had to admit, the sandwiches were pretty good. It had been a couple hours since breakfast, and there hadn't been a real good chance for lunch, what with the whole dragon burning down Hamittown thing.

"I'm not sure I understand the question," he replied, his voice mild but his eyes sharp.

"You wander into our camp in the middle of the night, making like you're some helpless traveler, but you get outta Mama's wards without waking anybody up, then you show up in a dragon's lair, acting for all the world like you...oh, shit."

Taryllan laughed, a sound much deeper than I expected given his slight frame. Or, I guess I should say, given the slight frame he currently wore. "By Mab, I think he's figured it out! My dear girl, he is much, *much* brighter than he seems to be. You may not have made a disastrous choice in a mate after all! It won't matter, since neither of you will ever leave this cave, but you can die knowing that your affianced is not a complete moron."

I jumped to my feet, yanking Bertha free of her shoulder holster, and squeezed off four quick shots. At that range, there was no chance I was going to miss, no matter how little the dude was. And I didn't miss.

He just didn't care. All four of the fifty-caliber rounds hit him right in the center of his chest, and they all just dropped to the ground, all their force expended. Taryllan gave me a little sideways cock of the head, as if to say, "What are you gonna do, I'm awesome," and smiled at me.

Smiled at me. The cocky little shit took four rounds from the world's most badass handgun, and he smiled at me. This was going to be harder than troll-wrestling.

"Now that we have that out of the way, which of you should I kill first?" Taryllan mused, waking around the table. Amy made as if to stand, but a twitch of the little wizard's fingers and she was frozen to her seat. I holstered Bertha and slid my hands into the caestae hanging from my belt. If I was going out, I was gonna go out fighting.

"Why are you even bothering, human?" he sneered. "You just watched your silly bullets bounce off my chest. You saw me immobilize your fiancée without breaking a sweat. And now you think you're going to *punch* me to death? Be reasonable, you idiot. Just sit down and accept your fate. If you behave, I'll kill you both quickly. If you make me work for it, I'll show you what happens to fools who accept Oberon's stupid quests. Then I'll go to Tisa'ron and bring it down around his pointy ears just to show that stupid git what happens when you try to rob an elder dragon."

He held up a hand to me, then waved it downward. "I said, *sit.*"

I stood there. Nothing happened. I expected some huge force to slam me into my chair, or to just squish me into redneck jelly right there, but all I felt was a little breeze, like an air conditioner kicked on over my head. Taryllan looked at his hand, like it was defective or something, and I decided it didn't matter what was going on, I needed to take advantage of it. I shot forward around the table and nailed the wizard with a running uppercut that looked straight out of a WWE ring. My iron-clad fist caught the diminutive spell-slinger right on the point of his chin, and he flew back about three feet before landing on his ass and sliding another foot or so backward.

"Ow!" he yelled, hopping to his feet. I was on him as soon as he was upright, pounding him with everything I had. I laid in heavy punches on his chest, stomach, and face, but he didn't go down. He didn't try to fight back, either, just staggered back more and more with a puzzled look on his face. After eight or ten of my best shots still didn't knock him down again, he reached up and slapped me with the back of his hand.

The little bastard just flicked his hand at me like a normal person would swat at a fly, and when he tagged me on the cheek, I thought my orbital socket might explode. It felt like getting hit in the face with a twenty-pound carp, and you really don't want to know what that feels like. I spun around and dropped to one knee, but didn't go completely down. Then I came back up and swung into him with everything I had, coming up from the ground with an uppercut that should have turned his jaw into shards of broken glass.

He grunted and took a step back. "Those are good gloves. That actually hurt. But this is becoming boring." He punched me in the chest, and I saw stars. I didn't just see stars, I saw the entire end sequence of *2001: A Space Odyssey*, complete with turtles all the way down. This time I went down, all the air gone from my lungs and maybe with a cracked sternum to boot.

"That's better," Taryllan said, walking forward to stand by my head. "I like you better down there. I think you should stay down permanently." He raised one foot to smear my head across the floor like joint compound but fell back on his ass when a blond missile slammed into his chest in a tackle that would make Reggie White come back from the grave to applaud.

Apparently, when he focused his time on kicking my ass, he lost his hold on Amy. And being the badass that she is, when she saw him about to rearrange the glory that is my face, she took him down with extreme prejudice. They went tumbling ass over teakettle all the way across the floor while I rolled over and struggled to my feet. I found my breath after a few seconds and probed my chest with a tentative finger. Nothing seemed broken, but it was going to be a couple weeks before I was back in any kind of shape to do the breast stroke. I got to my feet, shrugging out of my caestae and casting them aside. Not like they did any damage to the little bastard, anyway. I was almost upright, leaning on a chair to support myself, when the *crack* of breaking bone rang through the room, and I heard Amy scream in pain.

I spun around to see her writhing on the ground, clutching her shoulder. Her left arm hung limp against her side, and she clutched it with her right. Her face contorted with agony, and I saw nothing but red as I drew Great-Grandpappy Beauregard's sword and charged the son of a bitch that hurt my fiancée. As I ran at him, sword raised over my head, he looked at me and smiled. The scrawny bastard smiled at me while Amy lay there in pain.

"Well, then. Let's end this." He was surrounded by a glowing aura of red light that flared brighter and brighter until it blinded me, and when it faded, a red dragon the size of a bus with a head like a VW Beetle stood before me. "How do you feel now, human?" the dragon said, its voice loud enough to make the plates on the table rattle.

"I feel like turning your hide into a new pair of boots, asshole," I said, sprinting the last twenty feet to him. I was now officially fighting a dragon in a cave in Fairyland with a magical sword. It was like a bad game of *Dungeons & Dragons*, but if I died, I wouldn't be able to roll up a new Bubba.

14

———

So there I stood, sword in hand, in front of a no-shit dragon. The thing was big enough to snap me up in one bite like Jonah, then belch me out and flash-fry my ass before I hit the ground. Amy lay on the ground with either a broken collarbone, dislocated arm, or maybe something even worse. I couldn't even take the time to check on her because of the whole getting eaten by a dragon thing. Taryllan, now in his true form of Xythigax, looked down at me from his place near the roof of the cave, and if I knew anything about dragon facial expressions, he smiled at me.

So, new thing to note—dragons are assholes.

The asshole dragon in question lifted up one giant clawed foot and swiped at me. It wasn't much of an attempt, just a lazy slash through the air at about head height. I don't think he actually wanted to hit me; I think he just wanted me to get a look at the length of his claws. Well, I got a good look as I ducked under them. His foot had three front claws and one on the back and they were all longer than my hand. It would only take one shot to open me up from my navel to nostrils. I just had to make sure he didn't get that shot.

"Shield," Amy croaked from behind me.

I didn't turn around to look at her. "Yeah, babe. I'm gonna shield you from this assclown as long as I can. But after he guts me, you're probably on your own."

"No, you idiot, grab my shield!"

This time, I turned around, and Amy slid the shield Oberon gave her across the floor to me. She looked a little better, some of the color back in her face and her eyes clear. She still wasn't moving her left arm, but she was up on one knee now. I picked up the shield, remembering what Obie said about it protecting her from dragon breath. I saw Amy's eyes go wide and turned back to see Xythigax rear his head back, then thrust it forward in my direction. A gout of flame bigger around than my thigh shot toward me, and I brought the shield up just in the nick of time.

I don't know what I expected from Oberon's gift, but it performed past any expectations, especially for a gift given by my asshole grandfather who just learned I was his blood relation a few days before. But whatever his other flaws, the shield he bestowed upon my girl saved my bacon. Or really, it saved me from *becoming* bacon. I held the shield up right in the stream of fire, and it just disappeared. No heat, no little tendrils of flame licking over the edges to set my beard on fire, nothing. The fire was just *gone*.

Xythigax looked down at me, its eyes going wide. "Well, well, well," it said, its voice still perfectly understandable despite the redesigned face and jaw. "It seems my prey has a few advantages it didn't tell me about. Why did Oberon gift you with protection, when the rest of his hunters he merely sent in here to be slaughtered?"

"Maybe the rest of the hunters didn't have near my talents," I said, moving sideways to put myself, and the shield, between the dragon and Amy. She was way more mobile, now all the way up to standing, but she still didn't look like she had enough in the tank to dodge fireballs.

"No, that can't be it," Xythigax said without a second thought. I'll admit, I was a little pissed. I mean, I might not be some kind of faerie knight or magical critter, but I do all right for myself. I didn't have long to be offended, as the dragon refocused on me and shot out a string of a dozen little fireballs, no bigger than a volleyball. But they came fast, and they came at me high, low, and in between, so I had to duck, hop, and eventually crouch behind my shield to keep from getting roasted. When I dropped to one knee, Xythigax switched to a steady stream of flame, much longer and much wider this time. He poured on the flame for almost a solid minute, and by the time he had to stop to breathe, the shield's metal was glowing red from the heat. It still didn't pass any heat through to me, but it definitely didn't dissipate as much heat as the first time.

I ran to the side, thinking frantically. How do you kill a dragon? I didn't have a bow and arrow, and after shrugging off four rounds from Bertha, I didn't think I was gonna be shooting Smaug like the end of *The Hobbit* any time soon. I've played my fair share of video games, but almost always with Skeeter, so whenever we get to boss fights, I just do what he tells me to while he figures this kind of crap out. I mean, I guess it doesn't get any more "monster" than a dragon, but this thing was a couple light years outside of my wheelhouse. I skidded to a halt as Xythigax slammed a huge foot down in front of me, then I turned just in time to see its huge head swooping down on me. I flashed back to that damn *Dragon's Lair* video game from when I was a kid and remembered getting burned to a crisp more times than I could count. I slashed out blindly with Great-Grandpappy's sword and was stunned to feel it hit flesh and, after a second's resistance, cut right through it.

Xythigax was shocked, too, by the howl that came from his mouth. I stared at the blade, red dragon's blood hissing steam from the tip of the dark gray steel. "Holy shit, you can bleed?"

"What blade is that?" Xythigax said. "I have not seen it, and I know all the named blades of Faerie."

"Named blade? You mean like Sting?" This fight was getting more Tolkien by the minute. Next thing I knew, this scaly bastard was gonna ask me what was in my pockets. "You want to know this sword's name?" I flung Amy's shield to one side and gripped the hilt of Great-Grandpappy's sword with both hands. "This is Beauregard, and it's been in my family for more than a hundred years. And Beauregard here is gonna whoop your lizard ass!"

I sprinted toward the dragon, running like I was back at UGA chasing quarterbacks. He swiped at me with a clawed foot, but I met his stroke with the edge of my sword, and one fist-sized claw fell to the ground. Xythigax jerked his paw back, but I was on him now. I ran to the other leg, and instead of slashing at it, trying to bring him down, I just ran *up* his front leg, digging in with my sword any time my feet slipped. I got all the way up to his knee joint, then I planted my feet and jumped forward for all I was worth. I brought the sword down just behind his foreleg, stabbing the three feet of steel into his armored hide all the way up to the cross guard.

The dragon shrieked and thrashed his head, spewing fire all around the cave. I spared a fleeting thought for Amy, hoping she had time to get under a table or something, then it took all I had just to hang on. I sawed back and forth on the dragon's torso, right behind his shoulder, digging for where I hoped the heart was pumping away. He thrashed, jumped, and finally just flopped down on that side in an attempt to squish me like some stinging insect. That got me to let go, and I hit the stone floor hard and rolled away from the screaming dragon, who learned the hard way that when you put your whole weight on the thing that's stabbing you, all it does is drive it farther into you.

But it wasn't dead. It was hurt, but alive, and I didn't have a sword anymore. So when the dragon struggled to his feet, just the last couple of inches of Great-Grandpappy's sword protruding from its side, I stood there bristling with weapons, but unarmed. I had Bertha, but she wouldn't pierce his thick hide. I had a pair of silver-edged kukri, but they couldn't cut dragon scales. I had my Judge revolver, but a .45 long cartridge was no good against a lizard the size of an airplane. In essence, I was back where I started: staring up at a pissed-off dragon with nothing between me and certain death but my good looks and charm.

I was screwed. Again.

"You hurt me, human. That hasn't happened in centuries."

"It don't have to happen again. You just let me pull my sword out of your belly there, and I bet you'll bleed out pretty quick. Then nobody needs to get hurt anymore." Somehow my voice was steady. I don't have any idea how. I'd been in worse spots and come out of them somehow, but I had no damn idea how I was getting out of this one.

"Or I could smear your brains across my floor and use your carcass to staunch my bleeding. I think I prefer that solution." He reared his head back again, and I closed my eyes, thinking I'd probably drank my last beer, cleaned my last fish, and kissed Amy for the last time. *Well, at least I'll die with her knowing how I feel.*

"Bubba!" My eyes snapped open, and I turned to see Amy's shield flying at my face. I snatched it out of the air and dropped to one knee. I got the enchanted disk up just in time to block most of the flaming breath, although my eyebrows definitely got a good singe to them. Xythigax poured it on, hotter and wider than either of the other attacks. The shield started to heat up after about a minute, and soon I could feel the hairs on my arm start to singe.

I drew Bertha and reached around the shield, emptying the last few rounds in the general direction of its face. I knew they wouldn't do any good, but if I could distract it for a second, maybe I could get Amy and me back down the corridor and get a few seconds to rest. The bullets had no effect, and my sleeve started to smoke as the shield's magic finally gave up the ghost. The whole disk warped under the heat, and it started to fold over at the edges. I closed my eyes against the stinging smoke, then snapped them open again at a scream from behind me.

"Screw you, Xythigax! You leave my fiancé alone, you cheap Godzilla knockoff!" I looked to Amy and saw her standing with Joe's spear in her hand. She grimaced with every step, but she ran forward, planted her feet, and flung that magic spear right into the stream of fire. I watched the tip glow red, then white, then the spear flew straight into the dragon's mouth like a damn magical Sidewinder missile.

The fire cut off in an instant as the dragon shook its head and fought to dislodge the spear from its mouth. I flung the warped disk of metal that used to be a shield aside and shot Amy a grateful glance.

The dragon still struggled with the spear, now rolling onto its side to try and reach the haft with its forelegs. That was the opening I needed because it wasn't looking at me for a few seconds. I patted out my smoldering left arm as I ran back to the dragon and dashed up its side to the wound I'd made in its shoulder. I shoved my hands down into the hole and grabbed Great-Grandpappy's sword, pulling it free of the dragon's side with a crimson squelch.

At the same time I got the sword out of its side, Xythigax finally dislodged the spear from the roof of its mouth and turned to face me. I was still standing on its broad side, with nothing to hold me on if it stood up. But instead of standing up and dumping me to the floor, the pain-addled beast snapped at me with its huge jaws. That was all the mistake I needed. I sidestepped the giant head, reversed grip on my sword, and jabbed the newly-named Beauregard The Enchanted Blade right into the dragon's dinner plate-sized left eye.

I leaned in, driving the blade through the monster's amber eye and into its brain. The last thing Xythigax the dragon ever did was turn its head skyward and belch out one last blast of fire. Then it convulsed one time, snatching the sword from my hands, and died. I fell to my knees in the dragon's death throes, then just went all the way down to my butt and slid off the huge beast's side to the ground.

I made it all the way to where Amy sat on the floor holding her arm before my legs gave out. I plopped down right beside her. "We just killed a dragon," I said.

"Yeah."

"We ain't dead."

"No. Being dead probably wouldn't hurt this bad."

"Probably not," I agreed.

"Now what?"

"I reckon we get my sword, cut off its head, and go back to get Mama to heal you up. Then we find Oberon and get him to give us my sister."

"Well, there's only one problem with that," came a familiar voice from behind us.

I turned around to see Oberon standing in the cave, fresh as a daisy because he hadn't just fought a damn dragon. "What's the problem, Oberon? We killed the dragon. Now hold up your end of the deal and give me Nitalia."

"That's the crux of the problem. I don't have her," Oberon said. "But I know where she is," he added quickly when I drew Bertha and aimed it at his junk. He didn't need to know that she was empty, and I was aiming at his nuts because I was too exhausted to lift the gun any higher.

"Well, get to talking, Obie. Because if I'm not gonna shoot your dick off in a dragon cave, I'm gonna need a real good reason." I got all that out without slurring or stammering. Then I fell forward across Amy's legs and passed right the hell out.

15

I came to staring up at a cloudless blue sky, with Amy's face in the periphery of my vision. I'd woken up in worse places. Hell, most days I woke up in Fairyland seemed to be in a dungeon, so I really couldn't complain about lying on grass with birds chirping and a beautiful woman by my side. Except I knew I was still in Fairyland and had passed out inside a cave. I struggled to sit up, and Amy reached down to help me.

"You're heavy," she grunted.

"It's all muscle," I said, panting more than a little bit by the time we finally got me at least up sitting cross-legged on the grass.

"Your muscle jiggles a hell of a lot." Skeeter's voice came from my left, and I turned to see Mama and my other friends standing around. I reached upward, and Joe and Skeeter helped haul me to my feet. All the hurts and burns from my fight with the dragon were healed, and as I turned to Amy, I saw that she was using both arms. Either I'd been out for a couple months, or somebody had mojo'd up some healing magic on us. I raised an eyebrow at Mama, and she nodded.

"Yes, Robbie. When Oberon brought you back to me, there was some need for my healing abilities. Between my magic and his, we patched you up," Mama said with a smile.

"But your shield is a goner," Joe said.

"Yeah, that thing was pretty much melted to goo," Amy agreed.

"Did anybody get my sword?" I asked.

"I have it here," Oberon's voice came from behind me. I tried to spin around, but I was still pretty lightheaded, so after the ground stopped rolling around under my feet, I turned slowly to look at the Faerie Consort. He sat on a stump about ten feet away, a mug in his hand. He looked less regal than I'd ever seen him in his real skin, but a lot more comfortable. Maybe being the queen's boy toy wasn't all it was cracked up to be.

"Thanks for healing me," I said. "And Amy."

"It was the least I could do," he replied. "After all, you destroyed the Scourge of the Eastlands, Xythigax the Terrible."

"Yeah, well, I was pretty motivated. Now let's talk about finding my sister." I reached under my arm for Bertha, but the holster wasn't in its usual place. A quick pat to the small of my back showed that my Judge was missing, and I realized that I was completely unarmed. Not a problem. I rolled my head from side to side and loosened up as best I could. If I was going to have to beat the information out of him, so be it.

"Calm down, Robert," Oberon said, his voice tired. "I'm not going to fight you."

"Then this might hurt. Or you could just tell us where Nitalia is." I cracked my knuckles for emphasis.

Oberon laughed, which was about a million miles from the response I was looking for, and turned to Mama. "Oh, Ygraine, he is indeed your son! He has your fire and your drive to protect the weak. You should be proud."

"I am," Mama said with a smile. "I am also proud of my daughter, who we have traveled far to find."

"I know." Oberon's face fell. "Please know that I would have told you everything had I been allowed. But my queen, she is capricious, and when she saw the touch of Mab writ large upon your face, she was...less than inclined to be helpful to you. She demanded that I send you on this quest, and only if you survived would I be able to tell you what little we know of Nitalia."

"Well, we're alive, so start talking," I growled.

Oberon turned back to me and nodded. "Let's go sit down." He gestured toward a couple of picnic tables sitting in the middle of the smoldering remains of the town square. As we walked, he talked.

"Nitalia did come to Tisa'ron. She was not with us long, but I have seen her, some months ago. She was perfectly fine when she left our hospitality, although she did make a hasty departure when she learned of Titania's plans for her."

"To make her marry a prince of Summer and use her for leverage against Mab?" Mama asked.

"Of course," Oberon said, just like he was talking about selling a used car and not manipulating a person's life. The more time I spent around royalty, the more I liked rednecks.

Oberon went on. "I did not know where she had gone at first. I just assumed that she was somewhere within the Summerlands. But after our search parties found no trace of her, I began to be concerned."

"You mean after the soldiers you sent to drag her back couldn't find her," Mama said. Her voice was flat and her eyes cold, despite her taking on the aspect of Summer.

At least this time, Oberon had the good grace to look ashamed. "Yes, the first group sent after her was dispatched under orders to return her to Titania's 'care.' But when they returned empty-handed, I sent out a squadron of my personal guardsmen, this time with specific instructions to aid her in any way they could, especially if it meant getting her out of my wife's territory. They also returned with no trace of her."

"Why the change of heart?" I asked. I still wasn't real happy with Oberon, but it was starting to look like there might be a heart trapped under there after all.

"Titania is my wife, and my queen. I love her, but I also know exactly how fearsome she can be. When I saw the glint of battle in her eye, I knew that her plans for Nitalia went further than some minor jab at my former wife. Somewhere between Nitalia's arrival at Court and her disappearance, Titania decided to use her to destroy Mab. I couldn't let that happen. As little as I know of the girl, she is still of my blood."

"That didn't stop you from sending Bubba chasing after a dragon," Skeeter said with a scowl. "He's your blood, too."

"He is, but he also has brave companions with him, and I did bestow weapons upon him that allowed him to vanquish the beast."

"Still sent us chasing after a damn dragon," Skeeter grumbled. I knew my little buddy well enough to recognize that he wasn't going to just let this go, so I waved him quiet. He rolled his eyes at me, but shut up.

I turned back to Oberon. "So your guys couldn't find her, either?"

"They did not. But I uncovered something in the palace that I found particularly worrisome, and it spurred me to begin planning a major rescue expedition. Then you arrived, and my plans went sideways."

"Bubba has that effect on plans," Amy said. "What did you find?"

"A maid remembered seeing Robin Goodfellow near Nitalia's rooms the night before she vanished."

"I hate that little bastard," I said.

"A sentiment shared by many," Mama said. "But he has his uses, doesn't he, Father?"

Oberon looked embarrassed. "Yes, Daughter, he does. The Puck has been useful to the crown of both realms on more than one occasion. Unfortunately, his relationship with our Court has been... strained of late."

I leaned forward and lowered my voice. "Gramps, we don't know each other real well, but let me just lay this shit out for you. You need to say whatever it is that you don't want to say about Puck, or I'm going to beat it out of you. We need to find my sister so we can get the hell out of Fairyland because I can only assume I have missed almost the entire college football season by now, and I need to know how my Dawgs are doing with their new coach."

He looked at me, confusion written all over his face. "I honestly have no idea what you are talking about."

"He gets that a lot," Amy said. "But what's up with Puck? From what Bubba told us, he was pretty happy the last time you guys saw him. All married and stuff."

"That is exactly the source of the problem," Oberon said. "His wife, the Princess Alethea, was bound to the Summer Court. Puck is an unaffiliated Fae, a prince of the Lands Without Season, with a fine estate in the Shadowlands." He looked around the table like that was supposed to mean something to us. Mama looked pretty damn upset by this revelation, but the rest of us just looked like your Spanish teacher started trying to teach calculus.

"What the holy hell are you babbling about?" I asked. "What has that got to do with the price of tea in China?"

"I know nothing about tea, or China, for that matter. But the Puck's wife was tied to the Summerlands, and her tie could only be severed by Titania's blessing, or by Mab laying claim to her."

"Which would tie her to Winter," Mama said. "Then Mother could release her from her bond to Winter and she would be free of any ties to a Season."

"Exactly," Oberon said.

"So what's the problem?" Joe asked.

"Titania wouldn't release her from Summer, and Mab would not claim her over Titania's mark," Mama said, her face grave. Oberon nodded, as if that explained everything.

"That doesn't explain anything," I said. "What's the big deal? She's married to Puck, but she still works for Titania. No big deal."

"Expect that Summer Fae cannot live in the Seasonless Lands," Oberon said. "Our magic ties us to a Court, and if we spend too long in another Court's lands, we suffer the consequences."

"Those consequences are permanent, aren't they?" Amy asked.

"They are."

"So when she was stuck tied to Summer, she either had to stay in Titania's realm or die," Amy went on. Oberon just nodded.

"Okay, so Puck wasn't big on a long-distance relationship, but it ain't the worst thing in the world," I said.

"She's dead, Robbie," Mama said, her voice soft. Oberon nodded again.

I turned to him. "Wait, what?"

"I know Robin," Mama said. "He was a frequent visitor to Winter when I was young. He is a Shadow Fae, a Walker Between Seasons, unaffiliated but useful to both Courts. The Puck is a...problem-solver for Mab and Titania alike, the person they call when something or someone becomes...troublesome."

"An assassin," Joe said.

"Yes," Oberon said. "An assassin, a weapon, a tool to be used. Titania saw his love for Alethea as a hold on him, a way to secure his services for her alone. She told him that she would release Alethea from her service, but only if he swore fealty to Summer."

"And Mab promised to supplant Titania's claim on the girl if he would pledge to Winter," Mama said.

"Exactly," Oberon agreed. "The Puck, being a creature of great temper and possessing of a great desire to continue to play both Courts against each other, refused both offers, and took his bride back to the Shadow Keep."

"But all she had to do was leave and go back to Summer to be okay, right?" I asked. I knew what I was going to hear, but I didn't want to think it.

"Puck wouldn't allow it. Giving her up would mean losing to Titania, accepting defeat in a game played for centuries. So he imprisoned her within the Shadow Keep and stayed by her side every moment."

"Until she died," Skeeter whispered.

"Until she died," Oberon agreed. "Then he waited. The Puck is clever and patient. He knew eventually an opportunity for revenge would come along. And it did, in the form of your sister."

"He took her to get back at Mab for not helping save Alethea, but how would that hurt Titania?" Amy asked.

"If he hurts Nitalia for Mab's negligence, Mab will see it as Titania's fault."

"Because Titania did not release Alethea from her fealty," Mama said. "Then Mab will move Winter against Summer, and there will be war. My mother is many things, mad perhaps foremost among them. She would see Nitalia's death as a personal affront, and look to any cause that absolves her of guilt. She would blame Titania, and she would tear Faerie apart to avenge the insult. She cares nothing for my daughter, but killing Nitalia would be an insult, and her pride would not allow her to let it stand."

"So Puck is going to kill my sister to drive Mab into attacking Titania for letting his wife die? Seems convoluted," I said.

"Convoluted is one of the highest compliments in Faerie," Oberon said. "I do not wish to see my granddaughter harmed, but I cannot move against the Puck myself. Titania has forbidden it, and I am bound within the confines of the Summerlands until she sees fit to loosen my chains."

"So we have to go to the Shadow Keep to save Nitalia," I said. "How do we know she's still alive?"

"Her head has not been delivered to Mab's throne room," Oberon said.

"Well, that's pleasant," Amy said. "Okay, we can find her using Bubba's repurposed compass. Do we know when he plans to do the deed? It sounds like Puck has a flair for the dramatic."

"We are eight days from the anniversary of Princess Alethea's death," Oberon replied. "If I were a betting Fae, I would guess that is when he plans his revenge."

"So we've got a week to travel through a hostile realm of magic, invade something called the Shadow Keep, and kick a mystical assassin's ass before he murders my long-lost sister that I've never met," I said. I nodded, then stood up and looked around at my family and best friends. "Okay, gang. We've traveled to another dimension and killed a dragon. Now let's go save the faerie princess so we can go home." I turned and walked toward the pile of my weapons laying on the ground by one of the wagons.

Amy walked up next to me and started gearing up herself. "Gonna put our lives on the line against impossible odds."

Joe stepped up beside her. "Heading off into unspeakable danger to save someone we've never laid eyes on."

Skeeter leaned against the wagon and grinned at me. "Gonna kick a lot of ass and look good doing it."

I gave Skeeter a fist-bump and said, "Horrible danger? Terrible odds? Shitty rewards? Let's do this."

The End...for now

PART IV

SHADES OF GREY

1

The transition from the lands of Winter to the Summerlands had been subtle, a general warming and greening of the surroundings that I really didn't notice until Mama said something. Moving from Summer into the Lands Without Season was totally different. We rode up to a sharp line in the earth, a slash of demarcation where the color drained out of everything around us, dimming even the sun in a matter of seconds.

"This is as far as I can go, Robbie," Mama said from her horse beside me.

I reined in Buttercup, the cart horse they assigned to me, and turned to her. "What are you talking about? We've got to go in there after Puck and get Nitalia back."

"No, you have to get her, Robbie. You and your friends. I can't go into the Shadowlands. Puck is native to the Shadow, and his hold on the land is too strong. He would know it was me the second I set foot in his domain, and he would turn all his magic against us. And I would not be strong enough to stand against him. I am a creature of the Courts. I can move between Winter and Summer at will, but I cannot set foot in the Lands Without Season. The conflict between my magic and Puck's is too strong. It would kill me, and quickly."

"Then doesn't that mean it killed Nitalia just as fast?" Amy asked.

Oberon rode forward and answered. "No. Ygraine's daughter is less tied to the Courts than she is, not having lived among the royal houses. Her ties to us are weaker, and that benefits her now. She can survive in the Shadowlands longer thanks to that, and Puck may also be using his own magics to keep her alive."

"Because live bait is better than dead bait," I muttered.

"Exactly," Oberon agreed. "Your mother wished to accompany you this far, to see if her assumptions about the Shadowlands held true. Unfortunately, she was correct, and we must return to Tisa'ron."

"Well, I reckon we'll miss you, Obie," Skeeter said, before muttering "not" under his breath. Neither of my grandparents had done anything to ingratiate themselves to my friends on this trip, although at least Oberon hadn't gone out of his way to try and murder us.

"Can we talk, Robbie?" Mama asked me, slipping down off her horse.

I managed to get down off Buttercup without falling on my ass, which was a marked improvement over most of the times I tried to get off a horse, and I followed her to a stump a little ways off from where my friends waited. She sat down and looked up me, smiling.

"Sit down, Robbie. Sit with me, like you used to when you were little."

"I think you mean young, Mama. I'm pretty sure I was never little," I corrected, but I grinned when I did it. I sat down on the ground in front of her. "What's up?"

"I need to tell you some things before you go into Shadow looking for Puck and Nitalia. I cannot go with you, but I won't send you in there blind either."

"I've dealt with Puck before, Mama," I reminded her. "I'll be fine."

"You've dealt with him in his guise as Robin Goodfellow, the trickster. He may have threatened or intimidated, but he didn't try to actually harm you or those children he stole. That was Puck on his best behavior. This is something entirely different. This is Puck the Shadowborn, the murderer for hire, the killer for sport, the deadliest faerie in the history of this land. He was dangerous before this happened, but now he is likely completely mad and perhaps the most lethal foe you have ever faced, including the dragon Xythigax the Terrible."

I thought back to the first time I dealt with the legendary faerie trickster. He was fast, strong as hell, and teleported around like a really irritating X-Man, but I managed to bloody his nose and take him down that way. Judging from the look in Mama's eyes, I wasn't likely to get close enough to lay a finger on him this time. "What's changed? I mean, I know his wife died, so he's kinda unhinged by that, but why did that turn him so psycho?"

"It's not that the Princess Alethea died, it's *how* she died. The wasting from magical poisoning is horrifically painful and excruciating not only to endure, but to watch. She must have lived in agony her last few weeks, maybe even months, and Puck could do nothing to help her."

"Couldn't he just send her home?" I asked. That was the one thing that had bugged me about this whole deal ever since Mama explained it.

"She would not be allowed to return. She was a servant of Summer, and Titania released her to Puck as a result of a lost wager. A wager lost by Oberon, her consort." Mama laid emphasis on that last bit, and I sat there, letting the damp grass soak into my butt while I turned it all over in my head. Faerie politics are harder to follow than the conga line at a sorority party.

"I think I get it," I said. "Titania was being a bitch because her hubby screwed up and lost a bet, so she had to give away one of her subjects. Since Titania's batshit crazy, and kind of evil on top of it, she thinks of her subjects as her possessions, more like toys than people. She didn't like getting her Barbie doll taken away, so she wouldn't let Alethea come back to Summer to get well, and she wouldn't cut the bonds to Summer so she wouldn't wither."

"Exactly. And Mab would not intervene, as Alethea was one of Titania's rightful subjects," Mama added.

"Well, I reckon there was probably more layers to it than that," I countered. "Mab also thought that since this was a bet Oberon lost, she could either save her ex's bacon by bonding the Princess to Winter, then releasing her to be free, or more likely she could just let the girl die to keep Oberon looking like an asshole to his new wife." Maybe faerie politics weren't all that different from human junior high love affairs after all.

"That also played a part in the situation," Mama agreed.

"So, Puck watched the love of his life die a horrible death that could have been prevented if either of the rulers of Fairyland had pulled their heads out of their asses long enough to take a look around." The more I dissected the situation, the more Puck looked like the victim. Right up until the point where he kidnapped my half-sister and decided to let her die that same death to make Mab and Oberon feel bad for letting their grandkid die. I think everybody knew Titania would not give one single gold-plated shit about Nitalia dying, other than to be pissed off that Puck killed another child of Summer.

Mama cast her eyes aside. "The politics of Faerie have always been...complicated."

"Nah," I said. "I went to public school. I've seen bullies before. Your parents are assholes. Your stepmom is an even bigger asshole. Puck was justified in being pissed, but when he kidnaped Nitalia, he moved right into asshole territory, too. So now I gotta find him and do what I do to assholes. And that metaphor just went right off the rails into Awkward-Town, didn't it?"

Mama laughed, and her warm cascade of mirth sounded out of place this close to the grim border of Shadow. "It did, but I take your meaning. You mean to go into Shadow and deal with the Puck and bring your sister back safely."

"That's the whole quest, right? That's why I'm carrying this ring around, why they killed Aunt Beru and Uncle Owen, why Aslan brought us all into Narnia? Yeah, I'm gonna finish the quest, ruin Puck's day, and get all Jean Valjean up in this bitch and bring her home."

"Showtunes, Robbie?" Mama asked with a light smile.

"Hey, I'm multi-dimensional. Plus, Amy likes musicals, and my best friend is gay. I'm not what they call 'family,' but I'm damn sure an in-law." I smiled back at her, then reached up to pat her on the knee. I stood up and rolled my shoulders, then checked my guns. It was getting close to time to cross into the Lands Without Season, and I was getting antsy with all the talky stuff. "I'll get her back, Mama. You just go chill with Grandpa Obie, and we'll take care of it."

"You love pushing his buttons, don't you?" she said with a smile.

"Well, he was kind of an absent grandfather for a long time, so he deserves an extra helping of Bubba now that we've met, right?" I grinned down at her, then folded her in a giant hug.

She reached up, her slender arms wrapping around my waist. Well, partway around my waist, if we're being honest. "Be careful, Robbie. I want both my children to come back to me."

I pulled back and looked down into her eyes. "I guarantee it, Mama. Now let's go blow some shit up."

I walked back to the horses and noticed that everybody else was on the ground, too. "What's up, y'all? Did everybody have to pee all of a sudden?"

"The horses won't cross the border," Joe said, pulling his saddlebags off and throwing them across one shoulder.

"They are creatures of Summer, Robert," Oberon said. "They cannot abide in Shadow."

"Nice of you to tell us that ahead of time, Gramps," I grumbled. I looked over to Buttercup, but Skeeter waved me off.

"We got your pack all set, Bubba. Let's just get on the road," he said.

I started toward the border, but Oberon held up a hand. "Wait, there is something I must give you."

I turned back to him and looked at the ring he held in his outstretched palm. "Grandpa, I don't know about how things work in Fairyland, but even the most progressive places ain't gonna let me marry my own granddad. Besides, I'm not into dudes."

He looked at me for a long couple of heartbeats, then just sighed. "I don't understand all of the things you said, but I believe you are somehow subtly mocking me. Regardless—"

"Oh, it wasn't subtle," Skeeter interrupted.

"Not even a little," Amy agreed.

Oberon sighed again. It must be rough being the powerful ruler of a Faerie Court, and your grandson and all his friends just not giving a single shit. I still wasn't the least bit sympathetic. "Sorry, Gramps. You were saying?"

"I was saying that if you wear this ring, you will be able to escape the Lands Without Season via a teleportation spell at a thought. Simply say 'Tisa'ron' and you will be returned to our castle, along with anyone within the immediate vicinity."

"What's the immediate vicinity?" I asked. If I'd learned anything in my time in Fairyland, it's that magic is some finicky shit. I didn't want to pop out of trouble only to find that I left Skeeter, or worse, half of Skeeter, behind. "Do I have to be touching everyone who wants to come with me?"

"That would be best. The spell has a range of several feet, but if they are in direct contact with you, there is no chance for confusion."

"Well, God knows we have enough confusion in our lives already," Amy said. "Put on the ring, Bubba, and let's get moving. We're burning daylight, and we don't know how long your sister has before being away from Summer drains her completely."

"Your companion is correct," Oberon said. "We know that she still lives because Puck would certainly have delivered her corpse to her mother or me if she had died. But every day will see her grow weaker. You must proceed with haste."

"I got it," I said, reaching out and taking the ring. It didn't look big enough, but it slipped right on my finger, then the metal heated up, and it shrank down to fit my hand perfectly. I turned my hand over and tugged on it, but the ring was on there pretty good. "I hope you've got soap back at the castle, Gramps. This thing doesn't want to come off."

"The ring will disappear once its magic is used. So be wise, it has only one charge." With that, and not another word, Oberon turned and walked back over to his horse. He swung himself up into the saddle and turned his mount around. "Let us away. It pains me to be this close to the border with Shadow."

Mama glared at him but rushed through a quick goodbye to Joe and Amy, then gave Skeeter a fierce hug, holding him for several seconds before letting him go. She held him out at arm's length and said, "You take care of my baby, Skeeter."

He nodded, solemn for once. "Yes, ma'am. I always do."

She hugged him again, then looked at me. "Try not to do anything stupid, Robbie."

"No promises, Mama. I'll see you soon."

She nodded, then turned away, humming a tune from *Les Miserables* as she hopped up on her horse and they rode away, leading our mounts behind them.

I watched them ride away, then turned back to Skeeter, Amy, and Joe. "Alright, gang. Let's go to the dark side. I hear they have cookies."

2

———————

The Land Without Season looked a lot like the rest of Fairyland, only in a perpetual Southern November or February. It wasn't cold, just kinda chilly. It didn't snow, but there was persistent drizzle that soaked everything, but it wasn't cold enough to break out any heavy traveling gear. It was cloudy, but not the heavy snow clouds of winter, just a general overcast.

In short, it sucked. Walking through it sucked, making camp sucked, trying to get a fire started sucked, and after a morning riding and a pitiful attempt at cooking something for lunch, we were all pretty pissy.

"How much do you like your sister, Bubba?" Skeeter asked from behind me. "'Cause, this sucks enough that I don't know if I'd tromp through this much longer to rescue you, and I like you."

"I've never even met my sister, Skeeter," I called back over my shoulder. "I'm suffering through this shit on the off chance that I do like her."

"After slogging through this crap, she'd better pee rainbows and fart sparkles," Amy muttered beside me. "This has got to be the worst meet your in-laws trip in history."

"That reminds me," I said, looking over at her in a desperate attempt to change the subject and stem the tide of whining that I figured was about to bowl me over. "I still haven't met either of your parents. You've met both of mine. I think it's time we fixed that, just as soon as we get back to the right dimension."

"Bubba, the first time I met your father, he tried to kill me. And the first time I met your mother, your brother was trying to murder her, you, me, and most of Georgia. Meeting the parents hasn't really gone well for us, historically," Amy replied.

"That's why I was hoping you'd tell me your dad was a used car salesman in Scranton, or something nice and middle class like that. Is this the part where you tell me he's a necromancer, or kidnapped by aliens, or something really terrifying?"

"Like a hairstylist," Skeeter chimed in. "I'm pretty sure a makeover is his biggest fear in life."

I flipped my best friend the bird, but there was some truth to his words. I haven't shaved my beard since I got out of college, and I don't have any idea what my chin looks like these days. That's probably for the best, since I reckon it's got a couple of little bonus chins hanging out down there with it ever since I got old and fat. I turned to Amy. "You ain't said nothing. What's the deal? I mean, I don't even know if your parents are still alive, still married, divorced, nothing."

"It's not something I like to talk about," she said. "My dad is just an average guy. He likes to putter around in his little workshop, play around with some woodworking, make benches, turn old wooden doors into coffee tables, that kind of thing. He's not great at it, but it makes him happy, so I pretend not to notice when the picnic table he made for me wobbles a little, or when the picture frame doesn't sit quite flat on the mantel. But he's great. I love my dad. He doesn't love what I do, of course. I mean, what father wants his daughter hunting down and apprehending things that literally could rip her in half? But he's resigned himself to it, and we've reached a kind of 'don't ask, don't tell' detente. I don't tell work stories, and he doesn't ask questions."

"That's kinda cool," I said. "Does he like football?"

"He's a Colts fan. He grew up in Indy, and he and my mom still have a place up there, almost halfway between the zoo and the speed-way. We used to spend summers up there, he and I, to get away from the heat in D.C." This was more talking about her childhood than she'd done in all the years we'd been together, so I was inclined to do anything I could to keep her talking.

"So, you grew up in Washington?" Skeeter picked up his pace to walk on the other side of Amy along the wide road through Fairy-land. Skeeter's a nosy little shit on his best day, and when he's bored or uncomfortable, he's even worse. Being bored *and* uncomfortable, he was the perfect storm of curious.

Amy sighed. "I guess we've got nothing better to do than talk about my family, huh?"

"You know all about mine, as screwed up as it is," Skeeter said.

"Hey!" Joe protested from where he brought up the rear.

"Present company excluded, but even you have to admit, having somebody in your family you can literally call Uncle Father Joe is a little odd," Skeeter said.

I looked back at Joe, and we exchanged "what can you say?" shrugs. When my little buddy is right, he's right.

"And we ain't even going to get into the mess that's my family history, are we? I mean, my grandaddy Oberon, the friggin' fairy king, just took my mother, the fairy princess, back to Titania's castle while we trek through some kind of weird-ass Shadow Land looking for my long-lost half-sister, who would end up being my only living sibling, given the fact that I killed my brother for trying to take over the world. After he turned my daddy into a werewolf. Oh, and I killed him, too."

"You're hell at family reunions, ain't you, Bubba," Skeeter said.

"My family reunions involve a lot of solitaire, Skeet."

"All that's fair. I mean, given that, I guess my family is pretty normal. My parents are still married after forty-two years. Dad retired early, about ten years ago. He had a little money when he was young, invested well, and is doing pretty well for himself. I'm no big heiress or anything, but he's got enough socked away that he doesn't have to punch a clock. Mom still works, and probably will as long as..."

She looked away, and I cleared my throat. "Go ahead," I said.

Amy opened her mouth to answer, but then her eyes lit up. "What's that up ahead?" she asked, pointing down the road. Sure enough, peeking out of the gloom before us was a yellow light that looked like a lantern, but it bobbed and weaved through the air higher off the road than it should.

"Amy, you and Joe get off to the side of the road. Set up a flanking position, and shoot anything threatening. Me and Skeeter will wait here and see what it is." I reached under my left arm and popped open the snap on Bertha's shoulder holster. I had cold iron rounds loaded, designed to kill anything Fae that I hit.

"Why do I have to stand out here in the open like a sitting duck?" Skeeter protested. "I know you're an idiot, Bubba, but I'm not. I'm way better at the run and hide part than I am at the punch things part."

"Yeah, but nobody would walk through this shadowy shithole alone, and Joe's got the rifle. Amy's good with her pistol out to thirty yards, and you can't shoot worth a shit past ten. They can get off the road and back into cover while still being useful, something you don't have a chance at."

He looked pissed but didn't argue. Joe and Amy split off and took cover while Skeeter and I stood in the middle of the road, watching the light bob along toward us. After a few minutes, the fuzzy yellow light resolved into a golden glow, and I could see that it was a lantern mounted on a stick hanging beside the seat of a covered wagon.

"Ho there, travelers!" came a jolly voice from the mist.

"Howdy," I called back.

"Do ye mean to rob me, or are ye just afraid of an old man and his cart full of wares?" As the wagon rolled closer, I could see that it was indeed an old faerie man sitting on the buckboard. He had a blade at his side, but there wasn't any real evidence that he intended to use it.

"I ain't so much afraid of you, but I might have some concerns about who's riding with you," I said.

"Nobody here but me, friend. Why don't you tell your friends to come out of the woods, and I'll give you some idea the mess you're walking into about ten miles back that way." He jerked a thumb over his shoulder to indicate the direction he was riding from. Which, naturally, was the direction we were heading. Because we couldn't just walk to Puck's place, knock on his door, beat his ass, and rescue Nitalia. Oh no, we had to walk into some kind of damn revolution or some such bullshit.

I waved Joe and Amy in from the trees, and they walked over, their weapons down but still ready. They stood in front of the wagon with me and Skeeter, but off to each side, in case somebody tried to sneak in behind the cart and jump us. I'm not usually paranoid, but I have learned that if I assume everybody's out to get me and there really is a monster around every corner, my life is just a lot easier. Okay, so maybe that's the literal definition of paranoid. Whatever, don't judge.

"What's going on down the road, old-timer?" I asked, trying to look as pleasant and relaxed as I knew how. I figured I still probably looked like a mass murderer, but maybe I looked like, I dunno, a *pleasant* mass murderer. Like a clown. That kills people. Wait, that shtick's been done.

He stood up on the seat, and a transformation came over the little man. Instead of just a wizened little carter, he pranced across the narrow buckboard like a gymnast. He bowed deeply from the waist, popped back up with a top hat in his hands that I have no idea where he pulled it from, and tossed it high into the air. I watched it flip over and over as it rose up, up, and up, finally to drop back onto his head.

"Please allow me to introduce myself," he started.

I leaned over to Skeeter and said, "If he says he's a man of wealth and taste, start shooting." Skeeter, a lifelong Rolling Stones fan, nodded sagely.

The little man glared at me, then went on. "I am Terlindor the Splendiferous, the finest purveyor in Faerie. I have ointments, liniments, ligaments, testaments, testifies, fireflies, and flyswatters. I have gumdrops and gemstones, pendants and ink pens. I have weapons of war and instruments of seduction. I have the finest selection of goods in Winter, Summer, or The Grey. My prices cannot be matched, and my quality cannot be paralleled. I offer satisfaction guaranteed and a full money-back policy, no questions asked. Now, gents and gals, what can I interest you in this fine, albeit dreary, afternoon?"

I drew Bertha and pointed her at his nose. "Information. No magic, no splendiferousness. No selling, no buying, no snappy patter, no witty repartee. You tell us what we're walking into on the road ahead, then you move along. You give me any trouble, and I punch a hole in your chest with this cold iron slug, and I turn your insides to outsides, I turn your outsides to bloody mist, and I turn your wagon into your coffin. I'm a long way from home for a very long time, and I am tired of fast-talking faeries pulling hats out of their butts and baffling me with bullshit. So sit down, take off your hat, and spill your guts. Figuratively. Or I'll spill them for you. Literally."

Terlindor looked from me to Skeeter but found himself staring down the barrel of Skeeter's Mossberg. He turned to Amy and found a Smith & Wesson conversation ender trained on him. He didn't even bother looking over to Joe, but the priest had him covered, too. "Fine," he said, slumping down to the seat, all hint of glamour and showmanship gone. "But you can't blame a guy for trying to bring a little magic into your boring human lives."

"I might not blame you," I said. "But I'll damn well shoot you. I've had about as much magic as I can stand these past few months. Now get to talking, or I'll get to shooting."

"Okay, okay!" He held up both hands as if to ward off bullets with them. "Well, I reckon the first thing you're going to want to hear about is the zombies."

3

—————

I wanted to say, "No, I don't want to hear about any goddamn zombies. I want to hear about unicorns and puppies and kittens and fluffy bunnies that poop jellybeans." But I didn't. I'm not Bubba the Kitten Cuddler. I'm Bubba the damn Monster Hunter, and zombies definitely fall into the "monster" category, in Fairyland or in the real world. So I sighed the sigh of a man who knows he's heading into a shitshow and sees no way to get out of it, and said, "Tell me about the zombies."

"Well, my large and extremely surly friend, ahead of you on the road, about three hours of easy walking, lies the village of Dun Sheene. It's not much of a town, just a dozen or so homes, a smith who mostly fixes plows and makes horseshoes, and several hundred acres of farmland centered around a tavern and a church in the center of town. There can't be more than a hundred people living there at any given time. Most of the traffic comes from nearby farmers who bring in their grain to the mill and traders buying flour and taking it to larger towns or villages over in the Summerlands."

"Sounds nice, actually," Amy said. I looked over, and she had a little smile on her lips, like she was remembering something pleasant.

"It is, my lady, if your tastes run to the prosaic. Or it was, the last time I came through. This time, however, there was a very different feeling in Dun Sheene. The entire area felt as though a blanket of sadness and fear lay over the town. The feeling started several miles before I reached town, a general unease that grew oppressive the closer to Dun Sheene I drew. Finally, I entered the town, but none of the normal children rushed out to greet me. I carry a few bags of sweets, you see, to toss out to the children when I arrive in a new town, or one I haven't visited in a while. I find a little treat helps endear me to the young ones, and getting them out from underfoot endears me to their mothers."

"And if you have the love of the mothers, you have the coin of the fathers," Joe said with a nod. "It's another reason a strong Woman's Auxiliary is the lifeblood of a healthy church. If Mother goes to church on Sunday morning, the entire family goes to church."

"That's the damn truth," Skeeter said, rubbing his backside. "I remember how Mama used to lay into my hide if I didn't behave in Sunday School. But I'm sorry, Mr. Terlindor. Please go on."

The garishly clad merchant nodded, then said, "The town felt deserted, and yet I had the peculiar sensation of being watched with every step. I felt as if the farther I went into town, the less likely that I would be able to leave. Finally, as I reached the center of the village, I saw a figure waving to me from the church. I climbed down from my wagon and went over to the door, but found it barred against my entry. I didn't even know the church at Dun Sheene had a lock on the door."

He pulled out a handkerchief and mopped his sweating brow. It wasn't that hot, so I couldn't tell if he was overwrought from his experience with the zombies, or if running into a giant redneck with a gun had him sweating bullets. I reckon either one was a pretty valid response.

He went on with his tale. "A man spoke to me from within the church, exhorting me to leave town and send help. He told me that they were overrun with zombies, but they only hunted a night. So, the entire surviving townsfolk were taking refuge in the church, praying for some assistance."

"I would have expected most of them to be hiding in that tavern you mentioned, seeking aid from spirits of a different kind," I muttered.

Terlindor looked over at me with a sad smile. "According to the man in the church, some had attempted that very thing. But when I went to the tavern, I found nothing but a shattered front window and some smears of blood on the walls and floor. There were no towns-folk remaining."

"Well, shit," I said. "So we've got a whole town's population trapped in a church against nightly zombie raids, and they sent you out to find somebody to help them?"

"That is the situation in a nutshell, yes," Terlindor replied.

"I reckon y'all would take exception to me saying we oughta make camp here, sleep the night ten miles away from the shitload of zombies, and plow through in the morning, leaving the zombies to somebody else, wouldn't you?"

Skeeter was the only one who said anything, and all he said was, "Yes, I would take exception to that asshole plan." Joe just folded his arms and gave me the same steely glare he usually reserved for when I was confessing something particularly stupid and egregious. Amy was the one who tipped the scales, though. She knows how to get me every time. She gave me her "I'm disappointed in you" face, and all debate was over. It's not really fair, to be honest. She knows I can't handle the disappointed face. I can even hold out against the puppy dog eyes for a little while, but the disappointed face is an instant win for her. Good thing for me she doesn't drag it out that often.

"Okay." I turned back to Terlindor. "Did you see any of the zombies?"

"No. I did as the man suggested, and I got back on the road as fast as I could. I stopped only to water my horses. I didn't even take them out of the traces."

"Did the people in the church tell you anything about the

zombies?" Amy asked, slipping back into her role as federal agent investigator.

"No, my lady. They only said they were zombies."

"So, we don't know if they're slow zombies or fast zombies," Amy said with a frown.

"Do they even have fast zombies in Fairyland?" Skeeter asked.

"I hope not," I said. "Fast zombies suck."

Almost three hours later, Skeeter looked around the deserted town of Dun Sheene and declared, "The old dude was right. This place is creepy as hell."

I couldn't argue with him. It was creepy. There were eight or ten little cottages, cozy places with thatched roofs and wooden doors, but they all seemed to be locked up tight. The doors were shut, and the curtains drawn over every window. No children roamed the streets, and no one worked in the fields as we walked into the village. All the gardens were abandoned, and the fire in the forge at the smithy was dark and cold. If any place I'd ever been looked like the perfect setting for a horror movie, it was Dun Sheene.

"Fan out and check the buildings," Amy said, drawing her pistol. "If there are zombies, go for head shots. I don't know if lead will kill a Fae zombie, or if it has to be cold iron, but at the very least it'll slow it down until Bubba can get there and pulp its head." She looked over to me, and I nodded.

I pulled the pair of caestus from my belt and slipped the iron-banded gloves on. The knuckles had cold iron studs screwed into them, making my fists pretty damn lethal weapons against fairies. With the protection of the heavy leather and spikes, I wasn't afraid to punch a zombie to death, either.

Amy and Skeeter went left, and Joe and I went right. I flung the door to the first cottage open, and Joe darted inside with his rifle out and sweeping ahead of him before I even got the door all the way open. I followed, but it only took us a couple of seconds to see that the little house was deserted.

"Clear!" I called across the dirt path to the others.

"Clear!" Amy hollered back. Part of me worried about making so much noise in the middle of a zombie infestation, but the rest of me decided that dead things shouldn't be able to hear, so it didn't matter. I didn't know what kind of zombies we were dealing with, so I couldn't tell if they were still somewhat sentient or not.

We repeated the process half a dozen times, with each house proving to be as deserted as the last. After sweeping the dozen houses that made up the center of town and giving the blacksmith's shop and attached home a quick once-over, we gathered in the center of the street. "Well, there ain't nothing in here," I said.

"Yeah," Skeeter agreed. "If there's any people here at all, they're either in the bar or the church." He pointed to the two largest buildings in town, set off about twenty yards from the row of houses. One had a small porch in front of it and a glass door with a mug etched on the glass. Another dozen yards from the houses stood a structure that looked a lot like every small-town church in our world, right down to the white clapboard construction and the steeple.

"So far it seems that everything Terlindor has told us is true," Joe said. "Should we just assume that the rest is true as well and move on to the church?"

"Nah," I said. "You know what happens when you assume, right? You make an ass out of yourself."

"I don't think that's how that saying goes, Bubba," Amy said.

"Really? Ah, whatever. Either way, I'm all about investigating the bar first." I turned and took a step in that direction, but Amy stopped me with a hand on my arm.

"You sure you aren't just looking to pilfer some unattended booze, Bubba?" she asked.

"Would I do that?" I put on my best innocent face, but it didn't stop all three of my best friends in the world from standing right in front of me and nodding like a bobble-head Jesus on a trucker's dash.

"Well, maybe," I admitted. "But zombie hunting is thirsty work, so you can't blame a guy for trying."

"We do need to check it out," Skeeter said, unslinging the shotgun from his shoulder. "Why don't me and Bubba check it out while y'all negotiate with the fairies in the church to let us in?"

"What makes you think *we* should negotiate?" Joe asked.

"Uncle, who would you send in to ask somebody nicely, the preacher and the pretty girl, or the giant tattooed hillbilly and the black queen? Remember, there are no black people in Fairyland, so they might not know what I am and decide to shoot me on sight. And there's a better than even chance they'll think Bubba is a monster. Like a bugbear or something."

"I'm gonna choose not to be insulted, since I don't know what that is," I said.

"Good call," Joe said. "Fine. We'll go talk to the townsfolk in the church while you go make sure the alcohol is safe."

"I know exactly where it will be the safest," I replied, grinning.

"If you do your Fat Bastard impression from *Austin Powers*, you are going into that zombie nest alone," Skeeter warned me.

I stifled a "get in ma belly" roar and walked to the bar, a little disappointed that I didn't get to do my bit, but my spirits were lifted by the potential of booze in my near future. The bar was as deserted as every other building in town, but it had one noticeable advantage —a dozen bottles of whiskey sitting on a shelf behind the scarred wooden bar.

The whole place looked a little run down more than lived-in, like the town was a couple of drunks short of keeping the place prosperous. I pulled the stopper out of one of the bottles and had it almost to my lips when I heard something odd.

"Hey, what's that noise?" I turned to see a narrow door beside the end of the bar that we hadn't noticed before. There was a scratching noise coming from it, and it got louder and more frantic the closer I got to the door.

"Bubba, don't open that door," Skeeter warned.

"Skeeter, it won't be nothing. We've covered every inch of this place, and we haven't seen a single zombie. The old man said they don't come around until after dark, and we've still got a good couple hours of daylight yet." I put my hand on the doorknob and turned, pulling the door open.

I've really got to learn to listen to people. A pair of zombies lurched out of the door, and I had just enough time to look out the front window of the bar to see the sun dipping below the horizon as they came after me. I'll say it here, just this once, for posterity.

Skeeter was right, dammit.

4

———

"**S**hitshitshitshitshitSHIT!" I yelped, staggering back from the door and trying not to land on my ass with a couple hundred pounds of zombie fairy on top of me. The good news was that these zombies were the slow, stupid kind. The better news was that because they started off as fairies, they were pretty small and light. So once I had my balance, it wasn't too hard to keep them off me.

Skeeter was about as much help as I expected him to be, which is to say none whatso-damn-ever. He took one look at the zombies and hauled ass around the bar to the front door. I fended off the first zombie's snapping teeth by jamming my caestus into its mouth, then I drew Bertha from under my left arm, pressed the barrel of the big pistol to the side of the zombie's head, and made a fifty-caliber attitude adjustment.

Bertha is a loud lady of a pistol, and in confined spaces, it's even worse. When she barked, the zombie's head damn sure exploded, but I wasn't too sure what shape my eardrums were in. Either way, I swung her around and blew the shit out of the second zombie, and that was all anybody needed to write about that. I holstered Bertha, grabbed a bottle of whiskey from the shelf behind the bar, and walked to the door, where Skeeter was staring through the glass like he was watching *Avengers 7* or something.

"What is it, Skeeter?" I asked, but when he turned to me, I couldn't hear him. I shook my head and pointed to my ears, and he nodded.

"THERE'S A BUNCH MORE ZOMBIES OUT THERE," Skeeter yelled, pointing out the window. I looked over his shoulder, and sure enough, there were a couple dozen zombies shambling up the main street of the town. Where the hell they came from, I had no idea. There weren't any zombies in any of the houses in town, we hadn't seen any graveyards or anything like that, and we'd only been in the bar a few minutes before the sun went down. Which also seemed to happen too fast. I would have sworn we had a couple hours' worth of daylight left. Damn magical dimensions, screwing with time and shit like that.

I turned around in a circle, giving the interior of the bar a good look to make sure there were no more zombies inside, then walked to the door. "This is going to suck, Skeeter."

He winced, then nodded. I might have been talking a little louder than normal on account of the ringing in my ears, but it sure wasn't going to get better anytime soon. I stepped onto the small porch of the tavern and turned to Skeeter. "Get to the church and get inside with Joe and Amy. I'll hold them off until you're inside; then I'll come in and join you."

He moved his lips, but I didn't hear anything. I shook my head at him, and he pursed his lips, then yelled, "HOW WILL WE KNOW IT'S YOU AND NOT A ZOMBIE?"

"I'll be the one cussing. The zombies will just be moaning." He turned to run, but I grabbed the back of his belt. "Here, take this." I handed him my bottle of whiskey. "Don't you let Amy drink all that. I've been sober this whole damn trip, and if I survive a zombie attack in Fairyland, I intend to change that first thing."

Skeeter nodded and ran off up the street toward the church. I looked at the passel of zombies heading my way and let out a sigh. This was going to suck. I stepped down the two rickety steps onto the dirt path that passed for a main street and slipped off my caestae. I needed all my limited manual dexterity to change magazines as fast as possible, so my iron-clad gloves would have to sit this one out. I tossed the gloves onto the porch and drew Bertha. The zombies were about twenty yards away, so it was time to get to killing.

After taking out the two in the bar, I had five rounds left before I would have to reload. I made them count, steadying myself against one of the porch railings to give me more accuracy. I dropped four zombies with five shots, then ejected the spent magazine. I pulled a spare out from under my right arm and slapped it home as the horde shambled ever closer. Seven shots, five zombies down. The other two rounds did damage, but they weren't head shots, so they weren't kills. I mean, a shot in the shoulder from a fifty-caliber pistol will kill a human, and pretty much anything else in the world, but when you're shooting something already dead, you gotta be accurate.

I ejected the second magazine, letting it drop to the dirt next to its brother, and slapped another home. The mass of undead was less than ten yards away now, but I managed to drop another four before the slide locked open. I popped the magazine release and reached in my back pocket for my last clip. Seven shots left, and there were still a dozen zombies just a few feet away. This was about to suck.

The only upside to the zombies getting closer to me was that I hit six out of seven head shots this time, so I only had half a dozen zombies closing on me when I ran out of bullets. As much as it hurt me to treat her that way, I didn't even holster Bertha, I just dropped her to the ground and drew Great-Grandpappy Beauregard's sword. I didn't know if I was good enough to take out half a dozen zombies without a gun or some backup, but I sure wasn't just going to lay down and let the smelly dead bastards take me without a fight.

I stepped back up onto the porch, using the railings to funnel the zombies into a tighter kill box, and when the first one bumped into the steps and leaned forward, I sliced the top of its head off like I was Gallagher in Las Vegas. It dropped, fouling the steps of the one behind it, and I jabbed it through the eye socket like an oversized Michonne from *The Walking Dead*. It fell on top of its buddy, and I was building a nice little zombie barricade to hide behind. Until the porch railing to my left cracked and gave way and two zombies clambered up onto the porch beside me. Another one climbed over the pile of its buddies in front of me, straight into my sword.

Three down, but all three of the ones still standing were coming at me all at once. I backed up, but the porch was wide enough for two zombies to come at me at the same time, so I ducked under their grasping arms and lashed out with the sword. I don't know what the hell Great-Grandpappy made this sword out of, but it cut through muscle and bone like it was warm butter, and two zombies fell right off their legs onto the porch. I stabbed one through the back of the head, stomped the other one's skull flat, and stepped forward, driving the steel blade through the eye of the last zombie.

I wiped the blade down on a dead zombie's shirt, slid it back in the sheath over my shoulder, and picked up Bertha. I promised her a good cleaning as soon as we got back to anything resembling civilization and put her back in her holster. I picked up my caestae from the porch, clipped them to my belt, and looked over at the church to see if I could get a glimpse of Amy, Joe, or Skeeter. I'll admit to having a little bit of a desire for Amy to have seen me being all badass, but it was not to be.

"Hey!" I yelled down the street. "Hey! I killed the zombies! Y'all can come out now, it's safe!" I even jumped up and down and waved a little, hoping they'd see me and come on out. Nothing. At least, I thought it was nothing at first, then I saw the glint of a tiny bit of reflected twilight off glass in the church bell tower, and I realized that Joe was up there with his rifle.

I waved at him again, trying to catch his attention. He didn't wave back, but the rifle did *crack* as he shot at something.

"Hey!" I yelled. "What the hell are you shooting at? I killed all the...shit." I realized just how bad I had jinxed myself right about the time I turned around to see another horde of zombies, this one more than twice as big as the first, shambling up the street right at me. "Shit," I repeated, and hauled ass up the street toward the church.

I didn't get very far since zombies poured out of the spaces around all the houses and jammed the street between me and the church. Seriously, where did all these dead people come from? It was like every damn tree in the forest between the edge of Summer and here turned into an extra from *Z-Nation*. "Puppies and kittens, people," I muttered, jamming my hands down into the iron-wrapped gloves and drawing my sword.

I waded into the sea of zombies, really hoping these were magical zombies and not plague zombies. I don't mind chopping up any kind of walking dead things, but it's really hard to keep from getting bitten when you're fencing with dozens of dead assholes. So I just resigned myself to some flesh wounds and hoped the worst I got out of the deal was a heavy need for penicillin. After all, Skeeter was the closest thing I could find for brains, and he wouldn't be worth more than a light snack anyway.

The first zombies went down easy, heads flying from shoulders like I was warming up in a batting cage. I took down a good dozen of them in half the distance to the church, but my arms were starting to really burn. Bertha's a heavy girl, and emptying four magazines worth of ammo into zombie heads, followed up by chopping down ten or twenty more walking corpses was a hell of an upper body workout. Eventually I had to just slide my blade back into the sheath and wade in, fists swinging.

The problem with punching dead fairies, as opposed to live ones, is that they don't feel pain. You slam a live faerie in the face with a cold iron glove, he's gonna fall on his ass with a smoking handprint on his cheek. There might even be a little screeching, depending on how hard you hit. You hit an undead faerie with the same glove, you'd better crush his damn skull because he ain't going down easy. And skulls are pretty damn solid, even dead ones.

So I was getting overwhelmed pretty fast, despite beating the ever-loving shit out of some zombies. I was surrounded, and no matter how many I pushed down, bowled over, and stomped the shit out of, more of them kept coming. I made one last surge toward the church doors, but it was no use. I was stuck, hemmed in on all sides by clawing, biting, scratching zombies, and it was only going to be seconds before they took me down once and for all.

Until the sky split open with a roar of thunder, and zombies started dropping like flies all around me. Well, not exactly thunder. More like Joe from the steeple sniping zombies with his Remington 700 rifle. The *crack* of that rifle splitting the air above my head was the most welcome sound since I blew out my knee and the doc at the hospital taught me the word "morphine."

Three zombies right in front of me dropped in quick succession, and I snatched my right glove off with my left hand and drew my Judge revolver from the back of my belt. I went through the five shots in the cylinder in seconds, but at that range, I didn't miss, and five more zombies hit the dusty street, leaving me with a narrow path clear to the door. Two more shots from Joe dropped another pair of undead bastards, and I shoulder-blocked another one to the ground as I bull-rushed my way up the three steps to the church door.

It flung open just as I reached for the handle, and I heard Skeeter yell "DUCK!" even before the door was all the way open. I dropped to my knees and crawled through the left-hand door as Skeeter stood on the other side of the double doors, his shotgun blowing zombie heads to mist as fast as he could rack the slide.

Three seconds later, I was through the door and looking up at the unsmiling face of Agent Amy Hall, still the most beautiful woman in the world, even when she was pissed at me. "You scared the shit out of me, Bubba. I hope that trip to the bar was worth it."

I grinned up at her and said, "Well, I don't know yet, darling. But pass me that bottle, and I'll let you know."

5

Spoiler alert—the faerie booze wasn't worth fighting a bunch of zombies over. It was watery, and weak, and tasted like a blend of muscadine wine, cheap gin, and paint thinner. Which is basically cheap gin, so it tasted like cheap gin cut with muscadines. I hate gin and muscadines.

But I took a swig, spit the vile shit out all over the floor, and used the rest of the bottle to wash the worst of the zombie guts off my arms and legs. I checked my clothes and found no tears of any size, then peeled off my shirt to make sure I didn't have any tooth marks hiding in a tattoo or something. I splashed a little more booze on my arms for good measure, then pulled my shirt back on and turned to the inside of the church where a faerie preached stood in the center aisle with his mouth hanging open.

"Howdy, Padre," I said. "I'm Bubba. You seem to have a hell of a zombie problem around here."

He didn't speak, just looked way up at me. Like most of the Fae, he was shorter than me, and skinny. Admittedly, most of humanity is shorter than me, too, but this dude was downright petite. I stuck out my hand, looked at a little scrap of brain, or maybe a tiny piece of eyeball stuck to my thumbnail, and wiped it off on my damp jeans before extending my hand again.

He shook it, still staring up at me. "You have a tooth in your beard," was the first thing he said to me.

I reached up to my chin, felt around for a couple seconds until I found something too solid to be breakfast leftovers, and pulled it out. "Nah, Padre. I'm pretty sure that's a piece of skull. See how it's thin and curved, kinda like an eggshell?" I held the half-inch chunk of brainpan out to him, and he fainted dead away.

Amy shoved past me to the fallen priest, muttering something about not being able to take me anywhere.

"I didn't do nothing," I protested. "He was just helping me with a little personal grooming." Amy shot me a dark looked and knelt beside the priest, who was starting to wake up. In my girlfriend's arms, which, for the record, is where I like to wake up. I had to get the hell out of Fairyland. Now I was getting jealous of a preacher from a different species.

I looked back at the door where Skeeter stood with his shotgun at the ready. The double doors of the church looked like pretty sturdy wood, and there was a thick wooden bar laid across a couple of brackets set into the wall on either side of the opening. "Is that gonna hold?" I asked.

Skeeter kept his eyes on the door when he answered. "The preacher and the mayor both said it holds every night, but they also said this looked like way more zombies than they usually get."

"Nice of them to roll out the red carpet and invite a bigger band for us," I said. I turned to the two dozen faeries huddled in the front of the church. "Who's the mayor? I need some information," I called.

Nobody spoke up, but a round little man with a bald head save for two tufts of white hair poking out over his ears was working extra hard to look inconspicuous, so I assumed he was the mayor. I walked over to stand over him, not a difficult task since he was sitting on the floor, and a short dude to start with. "What's your name, Mr. Mayor?"

He looked up, and he got that look on his face that politicians get when they're about to lie. Which is to say that he looked like he was going to speak, then thought better of it. He stood up, straightened his bright red vest, and stuck out his hand. "I am Mayor Frumblecrump. I am in charge here. You are welcome to rest the night within our sanctuary, but once the sun rises, you must be on your way. It is no longer safe in Dun Sheene for outsiders. I'm sure you understand."

As if to punctuate his words, a loud *thump* came from the doors, and they rattled in their hinges. "Don't sound like it's real safe for anybody, Mayor," I said. "They usually this determined?"

"No," he replied. "Normally the dead come in much lower numbers, and they have never been so persistent in their assaults on the church. When I looked down from the steeple upon the crowd of dead surrounding you, I was certain you would not survive. I am happy to have been proven incorrect."

"Yeah, me too," I said. I sat down on one of the front pews facing the mayor and the gathered townsfolk. "Do y'all have any idea why they're here? What do they want? Are they magic zombies that somebody sent here for something? Or are they just asshole zombies that hang out in the woods all day and come back to visit every night?"

"That makes no sense, Bubba." Amy sat down next to me, her new buddy the faerie preacher in tow.

"Yeah," I agreed. "But nothing about this makes any sense. Zombies aren't like vampires. They don't have to hide from the sun. There are more zombies out there now than this village has living people, so where did they come from? If they're imported zombies, why didn't we pass any on the road? This is all crazy. If somebody conjured this many zombies, where the hell are they getting the parts?"

"Well, I can answer that much," Joe said, coming down a set of steps behind the pulpit. He sat down on the steps leading up to the altar and laid his gun on the floor in front of him. "The zombies you killed have all disintegrated. Same for the ones I shot from the bell tower."

"What?" My head snapped up, and I stared at Joe. "Disintegrated?"

"Yep. It looks like they were more golem than zombie, conjured from mud and moss, clad in human clothing, and sent here to attack the town. I watched some of them turn back into clumps of dirt when the magic left them. It seems that the only part of them that had a human component was the skull."

"So it's not that somebody needed a shitload of corpses, they just needed a shitload of skulls and magic. I don't know that I find that any less creepy," Amy said.

"That would take magic the likes of which I've never seen," the priest said from where he sat next to Amy. "Whoever wrought a spell of that nature would not only have to be completely amoral, but have no regard for life whatsoever and have incredible power."

"The kind of power that would let a person poke holes between worlds?" I asked.

The priest looked a little surprised at the question but nodded. "Yes, someone powerful enough to craft a world-breaching spell could probably handle magic on the necessary scale."

I looked around at Joe and Amy. "I reckon we know who we're dealing with, then."

"Yeah, and it makes sense," Amy said. "He knows we're coming after him, so he's throwing roadblocks in our way."

"Who?" Mayor Frumblecrump asked. "Who have you angered that has such power?"

"Puck," I said. "I've tussled with the little shit before, and he can definitely sling mojo on this level."

Every faerie eye in the room locked in on me when I said Puck's name, and more than one person leaned over to their neighbor and started whispering. "Let me guess," I said. "He's kinda like Voldemort."

The priest looked confused. "I don't know who that is, but we don't say that name here. Names have power, and using his willy-nilly can have dire consequences."

"Yep," Amy said. "Totally Voldemort."

"Voldemort is a fictional...never mind. I've met so many people since coming over here that I thought only existed in legends and tales that I can't even say that anymore," Joe said. "Voldemort is an evil wizard of legend in our land. It is said that merely speaking his name could focus his attention on you, and no one wants his attention."

"Then yes, the person who you spoke of is very much like that." Mayor Frumblecrump kept looking around, like he expected the little shithead to appear out of thin air. Hell, given the way my day had gone so far, I kinda did, too.

"Well, then we won't mention His Assholishness's name again," I said. "But it makes sense that he's set this whole mess up to screw with us."

"Isn't that giving him a little bit too much credit, Bubba?" Amy asked. "I mean, we've only been heading this way for a few days, so how would he have been able to put all this in motion? I mean, the zombies have been attacking the town for a long time now, right?" She turned to the mayor, who shook his head.

"The attacks started with just a few of the creatures about five nights ago."

"That's the night after you killed the dragon, Bubba," Skeeter said.

"So as soon as we didn't die in that stupid encounter, P—the person we're after knew we would be coming his way," I said.

"So he started the attacks in order to make sure we would come here?" Joe raised an eyebrow.

"He knows me," I said. "This is the kind of thing I couldn't pass up, especially if he set a certain merchant on the road to tell us about the trouble in town. Mr. Mayor, did you guys have a traveling merchant named Terlindor come through here early this morning?"

The plump faerie shook his head. "No. We have had no traders pass through in weeks. It's almost as if they knew what was happening and wanted to avoid any chance of getting caught up in our troubles."

"So we got suckered into coming here," Amy said.

"But why?" Skeeter asked. "I mean, sure, the goal looks like getting us eaten by zombies, but that only works if we're out there where the zombies are. As long as we stay holed up in here, we're safe and sound."

I didn't slap him, but man, it was tempting. As it was, I just glared at my best friend and reminded myself that he wasn't the field ops guy, he was the guy in the chair. Then I really wished he was back in a chair this time because then he wouldn't have jinxed us like that.

"You didn't just say that, did you?" Amy asked.

"Say what?" Skeeter looked around, but we all just shook our heads. Even the mayor and priest looked stunned at my little buddy's idiocy.

"You jinxed us, pal. We might have had a chance of staying safe, but you just ruined it," I said.

"Oh, come on, Bubba! You know that's a load of crap. Jinxes are bullshit, and we all know it. Nothing I said is going to have anything to do with whether or not those doors hold up against the zombies. And if they've held out the last few nights, there's no reason to think they won't hold out tonight."

I didn't answer. I just stood up, rolled my shoulders, and drew my sword. This was about to get ugly. As Joe walked over to his rifle, a loud *CRACK* came from the doors. We all turned to look, and sure enough, the bar was pushing into the room as one of the brackets began to tear loose from the wooden door frame.

"Yeah, Skeeter, it'll all be fine," I said. "You just move off to one side and get ready to shoot everything that comes through. I'll take the center aisle."

"I've got the right flank," Amy said, drawing her pistol and moving into position.

"I've got the high ground," Joe said from the pulpit. I looked up to see his rifle nested on what I assumed was some kind of holy book, barrel aimed at the doors.

We were as ready as we were going to get, and it was a good thing since about ten seconds later the doors gave way and all hell broke loose in the church.

6

The sturdy-looking bar across the doors pulled free of the frame and clattered to the floor. I knew things were about to go from bad to shitshow in about eight seconds. I was proven right when the wooden double doors split open with a loud *crack* and opened inward, spilling a horde of zombies into the sanctuary. The church looked remarkably like the ones I was used to back in Georgia, with two rows of pews, a wide center aisle, and narrow aisles down the sides of the room.

The townsfolk were clustered in the first few rows of pews, and Mayor Frumblecrump immediately started shuttling them up onto the pulpit area past Joe into the hallway that I assumed led either to the choir loft or some offices that hopefully would be secure. I had no such hopes for our security.

Guns barked all around me as Skeeter, Amy, and Joe started dropping zombies one after another. I just stood in the aisle, Great-Grandpappy's sword held with the point down, trying to stay relaxed for the last few seconds before the horde reached me. The aisle was about four feet wide, so the zombies couldn't easily come at me two abreast, but there were enough of them stumbling and shambling my way that I had no illusions about being able to hold out forever.

I thought about Mama, and Amy, and all the things I wouldn't be able to tell either one of them if I got turned into zombie kibble in Fairyland. Then I turned all that maudlin bullshit into anger, and the power of pissed-off redneck drove the weariness out of my arms and shoulders, and I started mowing down zombies like some kind of crazed Super-Michonne, only without the dreads and with way more belly.

My vision narrowed to nothing but hack, kill, hack, kill, lather, rinse, repeat. I lifted the sword, brought it down on a zombie head. Then I lifted it again and decapitated the next zombie. Then I shoved the blade through the eye of one zombie all the way into the skull of the shambler behind it and kicked them both backward off my blade. I don't know how long it went on, or how many zombies we killed, but after what seemed like a year and a half of chopping, suddenly there was nothing in front of me. I looked to one side, and Skeeter took out a zombie by smashing his shotgun butt through its face, but nothing stepped up to take its place. I turned to the other side and saw Amy fire her pistol into a zombie's face, dropping the last undead just as the slide on her service weapon locked open.

I spun in a slow circle, but there were no zombies left. Something brushed my ankle, and I looked down to see a hand clawing at my leg. There was one head lying off to my left between two pews, from a zombie I decapitated but never pierced the brain, so I took two quick steps over that way, stabbed my sword through its temple, and looked back at the hand. It lay motionless on the floor, so that hand must have been driven by that head. Okay, then. Problem solved.

"Did we win?" Skeeter asked.

"I can't tell," Amy said. "It looks like we've survived the first wave."

"First wave?" Joe's voice was incredulous. "That must have been fifty zombies! The only way we survived was the door made a natural choke point."

"The only way you survived was I let you."

My head whipped around to the door where a fat man leaned against the splintered frame. He was dressed all in black, with a rich purple cape, bad skin, and a goatee. If you looked up "douchebag" in the dictionary, you'd see his picture, right next to an entry that said, "see also: poseur."

"And who the hell are you?" I asked, leaning down to wipe my sword on a zombie's shirt.

"I am Marek, Lord of the Dead. Welcome to my domain." He stood up straight, then made a big, cape-sweeping bow. Like I said, douchebag.

"I think you might have mistaken yourself for somebody with some juice. I know who's running the show around here, and it ain't you, no matter how many sex-bots you're reanimating for yourself," I said. I stepped back one row and sat kinda sideways on the arm of a pew. He struck me as the kind of bad guy who pontificates, and I didn't feel like standing up for it. After all, I'd hacked a good three or four dozen zombies apart in the last two hours, so I needed a little break.

Marek flushed beet red at my insinuation that he banged dead people but kept most of his composure. "I may not rule the Land Without Seasons now, but I will very soon, and you shall be the instrument of my ascension." He actually held both arms out on the last word, making sure to grab his cape with both hands so it billowed out behind him dramatically. I revised my opinion of him. He wasn't a douchebag. He was an *uber*-douchebag.

"I don't think I want to have anything to do with your instrument, pal," I said. "I'm just here to get my sister back, kick a faerie's ass, and go home."

"But it is in that endeavor where you shall usher in the Age of Death!" He dropped his voice an octave on "Age of Death," and I started running out of ways to categorize the level of douche he was reaching. He was speeding toward DoucheCon One like a bullet train with no brakes, and I was tired, so I decided to move things along.

I got up from my seat, stepped around the mound of zombie parts lying in the aisle, and walked up to Marek. He was about a foot shorter than me, and at least two hundred pounds lighter. He was not a big faerie, and most of them are smaller than the average human.

I'm considerably larger than most humans, so when I loomed over Marek, it was some serious looming.

"Look, Marek. I'm sure you're a nice guy, or an evil necromancer, or whatever you want me to think you are. But I'm tired. I've been killing your zombies for the last couple of hours, my arms hurt, I've got a blister on my left palm like I haven't seen since eighth grade, and I'm out of ammo. So if you could just get to the point, I can tell you to piss off, and we can go our separate ways. Or you could just piss off. That would be fine, too."

He looked up at me, and I was close enough that he really had to cock his head back to look me in the eye. It was that or step back, and I guess he thought that would make him lose face. He probably didn't realize that all the humans in the room already thought he looked like an idiot, so he didn't have any face to lose, but whatever. He looked up at me, and I watched a whole catalog of emotions work across his face as he processed what I said. Finally I saw the muscles lock in his jaw, and I knew he'd come to a decision, and that I probably wasn't going to like it.

"I am bringing about a Renaissance of Death, with or without your help. I will tear down the Shadowlands and bring the Court de la Morte into being, if I have to slaughter every human and faerie within the domain of Shadow to do so! You cannot hope to stop me, human, so bend your knee and agree to aid me in killing the Goodfellow, and perhaps I will spare your female to be my queen."

I didn't bother answering. There was no point trying to reason with a guy who had more made up names for his make-believe kingdom than I had sacks in my whole college football career. Plus, as soon as he mentioned Amy as his queen, my vision went red and my fist kinda automatically flew at his jaw.

He staggered back a step when I slugged him, but he didn't go down. I was honestly surprised, given the difference in size, and the average toughness of the faeries I'd punched in the past few months. But Marek kept his feet and glared at me. "Insolent fool! For that, I shall kill you slowly."

He waved his hands in front of his face, and the air between his fingers started to glow with a sickly greenish-yellow light. I didn't bother waiting to see what kind of spell he was brewing, I just drew my sword and slashed down at his head in one smooth stroke. My plan was to do something kinda badass, like when Indiana Jones draws his pistol and shoots the guy doing all the ninja shit in front of him.

But my plans never really work out. This was no exception. What really happened was my sword flashed down, his hands went up, and as the blade struck the glowing sphere of energy, fire coursed up my every nerve ending. Now I've been set on fire a bunch, had bottle rockets shot out of my butt crack, been tazered in the nuts, and had a damn dragon breathe basically lava all over me, but I gotta tell you, the only thing that comes even close to the pain of that magical shit pouring through me was the time an offensive lineman for the LSU Tigers stepped on my nuts in his cleats in the fourth quarter of a football game back in college. They were down by four scores, so the game didn't matter, but he was all pissed off about my whole D-line making him look stupid for three quarters, so he just walked on my dick as I lay on the turf. I think one cleat went all the way inside my peehole, he stomped me so hard.

That's about what Marek's ball of piss-colored magic felt like, except it hurt like that everywhere, not just my sack. Even the inside of my ears hurt. I dropped to the floor, unable to do anything but try to remember how to breathe and hope I didn't shit myself too bad.

I couldn't even turn enough to watch the puny wizard as he walked past me to murder the rest of my friends. I just saw his ankles move past my field of vision and heard him pontificating some more through the sound of blood rushing in my ears. The only way I knew I wasn't dead was that I was pretty sure dead didn't hurt so damn much.

By the time I was able to scoot around on the floor enough to see what was going on, Marek had clubbed Skeeter to the floor, and Amy was retreating to the front of the church. I saw Joe come down from the pulpit and position himself between Marek and her, and I thought he was being nice and chivalrous by agreeing to die first.

"Out of the way, human, and I will let you live."

"I don't think so," Joe said. His voice was icy calm, the way he gets when he knows what's about to happen is going to suck, but it feels necessary. The last time I heard him talk like that, we were about to go kill my brother, and hearing that tone again gave me goosebumps.

"Fine, then. Die like your idiot friend." Marek raised his hands above his head, and his fists were wrapped in fire. He flung his hands in Joe's direction, but Joe just drew a sword from his belt and knocked the fireball aside like he was a kid playing tee ball. The flames winked out when they touched Joe's blade, and when the light dimmed, I could see his sword glowing with a brilliant blue-white light.

"You will not harm these people so long as I stand," Joe said, holding his sword in a guard position. "Leave now, and we will not pursue you. You can go back to whatever hole you crawled out of and scheme and plot against whomever you please. But if you strike at us again, I will be forced to destroy you."

Marek grinned. "Like you even could, human trash. I don't know what kind of lucky spell you cast, but it won't matter. I am power itself! I am Marek! I cannot be defeated! I am—" His words cut off in mid-pontificate as Amy put a round from Joe's rifle through his eye. The dead faerie dropped to the floor, and I never got to find out the last thing that he was gonna claim to be.

Joe turned to look at Amy, hands on his hips, which looked a little silly since he was still holding a sword. "I was giving him an opportunity to surrender and promise not to do it again!"

"And that's your job, Joe. You're the paladin, buddy. I'm the assassin. You try to redeem them; I assume they're just evil as shit and I kill them. We each have our roles. Sometimes yours is to be the distraction. Good job, by the way." She handed Joe his rifle back and hurried up the aisle to me.

"Bubba, are you okay?" She knelt beside me, then wrinkled her nose. "Jesus, these zombies stink."

"That might be me," I croaked. "I think he knocked the shit out of me. Literally."

"Ew. Well, other than some embarrassment, are you injured?"

"I'm so far past the point where I even consider that injury," I replied. "I'm fine. I'll just need to wash out these pants before we get back on the road."

"We're gonna need a little more than that," Skeeter said. He stood between two pews a few rows ahead of me, holding his right arm with his left. He looked ashen, and it wasn't for lack of lotion. Skeeter looked like he was about to pass slap out.

"Skeeter!" Joe cried, running to him. He got there, realized he was still holding the sword, and shoved it in his belt. "Skeeter, your arm is broken."

"Yeah, I noticed."

"We're going to have to set it."

"I was afraid you were going to say something like that. Is it going to hurt?" Skeeter started to say something else, then his eyes rolled back in his head and he slumped to the pew, unconscious.

I looked up at Amy, still not quite able to stand myself. "Well, shit."

7

———

"Now what?" I asked Amy.

"I don't know. We can't take him with us. He's going to be in a lot of pain, and his mobility is going to be seriously limited." She looked at Skeeter, who sat up on the pew with his arm splinted. He was conscious again, if a little drunk. I found one last bottle of whiskey hidden behind the pulpit, and it took pouring most it down Skeeter's throat to get him loaded enough for Amy and the town herbalist to set his arm, and that still involved a lot of screaming and thrashing. Joe and I held him down, but he was like a really loaded spider monkey before Amy finally got the arm bones back in an approximation of the right place.

"I'm sorry, guys," Skeeter said, his tone mournful and his words slurred. "I didn't mean to let the zombie douchebro break me."

"It's alright, little buddy," I said. "That guy had some serious mojo. If Joe hadn't gone all paladin on him, I don't know what we would have done. Speaking of which, can't you guys heal stuff?"

"It's not a *Caverns & Creatures* game, Bubba," Joe said. "I'm not some kind of holy warrior. I'm just a priest."

"A priest who swings a glowing white sword like some kind of bleached-out Jedi," I amended.

"I'll admit, I may have felt some sense of the divine flowing through me at the time, but it was Amy who struck the final blow for justice."

"Yeah, but assassins aren't known for their healing powers," I said.

"Fair point," Joe agreed. "But either way. I can't heal him, Bubba. I don't even know what made the sword glow. Your mother has healing magic. I don't."

I turned to the mayor. "Hey, Flumberstump."

He cleared his throat and looked affronted. "My name is Frumble-crump," he said, peering down his nose at me.

"Don't get all snooty on me now, Mighty Mouse," I said, standing up to my full height, which was almost two feet taller than the diminutive faerie. "Do you have a healer in town?"

"There is no healing in the Shadowlands." He shook his head sadly. "Our ruler has decreed that magic is forbidden, and all who practice it have either fled to Summer or Winter, or they live in hiding, afraid to use their gift. It is an offense punishable by death."

"Balls," I said, sitting back down. I looked to Joe. "Okay, then you two are out."

"Why does Joe have to stay?" Skeeter protested, weaving a little in his seat.

I lowered my voice and leaned closer. "Because I don't trust these assholes. You saw how Mayor Fumblefart looked at me. Now that they aren't in danger, I don't trust them not to turn you over to P-U-C-K as soon as we're out of sight. If Joe's still here, he can shoot them if they try anything too stupid."

Joe nodded. "I wouldn't feel right leaving you alone, Skeeter. You're my family. I can't leave you by yourself."

Skeeter got that boozy smile on his face that people get right before the awkward hugging starts and said, "Thanks, Joe. I wouldn't have said nothing if you all left, but I know what would have happened. Like I said, black dude in horror movies..." He started to topple over, but Amy caught him before he fell on his bad arm. She eased him down on his other side, and he curled up on the pew and started to snore.

"He's got the right idea," she said, looking at the snoring Skeeter. "There are a few hours left until daylight. We oughta catch some sleep while we can."

When dawn came, Mayor Crumblegrump woke us all up and told us that the pastor needed his sanctuary back to begin cleanup and repairs. I watched over the mayor's shoulder as the little faerie preacher shook his head and made apology motions with his hands as the mayor douched all over us.

"Fine," I said, stretching and listening the symphony of cracks that came from my back and knees after a night sleeping on a church pew built for people two-thirds my size. It didn't even make the top five list of most uncomfortable places I'd slept since coming to Fairyland, another reason I wanted to get back home. "We'll get going. Do you think any of your folks could spare some breakfast, or are we just supposed to handle your zombie infestation and then disappear like some kind of storybook assholes?"

"We have prepared food for your journey, Mr. Bubba," one of the townswomen said, walking up with a picnic basket. "And we will make sure that your friends are safe and *well cared for* while you continue your quest. We appreciate everything you all did for us." She kept shooting sidelong glances at the mayor, and I had a feeling that somebody wasn't going to be running unopposed next election. I felt a lot better leaving Joe and Skeeter now that I knew they'd be safe, so I took the picnic basket and held out my hand to the mayor. That didn't stop me from slipping my Judge revolver into Skeeter's hand as we hugged our goodbyes. I figured the faeries wouldn't try anything, but better safe than sorry.

"Mayor, I'm glad we were able to help. I hope you don't have any more zombie problems. But if you do, I hope I'm nowhere close when it happens." He stared at my hand for a few seconds, just long enough to make it awkward, then we shook. Feeling extra-asshole, I pulled him in for a tight one-armed bro hug and whispered in his ear. "If I get back here, and my friends aren't in absolutely perfect condition, I'll make you wish you were eaten by zombies."

"Fair skies and safe travels to you both," the mayor announced, his face pale and hands shaking. "Have no fear. We shall care for your companions until your return." Then he turned and bolted from the church.

I chuckled and headed up the aisle to the back of the church, Amy in tow. "What did you say to him?" she whispered.

"I just made my expectations for the safety of our friends very clear," I replied. "There might have been a promise of violence involved if those expectations aren't met."

"I can't take you anywhere, can I?"

"After we get done with this trip, you're damn right you can't. I plan to spend at least a month within ten miles of my cabin. I'm going to hunt, fish, drink beer, pee off my back porch, then drink some more. After that month, we can talk about plans for the future."

"The future?" Amy asked.

"Well, there is the little matter of a ring and the dates that are usually associated with that. And whether or not you're going to convert."

"Convert?" I didn't quite hear the brakes squeal in her mind, but almost.

"Yeah, convert. I mean, I know you're not Catholic now, but..."

"Bubba, you're about as Catholic as the Dalai Lama. You work for the Church, but the only time you go into a church is to kill something."

"That's not true! Sometimes I go into a church to hide from something that wants to kill me." I heaved a mock sigh. "I suppose we can table to conversion conversation until we get the guest list figured out. How many of your relatives do you think will come to the wedding?"

"Before we plan a wedding, let's plan an assault on a castle," Amy said. "And I think that looks like a good place to start." I stopped and looked where she was pointing. It was a wagon, one of the covered kind that had basically a little house attached, with a stage that flips down on one side and a roof that pops up to display a huckster's

wares. It was parked on the edge of the village and looked abandoned. Judging by the brownish stains on the seat of the wagon and
the back door, the last owner of the wagon had an eventful meeting
with the zombies.

"Doctor Parnassium's Physicking Phormula!" screamed the big
letters painted on the side of the wagon in garish colors. "Good for
what ails ya!"

"And what exactly do you think that's going to be good for?" I
asked. "You don't expect me to dress up like a fake doctor and BS our
way into Puck's castle, do you?"

"No, nothing like that," Amy said, and I heaved a sigh of relief. "I
expect you to play the part of my lovely assistant while I masquerade
as a doctor and talk us into the castle."

In what seemed to be the running theme of my conversations in
Fairyland, all I could really say was, "Well, shit."

8

———

I t took an hour to get the bloodstains off the wagon and another half hour to figure out how to hitch the horses to it, but once we finally got underway, the road was clear. We traveled the rest of the day to reach the castle, and the sun was low on the horizon when I stopped the horses to survey our surroundings. You would expect a castle in the capital city of the whole land to have a town built up around it, or at least bustle with activity.

Puck don't roll with anyone else's expectations, apparently, because this place looked deserted. There was no town at the base of the long, winding drive up to the hill where the castle sat, looking out over the land like a hulking gargoyle.

It was like something out of a horror movie, and not a gross one like *Saw* or *The Human Centipede*. No, this was old-school *Dracula* shit right here, the kind of castle that looks more like a painting than anything you could actually walk into. There was a windy road leading up to a wrought iron gate set into a stone wall high enough for me to see from a hundred yards away. This place wasn't some keep built for the defense of its citizenry; this was a lurking beast keeping a baleful watch over its subjects and daring anyone to come fight it.

"Well, looks like this costume was a waste of time," Amy said, poking her head through the curtains that led back into the wagon.

"Not from where I'm sitting," I said with a leer. She smacked me in the back of the head, but not real hard, and she smiled when she did it. I gotta say, my girlfriend rocked the sexy ringmaster getup we fashioned from the clothes left behind by the wagon's previous owner. She wore a bright red tailcoat with a corset underneath and her bra, no shirt. The tails hid her pistol that she had tucked into the waistband of her flowing skirt, which also obscured the pair of knives strapped to her calves. The only incongruous bit was her shoes, which were the sensible hiking boots she wore over from our world. The last driver of this wagon had obviously been a male faerie, and he had feet way too big for Amy to wear his boots, so we just hoped that her upper charms kept people distracted from her out of this world feet.

"I'll get changed," Amy said, ducking back into the wagon.

"Don't go to any trouble on my account," I called after her.

"Can't have you getting killed because you can't take your eyes off my boobs, Bubba."

"Oh, but what a way to go," I replied, then returned my gaze to the castle that awaited us atop the hill. I looked around to either side of the road, but it looked like the road was the only way in. It was a narrow ribbon of dirt and gravel, falling off to a steep canyon on either side. The kind of stuff you find deep in the European mountains, not on the formerly mild countryside we'd been riding through. Damn magical worlds, changing the geography right in front of my eyes.

Once Amy came back in her much more sensible and less distracting clothes, I pointed up the road. "We could leave the wagon, but it's not going to give us any better cover than just riding up there, and then we have to walk. I vote we ride."

"May as well. If anything is watching for us, it's already seen us," Amy agreed.

I clicked my tongue at the horses, flapped the reins, and finally leaned over to poke the right-hand one in the butt with the whip I found under the driver's seat. I wasn't going to whip an animal for not wanting to pull a heavy cart with my big ass on it, I totally got that concept. But I did need for the horsey to do its job, so I could get on with doing my job, namely saving my sister and shooting Puck right in his little asshole face. The horse looked back at me, and I swear I saw it trying to figure out how to flip the wagon over, but after one more poke in the butt, it started walking, and its buddy went along.

The road was steep and narrow, with treacherous switchbacks and steep drop-offs on either side. I decided not whipping the horse into a run had been a good idea since I had no real idea how to steer and didn't feel like trying to learn to fly when it really mattered. It took a solid couple hours of plodding up the hard-packed dirt road, but eventually we made it to the front of the castle. I climbed down, unhitched the horses, and set them loose. A smack on the butt, and each one turned and started to amble back down the road to freedom.

"What did you do that for, Bubba? How are we going to get back to everybody else now?" Amy asked.

I looked at her, puzzled. "Is this your first fantasy movie? That's not how this works. This is our point of no return moment, where I look grimly off into the clouds and mutter some whiny shit about there being no going back now, and we forge bravely on to fight the evil sorcerer. Then when we win, a magic portal appears to take us home, and all our hearty companions are returned with us. Or some other MacGuffin bullshit. Or we win, and the *deus ex machina* comes down to right all the wrongs perpetrated by the dastardly villain. We're not going to need those horses again, because I'm going to kick Puck in the balls so hard he wears his testicles for earrings, then he's going to let Nitalia loose and teleport us all back home."

She gave me a look that said she thought I was being stupid again, then sighed. "In other words, we're probably going to die in the next two hours, and it would be rude to leave the horses out here to starve."

"That is the other option, but I wasn't going to mention it."

"Let's just get this done. I really miss cable TV and toilet paper."

She turned to the castle and gestured toward the door. "I think this one's all you, sweetheart."

She was right. If ever a door had "Bubba" written all over it, the ones at Puck's castle did. They were huge, big enough to ride an elephant through, with two sets of handles. One set was down where a normal human could reach them, and another, much larger, set was about twelve feet off the ground. I really didn't want to see what came through here that needed those doorknobs. The doors were made of wood and bound with thick iron straps. The whole place looked an awful lot like it could withstand a tank. I just hoped it wasn't designed to withstand a hillbilly.

I walked up to the door, looking around to see if there was a smaller servants' entrance off to the side or something, but there wasn't. I squared my shoulders, gripped the human-sized knob, and turned. The door swung open like it was on glass, with no more effort than opening my refrigerator. The twenty-foot door swung open, and the darkness that was the Shadow Castle gaped before me.

"Well, that went better than expected," I said, then stepped over the threshold.

Immediately things stopped going better than expected as a seven-foot asshole in a suit of armor charged me out of the blackness. Fortunately, even in Fairyland, armored assholes are not also stealthy assholes, so I had some warning. But he was fast for a dick with a giant sword and a full plate armor, so I still barely had time to get out of the way before he was right on me, slicing down where my head was half a second before.

The six-foot blade sparked against the stone floor, and he slashed upward and sideways as he withdrew the sword, setting me to dance back out of range while I struggled to draw Bertha. I got the pistol clear of the holster, but he slapped me on the wrist with the flat of his blade, and my Desert Eagle went spinning across the floor. It was way too much to hope for that the gun would go off when it hit the deck and kill the rat bastard.

I ducked under his next big looping cut and charged the metal-clad dickhead. He was solidly built inside that tin can and almost held his ground against me, but I learned to shove, grab, wrestle, and generally beat the hell out of a man who was bigger, stronger, and a better athlete than me between the hedges at the University of Georgia, fighting for playing time behind an All-American defensive lineman. No way was some faerie in Ren Faire cosplay gonna keep his feet once I got hold of him. I shoved him back a few steps, then planted my right foot, shifted all my weight in that direction, and body-slammed the bastard to the floor in a thunderous clatter of metal and Bubba.

Of course, he didn't stay down. No, it can't be that easy. He couldn't just lie there and take a second to gather himself after getting flung to the ground while wearing full armor. No, he rolled over, scissored his feet around my knees, and dropped me like a bad habit. I went down in a heap and heard him clattering to his feet as I rolled over and scrambled back up, trying to keep an eye on my foe while looking around to see why Amy wasn't jumping in with at least some helpful advice, if not a couple of bullets to this asshole's head.

I didn't see Amy right away and decided she must have stayed outside where there weren't any animated metal-wrapped buttmonkeys running around. She's smart like that. I didn't have more than a second to think about it, though, because my cut-rate Colossus was swinging that giant damn pigsticker through the air again, trying to turn my innards into outards all over the nice clean, well, only moderately dusty, stone floor. I ducked and rolled forward, coming up a foot or so away from Bertha and scooping her up in a move that looked way more graceful in my head than I'm sure it did in real life, but I didn't die, so that was good.

I spun around and fired three rounds into the onrushing warrior's chest. He staggered back, but didn't go down, so I put two more into his face. That dropped him, but when he fell, the helmet split open down the middle to reveal...nothing. The damn suit of armor was completely empty, and it broke apart into pieces and rattled around on the stone floor like it wasn't trying to cut me into sushi seconds before. I kicked the breastplate, and it split apart from the backplate and clattered to the floor. Whatever was animating the armor, two fifty-caliber bullets to the face took care of it.

"Hey, babe, it's safe to come in," I called to Amy. No response. I turned to the door, but she wasn't there. That was odd. I walked over and stuck my head out the door, but there was no sign of her. I stepped back into the entryway and looked around the gloomy vestibule. She was nowhere to be seen, but something shiny glittered at me over by the right-hand wall. I walked over and knelt down, picking up a gold cross from the floor. I recognized it at once as Amy's and knew something was seriously wrong. She only ever took that necklace off to shower or sleep. I'd not seen her without it the whole time we'd been in Fairyland. If it was laying here in the dust, then it meant something was terribly wrong. No question about it, she dropped it here on purpose, hoping I'd find it.

I stood up and turned around, Amy's necklace dangling between my fingers. I spun around in a circle, looking up at the gothic architecture around me. The big chandeliers, the flying buttresses, the stained glass, all of it faded as a haze of red came across my vision. "PUCK!" I bellowed. "I'm coming for you, you pointy-eared son of a bitch! I'm coming, and I'm coming heavy. You've messed with my fiancée, you little shit, and I'm going to get her back, then I'm going to put a bullet right between your beady eyes!"

I jammed Bertha into the holster and headed down the hallway off the right side of the room, my fists now wrapped in the cold iron caestae and my blood full of an anger I hadn't felt in years. Somewhere in that castle was a demented faerie with my fiancée, and he was about to find out why you do not mess with Bubba.

9

"Amy!" I bellowed. There was no response, of course, but I had to try. I yelled myself hoarse, and the only answer I got was my own echo. The vestibule looked like something out of a gothic horror movie, with doors on three sides in the room leading deeper into the castle and twin staircases curving up in the middle of the room. The upper floors were shrouded in shadow, so I stuck to the door on the right side of the room, nearest where I found Amy's necklace.

The door was your basic medieval movie castle door, some rough-hewn timbers held together with metal bands and big triangular hinges set into one edge. I tried the knob, and it swung open into a large dining room, maybe thirty feet by twenty feet. A rectangular table dominated the room, looking like something out of the first *Batman* movie where Bruce Wayne has to walk the salt shaker all the way down to the other end to Kim Basinger. There were a dozen or more place settings, all empty, like the room was just waiting for the party to start, but judging by the dust on the silverware, it had been waiting a long time. Candles rested in holders down the center of the table, fused to the runner by mounds of wax from the long-burned tapers.

There was an air of sadness in the room, pervasive through the gloom, like something awesome was supposed to happen here, but the whole place was frozen in time before it could take place. I walked around the table, running my finger though the dust and examining everything. The sideboard was laid out with warming stones, just waiting for someone to bring out a multi-course meal and begin the feast.

Something flickered out of the corner of my eye, and I spun around, my fists clenching as I drew back my right. There was nothing there, just a tapestry twitching on the wall. I stepped up to it and took a good look at it, marveling at the detail they wove into the fabric. It was as gorgeous as any painting I'd ever seen, and my mouth fell open as I saw the images start to move.

It was a depiction of Puck and Princess Alethea, their meeting, their courtship, her capture at the hands of Oberon (depicted as a grossly obese troll-looking dude with a giant hooked nose), her rescue by me (depicted as a grossly obese ogre-looking dude with wild Hagrid hair), and their wedding. As I watched the scene play out before me, I saw Puck go to Oberon and plead with him to release her from her bond to Summer. Then I saw him go to Mab and beg for her to take Alethea into the Winter Court, so she could release her and save her life. I watched as both of the Faerie rulers (definitely some artistic license going on with their images) cruelly rejected Puck, and I watched him sit by her bedside as the lovely Princess Alethea withered and died.

I found my eyes strangely damp and shook myself to get my focus back. What Mab and Oberon did to Puck and his lady was shitty, but that didn't give him an excuse to take Nitalia, and it sure as hell didn't let him off the hook for laying hands on Amy. I was going to show him what this giant redneck could do when I found his ass.

Another flicker out of the corner of my eye, and this time when I turned, the door on the far wall was moving on its hinges, as if something had just gone through. I charged after it, not even thinking that it might be better to look before I leapt, and busted through the door into...a completely deserted parlor. Don't get me wrong, it was a very nice parlor, but I was still pretty pissed that whatever made the door move was either way too fast, or invisible.

The parlor was set up with several couches, an arrangement of chairs that looked like they were for an impromptu concert, and a huge grand piano. I walked over to the piano and plinked on a couple of keys, just like everyone who can't play piano does whenever they walk into a room with a piano. A rat the size of a chihuahua sprang out of the raised lid and launched itself at my chest, latching onto my shirt and beard with its surprisingly sharp claws and scrabbling up to my face, presumably to take a bite out of me.

I let out a yell that was way less manly than I wanted it to be and staggered back, swatting at my chest and the rat with my iron-wrapped hands. After several seconds of getting the shit clawed out of me, I got fed up with this bullshit and just belly-flopped onto the floor, crushing the rat beneath me. I cracked my chin a good one on the marble tile, but when I stood up, there was nothing left of Mr. Rat but a lifeless ball of fur and a whole lot of rat blood on my shirt and beard.

My shirt was in tatters, so I pulled it off and wiped as much blood off me as I could. Bertha's holster chafed a little without a shirt on, but shirtless I didn't smell quite as much like rat poop. It's remarkable how much crap can squeeze out of one rat, but the evidence was right there on what used to be my shirt. I looked around, but nothing in the parlor stood out as a viable clothing alternative, so I figured I'd just be showing off my tattoos and pelt of chest hair to the world until I killed Puck and got back to where we'd left all our spare clothes and gear with Joe and Skeeter.

This time, I didn't see any phantom movement, but I heard a door slam on the other side of the room. I looked toward the corner where the sound came from and saw a door painted to match the mural on that wall sticking slightly ajar. I hustled to it, tossing my shirt to the floor as I went.

On the other side of the door was a deserted kitchen, big enough to service a mansion that size. There was an island the size of an autopsy table in the middle of the room, with a rack over it holding pots that I swear you could cook an entire pit bull in. A rack of vicious-looking knives and cleavers sat in the center of the island, and I swear I saw the handle of one of the knives quivering as I walked in, as if someone had just slid it home. I made a quick lap around the kitchen, touching the cold stove, opening cabinet doors, peeking under the island, but there was no one there. I pulled open one small door that led to a pantry, then checked the door at the other end of the room. This one led to a long hallway, with several doors interspersed along its length. Figuring that led to the living quarters, I stepped into the hall, still desperately looking for someone to punch.

The hallway was deserted, with torches glowing from rings on the wall. I walked over to one of them to check it out and saw it was lit with a glowing yellow magical orb, not fire. That explained how they kept burning in a place where apparently no one lived, despite the fact that I kept hearing shit every time I turned my back.

About ten feet down the hall, I opened a door on the left into a guest bedroom. I didn't see anything, but when I stepped all the way into the room, something slammed the door shut, and a shadowy form rushed me. The shadow was thin, almost emaciated, and as it latched on to my upper arms with its smoky hands, I felt a chill go all the way to my bones. It felt almost like grappling with a ghost, only more substantial. I took advantage of the corporeality and slammed my fist into the shadow creature's gut. The second the cold iron hit the magical creature, it vanished in a puff of smoke and ash, leaving me rubbing flakes of ice off my arms and really hating that my shirt didn't survive the first room.

I sifted through the pile of ash the shadow monster left behind but found nothing to help me fight them or find Amy. Then I rummaged through the wardrobe in the guest room, but apparently Puck either didn't get many guests, or none of them left clothes behind. I hadn't held out much hope for finding anything that fit, since I was one of the largest people I'd run into in Fairyland, but it was worth a try. Stepping back into the hall, I caught sight of a shadow turning the corner some thirty feet ahead of me, and I took off in hot pursuit.

When I rounded the corner, four more shadows pounced on me, wrapping their frigid limbs around my arms and neck, slowing me down and making my fists go numb with the cold. I managed to dust two of them pretty quickly, but one got a grip on my weakened leg, and that sent the bad knee I thought Mama had healed into full lockdown. Apparently something in the Shadow Court screwed with magically repaired knee joints. I stumbled, clutching the frozen joint with both hands, then flailed at the shadow until I caught the corner of its head with one of the cold iron studs on my caestus and it vanished into a pile of ash. The last shadow went for my eyes, but I punched it into oblivion and dropped to the stone floor, trying to rub some feeling back into my bad knee. It only locks up when it gets really cold, and that's not much of a problem living in Georgia. Apparently, going to Fairyland and being attacked by heat-sucking shadow monsters is not good for old football injuries.

After a few minutes of massaging my leg, the knee unlocked with a loud *pop*, and I could bend my leg again. The pop came along with a knife of pain that blinded me for a few seconds, but when I could breathe and see again, I was able to stand up and continue my hunt.

The next several rooms turned out to be just more guest rooms, each as empty as the first, without even the lone shadow creature for me to kill. I did manage to find a robe in one of the wardrobes that I slipped over my arms and belted around my waist, looking more like Luke Skywalker's shirt or the top half of a karate outfit than a robe, but that's what you get when you're a good foot taller than most of the people who live in a dimension. It did provide some cushion from Bertha's holster rubbing under my arm and might help me not freeze to death if more of the shades got hold of me.

The fourth room I tried was locked, so I reared back and kicked the door in. The wood of the door exploded inward like I'd thrown a grenade, way out of proportion to the kick, but I just stepped through the now-empty doorway, my fists at the ready.

When I saw what waited for me in that room, I froze in my tracks. Standing in the center of the room, on a carpet that probably was worth more than my car, a wolfish grin on his face, was my kid brother Jason. The same kid brother that I killed in Athens almost two years ago. But now here he was in Fairyland, grinning at me the same way he'd grinned when he shoved Great-Grandpappy Beauregard's sword through my guts.

I opened my mouth to ask Jason what the hell he was doing alive, and here, but just then a bright pain exploded in the back of my head, and some asshole turned out my consciousness.

10

I t wasn't the first time I'd ever woken up face down on the floor with a blinding headache and no memory of how I got there, but it was the first time I didn't remember having a few drinks first. I was face down on a dusty stone floor, with torchlight flickering on my face. Dried blood crusted my face and had pooled beneath my nose, so obviously I wasn't dropped here very carefully. I was cold, but it only took me a few seconds to realize that was because the bathrobe I'd confiscated as a shirt was gone.

Dammit. I flexed my fingers and saw that my hands were bare. Whoever had knocked me out took my caestae, so I didn't have cold iron protecting my hands and helping me pummel faerie assholes to death. I rolled over, pressing my back into the cold stone, and reached for Bertha. Nothing. The usually comforting weight of my second-favorite girl in her shoulder holster was gone, as was the knife on my belt and my sword. I still had on my pants and my boots, but other-wise I was defenseless. Most of the gear could be replaced, but that shithead faerie was going to have to give me back my gun and sword.

"If you think I'm gonna thank you for not leaving me face down with lilies planted in my bare ass, you've got another think coming, you pointy-eared shitweasel," I called out toward the ceiling, which was a lot farther away than it had been in the last hallway I remembered before being knocked out. I struggled to my feet, rubbing the lump on the back of my head. I wasn't concussed, so whoever knocked me cold knew just how hard to hit me to put me down without causing any serious damage.

I was in a different corridor altogether, this one completely devoid of doors. There were just blank walls stretching a good twenty feet up into the air, with nothing above but blackness and more stone. Torches jutted out from the wall every eight feet or so, sticking out of rings in the stone. I walked over to them, and they were the same kind of magical light that I'd seen before, not real flame. That explained why it was not only cold as balls in here, but not smoky. I grabbed one of the torches and made to lift it out of the ring, but it was lodged fast. I pulled harder, but it didn't even wiggle. I planted a foot on the wall and pulled with both hands, but all I got for my struggle was a splinter.

Whatever. The hall was lit well enough without carrying a torch, but it would have been nice to have some kind of weapon, even if it was just a glowing stick. I sucked on my sore thumb and looked up and down the hall. It seemed to run about twenty feet in each direction, so I turned right and headed down into the featureless corridor. When I got to the end, I crouched down and peered around the corner, not wanting to get ambushed again. I didn't have to worry since that hall was just as empty as the one I was leaving. It ran about fifty feet in front of me, with a door set into the wall about fifteen feet ahead of me.

I crept to the door, as much as somebody my size can creep, and pressed my ear to it. Hearing nothing, I turned the knob and heard a very soft but distinctly mechanical *click* that seemed to come from the wall behind me. I've seen enough Indiana Jones movies and played enough video games to know that sound meant something bad was about to happen, so I dropped flat to the floor and skittered back from the door on my belly, just as the *swish-THUNKTHUNK* of a trap went off over my head. I looked up to see a pair of axes lodged deep in the door, one at just the right height for my knees, and the other right about where my neck was. Nice to know I got custom-designed traps built just for my size, since that upper axe would have floated right over the head of almost everyone I'd met in Fairyland.

"You missed, asshole," I yelled at the ceiling, my annoyance at almost getting chopped into thirds momentarily making me forget that I was trying to be all stealthy. I almost might have flipped off the empty air over my head in a fit of pique. I'm not sure if that's what it was, I've never had a fit of pique before, but that's what I always thought one would feel like.

Getting to my feet while avoiding the axes, I pulled them out of the door and tried to wiggle them loose, but they were attached to their mechanisms with some serious bolts. I couldn't even get them to move an inch, much less rip free to be useful to me. They pulled free of the door easily enough, though, and I swung them out of the way and opened the door. I twisted the knob and shoved the door open, swinging myself out of the way and pressing my back to the wall beside the opening, just in case Puck had a crossbow rigged up on the other side or some other such bullshit. When nothing shot out of the doorway, I stuck my head out and took a look.

The hallway stretching out in front of me was pretty anticlimactic, given that it looked just like the one I was standing in. Same stones, same torches in rings, same big ol' pile of nothing. It went about ten feet, then ended in a T-intersection. I checked the doorframe for trip-wires, and when I found nothing, I stepped through. Nothing fell on me or otherwise tried to kill me, so I walked down the ten feet and turned from side to side. I couldn't see any difference in the left and right hallways, so I turned left this time. This took me another ten feet, then the hall T'd off once more. I looked left and saw a dead end a few feet in front of me. The right-hand hallway stretched a good fifty feet before ending and turning to the right, so that was the obvious choice.

Before I took that obvious choice, I went into the little alcove to the left and searched over the stone walls to see if there was some kind of secret door, or mechanism to open a passage, or anything. If something was there, it was hidden way too good for me to find it, so after a couple of minutes of poking at stones, I turned and walked off down the long hall.

I'd gone about thirty feet when I froze. Under the faint whisper of air through the halls, barely loud enough to be heard over my footsteps, there was a sound. I couldn't tell what it was, just that it was coming from around the corner ahead of me. I pressed myself against the wall and crept forward, trying to move silently. It was admittedly a lot easier to move without making noise now that I wasn't carrying a bunch of weapons, but if given a choice between quiet and armed, I'll wrap myself in a tank every time.

When I reached the end of the hall and stuck my head around the corner, there was nothing there, just another corridor. I thought for a second that I saw something flit around the corner to the right about fifteen feet ahead of me, but when I blinked, it was gone, so I wasn't sure what, if anything, I saw. I crept along the passage, keeping tight to the near wall, and listening for anything that sounded out of place. Of course, I had no damn idea what this place was supposed to sound like, so I just figured anything I heard would count as "out of place."

As I reached the corner, I could see the hinges of another door set into the wall. I dropped to one knee and checked the door frame for traps as best I could, then tried the knob. It turned easily, without the tell-tale click of a trap being sprung for a change. I thought about it for a few seconds, weighing the benefits of a cautious entry versus a charge, then I shook my head.

"Nobody's ever called me Bubba the Ballroom Dancer," I muttered to myself, then took a couple of steps back and flung myself through the door. I dove into the room in another clumsy forward roll. They make that crap look so easy on the WWE pay-per-views, but when you're six and a half feet tall and close to three hundred fifty pounds, there's nothing easy about throwing yourself to a stone floor and then getting back up. But I managed to come to my feet with only a modicum of new bruises.

Only to find myself surrounded by skeletons with swords. Yep, skeletons. No shit, *Dungeons & Dragons, Evil Dead,* pick whatever movie you want, skeletons. There wasn't a scrap of flesh on them, and they even had the cliché red glowing eyes. And every damn one of them was armed to the teeth.

They didn't all have swords. No, we can't be *predictable* when we're building our stereotypical human-killing dungeon. Hell no. We have to have some skeletons with maces, a couple with quarterstaffs, four or five with swords, and one with a damn giant claymore that would give Mel Gibson sword envy. And, of course, I popped to my feet right in the middle of them.

The skeletons turned to me, their red eyes managing to look surprised, which was impressive without faces. I wasn't surprised because I'd dealt with Puck before and knew I was in for a shitshow the second the door didn't try to kill me. I reached out with my right hand for the nearest skeleton's shield and snagged the top edge of it. I played tug-of-war with the skeleton's shield on my left side while reaching out with my right and dragging another undead assclown toward my by his sternum. I picked the bag of bones up one-handed and flung him sideways, taking three other walking dead dickheads to the ground. They fell to the stone with a thunderous clatter, disassembling on impact.

"Gimme that," I growled at the skeleton holding the shield, and gripped the round metal disk with both hands. I gave a mighty yank, and the shield came free, arm still attached. I used the arm as a handle and smashed the skeleton to parts with its own shield. I had just shaken the finger bones out of the shield's grip when pain exploded across my upper back and shoulders. I sprawled face-first on the floor, rolling over and pulling the shield up just in time. I blocked the quarterstaff rushing at my skull and kept rolling over as the undead dickwhistle slammed the staff into the floor again and again, keeping me moving.

His buddies soon joined in with the Bubba-bashing, and in a few seconds, all I could do was curl up in a ball and turtle under the shield as best I could. A few shots got through, though, and soon my legs and arms started to go numb from the beating. Then something struck my shield with a mighty *CLANG*, and I felt the vibration all the way down to my balls. And not in a good way.

I figured that the big boss skeleton had arrived, so I braced myself for another shot. Sure enough, seconds later, my shelter rang like a church bell, but this time, I knew it was coming. It didn't make it hurt any less, but it made me mad enough to spring up half a second after the weight of the blade came off my shoulder, and spin around, using the shield's edge to shatter skulls and arm bones in a wide circle. I bashed two other skeletons in the head, sending their pieces to the corners of the room, then turned to the skeleton with the giant damn sword.

"Come get some, asshole."

11

———

He didn't have ears, but I coulda swore the boney asshole heard me lay down my challenge. He leveled his sword at me like a spear and charged, moving pretty fast for a guy with literally no muscles. When he came at me, the other remaining skeletons closed in from the sides, so I had nowhere to dodge. I didn't mind. I had no intention of trying to spin out of the way. I thought for a brief second exactly how stupid I was about to be, then lowered the shield and charged.

I slammed into the point of his sword and lifted the shield, driving the point of the blade to the sky. Then I let go of the shield completely, flinging it to my left, and I wrapped my arms around the skeleton's ribcage. I counted on the fact that since he had the biggest sword, he would have more magic pumped into him to hold him together, and I was right. He didn't fall apart as soon as I grabbed him like some of the other bags of bones; he held together all the way through my grabbing him under his arms, lifting, and spinning around to slam into the stone floor on top of him in a belly-to-belly suplex that would have brought tears to Magnum TA's eyes.

He had a lot of magic holding him together, but not *that* much magic. His ribcage exploded under me, and the big two-handed sword fell to the floor. I picked it up in one hand and pushed off the floor with the other, barely getting my head out of the way of a couple of maces and one broadsword that clattered to the stone behind me. I got to my feet in a whirl, slicing the claymore's blade through empty torsos and severing spinal columns as I went. I kept turning and turning, whirling the sword around me like a Ginsu-wielding Tasmanian Devil. With every rotation, more bones clattered to the floor, until finally I stood alone and dizzy as hell in the middle of a room full of shattered skeletons.

I staggered to a wall as the room spun, leaning against it to get my bearings, and heard a *thunk* from a door as it sprang open. I hadn't even taken the time to look for an exit, I was so focused on the fight. Probably a good thing because, apparently, this was a *Legend of Zelda* dungeon, where the door wouldn't open unless I killed all the bad guys. I took a couple minutes to collect a shield, a broadsword, and a mace, then tossed the claymore to the ground. It was a good weapon, but I'm not enough of a swordsman to use it, and it would just be dead weight in the tight hallways. Better to have something I could actually use to defend myself.

There were no traps on the door that I could find, so I stepped out into the short hallway. It looked just like all the others, and I gotta tell ya, I was starting to really feel like Puck overpaid for his decorator. I mean, what's the point of having a deadly dungeon maze if every corridor just looks like the one before it? Why not spice things up, add in some paintings of the people you killed before, just for variety and intimidation?

These are the things that go through your head when you're wandering through a dungeon waiting for the next thing to try to kill you. The only way to go was left, so I walked ten feet to the next T-intersection. "I went left last time, so we'll try right this time." Yeah, I started talking to myself. I couldn't really help it. I'd killed everything I saw, so there was nothing to banter with, so I was my only company.

I turned right and walked down twenty feet before the hall turned to the left. I stuck my head around the corner and was faced with nothing but black stone and another one of those damn magic torches, faux-flickering along like it was real fire or something. I've played enough *Baldur's Gate* to know that secret doors are a thing in dungeons, so I went down the short passage and pressed on the wall in a few places, then tried to turn the torch sconce. All I got was some rust on my hands, but no secret door. So, I went back the way I came, then continued down the passage, which stood clear for a good fifty feet before another coming to another T.

I looked in both directions, and the hall looked slightly longer to the left than the right, so I went that way. I kept tugging on the wall torches and pressing raised blocks, but I stayed disappointed in the lack of secret doors. They were everywhere in the video games, but I hadn't found a single one yet. If I didn't gut him, I was going to have a chat with Puck about getting sloppy in his design.

After another forty or fifty feet, the hall turned to the left, and after checking to make sure it was clear, I did too. After about twenty feet, I spied something different on the floor. I rushed toward it, not running, but walking fast and definitely not trying to open nonexistent secret doors. I got to the dark spot on the floor and realized that it was blood. I knelt beside it, then paused.

"Son of a bitch," I said, then looked up. "SONOFABITCH!!!" I yelled. I looked at the small puddle of dried blood on the floor, then at the flecks of brown next to it. It was my blood. This was the spot where I woke up with a bloody nose and a headache. I'd managed to walk around in a complete circle.

I sat down, leaned my head back against the wall, and cussed. I cussed Puck, Mab, Oberon, Titania, and every faerie in Fairyland that wasn't my mother. Then I cussed her. Then I cussed my own idiot self, Skeeter for getting hurt, Amy for getting kidnapped, and Joe for not doing anything cuss-worthy. By the time I circled back round to cussing Puck, most of my frustration had turned into a cold determination to wear that bastard's pointy ears on a necklace. So I got up, turned around the way I came, and headed off into the dungeon to do that very thing.

It was another half hour or so of walking, by my best estimation, and I finally came to another door. I'd spent the time marking my travel by bashing the mace into the wall under every torch. The metal dug a pretty good divot out of the stone every ten feet or so, and I was pretty sure that as long as Puck hadn't made the dungeon out of self-healing rocks, that I'd be able to recognize my trail if I started to double back on myself again.

This was an odd little hallway, where the passage kinda doubled back on itself in a U-turn with a wall as the divider but set into the opposite wall was a wooden door. The knob turned easily, and I pushed the door open and stepped aside in case there was a crossbow rigged on the other side or something. No arrows came whizzing by, so I stuck my head into the room.

It was dark. Not just dim, but darker than the inside of a black bear's butthole dark. There weren't any torches set into the walls in this room, so I couldn't see how big the space was, or if there was another door, or anything.

"You know, the smart thing to do would be to close this door and just leave it the hell alone," I grumbled to myself. "So, of course, I'm not going to do anything of the sort." I leaned in, holding onto the door frame, and something crunched under my feet as I took a step. I looked down, but the light from the hall seemed to get sucked up by the darkness as soon as it crossed the threshold. Did I mention I hate magic? Because I do. I friggin' hate magic, especially when somebody I don't like is using it. I don't love it when the good guys are using it, but when it's somebody like Puck? No damn thank you.

I couldn't figure out a way to get more light into the room, and I sure as hell didn't want to go in there blind, so I reached around for the doorknob and tried to pull the door closed. It wouldn't budge. Because of course it wouldn't. The door didn't have to be trapped; the door *was* the trap. As soon as I opened it, I was stuck. I had to either fight whatever was in the room or leave an open door full of monsters at my back while I hunted for Amy.

"Dammit," I muttered, and took a deep breath to try and calm my nerves. I'm not afraid of the dark, but I sure don't want to wander around in a magical dungeon if I can't see what's going to try to kill me.

After psyching myself up for a few seconds, I finally decided to step fully into the room. The second my entire body crossed the threshold, I was fully inside the room's magic, and I could see. I immediately wished I couldn't.

I took one look at what lay between me and the door across the room and turned around to leave. I didn't want those things at my back, but I didn't want to have to fight my way through them, either. I mentioned I hate magic, right? Well, I was reminded why when I turned around to find the door closed right in my face. Now there's no way in the normal world that door could have shut without knocking me down, but we were a long way from the normal world, and that previously unlocked door wasn't just locked tight, but the knob was gone, too.

I was not getting out of here without a fight. And judging by the clicking and skittering sounds behind me, every single critter in the room with me knew it. So I turned, very slowly, and looked at the dozen or so giant spiders that filled the twenty-by-forty room. They were about the size of ponies, with glittering green and black carapaces, and poison dripping from their fangs. Or maybe it was acid. I'm not sure which, but I knew it was something bad because every once in a while, a drop fell to the floor and sizzled on the stone for a few seconds.

That wasn't all, even though it was more than enough. Oh no, it couldn't just be huge spiders, that wouldn't be nearly nasty enough for Robin Poorly Named Goodfellow. Nope, he also scattered a couple hundred relatively normal-sized scorpions all along the floor, just to keep it interesting. That's what I'd heard crunching under my foot when I stepped into the room.

That's also what was crawling up my legs like my nuts were a homing beacon, jabbing little stingers into my boots like they were testing the soil to plant a row of beans. I reached down with my shield and flicked one off, watching as it soared across the room and landed in a puddle of spider spit. My suspicions of acid were quickly confirmed as the scorpion immediately turned black and started to smoke.

The nearest spider turned to me, all its eyes locking in on my position by the door, and it started forward, placing its little spider feet carefully as it advanced, not stepping on any of its poisonous cousins. I wasn't so careful, shuffling my feet around like I was trying to clog or two-step hoping to stomp as many scorpions as possible before the main event got to me.

Three spiders moved toward me, forming a triangle a few feet away. Their pincers clacked together excitedly, and they waggled forward and back, like they were trying to build up momentum to pounce. I could see the hairs on their legs twitching in the breeze they made as they rocked back and forth.

"Come on, Shelob," I growled. "Lemme show you what happens when you catch a real big damn hobbit." I readied my sword and shield, stomped a couple more scorpions, and hoped I could figure out a way not to become spider food in Fairyland. Then the spiders pounced, and it was on.

I caught the first spider on my shield and was surprised at how light it was for its size. I mean, I was expecting something that weighed about as much as a medium-sized dog, since the thing was at least the size of Great Dane. But nah, it was more like catching a chihuahua on a dinner plate. And then smashing the dinner plate into the wall and getting covered in slimy, nasty spider guts. The thing hit the wall with a *crunch* like a really sad bag of pretzels dropped onto the kitchen floor, and green ichor sprayed frigging everywhere.

The only upside to the spider showering a five-foot circle in acidic venom and nasty gut-slime was that the acid melted the scorpions, so I had a couple of places to put my feet while the rest of Clan Charlotte charged me.

In case you've never battled a horde of giant spiders in an enclosed space while tap-dancing on scorpions, and I hope you haven't, there are a few things you need to know. First thing— spiders are faster than you'd expect. These chittering little bastards were on me in a flash, covering the distance between us almost before I could bring my shield back around. Second thing—spiders are stupid. I'm not talking garden-variety dumb as a box of hair stupid. I'm talking faking a punt on fourth and thirty-five pinned up against your own end zone when you're the visiting team in Death Valley. So I mean *really* stupid. That was about the only thing that saved me. That, and the third thing—spiders will eat damn near anything, and they don't have the societal restrictions about cannibalism that humans do.

The stupid came into play when they all tried to rush me in almost a straight line instead of fanning out or taking advantage of the fact that they can climb walls. Peter Parker would not have been proud of his namesakes because not only did they not utter a single witty remark while trying to kill me, not a single wall was crawled in this fight. Nope, they rushed me in basically a double line of fang and hairy legs, allowing me to take out the first three or four of them just by slashing a sword through their little google eyes, stabbing them in the head, then pivoting around to bash the next one with my shield, then repeating the process.

That's when things got almost funny. Instead of trying to kill me, the spiders in the back of the line started chowing down on the corpses of the ones in the front. It was kind of like *Lord of the Flies*, except for bugs. The littler spiders, who apparently had been pushed to the back of the chow line for years and were damn tired of it, started eating the bigger spiders, the scorpions, and then started looking at each other all side-eyed like they thought anybody could be lunch. Except me. They left me alone, which gave me just enough breathing room to make my way around the room hacking and slashing like a bad horror movie villain, killing spiders with sword and shield and stomping scorpions to bits under my feet. I kept up my crazy-ass tarantella until my legs got tired, then I just grabbed my shield by the edges and slammed it into the floor, mashing three or four scorpions at a time.

I managed to get through the fight without getting bitten, stung, or doused with acid venom, and after about fifteen minutes of stomping, slamming, slicing, and a whole lot cussing, I stood alone, panting, in the middle of a roomful of disassembled arachnids. The walls were painted green with blood, and puddles of venom steamed on the floor. I walked over to the door opposite the one I entered through and tried the knob. Still locked.

"Okay, asshole. I killed all your pets. Open the damn door." No response. I looked around, trying to see if there was anything still moving in the room, but I couldn't see under all the carapaces and severed spider legs. I took a step toward the largest pile of spider carcasses, figuring if there was anything hiding under a corpse, that's where it would be, but just as I moved, a line of fire cut across my left shoulder.

"Goddammit!" I yelled, dropping my sword and slapping at my skin. My fingers came away covered in green fire as I wiped a big glob of the acid venom off onto my hand. I yelled louder as my flesh started to bubble and the agony set in, and I moved to wipe my hand clean on my thigh. Somehow, I managed to stop myself and wipe the acid off onto the wall instead. The last thing I needed was to burn off my leg to go with my scalded shoulder and mangled fingers. I got myself wiped down the best I could and examined the damage to my fingers.

The whole palm of my right hand was angry red, with blisters popping out along my first three fingers. My pinky and thumb were mostly unscathed, but wielding a sword was gonna be difficult, even if I hadn't dropped the hilt of my blade in another puddle of acid. I watched in horror as the bindings dissolved, and the dead spider's venom ate clean down to the steel.

"Shit," I muttered, looking at my hand. Then a really, really bad thought took hold. If venom dripped down on me from the ceiling, then that meant...I looked up. I didn't want to, but I looked up.

Remember what I said about none of the spiders climbing on the walls or ceiling? Well, one of them did. And it was the mac daddy of the bunch. This thing was easily six or seven feet around, and I swear it grinned down at me from where it hung, ten feet above and slightly in front of me. I looked up at the spider, then down at my destroyed sword, then at my blistered fingers.

"This is gonna suck," I said, then I pulled the mace from my belt, wincing as the rough leather wraps on the handle tore open the blisters on my fingers. "Come on, asshole," I called up to the spider. "Let's get this shit over with. I've got a woman to save and a fairy to kill."

So apparently giant spiders with acid slobber understand English. Who knew? Whether it really understood me or not, the boss spider dropped from the ceiling about five feet in front of me and lashed out with a leg aimed right for my face. I blocked with my shield and quickly realized that this one was a *lot* bigger, stronger, and heavier than the other spiders I'd made meat out of. Its foot smacked my shield hard enough to knock me back a step, and I had to hop to make sure I didn't step in a puddle of acid. While I was distracted, the spider swung another leg out at me, going low this time, and I had to jump to keep it from sweeping my leg.

"What are you, a Cobra Kai spider?" I grumbled, catching another strike on my mace and barely hanging on to the weapon because of the pain in my palm. I took another step back as its leg clanged off my shield again and barely caught myself as my foot slid in spider guts. This was fast turning into one of the worst fights I'd ever been in, and that includes the one where I ended up with a fistful of sasquatch dick.

The spider kept advancing, and I kept retreating. It struck; I blocked. It lunged; I swatted legs aside with my shield. The mace was almost useless, thanks to its short reach and my jacked-up hands. Every once in a while, I could parry with the mace, but usually all I did with that arm was wave it around trying to keep my balance as I danced backward away from a spider the size of a Volkswagen Beetle. Then it got worse. I took one more step back and felt something against my heel. A quick glance confirmed the sinking feeling in my gut—I'd backed up all the way into the wall.

There was nowhere else to go. I had solid stone behind me, a giant spider with acid dripping from its fangs ahead of me, and trying to dodge to the side would just put me right back in its clutches. Apparently, the same idea occurred to the spider because it decided that would be a great time to shift its weight onto its back four legs and lash out at me with four feet instead of two.

I took a deep breath, cast up a prayer to Great-Grandpappy Beauregard and everybody else who ever looked out for stupid rednecks, and did the only thing I could think of. I raised my shield up in front of my face, and I charged the big son of a bitch.

The spider slammed four giant spiky-hairy feet into the wall where I stood seconds before, and I rushed forward, slamming my shield right into its clicking, clacking mandibles. I wedged that rectangle of steel between the spider's nasty, dripping fangs, gripped my mace with both hands, and smacked the big bastard right between its eight google eyes.

The mace wasn't very long, so my reach sucked, and the angle was shit on account of my hand being all burnt to a crisp and having to reach around the shield, but it turns out that if you smack a giant spider in the eyeball with an eight-pound chunk of metal, you really don't have to hit it all that hard to do some serious damage. Or at least hurt like a mother. The spider shrieked as well as it could around a mouthful of smoking steel and reared up as it tried to skitter back, on the retreat for a change.

I wasn't having it. I knew if I let the thing get any kind of distance on me, I was screwed, blued, and tattooed. As long as I stayed inside the radius of its arms, it couldn't skewer me with its pointy-ass feet, but the second I took two steps back, I was going to find out what my insides looked like. Again.

So I hung right in there with ol' Auntie Shelob, staying in close where it couldn't kill me and taking whatever pot shots I could on its head. It skittered around the room backward like a Roomba on meth, and I stayed on it like body spray on a frat boy. It turned its head this way and that, trying to shake the shield out of its way so it could bite my face off, but it was wedged in there tight. I kept landing half-assed strikes to its noggin, and it kept slinging its head side to side and spraying my bare chest with acid. I was losing chest hair like a molting turkey, but the spider was getting more concussed with every shot. Finally, it went down on one foreleg, and I moved in for the kill.

Except the damn bug was playing possum. I hate it when the friggin' creepy-crawlies are smarter than me. It had chewed away enough of the shield to shake it loose, and when I came in high for a big overhand killing stroke, the spider opened its mandibles wide, dropping the pitted, scarred, and mangled shield to the floor, and turning those razor-sharp, acid-laced fangs my way. I looked down in horror as my hand descended toward the spider's mouth, and somehow, at the last second, I managed to change course just enough to swing the mace straight down on a fang and snap it off at the root.

"GODDAMMIT!" I bellowed as acid-venom sprayed up my arm, searing away skin and hair and cutting a line of fire through the tattoos on my right arm. I dropped that arm to my side, useless, and acting on nothing but adrenaline and sheer redneck fury, I snatched the mace out of my bleeding and smoking right hand with my left, spun around in place, reversed grip on the haft of the weapon, and stabbed it down through the spider's head like I was Van Helsing staking Dracula in his coffin.

The spider's skull collapsed in a wet *crunch*, covering my face in brains and spider eyeballs, and the monster fell to the ground, finally dead. I staggered over to a spot of clear floor by a nearby wall and slid to the ground as I watched the doors to the room pop open.

As my consciousness fled, chased clear of me by the agony shooting up my arm, I looked up at the ceiling and slurred out one last threat. "You'd better kill me in my sleep, you little bastard. Because if I wake up, I'm going to teach you a whole new kind of pain." Then the venom and the burns were too much, and I passed out.

13

——————————

I woke up tied to a post in the middle of a big room standing on my tiptoes with my hands bound and hung from a hook a few feet above my head. I blinked the crust from my eyes and looked around. Amy was strung up about ten feet away, looking pissed but pretty much okay. Skeeter and Joe were there, too, also hung up. Skeeter was only tied by one arm, but with his other one in a sling strapped to his chest, I didn't expect that to get us a whole lot of anything. I felt mostly okay, except for my right hand, which throbbed angrily in time with my heartbeat. My shoulders were screaming from holding up my bodyweight, and I felt a few bruises on my knees and legs, but in general, I could fight if I could just get loose. Admittedly, that didn't look real likely.

We were in a big throne room, fastened to wooden poles that just seemed to have grown straight out of the floors, or had the room built around them, or been stuck there with magic, because every shitty thing that happens to me has to be magic. Just once I'd like to get in a car wreck because a dog runs out in front of somebody and they rear-end me, or some such crap. Anything, really, just as long as there's nothing magical about it at all.

The room was huge, close to the size of half a basketball court, and we were in the middle of it, at least from what I could see by twisting around from my hook. Our posts were arranged in kind of a half-circle, with enough space between us that there was no way we could reach each other, not that I think we could do much by tapping our toes together regardless. Behind us were huge double doors and a long red carpet leading past where we hung, up to a dais with two thrones on it.

Puck sat on one throne, looking considerably worse for wear than the last time I saw him. His skin was completely gray now, and even though he was healthy, there was a general shabbiness to him that hadn't been there before. He was a dapper little guy last time we met, but now his clothes hung loose on him, and there were stains all over him like he hadn't bathed or changed in weeks. I mean, it's not like I was fresh as a daisy or anything, but he hadn't been traveling through a maze fighting skeletons and giant spiders.

On the throne next to him was a young woman, and she looked like death warmed over. She was pale, with a yellow cast to her skin that gave her a jaundiced look, and sweat poured down her face. She was unconscious, but not sleeping. No, she was trapped in some kind of fever dream, with her head tossing from side to side, and she would occasionally mutter something too low for me to hear. But even as rough as she looked, I could see a familiar shape to her nose and cheekbones. My mother's stamp was strong in her face. This was Nitalia, my sister, and by all indications, she was not doing well at all.

Puck must have seen something in my face because a slow grin stretched from one pointy ear to the other. "Ah, Bubba. So good to see you again. How have you found my kingdom so far?"

"Well, I turned left at Shitsville and followed the signs to Assclown Castle, and that led me straight to you." I gave him my best "go screw yourself" grin, and he launched himself off his throne like his butt was spring-loaded. I never even saw him move. He just did that annoying teleport thing, and suddenly he was standing in front of me.

"You think you're funny, human?" I think he tried to get in my face, but my face was about a foot taller than him, so all he really did was threaten my armpit, and given my exertions from the past few days, that probably went worse for him than it did me.

"I think I'm hilarious," I replied. I looked at the others. "What do y'all think?"

"Funny as hell," Skeeter said, his voice weak with pain.

"A real knee-slapper," Joe agreed. Amy didn't say anything, just gave me a grin that told me she hadn't given up hope yet.

Puck blurred out of sight in front of me and reappeared by Amy's pole, a wicked curved dagger in his hand. He traced the dagger along Amy's stomach, and I watched the fabric part under the razor edge. "Should I cut her this way first, Bubba? Or would you rather I slice down, then across? It lets the stomach open wider if there's some vertical space, I've found. It really lets the victim take a moment to see their entrails spill onto the floor before them. In my experience, that's how you get the really good screams." He put the tip of his knife in the center of her chest, right below her breasts, and started to draw it slowly downward, a tiny line of red welling up as he made just the shallowest cut across my fiancée's abdomen.

I didn't yell. I didn't cuss. I didn't even pull against my bonds. Instead, I let my blood go ice-cold and made my voice chill to match. "You want to put that knife away now, Shadowborn. You may be the Lord of these Shadowed Lands, but I have the blood of Mab and Oberon in my veins, and if you harm my loved ones, I swear by all the Seasons that I will visit vengeance upon you the likes of which you have never seen."

It was all bullshit, of course. I mean, I do have their blood, but I can't do any magic, and if I was going to get out of there at all, much less with all my people and my sister intact, it was going to take a whole lot of luck and a not inconsequential amount of bullshit. I had bullshit in abundance; now it was time to see about making some luck.

Puck whirled on me and blinked back to stand right in front of me. His knife pressed against my bare chest, and he glared at me. "Why shouldn't I just gut you right now and leave you hanging here with your intestines pooling around your feet to watch me slit the throats of those you love the best?"

That was it. All of a sudden, it all clicked for me. The little bastard wanted an out. He was in over his head, and he wanted somebody to give him a way out of it, a way to get back to where he used to be. He was hurting, and he wanted other people to feel his pain, but he also wanted to find a way back to being Robin Goodfellow, the Puck of the stories, not this crazed monster. And I knew just the out he needed.

"Because there's no challenge in it," I said, grinning down at him. "There's no sport to that, no *game*." Puck was a trickster at heart, and if I could give him a game to play, and maybe give him a chance to throw the game to put things back the way they used to be, there was a slim chance he could find his way back to some kind of light.

He looked up at me, a sly smile replacing the nasty leer on his face. "You propose a contest, human? You think there is some challenge that you could possibly best me at, in your weakened state?"

"I think there's half a dozen things I could kick your ass at, no matter if you chopped off both my arms, both my legs, hung me on a wall, and called me Art. But for now, let's keep it simple. We'll just have an old-fashioned fight. Barehanded, you and me. We scrap until one of us knocks the other out or kills him. Winner takes all, right here in your throne room. I beat your ass, we all walk out of here and you never come after me or any of my friends or family again. You beat me, then you get to kill me."

"I could just kill you right now," he said, drawing a circle on my stomach with his blade, then poking a couple of tiny holes in me for eyes, then carving a long arc right under the belly button nose. Yeah, the son of a bitch just carved a smiley face on my beer gut. Now I really wanted to kill him.

"You could, but where's the challenge in that? Aren't you *the* Puck? The one Shakespeare wrote about? The one whose exploits terrify faerie children in every Court? Aren't you the shit-hot trickster that makes Loki look like a schmuck with a joy buzzer and a couple of cheap card tricks?"

He turned away, tapping his knife on his chin and cheek,

smearing my blood there as he mumbled to himself. I shifted around, trying to get a little more balance on my tiptoes, and wrapped my hands around the cords binding my wrists together. That took a little strain off my shoulders and transferred my weight to my biceps, which was a tiny bit better, but not much.

"I think...that could be entertaining, human, if just to watch you struggle, and struggle, and then ultimately fail and have to watch everyone you love die anyway...I think, yes, I think..." He spun around, the dagger aimed straight at my gut. "I think I'll just rip you to pieces and let you hang here while I kill your friends!"

He stabbed for me, but I was ready for it. He was a trickster, a liar, and a general sack of shit. I just needed to give him a chance to double-cross me, and he took it. I grabbed hold of the rope tying my hands together and pulled up with all my strength. I haven't done a pull-up since summer two-a-days, but when my life depended on it, I hauled every bit of my fat ass straight up, kicked my legs out, and wrapped them around the little bastard's neck.

"Wha?" he croaked as I rested my legs on his shoulders and pulled him in close. I used him for a boost, lifted my hands over the hook I was hanging from, and pitched myself forward like some super-inflated Rey Mystery. Except I'm no luchador, and I barely managed to get myself rolled over without driving my head into the stone floor. It was clumsy as hell and hurt like a mother, but I managed to flip Puck off me and toss him ten feet across the throne room. He even had the courtesy to leave his dagger behind so I could cut my hands free.

Unfortunately, he left it buried in my right quadricep, and it hurt like a son of a bitch when I yanked it free. It hurt, but with a few seconds of determined sawing and a bunch of re-ruptured blisters on my right hand, I got my hands loose. Puck was still disoriented, so I ran over to where Amy hung from her own hook. I gave her a quick kiss, lifted her off the hook, and pressed the knife into her hands. I saw her eyes widen and knew my respite was over. "I love you. Now free the others and get the hell out of here," I whispered.

"I love you, too. Kill that pointy-eared bastard," she replied, and I turned back to face a very angry faerie assassin in his very own throne room.

"That wasn't very nice," Puck said, that nasty grin stretching back across his face. "For that, I'm going to hurt you a lot, and make it last for *years*."

"I don't know if you missed it, shithead," I said. "But I'm not a nice person. So come on, little man, let's get this shit over with. Just like the movie said, I'm here to chew gum and kick ass, and I'm all out of bubble gum."

Puck blurred out of sight, then reappeared right in front of me. He threw a kick at my injured leg, and it was on like Donkey Kong.

14

I let him land the kick, right in the big muscle where he'd buried a knife not a minute before. It hurt like a son of a bitch, but I clamped my right hand around his ankle and grabbed him around the throat with my left. I picked him up and spun in a half circle, building momentum as I slammed him to the stone floor flat on his back. He held his head up, so I didn't get the full concussion, but I think I heard a rib crack, so I took that as a partial win. He wriggled out of my grasp, trying to run away, but I limped after him.

With his jacked ribs, he wasn't nearly as fast as he was a few seconds ago, and it seemed like he couldn't teleport either. He came to that realization pretty quick and spun around, launching himself at my face like a psychotic spider monkey. He jammed a thumb into my eye, and I flung him off to the floor again.

Puck was a nimble bastard, I'll give him that. He managed to roll out of my throw a lot better than I ever could, and he pulled another dagger from somewhere in a boot, or maybe up a sleeve. I couldn't tell if he had anything strapped to his arms under the flowing sleeves of his billowy black pirate shirt, but it didn't matter. All I needed to focus on was the blade gleaming in the magical torchlight, the blade that he waved back and forth as the little bastard advanced on me.

"Is that supposed to scare me, shithead?" I laughed, sounding crazy even to myself. "Come on, you little bastard! I've fought dragons, redcaps, giant spiders, and reanimated skeletons. You think a faerie with a knife is enough to worry me? Bring it, you worthless little assclown."

Unfortunately, my bravado didn't seem to worry Puck at all, and he did bring it. He brought "it" in the form of a thrown knife right at my chest. I managed to twist so he caught me in the shoulder, but I couldn't get completely out of the way. I mean, I'm no Bruce Lee, and this wasn't a movie. Knives move *fast*, and I'm a big target. I got lucky, though, and the knife pierced my shoulder but didn't bury itself there. I bled a bit but still had a little use of the arm, and the bleeding wasn't a gusher, so he missed the artery.

I turned around and picked up the knife, then dropped to one knee and spun around as he charged again. Surprising no one, the faerie assassin had another knife in his hand, and I was starting to run out of places to imagine he was pulling them from. At least not really uncomfortable places, anyway. I caught his overhand strike with my left arm, but that arm had a fresh knife wound for him to jam a thumb into, and I screamed like a soccer mom at a Backstreet Boys concert. My shriek caught him off guard, and I was able to bury my knife in the side of his thigh, giving us a matching set. I twisted the blade, then pulled it out, falling backward as Puck slammed an elbow into my nose, filling my vision with white stars and sending blood pouring down my face.

I slammed flat on my back with a broken nose, a stab wound in my leg, another one in my shoulder, and acid burns all over my right hand and arm. Puck grinned down at me and dropped a knee into my gut, then stabbed down at my throat.

So I made sure my throat wasn't there when his knife landed. I clubbed him in the side of the head with my weakened left arm and rolled to the right. That let me push off with my uninjured leg, giving me enough strength to throw the faerie off me and give me a second's breathing room.

But just a second, because Puck was out for blood. He rolled over and kept rolling, spinning to his feet, and throwing his blade at me. Lucky for me, I kept on rolling too, so all he did was score a bloody line across my back that I hardly noticed through all the other pain I was in.

I scrambled to my feet, wiping tears from my eyes and breathing heavily through my open mouth. Puck reached around to the small of his back and brought his hands out with two more daggers, making me *really* wonder where that sheath was and how many daggers he could fit up there. I didn't have long to think about it because he darted in to me, blades and feet flying. I checked one low kick with my left leg and got a slash across my thigh for my troubles.

I responded by snatching the front of his shirt with my left hand and pulling him in close. When he was pressed up close to me, with his face just under my chin, I sucked in a big breath, pressed my right thumb to one nostril, and blew a jet of bloody snot right into his face. I learned that trick playing against Alabama. Nothing freaks a quarterback out more than a face full of someone else's boogers and blood.

It works on faerie assassins, too, in case you were wondering. Puck's hands immediately went to his face, and I landed two hard shots to the side of his head before he lifted a knee into my balls and had to let him go.

Puck danced back, hands flailing at his face, and I took the momentary respite to put my thumbs on either side of my nose and *crunch* it back into place. It hurt like a mother, but I could kinda breathe through it again. I blew another gobbet of bloody snot to the floor and turned to Puck. It was time to finish this shit.

He must have had the same idea because he flipped the dagger from his left hand at me, then leapt after it, his right-hand blade held low and ready to cut me from nuts to neck. I got crazy lucky and swatted the knife out of the air, then tangled with the tricksy bastard as he slammed into me. I got my right wrist between his knife and my ballsack and punched him in the eye with my left fist. I didn't have enough room to get much on it, but it doesn't take much when you're putting your knuckle in someone's eye. Puck danced back, but I stayed with him. I was tired and hurting all over. If I let him get room to maneuver, I was dead, and that meant everybody I cared about was dead. That wasn't gonna happen. Not today.

"NOT. TODAY!" I bellowed, and dug down deep for the last shreds of strength I had. I bull-rushed him, and this time, he didn't get out of the way fast enough. I caught him around the chest and picked him up, driving him backward toward the stone wall. I slammed him into the wall like I was trying to run right through the bricks, and I heard a *lot* of ribs break on impact.

"Take that, you little shit," I growled into his face. Then it hit me... he was *smiling*. What the hell?

"I will, you ignorant mortal. I will take it, and I will heal...eventually. But will you?"

That's when I felt it. The fire in my side, spreading from just below my armpit up and down my right ribcage. The shortness of breath, the tightness in my chest...the son of a bitch had stabbed me. I looked down, and sure enough, there it was. Buried in my side, angled up through my ribcage, was the hilt of his last dagger. I couldn't see anything but the hilt, that's how far he had it lodged into my chest, and judging by how hard it was getting to breathe, he pierced a lung.

I stepped back, my hand falling to my side, and I dropped to one knee, then both. I couldn't make my legs work. This was bad. Really, really bad. I knew enough not to pull the knife out because it might be the only thing keeping that lung inflated, but that was about all I could keep straight in my head.

Puck grinned down at me, then snatched the dagger from my left hand. His movements were halting, and he was panting from the pain of his crushed ribs, but he lifted the blade over his head and smiled a sadistic Hannibal Lecter smile. "You were a worthy opponent, Bubba. One of the best I ever faced. But you can't best the Lord of Shadows in his own domain. You are, after all, just a part-faerie, part-human mongrel, son of neither realm. You had no hope against one of the true Masters of the Fae."

I watched him take a deep breath and closed my eyes before the knife came down. Then there was a loud *crack*, and I heard something clatter to the floor beside my knees. I opened my eyes, and Puck stood there over me, his smile gone and a neat round hole in the center of his chest. I watched as two more holes appeared, followed almost instantly by two more *cracks*, and Puck staggered back, hit the wall that was now covered in blood from the exit wounds, and slid slowly down to sit in a spreading puddle of his own blood, his eyes wide and staring at me in amazement.

"Wha...?" he managed to say, then I heard the quiet slap of hiking boots on stone come up behind me. Amy put a hand on my shoulder and glared down at the dying faerie, my Judge revolver still smoking a little in her right hand. "He might be a mongrel, but he's my mongrel. And I'm all human, with a pistol full of cold iron for your sorry ass." She leaned over and pushed Puck on the shoulder. He slumped to the side, stone cold dead.

Amy knelt beside me. "Don't you die on me, Bubba. You hear me?"

I grinned at her. "I don't...think I get to make that call this time, darling," I said.

"The hell you say, you giant redneck son of a bitch. You suck it up, you great big pansy, because we have to get back home so you can marry me and we can grow old together and teach our babies how to hunt monsters."

I locked in on that word, "babies," and clung to it like a life raft. I wasn't going to die in Fairyland. Not at the hands of a second-rate Shakespeare character. No damn way. I sucked in as much air as my damaged lungs would hold and straightened up. I couldn't stand, but I wasn't going to fall over, either. Probably not in the next thirty seconds. "Get everybody over here. Now," I panted.

Amy waved Joe and Skeeter over, and a few seconds later, they huddled down, Joe carrying Nitalia and laying her on the floor next to me. I put a hand on her leg, everybody else touched me, and I clenched my fist, activating Oberon's magic ring and hoping this wasn't just another damn faerie trick. I felt the magic swirl around us, then a bright light engulfed me, and I passed out. Again. This was really starting to become a habit in this dumbass dimension.

EPILOGUE

I woke up not dead, so that was a good start. I was also butt-naked in an unfamiliar bed, so apparently unconscious me had a lot better time in Fairyland that conscious me did. I sat up, noticing that I didn't hurt nearly enough for the injuries I sustained, so I assumed that either somebody slapped some faerie healing on me, or I'd been in a coma for about a year. I looked down at my right arm, and since the hair was still missing where the acid burned it all off, I figured it was faerie healing.

Once I'd been awake for about thirty seconds, I realized what every guy realizes almost immediately upon waking—I had to pee like a racehorse. I swung my legs around, threw off the blankets, and stood up, looking for my pants. I found a reasonable facsimile of underwear and pants laying on a chair and shrugged into a loose shirt that lay next to them. Then I started looking around the bedroom for a bathroom, or at least a chamber pot. I opened a door in the near wall and found a bathroom.

That's when it hit me. This was *my* bedroom. And *my* bathroom. I took care of business, then took a better look at the clothes I threw on. These weren't some faerie recreations of my clothes, made out of magic and a mediocre understanding of just how big I really am;

these were my favorite jeans, my Stone Cold Steve Austin t-shirt with the hole in the left armpit, and even my boxers.

I walked back out into my bedroom and looked around. Sure as shit, that was my bed, my chair, my chest of drawers that I'd had since I was a teenager, complete with the band stickers I tried unsuccessfully to peel off when I got out of college. I was home. Hell, I even saw Bertha lying on the chair, with my sword standing in the corner by the dresser. I felt the emotions well up inside me, and I sat down on the edge of my bed, overwhelmed. I sat there for a couple of minutes, just taking it all in, trying to put everything together.

I was home. I'd gone to Fairyland, fought knights and goblins, battled a dragon, and danced in front of the Winter Queen. I'd survived a psychotic dungeon, battled zombies (okay, that one didn't require a trip to another dimension), and beaten a crazed trickster faerie. And we'd rescued my sister in the process.

That thought spurred me to move, and I got up and walked out into the hall. I heard voices coming from my living room, and even better, I smelled bacon. I walked down the hall to see Mama, Skeeter, Joe, and Amy all sitting at my kitchen table, plates of food piled high in front of them.

"I told you bacon would get him moving. I've never known Bubba to miss fried pork product," Skeeter said, gesturing with his knife. His arm was out of the sling, so I reckoned I wasn't the only one who got some magic healing.

"Welcome back to the land of the living," Joe mumbled around a mouthful of eggs.

I didn't get a chance to answer because my arms were full of a blond woman who took four running steps and launched herself into my arms. Amy wrapped her arms around my neck, her legs around my waist, and her lips around mine. She laid a kiss on me that would have woken me up even if I had died in the Fairyland castle. I staggered back a step, then caught my balance and returned her kiss with a fervor that I didn't know I had in me.

We made out for a long second, then I heard someone clear their throat behind Amy. I pulled away and looked over my fiancée's shoulder at Mama, who stood at the table smiling. "Good morning, dear. Would you like some breakfast?"

That almost broke me, right there. Just the words and the tone, so normal, like nothing had ever happened, brought me back to Sunday mornings at our house growing up when Mama would lay out a spread of bacon, eggs, grits, and cathead biscuits with honey and sugar. Me and Jason would eat ourselves stupid and then try to sit still through Sunday School with all the sugar from the biscuits running through us. Jason usually managed better than me. A tear welled up in the corner of my eye, but I dashed it away and managed to mumble a "yes, ma'am" without completely losing it.

Then I saw Nitalia, sitting at the table looking up at me from under a waterfall of hair with big green eyes and a nervous expression on her face. "Hello, brother," she said. "Thank you for—"

That was all she got out before I basically tackled my kid sister. I took two giant steps forward, leaned down, and swept her up into a huge bear hug. After about half a second, I noticed what I'd done and let the chair clatter to the floor. I held on to Nitalia, though, wrapping her in my big arms and crushing her to my chest.

"I bet you're glad I insisted on giving him a sponge bath now," Amy said laughing from behind me.

"We all figured that was just so you could fondle your boyfriend," Skeeter said. The *thwack* of her slapping him was all the confirmation I needed that we were back in the real world.

After a few seconds, I set Nitalia down and took a step back, keeping my hands on her shoulders. "You look better."

"Oberon healed me. He was very...contrite when we returned to the Summer Lands."

I grunted. "He doesn't strike me as the contrite type."

Nitalia leaned in and whispered, "I don't know if you know this, but our mother can be very persuasive."

"You know I can hear you, right?" Mama said from the stove.

"She used to do that crap to me all the time growing up," I said.

Nitalia chuckled. "Me too."

I bent down and straightened her chair, then sat down at the table between Amy and Nitalia. I couldn't take my eyes off the faerie woman. I had a *sister*. Hell, I was pretty excited just to have some family again, even if they couldn't live in my dimension. Maybe we could set up a magic door or something.

Nitalia did look better. The jaundice was gone, and her hair, which hunk lank and greasy when I saw her in Puck's throne room, was now full, dark and glossy, with some curl to it. She was taller than Mama, but still normal-sized for a full-blooded faerie, so about medium height and slim for a human.

Her eyes had a little bit of a haunted air to them, and she jumped a touch whenever somebody scraped a chair across the floor, or a fork clattered too loud against a plate. I wasn't surprised. The kind of trauma she went through leaves scars. I would have been more worried if she *hadn't* shown some signs of PTSD.

"How long can you stay?" I asked. "Without getting sick, I mean."

"Not long," Nitalia said. "Mother knows best the limitations of our travel to this world, but after having been away from the Summer Lands for so long, I will begin to fade again within a few days."

"I'm surprised you're able to be here at all, honestly," I said.

"I have some, how do you say it? Juice, with the Prince Consort of Summer," Mama said. I looked over at her, and she gave me a grim smile, twirling a paring knife between her fingers. "But we will depart right after breakfast. Nitalia has a life to return to, as do all of you."

"I just wanted to make sure you were whole before I left," Nitalia said. "And to thank you. Not many would have done what you did, braving another world for a stranger."

"You ain't a stranger, sis," I said, shoving a piece of bacon in my mouth and moaning a little as the perfectly crisped slice of heaven exploded on my tongue. I swallowed, then washed it down with a sip of OJ. "You're family. Family takes care of one another." I looked around the table at the nodding heads and knew I was speaking truth.

Nitalia stood up, threw her arms around me, and hugged me tight. "Thank you, brother. I will miss you."

"But not just yet, and not for long," Mama said. "After all, we have a wedding to plan." She smiled at Amy, and the womenfolk's faces lit up. It looked like I was in trouble. I mean, with literal faerie princesses planning the wedding, I was gonna have to wear something embarrassing, I could feel it. I just hoped I could avoid tights.

I decided to change the subject before somebody started talking about flower arrangements. "How long have I been out?"

"Not long," Skeeter said. "Just one day and one night."

Amy looked over at me. "You teleported us back to Titania's throne room, and Oberon's people leapt to action. Your mother healed you, and his court healers fixed Skeeter's arm. Then they sent us home. You slept through all the boring bits, but you're an honorary Knight of the Summer Court now."

"Couldn't have done it without you guys. Especially you, Skeet. Nice job smuggling the pistol in," I said.

"Nobody ever checks the sling," he replied. "Faeries aren't any smarter than humans when it comes to that."

"And good job not trying to shoot Puck yourself. I was too hurt to live through a bullet wound, too," I said, grinning at my buddy. There was very good reason Skeeter was always on the shotgun.

"As soon as Amy cut me down, I gave her the gun."

"And she saved my ass," I said. "Thanks, babe." I gave her a quick kiss on the lips, then turned back to Mama. "So that's it? We're home, we're healed, and you and Nitalia have to go back to Fairyland, just like nothing ever happened. Sounds like a pretty good deal."

"Well…" Joe said.

I looked around the table at my family and friends. "What's the deal? Did somebody die while we were gone? How long were we gone, anyway? Last time I went into Fairyland, two days over here was a couple weeks there."

"You're right," Mama said. "Time moves differently in Faerie than here in your realm, like I mentioned. What I didn't tell you was that crossing from Winter to Summer, and into Shadow and back…that complicates things."

"What do you mean?" I asked.

"The boundaries between the Courts are more than just within

Faerie. They connect to your world in different places." Mama wasn't meeting my gaze. I felt like there was something she wasn't telling me.

"So what?" I asked. "Who cares where the Courts touch our world, as long as we got home okay."

"They touch in different places in space...and time."

"Oh," I said. Then I shook my head. "I still don't get it."

"Moving between the Courts changed the way time moved between the Realms. Had your travels only occurred in Winter or Summer, then you would have been gone mere days in your world. But when you stepped into Shadow, something changed."

"Okay, Mama," I said, putting another piece of bacon in my mouth and talking as I chewed. It was rude, I know, but bacon excuses a lot of sins. "Cut the crap. How long were we over there?" I looked around the table. Nobody would look at me. They all apparently knew the deal already. I guess that's another benefit of not almost dying and needing a shitload of healing magic and sleep.

"Every day you were in Faerie accounted for close to four days here in your world," Mama said.

I sat back in my chair and laid the strip of bacon on my plate. I looked around, doing some rough math in my head. "We were in Faerie for what, four or five months?"

Joe nodded. "Something like that."

"So...how long were we gone on this side of the magic curtain?" I looked to Amy.

"We were gone for a year and a half, Bubba. We were missing for eighteen months." She looked like there was more, so I motioned for her to go on. She didn't speak.

"Okay, we were gone for a long time...wait, were we declared dead? Did we all just fake our own deaths?" I asked.

"No," Skeeter said. "That takes a lot longer. And since you and I own our places, and folks around here know what we do...well, my dad paid my light bill, and you've got a generator. That's what we're working off of right now, so that's good."

"But you..." I turned to Amy.

"Yeah, I kinda don't have an apartment anymore. Or a car. Or a job, for that matter."

"Holy shit," I said. "They fired you? Well, I guess they thought you were dead. Damn. Getting that straight is gonna suck."

"That's...not all," Joe said. "Amy isn't the only one with bad news on the employment front."

I stared at him. "Really? I thought being a priest was like a lifetime appointment."

"It is," he said, holding up his hands. "I've spoken with the Cardinal and explained what happened. He understands, and I'll likely be reinstated once they are done with all their investigations."

"Okay, then that's good. It's gonna suck, but I've got a little money put back, and once the feds and the Church get all their ducks in a row, you guys will be back square in no time. Right?"

"Well...kinda," Amy said. "We're not the ones with the problem."

"What do you mean?" I asked.

"The Church wasn't happy to find out that their Hunter for the region was in Faerie for a year and a half, but they were a lot less happy when they learned that he's also part faerie with blood ties to two different Courts and their rulers," Joe said.

"What are you saying, Joe?" I asked, leaning forward with my elbows on the table.

He wouldn't meet my eyes. "Bubba, effective immediately, you are no longer the Regional Monster Hunter of the Holy Roman Church. It is the opinion of the Church that your faerie blood makes you untrustworthy by your very nature. I'm sorry, Bubba. You're fired."

"Holy shit," I said. I turned to Amy. "Well, I hope DEMON is hiring because I'm gonna need to get my beer money from somewhere."

She wouldn't look at me. "What?" I asked.

"The government agrees. They will not allow a nonhuman to be a part of the Department under any circumstances, nor will they allow any agent to use a nonhuman as a consultant on anything more than an extremely limited basis."

"Well, that sucks," I said, looking around the table. "What the hell am I supposed to do for money?"

"We," Amy said, her voice small.

"Huh?" I turned back to her.

"What are *we* going to do for money. That's what you meant to say. Because they won't let any of their agents consort with a nonhuman, either."

"Wait, what?" I started to stand up, but Amy put a hand on my shoulder. "You're saying that they won't let you be with me and be an agent?"

"That's exactly what I'm saying. I turned over my badge and gun yesterday. As of this morning, we're unemployed."

"We all are," Joe said. "I told the Cardinal that if the Church didn't want my best friend because of some racist bullshit, then the Church could kiss my ass." I hadn't noticed that he wasn't wearing the collar, but I certainly noticed the less than priestly language. I guess he really had quit.

"So...welcome home, now you're fired?" I said, looking around.

"Pretty much," Skeeter said. "I guess the only real question now is...now what?"

I looked around the table, at my family by birth and by choice, and I felt a smile creep across my face. "I don't know, Skeet. But I know this much. It don't matter what they throw at us. With y'all by my side, I can handle it. Now gimme the rest of that bacon."

We finished breakfast, with everybody throwing out ideas for how to earn a living in our new reality, and I didn't care if I never found another job, as long as I could live in a cardboard box next to these people. I was halfway through the breakfast dishes when there was a knock at the door.

I looked at Skeeter, but he looked as confused as I did. "I ain't expecting nobody."

I walked unarmed to the door. Not something I usually do, but I'd just survived a lot of shit and was feeling pretty damn invincible. All that went away when I saw the giant hairy man standing on my porch.

"What's up, Barry?" I asked the sasquatch. I hadn't seen Barry since him and the remnants of his tribe helped me stop my brother from taking over the world a couple years ago.

"I need your help, Bubba. The Wild Hunt has come to our forest, and they are hunting sasquatch."

Well, shit. That had to be like the world's shortest retirement.

THE END - FOR NOW

If you enjoyed this book, please leave a review on Amazon, Goodreads, or wherever you like.

If you'd like to hear more about or from the author, please join my mailing list at http://eepurl.com/fV4In.

You can get some free short stories just for signing up, and whenever a book gets 50 reviews, the author gets a unicorn. I need another unicorn. The ones I have are getting lonely. So please leave a review and get me another unicorn!

ACKNOWLEDGMENTS

Thanks as always to Melissa Gilbert for all her help, and for trying in vain to teach me where the commas go.

Thanks to Natania Barron for her amazing cover designs.

As always, thank all of you for reading, and thanks especially for taking this journey to Fairyland with me and Bubba!

The following people help me bring this work to you by their Patreon-age. You can join them at Patreon.com/johnhartness.

Sean Fitzpatrick
Amanda Justice
Noah Sturdevant
Mark Ferber
Andy Bartalone
Nick Esslinger
Sharon Moore
Wendy Taylor
Sheelagh Semper
Charlotte Henley Babb
Andreas Brücher
Sheryl R. Hayes

Amaranth Dawe
Butch Howard
Lawrence Nash
Delia Houghland
Douglas Park Jr.
Travis & Casey Schilling
Michelle E. Botwinick
Carol Baker
Leonard Rosenthol
Lisa Hodges
Patrick Dugan
Mark Wilson
Darrell Grizzle
Kenneth Dick
Liberty Becker
Kimberly Richardson
Aloof Fox
Arthur Reisfeld
Kristie McKinely
Melissa Cole
Leia Powell
Jeremy Snyder
Candice Carpenter
Theresa Glover
Salem Macknee
Jared Pierce
Vikki Perry
Valentine Wolfe
Noella Handley
Don Lynch
Jeremy Wilhoit
D.R. Perry
Andrea Judy
Anthony D. Hudson
John A. McColley

Dennis Bolton
Shiloh Walker/J.C. Daniels
Andrew Torn
Sue Lambert
Emilia Agrafojo
Tracy Syrstad
Samantha Dunaway Bryant
Steven R. Yanacsek
Scott Furman
Rebecca Ledford
Ray Spitz
Lars Klander

STAY IN TOUCH!

If you enjoyed this book, please leave a review on Amazon, Goodreads, or wherever you like.

If you'd like to hear more about or from the author, please join my mailing list at http://eepurl.com/fV4In.

You can get some free short stories just for signing up, and whenever a book gets 50 reviews, the author gets a unicorn. I need another unicorn. The ones I have are getting lonely. So please leave a review and get me another unicorn!

ABOUT THE AUTHOR

John G. Hartness is a teller of tales, a righter of wrong, defender of ladies' virtues, and some people call him Maurice, for he speaks of the pompatus of love. He is also the best-selling author of EPIC-Award-winning series *The Black Knight Chronicles* from Bell Bridge Books, a comedic urban fantasy series that answers the eternal question "Why aren't there more fat vampires?" In July of 2016. John was honored with the Manly Wade Wellman Award by the NC Speculative Fiction Foundation for Best Novel by a North Carolina writer in 2015 for the first Quincy Harker novella, *Raising Hell.*

In 2016, John teamed up with a pair of other publishing industry ne'er-do-wells and founded Falstaff Books, a publishing company dedicated to pushing the boundaries of literature and entertainment.

In his copious free time John enjoys long walks on the beach, rescuing kittens from trees and getting caught in the rain. An avid *Magic: the Gathering* player, John is strong in his nerd-fu and has sometimes been referred to as "the Kevin Smith of Charlotte, NC." And not just for his girth.

Find out more about John online
www.johnhartness.com

ALSO BY JOHN G. HARTNESS

The Black Knight Chronicles - Omnibus Edition

The Black Knight Chronicles Continues - Omnibus #2

Scattered, Smothered, & Chunked - Bubba the Monster Hunter Season One

Grits, Guns, & Glory - Bubba Season Two

Wine, Women, & Song - Bubba Season Three

Year One: A Quincy Harker, Demon Hunter Collection

The Cambion Cycle - Quincy Harker, Year Two

Damnation: Quest for Glory Part 1 - Quincy Harker Year Three

Fireheart

Amazing Grace: A Dead Old Ladies Detective Agency Mystery

From the Stone

The Chosen

FALSTAFF BOOKS

Want to know what's new
And coming soon from
Falstaff Books?

Try This Free Ebook Sampler

https://www.instafreebie.com/free/bsZnl

Follow the link.
Download the file.
Transfer to your e-reader, phone, tablet, watch, computer,
whatever.
Enjoy.